"Important"

This important and fact-filled book will help thousands to have a better understanding of glaucoma.

Lorraine H. Marchi
Founder/Executive Director
National Association for Visually Handicapped

"Comprehensive"

This is the best written, most comprehensive book available on coping with glaucoma. It contains valuable practical information not available in any other single source.

Ben C. Lane, O.D.
Director
Nutritional Optometry Institute

"Solid Information"

Comprehensive and solid information for the person living with glaucoma. Ms. Marks and Ms. Montauredes have clearly done their homework.

Tara Steele
Executive Director
Glaucoma Research Institute

"Excellent"

Edith Marks provides an excellent explanation of why mass glaucoma screenings are so important and why managing this disease means more than a simple intraocular pressure check.

Dick Hellner
Prevent Blindness America

“Clear and Concise”

This book provides the reader with a comprehensive and accurate overview of many simple and complex medical conditions, diagnostic tests, and eye operations in a clear and concise way, so that it can be easily understood by the lay person.

Mollie M. Hyman, M.S.
Registered Dietitian and Glaucoma Patient

“A Must”

This book is a must for African Americans who have glaucoma. I know from my own experience with family that glaucoma is four to five times more prevalent in people of my race. Edith Marks has done a remarkable job in bringing this information to the public.

Beverly Johnson
Supermodel

“Extraordinary”

Edith Marks writes with an extraordinary balance of intelligence, respect, and empathy. Until now, there has been no source for persons with glaucoma to use to educate themselves as to accurate medical details, the risks and benefits of standard treatments, and the complementary methods available that allow patients to help themselves.

Barbara S. Friedman
Attorney and Glaucoma Patient

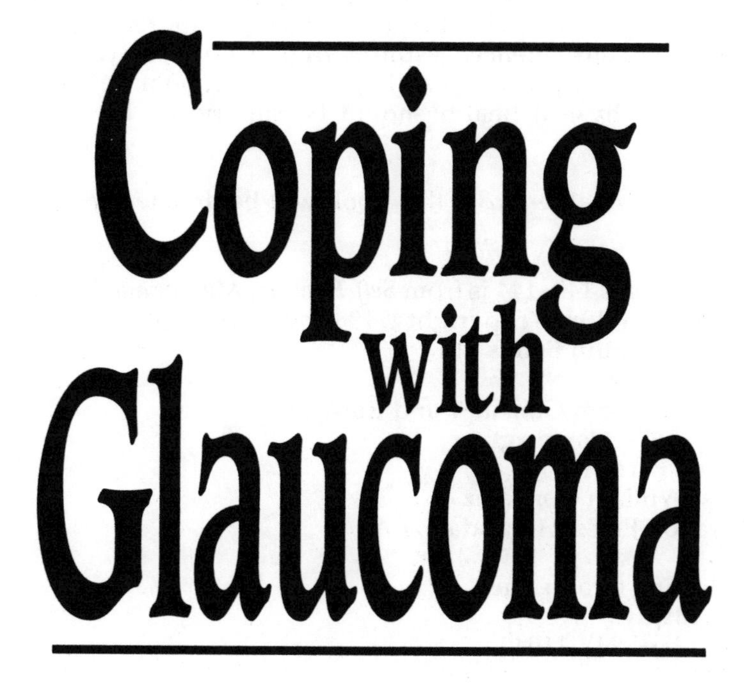

Edith Marks
with Rita Montauredes

Avery Publishing Group
Garden City Park, New York

A portion of the royalties from this book will be donated for research on glaucoma.

Cover design: William Gonzalez and Rudy Shur
Editor: Amy C. Tecklenburg
Typesetter: Al Berotti
Illustrations: William Gonzalez
Printer: Paragon Press, Honesdale, PA

Avery Publishing Group, Inc.
120 Old Broadway
Garden City Park, NY 11040
1-800-548-5757

Publisher's Cataloging-in-Publication Data

Marks, Edith

Coping with glaucoma ; a guide to living with glaucoma for you and your family / Edith Marks with Rita Montauredes. —1st ed.

p. cm.
Includes bibliographical references and index.
ISBN: 0-89529-804-X

1. Glaucoma I. Title

RE871.M37 1997 617.7'41
QBI97-40695

Printed in the United States of America.

10 9 8 7 6 5 4 3 2 1

Table of Contents

This book is dedicated to the members of
The Glaucoma Support and Education Group,
without whom *Coping With Glaucoma*
would never have been written.

Acknowledgments

Our "thank-you's" for making the publishing of this book possible range far and wide. Thanks beyond measure for invaluable assistance, encouragement, and insights to: Dr. Max Forbes, professor of ophthalmology and director of glaucoma services, Harkness Eye Institute, Columbia-Presbyterian Medical Center; Dr. Jeffrey Liebman, clinical associate professor of ophalmology and associate director of glaucoma services, New York Eye and Ear Infirmary; and Dr. Robert Ritch, chief of glaucoma services, New York Eye and Ear Infirmary. Without their active consultantship on the medical information for this project, we would not have been able to accomplish it.

A heartfelt thanks to those who believed that this book would be an important contribution to the care and management of glaucoma by persons afflicted with the disease: Rudy Shur, managing editor, Avery Publishing Group, for his encouragement and direction; Amy Tecklenburg, editor, Avery Publishing Group, for her incredible precision in shaping up the manuscript; and B.K. Nelson, literary agent, for believing that the manuscript deserved to be published.

A special thanks from the heart to my husband, Jason, for his editing, championing, and for bearing with me through the long period of researching and writing this book; and to Tom, Rita's husband, for his moral and spiritual support of both Rita and myself.

An appreciative thanks to Tara Steele, director of The Glaucoma Research Foundation; from whom we learned much about the vicissitudes of glaucoma; John Corwin, executive director of The Glaucoma Foundation, who enthusiastically has helped the facilitation of putting the book together and getting the word out; Thomas F. Furlong, director of public relations, who invited me to attend my first ophthalmological research conference; Marie Burack and Bill Hurley, formerly with Prevent Blindness America, New York, and Joe Basile, president and chief executive officer, and Becky Friend, director of community service, Prevent Blindness America, New York, and Richard Hellner, president of Prevent Blindness America, all of whom have supported this project.

It would be impossible to name all those who directly or indirectly contributed to this book, but we especially want to acknowledge the following, who gave freely of their advice, shared some of their latest research with us, and in general helped us in many ways to accomplish our mission: Christine Alexander, M.S., A.B.D.E., pharmacist and columnist, N.Y. Carib News; Dr. Deborah Banker, holistic ophthalmologist and author of *The Best Preventative Eye Care of Western, Oriental, and Holistic Medicine*; T. Joel Byars, O.D., president of the American Optometric Association; Dr. Bruce Cameron, assistant professor of ophthalmology, State University of New York Health Science Center, Brooklyn; Sally Campbell, librarian, Herskell Library for the Blind, New York; Gerard Clemente, editor, *The Trends Journal,* Trends Research Institute; Annelies de Kater, Ph.D., of the department of ophthalmology, University of Texas at Dallas; Judith Duchateau, Esq., of the American Academy of Optometry; Dr. Evan B. Dryer, assistant professor of ophthalmology and acting director, Glaucoma Consultation Service, Massachusetts Eye and Ear Infirmary; Dr. David Epstein, professor and chairman of the department of ophthalmology, Duke University Medical Center; Sylvia Elbaz, certified nutritionist; Michael Fisher, O.D., director of low-vision services, The Lighthouse, New York; Saul Friedman, Ph.D., of the New York Commission for the Blind; Dr. Douglas Grayson, attending surgeon at the New York Eye and Ear Infirmary; Dr. David S. Greenfield, clinical assistant professor of ophthalmology and neurology, New York Eye and Ear Infirmary; Dr. Kevin Greenidge, chairman of the department of ophthalmology, State University of New York; Dr. Arlene Gwon, medical researcher at Allergan Laboratories; Dr. Alyson Hall, attending physician at the New York Eye and Ear Infirmary; Alon Harris, Ph.D., director of the Glaucoma Research Diagnostic Center, Indiana University; Dr. Raymond Harrison, chief emeritus of glaucoma surgery, Manhattan Eye and Ear Hospital; Richard Hellner, president of Prevent Blindness America; Charles Hollander, O.D., director of Sight Improvement Center, Inc., New York; Dr. Raphael Klapper, chief of glaucoma service, Manhattan Eye and Ear Hospital; Bob Kuska of the National Eye Institute; Ben C. Lane, O.D., nutritional epidemiologist, Columbia

University School of Public Health, New York; Mindy Levine, C.S.W., consultant with the National Association for Visually Handicapped, New York; Dr. Mark Lister, attending physician and director of cornea and cataract services, Metropolitan Hospital Center; Dr. Richard Mackool, director of The Mackool Eye Institute; Dr. Wayne March, professor and chairman of the department of ophthalmology and visual sciences, University of Texas at Galveston; Lorraine Marchi, founder and executive director of the National Association for the Visually Handicapped; Dr. Bruce Martin of The Glaucoma Research and Diagnostic Center, Indiana University; Yvanne Mertelly, pharmacist, Westerly Pharmacy, New York; Steven C. Miller, O.D., director of the American Optometric Association; Frances Neer, writer and researcher on glaucoma; Priscilla Nemeth, managing editor of *Lifetimes*; Dr. Peter Netland, assistant professor of ophthalmology at Harvard Medical School; Marilyn Newman, orientation mobility specialist, Touch Technique; Fred Nurock, consultant, statistical research; Alberta L. Orr, national program assistant with the American Foundation for the Blind; Ruth Fangmeier, associate director of The Lighthouse National Center for Vision and Aging; Dr. Michael Patella of Humphrey Instruments; Dr. Harry A. Quigley, director of glaucoma services at Dana Center for Preventive Ophthalmology, Baltimore; Dr. Joseph Rizzo III, assistant professor of ophthalmology at Harvard Medical School; Ruth Sackman, president of the Foundation for Alternative Therapies; Mansoor Sarfarazi of the University of Connecticut Health Center; Dr. Liviu B. Saimovici, an ophthalmologist practicing in New York City; Meir Schneider, Ph.D., director of the Center for Self-Healing; Dr. Jeffrey Schultz, director of glaucoma services, Montefiore Medical Center; Dr. Bernard Schwartz, professor emeritus, Tufts University, Boston; Dr. Paul Sidoti, assistant professor and attending physician at the New York Eye and Ear Infirmary; David Steinberger, administrator, New York Eye and Ear Infirmary; Joseph Trachtman, O.D., investigative researcher and author of *The Etiology of Visual Disorders*; Dr. Gary Todd, ophthalmologist and author of *Nutrition, Health & Disease*; Manley West, Ph.D., pharmacist in Jamaica, Wisconsin; Mark Usland, manager of technical evaluation services, Technology Center, American Foundation for the Blind; Steve Wong, computer consultant; Ran C. Zeimer, Ph.D., director and professor at the Ophthalmic Physics Laboratory, The Wilner Institute, Johns Hopkins University, Baltimore.

Foreword

The story you are about to read is true—but it didn't have to be. For the blindness from glaucoma that has afflicted millions around the world could have been prevented, in more than nine out of ten cases, by early detection and treatment. Glaucoma is in fact the world's number one cause of *preventable* blindness.

This is a story about the "silent thief of sight"—an insidious eye disease that strikes without warning, without symptoms. Fifty million people worldwide have glaucoma, and as the population both grows in numbers and lives longer, the incidence of the disease is on the rise, indeed accelerating. Yes, everyone knows someone with glaucoma. And yet, for some reason, it has not become a part of our collective public health consciousness.

Not yet, that is. Now, Edith Marks, with Rita Montauredes, has brought us, at last, the first comprehensive treatment of the subject of glaucoma written for the general public. As fate would have it, her book arrives in, and in turn advances, a period of unprecedented public attention to this shy, sly disease. Public personalities, including former President George Bush, have begun to speak out. Nationwide media attention was drawn to the sudden retirement from major league baseball of Minnesota Twins all-star Kirby Puckett, who at the age of thirty-five discovered he had glaucoma.

In this book you will find more information about glaucoma than can be found in any other single source for the lay reader. Ms. Marks starts at the beginning and takes us through a thorough discussion of her subject, encompassing a vivid description of the miracle that is the eye, a survey of the many kinds of glaucoma, a review of the diagnostic tools doctors use, and the wide array of treatments available, from eye drops to lasers to surgery.

This book is more than informative—it provides the energetic, positive outlook that is in fact quite important to the glaucoma patient's management of the disease. Perhaps this vital dimension arises not only from Ms. Marks' ability as a writer but also from her and her colleague's personal interest in the subject: Ms. Marks has already lost a portion of her eyesight, and Ms. Montauredes has lost most of hers, to this disease. You will find in this book not only the facts and figures of glaucoma, but the courageous example set by its author, as she responded to her sudden challenge with a determination to help others—through research, writing, organizing, and conducting support groups, and, most of all, showing us how glaucoma patients can take charge and help to save their own eyesight.

Hopefully, coming as it does amid increasing public interest in the disease, this book will also help to inspire the majority of our population who have never been to an eye doctor, or who haven't been in a long time, to have regular eye exams. A glaucoma test is simple, painless, and quick. It can save your sight. Edith Marks tells us all about it in the pages that follow.

John W. Corwin
Executive Director
The Glaucoma Foundation

Preface

Glaucoma! The word struck fear into my heart. Pursuing a successful career in special education, I wanted no interference from my eyes. I could not afford to take time out to care for myself when the kids and teachers needed me. So for a year, I denied that I had the disease. My husband, who was as unaware as I at the time of the implications of a glaucoma condition, did not press me to seek specialized help. Only when I returned to the ophthalmologist who had treated my eyes for the retinal tears that had preceded the onset of glaucoma did the full impact of the disease bear down on me. I had already lost some sight in my left eye.

Rita, who worked with me on this book, found that glaucoma messed up her life immediately. She was stricken with polymorphous dystrophy, a rare form of the disease, at the age of thirty-two. Rita, then involved in a family crisis, also denied that anything could be wrong with her eyes. Not until one eye refused to open one morning did she take herself to an ophthalmologist, who treated her for glaucoma. A year later, Rita had the first of a series of operations, each of which left her more devastated than the one before. She came to feel that she had been reduced to an eyeball. Her husband, who had been blinded by the excess oxygen once given to premature infants, had lived in a dark world all his life and could not quite comprehend Rita's dread of what seemed to be at that time the inevitable—the loss of her sight.

Rita and I met at a support group in New York City. By the time I found the support group, I had already had laser treatment and one eye operation, and I had retired from my job. Rita had lost the vision in one eye. Her attitude toward doctors and the entire medical profession was definitely antagonistic; Rita felt disabled, like a nonentity, and blamed the doctors for her condition. But we both wanted to know more about our conditions, and we also longed to hear from other people who had had similar experiences. What we found were the same kinds of fears, trepidations, stories, and, yes, some successes, among members of the group. Each participant had a different story to tell, for each person's glaucoma is unique. Some of us fared quite well. Others did not, and were losing sight despite medical interventions. Each of us wanted to know more about glaucoma and particularly about the form of glaucoma affecting him or her.

We learned that we, the members of our support group, are a tiny segment of some 3 million Americans who have glaucoma, although half of those affected do not even know they have it. Most of us are over thirty-five years of age; many of us are African-American. Many of us are diabetic, myopic, and/or genetically predisposed to glaucoma. We are the "risk" people. Sixty-eight percent of us are sixty-five years of age or older; 25 percent are between forty-five and sixty-four; and 7 percent are between eighteen and forty-four. Children and young people also can get glaucoma, and Prevent Blindness America, an organization that tracks incidents of blindness, reports that glaucoma is increasing among younger members of the population. This increase may be due more to the growing awareness that the disease can exist at younger ages, and also possibly to the screening efforts for glaucoma by Prevent Blindness America, than to an actual increase in the incidence of the disease.

Untreated, glaucoma can lead to legal blindness. This is a term used to characterize a person whose vision, with correction, is 20/200 or worse. Such a person can see only the big "E" on the standard eye chart, or no more than 20 degrees peripherally (often referred to as tunnel vision). Unfortunately, some of the members of our group, even with treatment, have succumbed to legal blindness.

One of the purposes of our support group has been to invite a speaker to each meeting. Members of the eye care profession accommodated us, and we listened to doctors, nurses, pharmacologists, nutritionists, psychologists, and hospital administrators who shared their thoughts with us. We pestered the good doctors and practitioners with questions about our individual treatments, our medications, our prognoses, our diets, and our lifestyles, seeking to solve the riddle that confused and terrified us.

Both Rita and I profited from our group experience. I became the group's newsletter editor. Rita chose an advocacy role, seeking better solutions for persons with low-vision problems. Anyone we met who had glaucoma, or who had friends or family members who had glaucoma, wanted to know more about this disease. Thus, the idea of researching and putting together this book was born.

In our research, we discovered answers to many of the questions that members of the group had posed: the reason for the diagnostic tests; what the recommended medications (and their side effects) were; and what the state of research into the causes of glaucoma was. We looked into complementary therapies and, in so doing, began to take charge of our own lives. Our prognoses improved, as did our outlook on life, and we found ourselves in agreement with the premise advanced by Dr. Bernie Siegel, a well-known author and advocate of self-healing, that patients who become partners with their doctors in the treatment of their conditions appear to have better outcomes.

These investigations led to the shape of this book. By providing the "yin" and the "yang"—the two halves of the whole, neither of which can function well without the other—we hope to provide you with as many answers as possible for living with glaucoma, and we hope, eventually healing the condition.

Edith Marks
New York, New York

CHAPTER 1

The Engineering Miracle

Our sight is the most perfect and the most delightful of all the senses. It fills the mind with the largest variety of ideas, converses with its objects at the greatest distance, and continues the longest in action without being tired or satiated with its proper enjoyments.

Joseph Addison (1711)

When I was told that I had glaucoma, despite my initial reaction of denial—how could this happen to me?—I found I wanted to learn more about my eyes. Overnight, they had changed from alluring objects to be enhanced with mascara, eyeliner, and the like, into worrisome medical problems. Rita found herself going through the same transformation. Both of us found that we wanted to know more about the eyes and how they work.

If you think of the eye as a camera, you can grasp some elementary information. Light enters the pupil (comparable to the shutter on a camera), is focused by the lens, and falls on the retina (comparable to the film), where the image is recorded, and presto! You see.

Rita and I soon discovered, however, that a lot more goes on inside this amazing organ. The eye is about an inch in diameter, weighs only a quarter of an ounce, and is less than one-half cubic inch in volume. Yet inside this small container are organs that ensure that your eye is kept properly irrigated, that it filtrates (removes fluid efficiently), and that it sends a steady flow of signals to your brain to interpret what you see. Actually, the eyes are extensions of the brain, with the optic nerve forming the bridge between the retina and the brain.

The eyes are designed to give you maximum seeing power. When you roll your eyes at your husband's latest corny joke, it is the extraocular muscles that do the work. These muscles move the eyes up and down and from side to side. And to make sure this action runs smoothly, the eye is surrounded with a cushion of fat that serves essentially the same function as oil around a ball bearing.

As with every other part of your body, every unit of the eye has its own particular job to do, but is also dependent upon every other unit for the whole affair to run smoothly. The blood vessels and tissues of the eye are neatly organized into three layers (see Figure 1.1). The outer layer is the *sclera,* the tough white membrane that covers the entire eye. The middle layer is reddish-blue in color and is called the *uvea,* after the Latin word for grape. The uvea contains the *choroid* (blood vessels), the *ciliary body,* and the *iris,* which, although visible from the outside, is actually a part of the inner eye. The *pupil* is the round dark area in the center of the iris. The *lens* sits just behind the iris and the ciliary body lies behind the iris and is attached to the sclera. The inner layer, extending three-quarters of the way around the eye, is the *retina.* It contains the tiny nerve cells that capture the images you see and sends them to the *optic nerve,* which is the eye's pathway to the brain. The large central space inside the eye, behind the lens and enclosed by the three layers, contains the *vitreous body,* a gel-like substance whose job is to keep the eye rigid.

The vitreous body, optic nerve, and retina are collectively referred to as the back part, or the posterior segment, of the eye. The area bounded by the cornea, iris, pupil, and lens is filled with a fluid called *aqueous humor,* which is produced by the ciliary body. This area is called the front, or the anterior chamber, of the eye. The drainage area, consisting of the *trabecular meshwork* and *Schlemm's canal,* is situated in this section of the eye. Now let us look in detail at some of the structures of the eye most important to an understanding of glaucoma.

THE CORNEA

The eye is not a perfect sphere, but protrudes slightly in front. A small transparent membrane, the cornea, is fused onto the front. The cornea is roughly the size of a dime, but only one-fiftieth of an inch thick. The rest of the eye is covered with the sclera. When you look at your eyes in the mirror, it is the sclera you see; because the cornea is transparent—necessary to allow light to enter—you are unaware of its presence.

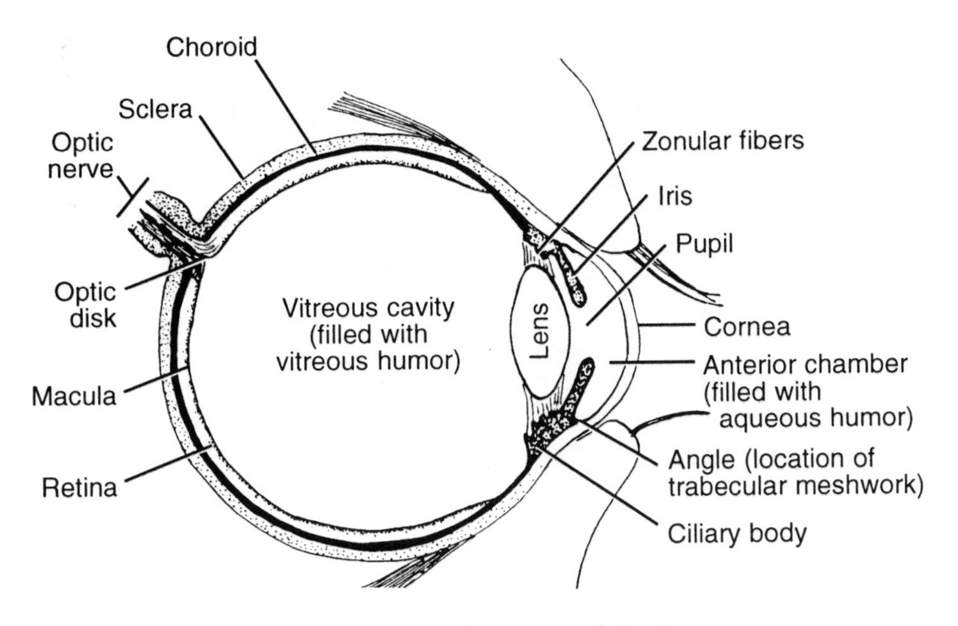

Figure 1.1 Anatomy of the Eye

THE IRIS

Behind the cornea is the colored part of the eye, the iris. Lovers and poets write odes to the eyes of their sweethearts, comparing the colors of the iris to gems, flowers, the sky, or whatever. The color of the iris is a result of the amount of pigment it contains. If it has a little pigment, the iris is blue; if it has a lot of pigment, the iris is brown.

But the iris does much more than stimulate romantic fancies. It is busy during all of your waking hours, contracting and expanding its dilator muscles, depending on whether you are in bright light or in dim or dark surroundings. By regulating the size of the pupil, the opening in the center, the iris directs light onto the retina. Fluid also drains by flowing across the iris. This route of outflow is called the *uveascleral route*.

THE LENS

The lens sits in the middle of the eye, behind the pupil. It focuses the light onto the retina so that you see clear images. The lens is a remarkable instrument that adjusts from reading fine print to reading a name on a movie marquee 100 or more feet away. Tiny ligaments (strands of connective tissue) called *zonular fibers* keep the lens suspended in place.

The lens is a mass of tightly packed transparent cells packaged in a capsule. These lens fibers continue to grow throughout life. When the lens is interfered with in some way—through manipulation, injury, exposure to certain kinds of medications or ultraviolet rays, or just plain aging—the lens fibers may respond by becoming opaque, like a piece of plastic that has aged. This is how cataracts form.

THE LACRIMAL GLANDS

Shedding tears is a normal process, and a good cry now and then relieves tension. It is the lacrimal glands that produce tears. Tears work constantly to bathe the outer surfaces of the eyes in fluid, keeping them healthy and comfortable. These secretions flow across the cornea and empty into small ducts, called *puncta,* that are found in the inner lower corners of the eyes, next to the nose. If your eyes become irritated, tearing results.

THE VITREOUS BODY

The vitreous body is a gel-like substance that, although fluid, acts like a semisolid structure, keeping the eye rigid. The vitreous body is mainly inactive. As we age, the gel often breaks down a bit. If this occurs, you may see little specks, called *floaters,* that sometimes interfere with vision. Most of the time, these are harmless, although if you begin to see a lot of black floaters, you should consult your ophthalmologist, as it may signal that your retina is in trouble. A heavy shower of floaters can be a sign of a detaching (or detached) retina.

THE CILIARY BODY

The ciliary body is a ring-shaped structure that is joined at one end to the iris and at the other to the retina. It consists of layers of cells arranged in about seventy folds that look like tiny sausages. These are the *ciliary processes,* and they are responsible for producing the aqueous humor. The aqueous humor is a wonderful brew of oxygen and nutrients, among them vitamin C, minerals, glucose, and adenosine triphosphatase (ATPase), a vital metabolic enzyme.

Attached to the ciliary body is the ciliary muscle. This muscle contracts and expands, depending upon what your eyes are focused on. In doing so, it loosens or tightens the zonular fibers that hold the lens in place, which serves to focus the lens.

The ciliary body is one of the key players in the glaucoma picture because it is responsible for maintaining the intraocular pressure (the pressure within the eye). For proper pressure to be maintained, the rate at which the ciliary body produces aqueous humor must match the rate at which the aqueous humor leaves the eye through its various filtration channels. If the system fails, trouble ensues.

The system may fail in a number of ways. Fluid produced by the ciliary body must squeeze through a very narrow space between the lens and the iris. If something in the eye causes this space to narrow even further or close altogether, the fluid that becomes trapped or limited in its outflow pushes the iris forward into the trabecular meshwork, through which the fluid is supposed to drain out of the eye. In this position, the iris blocks the trabecular meshwork, a situation that can lead to the type of glaucoma called angle-closure glaucoma in susceptible individuals. If the meshwork becomes plugged up in some way, the flow of fluid out of the eye and into the bloodstream is hampered as well.

Whatever the particular scenario, when fluid cannot easily exit the eye, it builds up in the front of the eye and presses against the scleral walls. In adults, these walls are quite rigid, so this cannot be observed from the outside. In infants, however, because the sclera is still quite elastic, aqueous accumulations cause the eye to bulge outward, creating what is commonly called "cow's eye." Whether visible or not, the presence of excess fluid pressure signals danger, for when the fluid cannot escape, the pressure it creates presses against the fibers of the optic nerve.

Our body's chemistry is remarkable: It is designed to instruct itself to do the right thing. Normally, fluid buildup in the eye is matched by an increased level of outflow sufficient to maintain a steady state. In those of us who have glaucoma, however, this adjustment may be distorted or incomplete. The reason for this is not always apparent. It is known, however, that blockage in the trabecular meshwork causes pressure to rise, and that minute bits of cellular debris in the eye can clog up the meshwork. Scientists are investigating the role of the cilary body in this process, as well as how the presence of certain proteins, vitamins (such as vitamin C), bicarbonate, peroxide, and other substances affect the eyes. Glaucomatous eyes (eyes affected by glaucoma) appear to react differently to these substances than normal eyes do. Other researchers are looking into the way ciliary muscle cells regulate the outflow of aqueous humor. These are only a few examples of the explorations of the workings of the ciliary body currently underway.

A great deal is happening in glaucoma research, and hopefully will lead to the development of new and effective treatments for the condition.

THE TRABECULAR MESHWORK AND SCHLEMM'S CANAL

One of the first medical terms I heard when my glaucoma was diagnosed was *trabecular meshwork.* At first, I was not convinced that it could be the seat of my problem. Since then I have had laser therapy treatments and filtration operations that have proved it to be at least partially true.

This tiny bit of tissue (less than one-eighth inch in size) can be compared to a one-way spongelike tissue valve. It is located in what is called the *angle,* the place where the iris and the cornea meet (see Figure 1.2). It is very thin and spongy, about one-fiftieth of an inch wide, and consists of an interlacing of tiny beams of tissue (the word *trabecular* comes from the Latin for "beam"). The beams contain a core of collagen and cells. The meshwork is punctured by openings of different sizes. A gel-like substance fills these spaces. Aqueous humor drains through these structures and into Schlemm's canal, which is a ring-shaped network of passages. From there the fluid drains into the bloodstream by means of tiny veins.

Glaucoma can occur if this drainage system clogs up. It's a little like putting a stopper in your sink; if the faucet is not turned off, water will overflow and spill out of the sink. Inside your eye, however, the liquid cannot escape, and as more of it accumulates in the anterior part of your eye, pressure builds. This accumulation of liquid elevates the pressure in your entire eye. The pressure in turn leads to the loss of nerve cells in both the retina and the optic nerve.

What causes the trabecular meshwork to go wrong? Flexibility is an important feature of the meshwork, but with age, it can become too sclerotic (rigid) or too flaccid (limp) to function properly. Excessive scarring, whether a result of injury or a consequence of surgery, may also contribute to lessening the meshwork's efficiency in removing liquid. Researchers have discovered that in persons with normal vision, about half of the cells in the trabecular meshwork disappear by the age of eighty. However, persons in midlife who have glaucoma apparently also have fewer cells. In other words, it appears that the trabecular meshwork ages prematurely in people with glaucoma.

When glaucoma strikes, the tissues become more granular and develop a substance called plaque. As glaucoma worsens, the entire

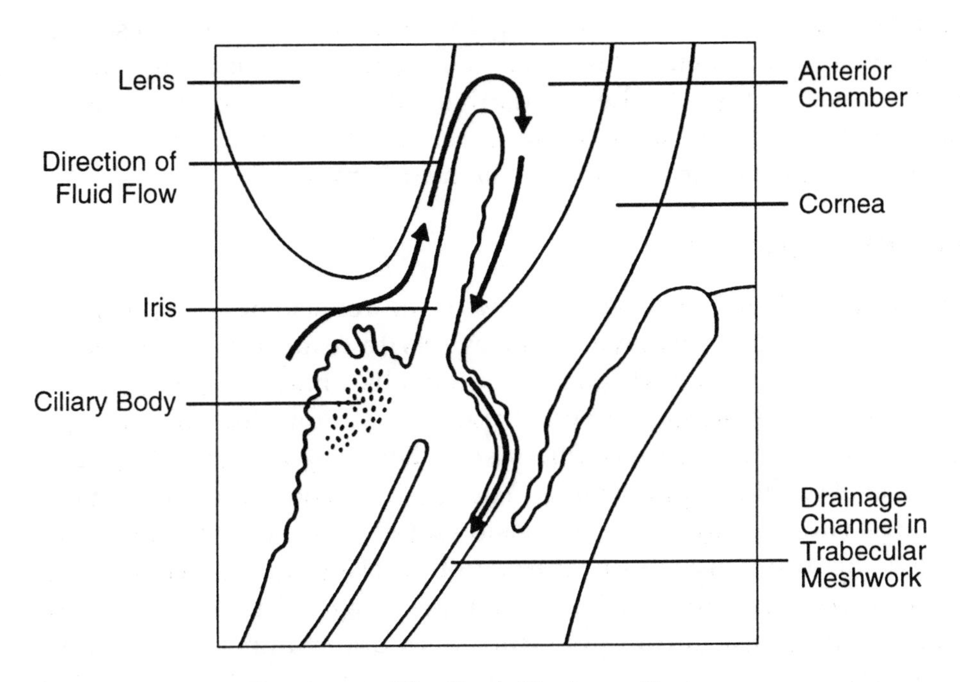

Figure 1.2 The Eye's Drainage System

meshwork becomes a mass of granular matter and collapses in on itself. Also, when cells die, they fuse together and are apt to block the openings through which the fluid flows. While many theories are still speculative, with certain forms of glaucoma the answers are evident. With pigmentary-dispersion glaucoma, for example, it is believed that pigment from the iris lodges in the outflow channels of the trabecular meshwork. With exfoliative glaucoma, the same thing happens with flakes resembling dandruff that peel off, it is believed, from tissues within the eye. (More about these conditions in Chapter 2.)

Steroids and other chemicals can have a profound effect on the cells of the trabecular meshwork as well. Increased levels of steroids can cause cells to change into irregular shapes that inhibit fluid movement. Scientists have found a sensitive response to the steroid drug dexamethasone in 95 percent of patients with open-angle glaucoma. Dexamethasone is found in numerous prescription and over-the-counter medications used to control rashes, inflammation, and allergic reactions, among other things.

Finally, there is research now underway looking at many factors that may hamper the ability of the trabecular meshwork to function properly. The oxidation of substances within the cells of the meshwork, and the body's ability to protect against it, is one avenue of research. The transport of electrolytes into and out of the cells of the eye is also under investigation. As these and other subjects are explored, we can hope that answers to some of our questions concerning the causes of glaucoma may be forthcoming in the near future.

THE RETINA

The retina, a layer of nerve tissue with the consistency of wet tissue paper, is the innermost layer of the eye. With respect to vision, this is where the real action is. Millions of retinal cells—nature's microchips—constantly flash messages to your brain. These countless bits of information are carried on nerve fibers, somewhat like electrical impulses that travel on fiber-optic strands. Your brain decodes these messages, much as your telephone and television set decode electrical impulses.

For this transmission of information to the brain, the cells of the retina are divided into two basic cell types: the *rods* and the *cones.* The rods function best in dim light, the cones under lighted conditions. There are about 7 million cones and 125 million rods, a total that is—imagine—equal to about half the number of people living in the United States.

The cones are snappy little numbers that spring to attention the moment light hits them. They handle fine details and color. The rods, on the other hand, are laggards, taking about ten minutes to come to attention when you enter a dim or darkened room. Their job, in addition to helping you see in the dark, is to distinguish black and white.

That's not the whole story. Your sight is further refined by the connection of each rod and cone to a type of cell called a *bipolar cell.* The job of the bipolar cells is to relay messages to the over 1.9 million *ganglion cells,* which carry the messages to the brain. The bipolar cells have a lot of responsibilities. They are divided into two types, the *magno cells,* numbering about 10 percent of the total, and the *parvo cells,* which are much more numerous at 90 percent of the total. The magno cells make it possible to distinguish shapes in indistinct light and to see in the dark. Thanks to these cells, you can find a penny on a wood floor in dim light, locate that black jacket in the back of your closet, or see your dog Fido in a field at night. Loss of magno cells may impair your ability to read, causing difficulty in separating the details of letters, spaces, and the breaks between words. The parvo cells fill in the details, like a painter adding texture, line, and color to the basic sketch.

Since there are fewer ganglion cells than there are rods and cones, several hundred rods and cones are connected to each ganglion cell, forming a field around the cell. If you were to lose ganglion cells, it would affect your ability to see well in dim light, cause difficulty in contrasting similar shades of color, and make detail fuzzy. Cataracts can cause similar symptoms. Before my cataract operation, I bought rose-colored towels that I had thought were beige. When I saw color again, I had to redo my bathroom scheme.

The *macula,* in the center of the retina, contains the richest supply of ganglion cells. It is the hub of sight. If you lose cells in this region, it robs you of the ability to see things in the center of the visual field and compromises your ability to fixate (to focus the eyes on a specific point or object). You need to fixate in order to read, for example. Otherwise, the letters seem to jump around on the page. Macular failure is a condition most often associated with age-related macular degeneration (AMD), a disease that primarily affects the elderly. With glaucoma, damage to the macula generally does not occur until the final stages of the disease. Glaucoma patients experience visual loss in their peripheral areas first. Unfortunately, there are fewer cells in this area, so if you lose any of them, your peripheral vision decreases. While this type of vision loss is not as disabling as the loss of central vision experienced by people with AMD, it is, nevertheless, worrisome, for you find your side vision, and your top and bottom vision, falling away.

Plumb in the center of the macula is a tiny body of densely packed cone cells, each with its own connecting ganglion cell. The fact that each cone cell in this area gets its own ganglion cell is an indication of how important this area is for seeing. This body, the *fovea,* is your spyglass; it makes you able to spy a bird in a treetop, see a statue decorating the corner of a high building, or look miles into the distance on a clear day. Birds of prey, such as hawks and vultures, possess not one, but two, foveas that act as magnifiers, enabling them to locate objects that even the sharpest of human eyes cannot detect. Such birds can detect the presence of a creature that might become dinner from 9,000 to 13,000 feet in the air.

Perhaps the most remarkable feature of our sight apparatus is that the eye produces actual images on the retina. A tiny inverted image appears continuously during the act of seeing. This image is slowed down or speeded up depending upon the strength of the light source, the eye's ability to fixate, and the general health of the rods, cones, and nerve cells. For example, in dim light, you may find it takes a bit longer to discern the outlines or details of an object. A similar situation occurs if you have cataracts or have trouble fixating because of a loss of cone cells in the eye. You may find yourself needing more time to, say, read a menu in a dimly lit restaurant or read the subtitles in a foreign movie. When I watch a movie with subtitles, I often want to yell, "Slow down!" If there are two-line subtitles, I can manage to get through only the first line before the film moves on.

THE OPTIC NERVE

The optic nerve transmits messages from the retina to the brain. Nerve fibers called *axons* extending from the ganglion cells are bundled into packages of about 2,000 each to form the optic nerve and its head. The bundles are separated by tissues that have narrow openings.

Second to worrying about the condition of the trabecular meshwork, we glaucoma patients worry about our optic nerves. Any undue pressure, chemical imbalance, genetic abnormality, or lack of circulation can damage the cell structure of the optic nerve. The greater the number of cells lost, the less we see. One reason for the extreme fragility of the optic nerve is that when the nerve fibers enter it, they bend at a 90-degree angle, which leaves the fibers in a vulnerable position. Another problem is that the nerve cells, while several inches long, are extremely thin—about one one-thousandth of an inch in diameter. Any compression of these delicate fibers damages them, and if the compression is constant, the nerve cells die. Once damaged or destroyed, these nerve cells do not regenerate. In the future, with advances in nerve-cell regeneration (progress has already been made in animal studies and in some cases of spinal cord injury), regeneration of the nerve cells in the eyes may become possible.

When your eye doctor dilates your eyes, he or she can see your optic nerve and determine whether any damage has occurred. What your doctor looks for is a phenomenon called *cupping.* To remain healthy, the optic nerve must have a good supply of blood. A healthy optic nerve looks something like an overhead view of a white cup sitting on a pink or red saucer. If the blood flow is diminished, the white area becomes larger. The larger the cup and the smaller the rim of the saucer, the greater the damage.

Blood pressure plays a role in regulating blood flow to the optic nerve. As we age, our autoregulatory capacity—that is, our bodies' ability to regulate blood pressure—weakens. If blood pressure rises or is variable, it can cause a change in intraocular pressure. In addition, decreased blood flow resulting from cardiovascular disease can affect the optic nerve. During sleep, your blood pressure may drop, or a vascular problem resulting from cardiovascular disease such as arteriosclerosis or arterial hypotension may reduce blood flow. If this happens, your optic nerve may suffer. Strange as it may seem, both high and low blood pressure can lead to optic nerve damage.

WHAT DOES THE FUTURE HOLD?

We glaucoma patients and our families worry about our losing our sight. We measure the years left to us by the health of our eyes. And we constantly ask what is being done to find solutions. It is encouraging to find that researchers are focusing more and more on locating the underlying causes of glaucoma. Spurred on by the National Eye Institute's guidelines and by the funding flowing from that organization, and from nonprofit organizations dedicated to glaucoma research—and by their own inner voices, which are telling them they are treating symptoms rather than the cause—scientists are delving into the very essence of life to find answers. They are studying how cells interact, how the immune system affects the eye, how the intricacies of blood circulation function, and, perhaps most exciting, the genetic roots of various forms of glaucoma. What we eat, where we live, the air we breathe—all of this may one day be found to have an effect on the eye's functioning.

One cannot help but be awed by the complexity and versatility of this all-important organ, the eye. Yet as long as our vision is good, most of us consider our ability to see to be unremarkable. Not until our vision is threatened do we begin to seek to understand the many things that may affect our eyesight. In the next chapter, we will look more closely at the glaucomas and find that, although not infinite in its variety, glaucoma is a condition that has many different faces.

CHAPTER 2

Shedding Light on the Glaucomas

No object is mysterious. The mystery is in your eyes.

Elizabeth Bowen (1935)

Many people have the impression that (to paraphrase Gertrude Stein) glaucoma is glaucoma is glaucoma. But is it? Not really.

Glaucoma is now believed to be the end product of a number of distinct structural and systemic diseases characterized by high pressure inside the eye and optic nerve damage. This pressure can damage and even kill the sensitive nerve cells in the back of the eye, causing loss of sight. Glaucoma is not a new disease. The ancient Greeks gave us the term glaucoma, which they used to describe all eye diseases leading to blindness. In the first several centuries A.D., cataracts, which are amenable to treatment, began to be distinguished from glaucoma, which could not be treated. The association of glaucoma with increased pressure in the eye is often attributed to Richard Banister, an English oculist and author of the first book on ophthalmology in English, who made this observation in 1622 (although there is some evidence that earlier Arab physicians may have known this as well). Banister noted that if you felt an eye with glaucoma by rubbing on the eyelids, the eye felt more hard and solid than normal.

Today, a diagnosis of glaucoma is based on three factors: intraocular pressure (IOP), the pressure within the eye, which is typically elevated; characteristic changes in the visual field, specifically a loss of peripheral vision; and signs of damage to the optic nerve. Very often the first indication that glaucoma may be present is an increase in IOP. Since the 1930s, eye doctors have distinguished between two primary forms of the disease: open-angle and narrow-angle glaucoma. These determinations were based on the width of the angle formed by the meeting of the iris and the cornea (see page 6). Grades I and II glaucoma (glaucoma in the presence of 10-degree and 20-degree angles, respectively) were designated narrow-angle glaucoma; grades III and IV glaucoma (glaucoma in the presence of 30-degree and 40-degree angles, respectively) were termed open-angle glaucoma.

Angle-closure glaucoma—glaucoma caused by a narrow angle and/or close proximity of structures within the eye to each other—may be considered a structural problem. Open-angle glaucoma is divided into a number of different varieties. The most common type of glaucoma is *primary open-angle glaucoma.* The other glaucomas that make up the open-angle family are variously called structural or secondary, or glaucoma as an end product of a disease. Today, researchers have recorded more than a dozen distinct forms of glaucoma, and there may be more. Some scientists claim that they can differentiate between as many as forty different types of glaucoma.

Although primary open-angle glaucoma accounts for the majority of cases of glaucoma, many people do have other forms. Certainly this is true of the participants in our glaucoma support group. Both Rita's and my glaucoma may be related to systemic disease, for example. As the differences among glaucomas become clearer, and the root causes are better identified, researchers may be able to develop specific treatments for controlling each individual type of glaucoma.

Rita and I have found that knowing more about the particular forms of glaucoma that afflict us has helped us to deal with our conditions. This desire to know more resonated among the members of our support group, for we all found that when we learned about medications, laser procedures, and operations, we could cope better with the care and management of our individual glaucomas. Furthermore, sharing our experiences helped us to realize that we were not alone. Our individual histories helped us all to come to terms with our conditions. Here are some of our experiences—and profiles of some of glaucoma's different faces.

PRIMARY OPEN-ANGLE GLAUCOMA

Primary open-angle glaucoma (POAG) is the most common form of glaucoma. It affects 1 percent of the U.S. population over the age of forty. It is called primary because no underlying disease has been identified as the cause of the condition. However, a genetic discovery at the University of Iowa College of Medicine in 1997 sheds new light on the possible origins of POAG. A mutation in a gene identified as TIGR, located on chromosome 1, was found to result in the manufacture of a protein that gums up the trabecular meshwork. When the trabecular meshwork fails to do its job—that of removing aqueous humor from the anterior chamber—the fluid builds up, causing pressure that ultimately results in damage to the optic nerve. This mutation is believed to be only one genetic factor that may be responsible for POAG. Others have yet to be identified. What is known for certain are a number of risk factors that predispose an individual to developing POAG. These include a family history of glaucoma (one or more family members who have had the condition); myopia (nearsightedness); being over thirty-five, and being of African-American descent. Statistically, African-Americans are four times more likely to develop glaucoma and eight times more likely to succumb to blindness than members of other ethnic groups.

A diagnosis of high intraocular pressure is not necessarily a diagnosis of glaucoma. If your eye doctor finds that your IOP is higher than 22 millimeters of mercury, or 22 mm Hg (10 to 21 mm Hg is considered normal), he or she will then check your optic nerve and your visual field (how far you can see from side to side and up and down while you stare at a fixed point). If you have no vision loss, you may have what the doctors call ocular hypertension—that is, pressure above the normal range. This condition may or may not lead to glaucoma, but it puts you in the category of "glaucoma suspect." As a glaucoma suspect, you will need to have your eyes monitored regularly to determine whether your ocular hypertension is benign or whether it has developed into glaucoma. A National Eye Institute research study now in progress may help to determine whether persons with high tension but no vision loss can be expected to remain free of glaucoma or not, but in the meantime, persons with high tension are advised to see their eye doctors regularly to assure that their vision is unaffected by their higher tensions.

On the other hand, if your doctor finds vision loss and optic nerve damage, glaucoma will likely be diagnosed and immediate treatment recommended, for if the pressure in your eye rises, it can compress the nerves in the retina and crush them.

> Sally, afraid that she might get glaucoma, began having her eyes checked yearly, starting at the age of thirty-five. In her mid-forties, her fears were confirmed; her ophthalmologist told her she had open-angle glaucoma. This was the same diagnosis given to her father on his eighty-third birthday. Sally was wise to have her eyes checked periodically, for glaucoma is said to run in families.

If you have POAG, you should visit your eye doctor regularly for checkups. At times, even if you are on medication, the pressure in your eyes can creep up, and you may need further intervention such as laser therapy or a filtering operation. Many of us at first do not realize the gravity of glaucoma, and only the urging of our friends and family impels us to seek out a doctor specializing in the treatment of the disease. I was one of those people. When my condition was first diagnosed, I ignored it. Only when my sight worsened, and my friends got worried and insisted I see a specialist, did I begin to take my ailment seriously. Yet eye doctors feel strongly that primary open-angle glaucoma, when caught early, can be controlled. Sally, now sixty-seven, has lost only a tiny bit of her sight. She is one of the lucky ones.

Some people, like Sally's father, do not develop glaucoma until they become senior citizens. If glaucoma develops in later life, you can probably expect to retain your sight with the help of medication and medical interventions when necessary.

GLAUCOMAS CAUSED BY THE FORMATION OF THE EYE

Two types of glaucoma, narrow-angle and pigmentary dispersion, result from the configuration of the eye. In all likelihood, these types of glaucoma are inherited.

Narrow-Angle Glaucoma

Narrow-angle glaucoma occurs when the angle formed by the iris and cornea is less than 20 degrees wide. In contrast, people with no structural problems have at least a 40-degree opening. Not all people with narrow angles develop glaucoma. However, if you have narrow angles, you should be monitored by an eye doctor because this condition makes you susceptible to an acute angle-closure glaucoma attack if your angles should become blocked. The people who are most likely to have narrow angles are those with hyperopia (farsightedness). This wonderful facility for seeing long-distance is made possible by a smaller, rounder eye—which, unfortunately, results in a narrower angle because there is less room in the front of the eye.

Narrow-angle glaucoma can be chronic, in which case it is called *chronic angle-closure glaucoma,* or it can produce an acute glaucoma attack called *acute angle-closure attack.* Chronic angle-closure glaucoma occurs if the iris begins to move into the angle formed where the iris and cornea meet (see Figure 2.1). This movement of the iris is the result of a whole sequence events. To get to the anterior chamber, the aqueous fluid must squeeze through a tiny opening between the iris and the lens. As we age, the lens becomes larger, which narrows this tiny passage and hampers the flow of aqueous fluid. The decrease in fluid outflow in turn leads to a buildup of fluid behind the iris, which presses the iris forward into the angle. Furthermore, when this situation occurs, scar tissue slowly forms between the iris and the drainage area, and eventually the accumulation of scar tissue covers the drainage area. This prevents the remaining fluid from leaving the anterior chamber and results in an even greater buildup of pressure.

With an acute angle-closure attack, the scenario is much the same as in the chronic condition, except that dilation of the pupil adds a serious consequence. When the pupil enlarges, the iris is forced to fold back, increasing its thickness and bringing it even closer to the outer and inner walls of the angle. Dilation of the pupil is an autonomic (involuntary) response to dim light, drugs, stress, fatigue, anxiety, excitement, close work, upper respiratory illness, and a number of other ordinary situations. For most people, it is a normal condition, and unless you are a glaucoma suspect, it does not present a problem. A subtype of angle-closure glaucoma is called *malignant glaucoma.* In this condition, the ciliary body rotates and blocks off the flow of fluid. This is most likely to occur following a filtering operation or cataract-removal surgery.

An acute angle-closure attack is serious business. Intraocular pressure can rise as high as 80 mm Hg and cause permanent damage to the eye. Scars can form on the angle, the optic nerve can be partially destroyed, and cataracts may form. Immediate treatment to reduce the pressure is vital for preserving vision.

Natalie, age sixty, went into her bathroom one night. She saw tiny lights dancing before her eyes, and she could not see the

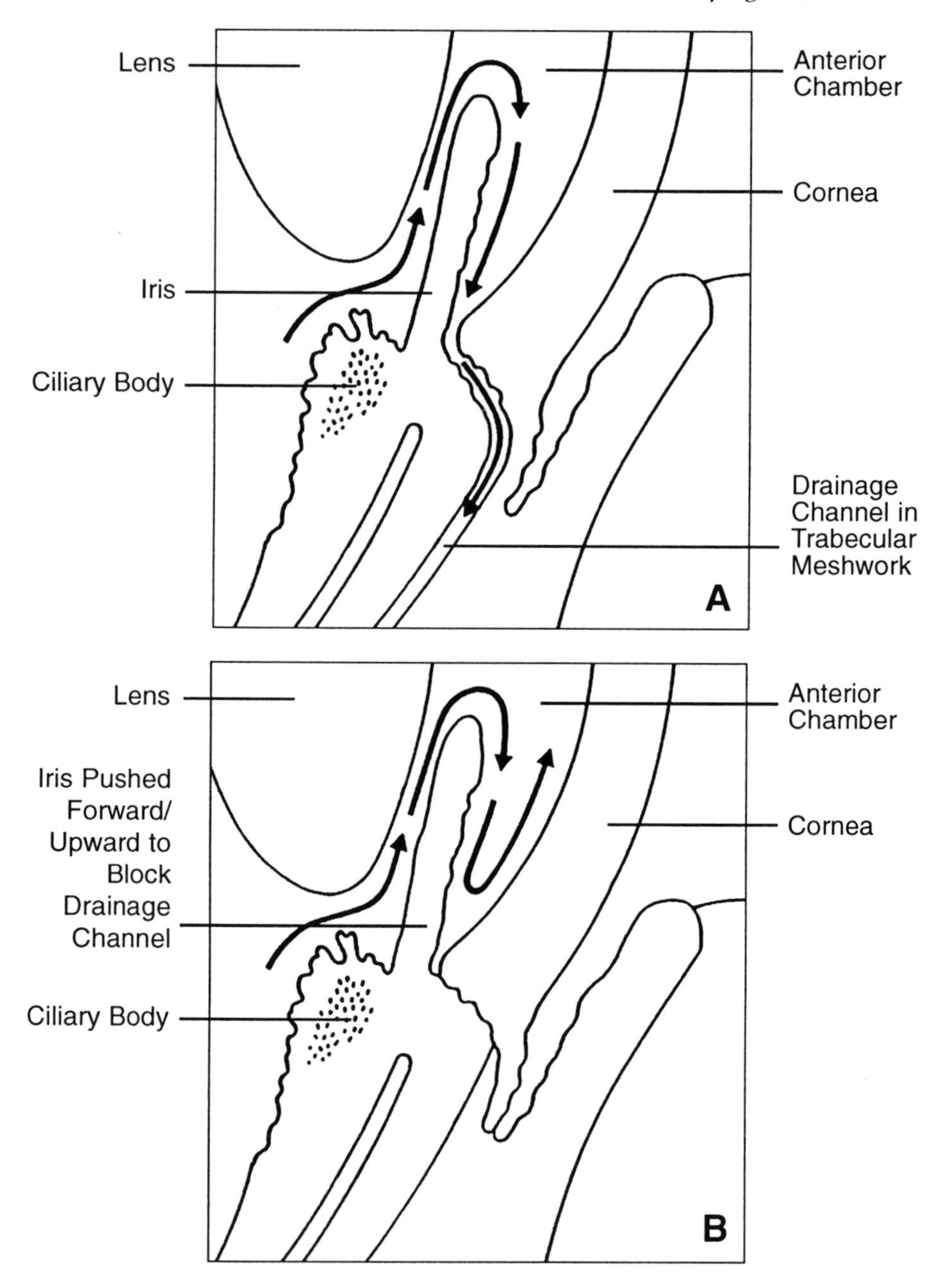

Figure 2.1 How the Iris Can Move Into the Angle

In a healthy eye, fluid secreted by the ciliary body squeezes through a tiny opening between the lens and the iris to enter the anterior chamber, then drains out through the trabecular meshwork (figure A). If the tiny opening narrows, however, fluid can build up behind the iris and push it forward and upward into the angle (figure B), closing off the drainage channels. Fluid then accumulates in the anterior chamber as well and IOP rises.

sink or the bathtub. When she turned the light on, the phenomenon disappeared, and she forgot about it. But the lights did not disappear for good. Several days later, she saw them again, and now her head ached. Alarmed, she called her ophthalmologist for an appointment. Her doctor discovered she had a pressure of 65 mm Hg in one eye and was in danger of losing the sight in that eye. He recommended immediate treatment, for Natalie had narrow-angle glaucoma.

When people talk about the horrors of glaucoma, they are generally referring to narrow-angle glaucoma. It seems to come out of nowhere. One day you're fine; the next day you're in danger of losing your sight. Unlike POAG—which is so symptomless that eye doctors call it "the sneak thief of sight"—narrow-angle glaucoma virtually shouts at you that something is wrong with your eye. You may see strange light effects, like Natalie did, or you may see halos around electric lights. You may very well have a terrible headache centered around the area of the affected eye. If you have any of these symptoms, take yourself *immediately* to an eye doctor or to the emergency room of a hospital that has an eye clinic. Insist that an eye doctor who understands the gravity of glaucoma attacks diagnose your condition. It is important that you get attention immediately, or you may lose your sight in the affected eye.

Who is most likely to have a narrow-angle problems? Worldwide, Asians head the list. In this country, narrow-angle problems are more prevalent among African-Americans, although in the majority of cases, their glaucomas are of the chronic angle-closure type rather than acute angle-closure attacks. The reason for this appears to lie in the fact that African-Americans have irises that are thicker and more rigid than those of other groups. This slows the movement of the iris into the angle when dilation or other problems occur in the eye.

Narrow-angle glaucoma must be monitored carefully by an ophthalmologist. Any sign that the iris is moving into the angle may require some form of treatment. It should be remembered, too, that glaucoma plays no favorites. While the condition is more common among those of African ancestry, no one of any race or ethnic background is exempt.

Persons who are under fifty and develop narrow-angle glaucoma are sometimes diagnosed as having *plateau iris.* In this condition, the iris is pushed forward by the ciliary body. In some people, the ciliary body is in a more forward position than normal, and its projections, called ciliary processes, butt up against the iris and push it into part of the angle.

Pigmentary-Dispersion Glaucoma

Pigmentary-dispersion glaucoma is a type of glaucoma also involving the anatomy of the eye. In persons with pigmentary-dispersion glaucoma, the angle is typically open. It may, in fact, be unusually wide, contributing to a concave rather than a convex-shaped iris. This configuration causes the iris to rub against the lens and the zonular fibers that hold the lens in place. This action releases pigment from the iris. It's like grating the rind of a lemon to make lemon zest. The particles of pigment circulate in the aqueous humor and eventually end up in the trabecular meshwork, where they clog up the pores. Open-angle glaucoma that occurs before the age of fifty is usually pigmentary-dispersion glaucoma.

> Ben, age thirty-four, discovered his own glaucoma. Ben is the type of person who always asks the important questions and quickly apprehends the most technical details. And when Ben discovered he had glaucoma, he immediately knew the steps that should be taken. Since the ophthalmologist he saw at that time did not recommend a visual field exam to check for vision loss, Ben asked that he be given one. This test did show a defect, and Ben immediately switched to another ophthalmologist, who diagnosed Ben's condition as pigmentary dispersion.

Ben falls into the category of persons who are most susceptible to this form of glaucoma. He is a myopic (nearsighted) male in his middle thirties. Pigmentary-dispersion glaucoma most often strikes myopic males in their twenties through early thirties. Doctors believe the reason for this is that the eyes of males expand and grow larger than those of females. As the eye grows larger, the iris rubs against the zonular fibers, the ligaments that keep the lens in place. This action strips off pigment from the iris. Once freed, these stripped-off bits of pigment attach to other parts of the eye—the lens, the ligaments, the cornea, and, unfortunately, the trabecular meshwork, where they clog up the pores. Although males appear to be more susceptible to this type of glaucoma, women can develop it as well. When they do, they fare about the same as men.

If you are diagnosed as having pigmentary-dispersion glaucoma, dilation of the pupil is a danger. You should be cautious about having your eye dilated if you happen to see an ophthalmologist other than your regular physician. You may also want to limit your exposure to dim light. However, if you are taking a miotic drug (a drug that constricts the pupil, such as pilocarpine or carbachol, which are commonly prescribed for glaucoma), you needn't worry about dilation. Bouncy exercise is also thought to release pigment, so it is probably best to choose less jarring forms of exercise, like power walking and stretching rather than running or doing aerobics.

The good news about pigmentary-dispersion glaucoma is that in some cases it becomes a self-limiting disease. That is, unlike other forms of glaucoma, as you grow older, the effects of the glaucoma decrease because age-related changes in the eye decrease the likelihood of pigmentary release. That gives the phagocytes, cells that act as your body's clean-up crew, the opportunity to tidy up the meshwork. And as long as they don't sweep up some good cells in the trabecular meshwork in their zeal, you're free and clear.

It is possible to have pigmentary dispersion but not develop glaucoma. Ben's sister has the syndrome and she is free of the disease. Scientists believe that a gene exists for this condition but they have not yet located it.

SECONDARY GLAUCOMAS

Glaucomas that arise as a result of other, systemic diseases are called secondary glaucomas. Some of these diseases are more readily identifiable than others. The picture is further complicated by the fact that while some people with certain diseases develop glaucoma, others do not. On the other hand, some people (myself included) can name several conditions, such as exfoliation and retinal detachment, as possible causes of our glaucomas. Rita feels that a heavy steroid intake for a chronic condition in her youth may have been a chief contributing cause of her glaucoma.

Nevertheless, the picture of what causes certain types of glaucoma, such as exfoliative syndrome, uveitis, and low-tension glaucoma, are not yet in sharp focus, although they are gradually becoming clearer. Better understood are the glaucomas resulting from vascular (blood vessel) problems such as diabetic retinopathy. Here we shall consider a number of conditions that can give rise to secondary glaucomas.

Exfoliation Syndrome

Exfoliation syndrome results from a flaking of cells within the eye. They are thought to come from the epithelial (lining) cells in the front of the eye. These flakes look like dandruff, but they are not so benign. Like the pigment flakes in pigmentary-dispersion glaucoma, they settle in the trabecular meshwork, where they gum up the works, even though persons with exfoliation syndrome usually have wide-open angles.

When the ophthalmologist treating me for retinal tears diagnosed *pseudoexfoliation* of my eyes, I dismissed the information as irrelevant. My husband, who was with me at the time of the examination, did not take this information lightly. He looked the word up in the dictionary and told me it meant flaking. Even then, I did not become overly concerned—until I developed glaucoma in the eye that had the greatest amount of exfoliation. That was when I discovered that this form of glaucoma is one of the most insidious, for, in many cases, it is hard to control and can lead to blindness.

For a long time doctors referred to exfoliation syndrome as pseudo-exfoliation to distinguish it from another condition in which exposure to excessively high heat caused a flaking of the lens that led to cataracts. Today most doctors have dropped the *pseudo* from the term and refer to the condition as exfoliation. Although some people have exfoliation and do not have glaucoma, the medical community believes that it is the exfoliation that causes the glaucoma. The course of treatment recommended for exfoliative glaucoma is much the same as that for primary open-angle glaucoma, including medication, laser treatment, and/or surgery.

As scientists continue to study this condition, however, newer and more effective treatments may one day be developed. Researchers are trying to determine the precise composition of the fibers that make up the exfoliated flakes and their effect on other cells. They are also trying to analyze just what causes the cells to be shed. Studies have located exfoliation in other organs of the body as well, including the heart, kidneys, and lungs. With answers as to the exact nature of exfoliation syndrome, treatment for the condition may change for the better.

Uveitis

Uveitis is a generic term that denotes an inflammation inside the eye. The uvea is the middle layer of the eye that incorporates the choroid (blood vessels), the ciliary body, and the iris. The suffix *itis*—as in tonsillitis, bursitis, or arthritis—means "inflammation."

A viral infection may cause this disorder, but in many cases no virus can be identified. There is some evidence from recent studies that an antigen (a substance, usually a protein, that provokes the formation of antibodies) found in the retina may be the cause. If so, that would put this disease in the autoimmune category. An autoimmune disease is one in which the immune system for some reason attacks the body's own tissues.

> Mary had once been a stage actress. In the roles she played, she used her wonderful eyes to display the emotions of fear, anger, love, tenderness, and joy. With age, the eyes that had served her so well began to trouble her. She developed uveitis, and within a short time thereafter, glaucoma followed. Mary still cannot understand what caused her significant sight loss. She was told that her high pressures of 40 mm Hg might have resulted from taking too little anti-inflammatory medication for her uveitis, or, conversely, they might have been caused by the medication. Or her problems might have been directly related to the inflammation itself.

The mechanism by which uveitis leads to glaucoma is not clearly understood, and not all persons who have uveitis develop glaucoma. But when glaucoma does occur, it appears to be due to the effects of inflammation on both the ciliary body and the trabecular meshwork.

According to one theory, the inflammation of uveitis itself leads to glaucoma. In uveitis, the ciliary body becomes inflamed. The ciliary body, remember, produces the aqueous fluid. When inflammation of the ciliary body occurs, the production of aqueous fluid slows down. This situation can cause structural changes in the eye. Inflammation also summons up the body's defenses, causing white blood cells that act as scavengers to rush in to mop up the debris produced by the inflammation. But these "do-gooder" cells can pile up and land on the cells of the trabecular meshwork, and they, along with the inflammatory materials not absorbed by the white cells, can overburden the meshwork. The cells of the meshwork do their best to regenerate new versions of themselves to replace those lost due to all this activity, but with each bout of uveitis, the cells of the trabecular meshwork become less able to make new cells that will filter out the unwanted materials.

The result of a series of attacks of uveitis is a weakening of the trabecular meshwork, and the materials they would otherwise get rid of are left in the meshwork to clog it up. Intraocular pressure then rises, for the aqueous fluid is blocked from leaving the eye through the drainage system.

Another theory explaining how inflammation leads to glaucoma focuses on prostaglandins, hormonelike substances that are important for many bodily functions. Yet the presence of too many prostaglandins is known to increase eye pressure. To make some prostaglandins, your body uses a fatty acid called arachidonic acid, which is also contained in certain medications. Thus, the theory goes, if you have uveitis and also take medications that contain arachidonic acid, your body may be producing more prostaglandins than is healthy. Because of this, some experts recommend that people with uveitis take an aspirin along with any other medications they must take. The aspirin blocks the synthesis of prostaglandins.

Still another theory, this one based on animal studies, concerns free radicals. We hear a lot about free radicals these days. A free radical is a molecule or a fragment of a molecule that, due to its chemical structure, is highly reactive. If there is an excess of free radicals, they may damage the body's cells and tissues. (More about free radicals in Chapter 10.)

If you receive a diagnosis of uveitis, you should ask your eye specialist to check also for glaucoma. By the time Mary learned she had glaucoma, her uncontrolled uveitis had already caused structural damage to her eyes. Persons with uveitis do not always develop glaucoma, but if you develop this disease, it is worth it to check out the possibility. Doctors often find that with early treatment, glaucoma can be controlled.

Normal-Tension Glaucoma

What a surprise! After all the talk about high intraocular pressure, along comes a glaucoma that defies the rules. Normal-tension glaucoma (or low-tension glaucoma, as it was once called) appears to be a disease of the optic nerve. For reasons not yet clearly understood, the optic nerve begins to die, despite intraocular pressures that are in the normal range (10 to 21 mm Hg).

> Jacquelyn loved to visit art galleries and go to concerts. She also enjoyed folk dancing. Accustomed to perfect sight, she

complained to her ophthalmologist that her eyeglass prescription needed correction. He found nothing wrong with her eyes other than a few floaters, which he said were of no consequence. He measured her intraocular pressure and declared her free of glaucoma, for her pressure was an enviable 12 mm Hg. Yet a year later, she had lost a wedge of sight. "Why?" Jacquelyn asked. "Why, why, why?" In the next five years Jacquelyn lost 50 percent of her vision despite conventional glaucoma treatments.

Theories about the underlying cause of this disease range widely: a misshapen optic nerve head, hemorrhages of the optic nerve disc, a diminished blood supply to the optic nerve, myopia, low blood pressure, high blood pressure, vascular disease, a sedentary lifestyle, carotid artery disease, and migraines, and possibly transient high intraocular pressures during different times of the day and night. Some scientists also speculate that a glaucoma crisis that goes undetected but that leaves a cupped nerve head (see Chapter 1) and substantial visual field loss may be to blame.

Since there are so many variables associated with normal-tension glaucoma, many eye doctors now recommend that anyone with this condition undergo a complete physical examination by a medical practitioner familiar with cardiovascular and neurological disorders. The examination should include blood tests (complete blood count, serum chemistries, erythrocyte sedimentation rate, and carotid blood evaluation), and computer tomography (CT scan.)

Some eye doctors speculate that normal-tension glaucoma may be a totally different disease from other types of glaucoma, and may not even belong to the same family of disorders. However, until the causes of this optic nerve deterioration are sorted out, most ophthalmologists continue to treat this condition as glaucoma. They reason that, for reasons unknown, some eyes may simply be extremely sensitive to pressure. Since pressure is still largely considered one of the major culprits in glaucoma, they recommend reducing intraocular pressure even further, to the low teens or even the high single digits, between 8 and 12 to 14 mm Hg. One recent study indicated that the medication betaxolol (Betoptic) may be helpful in preventing damage to the optic nerve. A series of studies has suggested that breathing in air enriched with carbon dioxide can raise the pulse rate of normal-tension patients, resulting in improved visual field tests.

The Neovascular Glaucomas

Neovascular (literally "new-blood-vessel") *glaucoma* describes the end product of several diseases that affect the orderly flow of blood to and from the retina. Diabetic retinopathy, central retinal vein occlusion (CRVO), and carotid artery occlusive disease (CRAO) are the most common of these diseases. They occur when the fine balance between stimulation and inhibition of the carotid arteries (which bring blood from the heart to the head) and the central retinal vein (which returns the blood from the retina to the heart) become impaired. Each of these diseases is associated with systemic problems that result in blockage to either the central vein or the carotid arteries. When blockage occurs, the regular blood vessels are starved of oxygen. In an attempt to restore circulation, the body responds by releasing substances that stimulate the growth of new blood vessels. But these vessels are misdirected and extremely fragile. They are easily ruptured, leading to hemorrhaging, and they grow wildly over the retina, iris, optic nerve, and trabecular meshwork. This process is called neovascularization.

Not all patients who have diabetes, CRVO, or CRAO develop glaucoma, but when glaucoma becomes part and parcel of these diseases, it needs to be treated. As a result, anyone who has any of these conditions should be sure to see an ophthalmologist regularly, for glaucoma may develop at any time.

Diabetic Retinopathy

Carlos, a diabetic, has already lost half of his right leg to the disease. He fears his sight may go next.

George came to the glaucoma clinic where Rita worked, complaining that he had "bugs in his eyes." Upon examining him, the ophthalmologist discovered that George had lost sight in his right eye to the point where he could barely count the fingers of a hand placed before his eyes.

Both Carlos and George suffer from type II adult-onset insulin-dependent diabetes. Carlos, who visits his ophthalmologist regularly, is on top of any eye condition that may develop. George, who took his insulin faithfully but neglected to see an eye doctor, has practically lost the sight in one eye due to diabetic retinopathy.

Diabetic retinopathy is a complication that affects one of every two patients with diabetes to some extent. In this condition, errant blood vessels travel to places they do not belong—they grow over the iris and the drainage channels, where they clog things up, and over the retina, where they damage nerve tissues.

Fortunately, an ophthalmologist can prescribe certain medications and/or laser treatment to curb the excesses of the retinal vein. And if the blood-sugar level is kept under control, it may be possible to avoid this disease. A study that followed 4,000 diabetics for twenty-five years found that those patients with good blood-sugar control did not develop diabetic retinopathy as frequently as those with poor sugar control.

According to the U.S. Centers for Disease Control and Prevention, 40,000 diabetic patients will lose their vision this year. If you have diabetes, you should see an eye doctor regularly. Spread the word to family and friends who have this disease to follow your example. Some people are unaware that they have diabetes, but do have a history of hypertension. Both Carlos and George have hypertension, and George also has arteriosclerotic heart disease. These conditions are often part and parcel of diabetes.

While laser treatment and/or surgery are often sufficient to protect you from blindness due to diabetic retinopathy, researchers are seeking other means to achieve even better results. One exciting prospect involves transplantation of insulin-producing pancreatic cells, a subject of current research at Duke University. The hope is that transplantation of these cells into the retinal space may allow for minute-to-minute blood-sugar control. There is also a drug, pentoxifylline (Trental), that is now the subject of clinical trials on its effectiveness in slowing the progression of early diabetic retinopathy. In addition, effective early screening for diabetic retinopathy may soon be available through the Internet. A group of researchers at the Oklahoma University Health Sciences Center are working to develop technology that makes it possible to transmit images of a patient's retina to a reading center for professional review; a report would then be returned to the doctor treating the patient, all during the time the patient is being examined.

Central Retinal Vein Occlusion

Central retinal vein occlusion disease (CRVO) is a condition in which the central vein in the retina, which sends blood back to heart, becomes blocked. People at greatest risk of developing CRVO are those with high blood pressure, diabetes, polycythemia (a blood disease), or any other condition that affects blood flow. CRVO usually occurs in persons over sixty, but may also be diagnosed in younger patients.

There are two kinds of CRVO. In the first, the retina is deprived of its blood supply because of blockage of the central retinal vein. In the second, the retina is unaffected. It is with the first type of CRVO that we are concerned, because it is this type of the disorder that often leads to glaucoma.

In this type of CRVO, an inadequate supply of blood supply starves the retina of oxygen, leading to neovascular glaucoma. There may be no immediate signs of glaucoma, for there is a latency period with this condition. As a result, it has been called "100-day glaucoma." Nevertheless, 80 percent of those diagnosed as having occlusion do go on to develop glaucoma within six months. If you are older, your risk is greater, but if you are younger, you are not exempt. Researchers have found that younger patients' pressures can rise to very high levels at certain times of the day, putting them at risk. Scientists speculate that this condition may stem from hypertension, abnormal glucose tolerance, and/or high blood cholesterol levels.

Carotid Artery Occlusive Disease

Carotid artery occlusive disease (CRAO) is the third leading cause of neovascular glaucoma. This disease is caused by atherosclerosis, or hardening, of the carotid arteries, the two major blood vessels that carry blood to the head. If these arteries become hardened or narrowed, the amount of blood flow is reduced. In severe cases, blockage may occur and the blood flow can be cut off completely. It is believed that neovascularization occurs with or is a forerunner of this disease.

Severe cases of CRAO can lead to blindness, for if there is no blood supply to your retina, the retinal tissues can die. Symptoms of CRAO-induced glaucoma include suddenly cloudy vision and a very high intraocular pressure, sometimes as high as 60 mm Hg.

Since all three of the syndromes discussed here—diabetic retinopathy, CRVO, and CRAO—may be present in the same eye, it can be difficult to determine the primary source of spreading blood vessels. Three-quarters of patients diagnosed as having neovascular disease are thought to have carotid artery occlusive disease also. This condition deprives your blood vessels of a much-needed blood supply. If your doctor suspects that you have this disease, you should see a cardiovascular specialist.

Diabetic retinopathy, carotid artery occlusive disease, and central retinal vein occlusion are all syndromes that can cause glaucoma. How? There is a common pattern. Tiny tufts of new blood vessels along the edges of the pupil grow into larger vessels. These travel from the iris into the angle, where they join up with the ciliary body artery. This union produces more new vessels that grow all over the trabecular meshwork, like an ivy plant growing up a brick wall. Linked to these vessels is a fibrovascular membrane (a bundle of tiny blood vessels) that may block the trabecular meshwork, thus causing a secondary glaucoma. The membrane may also contract and cause adhesions between the iris and the drainage system. When the membrane starts to contract, various sites along the iris become scarred, and if enough of these scars form, they may act like a zipper, closing off the angle.

It is possible that the abnormal growth of new blood vessels in the eye may be stimulated by an as-yet-unidentified substance in the aqueous humor produced in response to damage to the iris. Another, perhaps more appealing, theory now gaining acceptance among researchers involves the effect of the available blood supply on the eye. Researchers searching for means of fighting these diseases are targeting a type of protein called vascular endothelial growth factor (VEGF). This substance is capable of stimulating retinal blood vessel growth, Moreover, researchers have found that the concentration of VEGF is dramatically elevated in patients who have abnormal blood vessel growth, but low in those who do not. They are currently experimenting with compounds to decrease VEGF activity. If this effort succeeds, it is possible that a drug may one day be developed that will halt the progress of neovascularization.

GLAUCOMA AND RETINAL DISORDERS

Three months after I underwent photocoagulation (laser treatment) to repair a tear in the retina of my left eye, the doctor who performed the surgery gave me some unpleasant news. "I'm sorry," he said. "You have glaucoma in that eye." *He* was sorry! Imagine how I felt! I had thought the laser therapy would solve my eye problem, but lo and behold, I now had another problem—a much worse one, as I later found out.

At the same time, the doctor observed that I had something he called pseudoexfoliation of the lens (see page 22), but I was much too worried about the glaucoma to think much about pseudoexfoliation. I later discovered, though, that this pseudoexfoliation could be a main factor contributing to my glaucoma. With me, as with many of the other members of our support group and the hundreds of people I have since spoken to, doctors find it hard to pinpoint just what is causing the glaucoma. My glaucoma could have come from my myopia, from my retinal problem (which itself might have been due to myopia, since myopia often results in thinner, more easily torn retinas), from the laser treatment, from the steroid eye drops I used after the laser treatment (doctors now know that with certain susceptible people, steroids will cause a rise in pressure inside the eye), or even from the birth-control pills I took during my middle to late thirties.

A more clear-cut case of glaucoma related to a retinal disorder may occur if you have a detached retina and your doctor performs a laser procedure called scleral buckling. While this treatment seals the retina back in place, it puts you at risk of developing glaucoma. Other retinal problems that can lead to glaucoma include birth defects, diseases of the vitreous body, and AIDS. With AIDS, glaucoma may result from an opportunistic infection with cytomegalovirus, which attacks the retina.

If you have a retinal problem, be sure to call this to the attention of any doctor or other eye care professional you consult. It is a good idea to bring along your records whenever you see any physician for the first time.

MIXED SYMPTOMS

At times, glaucoma can take forms that make it difficult to diagnose correctly. Many of us have experienced this dilemma.

> When Dorothy was thirty-five, a persistent pain in her right eye and right ear drove her to seek medical help. One otologist (ear specialist) told her she had polyps growing in the sinus cavity of her right eye; a second could not find the polyps. She visited two ophthalmologists and received two differing diagnoses. One claimed he found a pressure of 30 mm Hg in her right eye. That would ordinarily put her in the danger zone, although some people with even this high pressure have been known to free of glaucoma. A second doctor recorded normal pressure. Eventually, Dorothy—after seeing several more ophthalmologists—learned she had narrow-angle glaucoma, pigmentary dispersion, and possibly low-tension glaucoma as well.

Dorothy's case illustrates what is now recognized as an array of symptoms that may take different forms. One of these unusual forms of glaucoma mimics open-angle glaucoma and is often mistaken for it. As in open-angle glaucoma, the intraocular pressure rises slowly. However, unlike open-angle glaucoma, in which the iris is static, in this condition the iris moves slowly into the angle and pushes against the trabecular meshwork, adhering to it and eventually closing off the chamber.

CORNEAL PROBLEMS LEADING TO GLAUCOMA

Abnormalities in the cells lining the cornea characterize a range of diseases that can lead to glaucoma. Some of these are referred to collectively as *iridocorneal endothelium syndrome,* or ICE syndrome. The most common are *progressive iris atrophy, Chandler's syndrome,* and *Cogan-Reese syndrome.* One of the least common, which may or may not be part of ICE syndrome, is *polymorphous dystrophy.* In most cases, the first three of these disorders are unilateral, affecting only one eye, although the other eye may have some defects as well. Fortunately, these defects do not follow the pattern leading to glaucoma.

Each of these disorders affects the eye in a different way, although the underlying causes are similar. The predominant feature of progressive iris atrophy is a deformed pupil resulting from a wasting away of the iris. A blockage in the flow of blood to the iris is thought to be responsible; when the iris is starved of blood, it thins out and cannot hold its shape. A change in the shape of the pupil may be a sign that this condition is developing. Progressive iris atrophy most often strikes young women in their twenties and thirties.

With Chandler's syndrome, iris atrophy also occurs, but it may be mild. The main feature of this syndrome is edema (swelling as a result of fluid buildup) of the cornea. With Cogan-Reese syndrome, iris atrophy occurs as well, but the most distinguishing feature is the appearance of pigmented nodules on the surface of the eye.

> While applying mascara, Leona noticed that the pupil of her left eye seemed larger than that of her right eye.
>
> "Bill," she asked her husband, "am I imagining things, or are my eyes different?"
>
> Bill looked into her eyes and declared they were beautiful as always.

"But," Leona persisted, "one pupil is larger than the other, isn't it?"

Bill looked again, and then pointed out to his wife how his right hand and right foot were larger than his left hand and left foot. "It happens," he said, "all over the body."

Leona would have left it at that, except that her eye began to hurt and then her vision blurred. Accompanied by Bill, Leona went to an ophthalmologist for an examination. She was told she had a condition called iridocorneal endothelial syndrome, also known as ICE syndrome. Both Leona and Bill were flabbergasted. Leona wasn't yet twenty and she had a serious eye problem. Now, ten years later, Leona has lost most of the sight in the affected eye, but her other eye remains perfectly normal. She has learned that this is typical of what happens with people who have this particular form of ICE syndrome.

The causes of ICE syndrome may lie in a defective eye that does not develop properly after birth. Some scientists suggest that a viral infection may be to blame. Whatever the reason, once the disease is present, doctors believe it generates the development of a membrane that closes off the angle or covers the trabecular meshwork. When this happens, glaucoma develops.

If you are diagnosed as having glaucoma as a result of ICE syndrome, your doctor will probably follow the standard glaucoma treatments, and you should see your ophthalmologist regularly. You may notice, if you have this particular type of glaucoma, that when you wake in the morning, your vision is blurred. This effect is due to edema of the cornea. During the day, this edema subsides and you begin to feel more comfortable. However, as the disease progresses, the edema may not disappear during the day. That may be your first indication that you have high pressure in your eye. Needless to say, if this occurs, you should see an ophthalmologist as soon as possible.

Not all corneal diseases are considered forms of ICE syndrome. *Axenfeld-Rieger syndrome,* although similar to ICE syndrome, differs in two ways: It often involves both eyes rather than just one, and it is considered to be a congenital abnormality. Another corneal condition that may or may not lead to glaucoma is *Fuch's endothelial dystrophy.* If you have this condition, you may have heard your ophthalmologist refer to it as "corneal guttate," which is the name given to the wartlike growths it causes to appear on the cornea. You may be one of the lucky ones and not suffer vision loss from this condition. If you do go on to develop glaucoma, you may have either open-angle or narrow-angle glaucoma. Since such a small number of people contract this form of the disease, there has been comparatively little research done to track down other factors that contribute to it.

> Rita awoke one morning, at age thirty-two, to find she could not open her right eye. Prior to this incident, a speck of dirt had gotten into her left eye. Unable to use this eye for an hour, she noticed that with her right eye, she was seeing halos around lights and candles whenever she looked at these objects. She later found out that she had a congenital disorder called polymorphous dystrophy, although it was not diagnosed until a year after the incident that sent her to the doctor. Rita had also taken steroids from infancy to the age of twenty-two, and she is nearsighted. Just before her diagnosis of glaucoma, she experienced trauma to her eye.

Rita is one in a million—that is, she is the one in a million people who gets polymorphous dystrophy. Both of her eyes are affected, and her corneal abnormalities are severe. In polymorphous dystrophy, iris problems occur along with corneal complications that cause an excess of cellular debris to accumulate and clog up the trabecular meshwork. This syndrome is usually bilateral, affecting both eyes. Because of the low incidence of this disease in the general population, research on polymorphous dystrophy has been sparse, and since so little is published about it, ophthalmologists may misdiagnose it—as Rita, unfortunately, discovered.

From the time her left eye first began to trouble her, Rita was in constant excruciating pain, and despite medical and surgical therapy, she lost the sight in that eye. Doctors attempting to halt the deterioration of her eye performed a total of two laser procedures and eleven surgeries. Although polymorphous dystrophy usually occurs in infancy or early childhood, Rita did not experience her first symptom until she turned thirty-two.

What do we know of this disease? Very little. There is some speculation that it may be virus-induced, or it may be a result of a genetic abnormality. Rita had vague eye problems during her childhood. It may never be possible to know, but she wonders whether her condition might have resulted from her surgical experience, the use of steroids for asthma in her childhood, or some combination of events.

She has now lost one eye to glaucoma and her other eye is in serious trouble.

MEDICALLY INDUCED GLAUCOMAS

Some glaucomas result from medical interventions that were meant to cure other problems. These are so-called side effects that, unfortunately, can create chronic and long-standing difficulties.

Post-Cataract Glaucoma

> At the age of sixty-five, Jim had his cataracts removed. Both he and his doctor were satisfied with the result. A slight increase in intraocular pressure, a condition that may follow surgery, soon subsided. Yet when Jim returned for his yearly checkup, his ophthalmologist did a routine check for glaucoma and discovered he had high pressures in both eyes.

Post-cataract glaucoma now occurs less often than it once did, due to new techniques for removing cataracts. But it still happens. A cataract operation can precipitate an attack of narrow-angle glaucoma by causing a slight shifting of the parts in the eye, and these—the pupil, the ciliary body, or even trapped air—can block the angle through which the aqueous fluid flows. In addition, surgery to remove cataracts can have the effect of undoing surgery for glaucoma. The complex connections between cataracts and glaucoma, and the treatments for these two conditions, are discussed in detail in Chapter 8.

Ghost-Cell Glaucoma

Ghost cells are blood cells that have degenerated, usually following an operation to stop the vitreous body from hemorrhaging. Sometimes a cataract operation or trauma to the eye can also leave ghost cells. These cells are khaki in color and they serve no purpose; that is why they are called ghost cells. Since they have no home, they often end up in the angle, where they close up the outflow passages. If this happens, the eye must be treated for glaucoma, for the intraocular pressure will rise fast.

Post-Corneal-Transplant Glaucoma

If you need a corneal transplant, you face the same risks as with cataract surgery. Once the eye is operated on, a chain of events can occur. The more operations you have on your eye, the greater the risk, for with each intervention, your eye loses some of its resiliency. If a corneal transplant is a first-time procedure on your eye, chances are that even if you experience a rise in intraocular pressure following surgery, you will not develop glaucoma. Usually this increased pressure lasts no more than a week following the operation. However, if the elevated pressure persists, then you need to pay attention to the glaucoma that has resulted from the procedure.

Steroid-Induced Glaucoma

Steroids are drugs that resemble the famous Dr. Jekyll and Mr. Hyde. On the one hand—the Jekyll part—the adrenal gland produces special beneficial steroids that your body needs. The Hyde part arises with the introduction of medications containing these substances. In some cases, these can successfully heal a condition, but in other cases, they can do damage to the eyes.

Many medications contain some form of steroid. Steroid-containing eye medications abound, and are used to control inflammation, relieve obstruction of the tear ducts, abolish contact lens discomfort, and heal blepharitis (an inflammatory condition affecting the eyelid) and conjunctival hyperemia (dilation of blood vessels producing redness of the conjunctiva, the thin, transparent membrane that covers the front of the eye and the insides of the eyelids). Steroids from ointments used for skin problems can find their way into your eyes if you touch your eyes after applying the ointment. And if the adrenal gland itself, which manufactures steroids, develops tumors, they can cause the gland to produce an overabundance of steroids. There have been instances in which an individual's gland problem was corrected, and that person's eye pressure dropped and no longer showed signs of glaucoma.

Why are steroids harmful? Studies indicate that they hamper the outflow of fluid from the eyes. They are thought to do this by affecting the metabolism of a type of complex carbohydrate called glycosaminoglycan. If these carbohydrates cannot be catabolized (broken down), they clog up the trabecular meshwork. A second problem caused by steroids involves an enzyme found in tears. This enzyme governs the production of compounds important for healthy functioning of the eyes; when the enzyme is deactivated or slowed down, the production of these compounds is inhibited. Other studies focus on the effect of steroids on phagocytes, cells that act as your body's sanitation crew. Steroids suppress the activity of the phagocytes, and as a result cellular debris accumulates in the trabecular meshwork, causing blockage.

It is believed that people who have open-angle glaucoma are more susceptible to the effects of steroids, but it is unclear whether steroids cause the glaucoma in the first place. In some cases, it is difficult to distinguish between normal-tension glaucoma and steroid-induced glaucoma, and only a medical history will reveal the steroid source.

Episcleral Glaucoma

Did you know that playing the trumpet may be hazardous to your eyes? People who play brass instruments, especially trumpeters, may find their eye pressures rising when they blow into their horns. A group of researchers at Northwestern University in Chicago evaluated the intraocular pressure of musicians while playing their instruments and at rest, and found a mean rise of 9 points in IOP, from 17 to 28 mm Hg. Unlike other glaucomas, in which the trabecular meshwork is blocked, obstruction in this case takes place in the episcleral veins. The episcleral veins are the final pathway of the ocular outflow system. Blowing hard causes an increase in episcleral venous pressure that results in a parallel increase in IOP. Swinging a baseball bat can also cause a rise in IOP. Kirby Puckett, a celebrated baseball player with the Minnesota Twins, suddenly lost one eye to glaucoma and had to retire from the game. The standard medical treatments for glaucoma do not alleviate this condition. Only a trabeculectomy (creation of a bypass channel in the trabecular meshwork) will relieve the pressure.

The recognition that many forms of glaucoma are the end products of other diseases is currently taking hold in the medical and ophthalmological communities. Once broadly defined as open-angle, acute angle-closure, chronic angle-closure, and congenital, glaucoma has now splintered into a wide variety of what scientists call syndromes—not diseases as such, but specific sets of conditions in the eye that follow particular patterns. Some ophthalmologists claim that at least forty different types of glaucomas exist, and perhaps there are more yet to be discovered. With the aid of new technological equipment and the work of scientists from other disciplines collaborating with the eye specialists, identification of these syndromes, and better explanations for existing syndromes, will no doubt be forthcoming.

Glaucoma is certainly more complicated than the common description of "high pressure." Intraocular pressure does indeed affect the nerves in the back of the eye, and if these nerves are compressed, they wither and die. Ophthalmologists now refer to glaucoma as a disease of the optic nerve. But glaucoma, and the questions it raises, are extremely complex. Teasing apart all the factors that relate to this medical condition is a very tricky proposition. Genetics most certainly plays a role. We know that what happens in early life has a deep effect on both our physiology and our behavior—so profound that the effect appears to be an innate trait. We also know we are not immune to environmental insults in the form of pollution, pesticides, and toxic materials that we are exposed to daily. We do *not* know how the many forms of viruses and parasites that exist can affect the eyes. How then can we position ourselves to garner the best care for our glaucomatous eyes? We will examine these issues in the chapters that follow.

CHAPTER 3

Wrong Signals—Glaucoma in Infants and Children

The joys of parents are secret, and so are their griefs and fears; they cannot utter the one, nor they will not utter the other.

Francis Bacon (1625)

Prospective parents imagine giving birth to a baby whose big, bright eyes will fill them with joy. Although many parents may be vaguely aware that handicapping conditions strike one-tenth of the entire population, the possibility that it might happen to their child seldom crosses their minds. Other parents, more familiar with birth defects, pray that their children are developing free of disease or other problems. But whatever a parent's degree of knowledge about birth defects, the diagnosis of a congenital problem in a child is both shocking and surprising.

Three days after their daughter was born, Frank and Joan were told that their child had congenital blindness and would never be able to see. They were stunned. Reluctant to accept this diagnosis, they took the baby to three different hospitals before they encountered a glaucoma specialist—who, after medical treatment, was able to improve the child's vision to 20/80 with corrective glasses. Unfortunately, glaucoma turned out to be only one of the birth defects in this child, a not uncommon situation.

While it certainly occurs less frequently than adult-onset glaucoma, 1 baby in 10,000 is born with glaucoma. In many of these cases, glaucoma is but one of multiple birth defects that may afflict the infant.

Various diseases, such as Marfan syndrome (a disease that affects the heart and skeleton as well as the eyes), Sturge-Weber syndrome (a congenital disorder characterized by unusual clusters of blood vessels), and some dozen other syndromes, as well as prenatal exposure to rubella (German measles), can all produce glaucoma. Glaucoma may also result from tumors, inflammation, or trauma.

Making eye contact with your infant is perhaps one of a parent's greatest pleasures. The large, luminous eyes of your baby capture your love, bonding this tiny bit of humanity to you. When a child is born, his or her beautiful eyes are still in the process of developing. During the period from infancy to about four years of age, and especially in the first six months or so of life, the collagen fibers in a child's cornea are softer and more elastic than those of an older child or adult. The trabecular meshwork and the iris too undergo changes, and these structures within the eye do not become fully formed until the child is about six months old. If elevated pressure caused by blockage of the drainage area—that is, glaucoma—occurs during the critical early years of life, a child's eye may expand into a bulbous orb that is often called "cow's eye." Other symptoms of glaucoma that may be identified in an infant or toddler include unusual sensitivity to light, tearing, and a slight haziness or cloudiness of the cornea. If a child develops any of these symptoms, he or she should be seen by an ophthalmologist as soon as possible.

Infantile glaucoma is divided into three categories. The first is primary infantile glaucoma, which is congenital (present from birth, but not necessarily inherited) and is caused by a failure of the fluid to exit the eyes due to blockage of the trabecular meshwork. The second category includes infantile glaucoma associated with other congenital diseases or what are called anomalies. The third type, secondary infantile glaucoma, includes glaucomas that result from conditions such as tumors and inflammation of the eye.

PRIMARY INFANTILE GLAUCOMA

Congenital glaucoma, or primary infantile glaucoma, is caused by an isolated maldevelopment of the trabecular meshwork. Although this is the most common of the infantile glaucomas, it still occurs in only about 1 in 30,000 babies. In approximately 50 percent of affected infants, the iris is inserted into the trabecular meshwork or is mislocated in front of the scleral spur. Other possible problems include an iris that does not fully develop, blood vessel irregularities, and a cornea that is either too small or too large. Any of these deformations will affect the development of an infant's eye. A mutation in a gene known as CYPIBI, located on chromosome 2, has been identified as responsible for up to 85 percent of all cases of primary infantile glaucoma.

The recommended treatment for primary infantile glaucoma is surgery, performed one to two weeks after birth. The earlier action is taken, the better the outcome is likely to be. (The surgical procedures used to treat primary infantile glaucoma are discussed in Chapter 7.)

Most often, it is the pediatrician who discovers that a child has primary infantile glaucoma. In some cases, a pediatrician may mistakenly identify the problem as conjunctivitis, an inflammation of the membrane covering the eye. If you suspect that your baby's eye condition may be more serious, you might consider consulting an ophthalmologist (a pediatric ophthalmologist, if such a practitioner is available), if for no other reason than to assure yourself that your baby does not have glaucoma.

GLAUCOMAS ASSOCIATED WITH CONGENITAL DISEASES

There are a number of congenital conditions that can cause glaucoma in a child. Such conditions may or may not be inherited, but are present at birth or shortly thereafter. Although other parts of the eye are initially involved in these diseases, they ultimately result in glaucoma because they impair the eye's drainage system.

All of these conditions occur much less frequently than primary infantile glaucoma. In many cases, they are difficult to treat because they involve incomplete development of parts of the eye. When glaucoma does occur, treatment usually follows the same protocol as with primary infantile glaucoma.

Familial Hypoplasia of the Iris

This disease is hereditary, and is characterized by an underdevelopment of the iris structures of the eye. Glaucoma results when the maldeveloped iris blocks the trabecular meshwork. Although the defect is present at birth, the glaucoma may occur at birth or at any time thereafter, even in late adulthood. Apparently, however, no one who has this disease escapes glaucoma in the long run. Children with glaucoma as a result of this condition tend to respond well to surgery. If glaucoma strikes in adulthood, laser treatment and/or surgery may be performed to control the pressure.

Aniridia

Aniridia means absence of the iris. This is a rare condition that develops around the twelfth week of pregnancy and affects both eyes. The iris may be completely absent except for a small stump. This stump moves forward and adheres to the wall of the angle, obstructing the trabecular meshwork and resulting in glaucoma. The cornea also may be affected. It may become cloudy—a condition believed to stem from the same defect that prevents the iris from developing—and cataracts may also be a problem. Although most people with this condition have visual acuity in the range of 20/200, which is considered legally blind, there are some rare individuals who have normal vision. There is one form of aniridia that is known to be genetic in nature, caused by deletion of part of chromosomes 11 and 13. This type of aniridia is associated with mental retardation.

Glaucoma resulting from aniridia is difficult to treat, for if medical therapy fails to control the pressure, the next step—surgery—is considered hazardous because these eyes are extremely vulnerable and surgery may produce further injury. Cataract extractions and corneal transplants are risky for the same reason.

People who have this disease often lose their sight entirely. The one good piece of news about this disease is that it occurs rarely, in as few as 1 in 50,000 to 1 in a million children.

Axenfeld's Syndrome

With Axenfeld's syndrome, the cornea has defects and lesions, the iris may be undeveloped, and strands of the iris may bridge the angle, causing blockage of the drainage system. About 50 percent of persons who have Axenfeld's syndrome develop glaucoma.

> While she was away at college, Lillian, who was myopic and needed corrective lenses, began to think she needed stronger glasses because she could no longer read the writing on the chalkboard. She consulted an ophthalmologist, who told her that she did indeed have a problem—a marked difference in vision between her right and left eyes. A more detailed examination revealed optic nerve damage in her right eye and an intraocular pressure of 40 mm Hg. The ophthalmologist offered a tentative diagnosis of Axenfeld's syndrome, which, unhappily, proved to be the case. Lillian is now forty-five, and her left

eye has remained unaffected, but her right eye has deteriorated to "count fingers"—she cannot read anything on the standard Snellen exam chart.

As with Lillian, it is perfectly possible to lead an active life with this syndrome, and it may not be diagnosed until late adolescence or early adulthood. When it is diagnosed in infancy, surgery may cure the problem. Later in life, medication, plus operations if needed, are the recommended treatment.

Rieger's Anomaly

Rieger's anomaly is a term that refers to immature development of the cornea and to a scar that forms between the iris and the cornea. In addition, the iris may be deformed, having more than one pupil or a pupil displaced from the center. Because of these structural defects, sight is impaired. Glaucoma occurs because the passage of fluid is blocked by the eye's malformations. The recommended treatment includes medication and, when this is no longer effective, surgery. A child with Rieger's anomaly may also have an umbilical hernia and/or facial abnormalities such as undeveloped cheeks or missing or misshapen teeth.

Peter's Anomaly

This condition affects the cornea. The central portion of the cornea becomes abnormally thin and parts of the iris attach to the periphery of the cornea. The cornea may also become opaque. In the more serious cases, the front of the eye (the anterior chamber) is flattened, which causes the iris and cornea to stick together, blocking the drainage passages and causing glaucoma. Not all cases are severe enough to either impair vision or cause glaucoma, but if the cornea becomes opaque and glaucoma does develop, action must be taken to preserve a child's sight. A corneal transplant at an early age (before the child is six), followed by fitting the child with corrective contact lenses, prevents amblyopia (disuse of the affected eye).

Sturge-Weber Syndrome

This syndrome involves the presence of errant blood vessels on the conjunctiva and iris, and in the anterior chamber angle, the choroid (the layer in the eye carrying the blood vessels), and the retina. This vascularity, as it is called, may also be found in an affected child's cheeks, tongue, and gums. Children with this syndrome may also have tumors on the meninges, three membranes that surround the brain and spinal cord, and be subject to convulsive seizures.

Glaucoma may occur in infancy. When it does, it is similar to primary infantile glaucoma, and surgery will usually control the problem for a period of time. However, as the child ages, glaucoma may return, for the original problem of errant blood vessels remains. For some patients, it may be more difficult to treat the glaucoma when it reappears because of the blood-vessel problem (an operation may cause additional proliferation of blood vessels). While it is generally believed that eyes affected by Sturge-Weber syndrome have a poor prognosis, a 1989 study conducted by the Glaucoma Research Foundation revealed that early surgery (as soon as the disease is detected) yielded the best outcome for these patients.

Marfan Syndrome

This syndrome is an inherited disorder of the connective tissue that also affects the musculoskeletal and cardiovascular systems. A person with Marfan syndrome may have an irregular gait and an unusually tall, lean body with long toes and fingers. The joints may be abnormally flexible, the feet flat, the shoulders stooped, and the lens of the eye dislocated. Some researchers believe that Abraham Lincoln had a mild form of this disorder.

The dislocation of the lens in Marfan syndrome can block the pupil and the outflow channels of the eye. Glaucoma may also occur if a malformation causes other tissues from the uvea or the iris to move into the angle, blocking the drainage passage. Both medical and surgical treatment may control the glaucoma. If surgery is indicated, an ophthalmologist specializing in surgery of the vitreous will most likely do the operation, for the problem lies in the back of the eye. Vitreous surgeons have experience with this part of the eye. Because this syndrome affects the entire body, the coordination of treatment among orthopedists, cardiologists, and ophthalmologists is recommended to achieve the best possible results.

Neurofibromatosis

Neurofibromatosis, or von Recklinghausen's disease (sometimes colloquially called "elephant-man disease"), is characterized by multiple pigmented areas, something like freckles, that may appear anyplace on the body. Tumors may appear in late childhood, and although in most cases they are benign, there is no cure for them.

In rare cases, this condition also involves a disrupted pupil. When glaucoma strikes infants with this disease, the condition resembles primary infantile glaucoma. Later in life, the iris may move into the angle and block the drainage area. In some cases the tumors may reach deep into the cranial nerves that control vision and blindness may result. Surgery is the recommended treatment.

Marchesani's Syndrome

Marchesani's syndrome, or spherophakia, is a rare form of glaucoma that may occur in obese individuals and occasionally in the mentally retarded. It is considered to be an inherited condition. Children with this syndrome have a lens that is spherical in shape. It may also be smaller than a normal lens. From early childhood on, the lens may become dislocated and move into the front of the eye, blocking the drainage pathways and causing glaucoma. When such blockage occurs, an ophthalmologist will likely recommend surgery to create a new outflow passage.

Homocystinuria

This is a condition that is sometimes misdiagnosed as Marfan syndrome or Marchesani's syndrome, but that has its own special characteristics. It is caused by an inborn error in the metabolism of amino acids. Children afflicted with this syndrome may be mentally retarded, experience seizures, and have skeletal deformities that eventually lead to osteoporosis. Glaucoma may occur because of pupillary block, a condition in which the aqueous fluid is unable to squeeze between the lens and the iris in its passage from the back to the front of the eye. Fluid then builds up behind the iris and pushes the iris forward into the drainage channel.

Congenital Rubella

This condition results in infants whose mothers are infected with the rubella (German measles) virus during pregnancy. It is especially serious when this happens during the first trimester of pregnancy. An infant with congenital rubella may have a number of medical problems resulting from damaged organs and blood vessels. The virus can damage the tissues of developing inner ear, the lens of the eye, and the teeth.

If the virus affects a baby's eyes, a condition resembling primary infantile glaucoma may result, characterized by poor drainage of the trabecular meshwork where the cornea and iris meet. This is usually treated with surgery. Congenital rubella may also cause an infant to be born with corneas that are clouded, but without glaucoma. In this case, surgery for glaucoma is unnecessary, but cataract removal may be called for. A third possiblity involves inflammation of the eye; debris from the inflammation may block the trabecular meshwork and elevate the eye's pressure. Medication will often relieve this situation.

Once a common problem affecting 2 percent of all infants born, congenital rubella occurs much less frequently today because of the introduction of the rubella vaccine. The number of affected babies has now dropped to well below 100 in a year in the United States.

SECONDARY INFANTILE GLAUCOMAS

As with adults, there are certain eye conditions that can expose a baby's eyes to the possibility of glaucoma. These are called secondary glaucomas, because the resulting glaucoma is preceded by another eye problem. These problems include inflammation, tumors, and trauma to the eye. In some cases, with tumors and trauma, the glaucoma may be reversed once the primary situation is corrected. In other cases, such as inflammation, damage to the eye may be permanent and result in lifelong glaucoma.

Inflammation

Babies are not immune to inflammation of the inside of the eye. Why inflammation occurs in babies is not clear. With adults, some researchers believe that prostaglandins, a group of naturally occurring body chemicals, may be the cause. If so, the same factors may affect infants' eyes. When inflammation does occur, the trabecular meshwork becomes damaged because of the influx of debris from the inflammatory materials. Blockage occurs and pressure rises, leading to open-angle glaucoma. Another problem, called pupillary block, may occur if the iris and lens adhere (stick together) early in the inflammatory scenario. When this happens, the margins of the pupils adhere to the lens. This closes up the route by which the aqueous humor flows from the back of the eye, where it is manufactured, to the front of the eye. This situation results in angle closure. Treatment for both conditions follows the adult protocols of medication and/or surgery.

Tumors

Xanthogranuloma, a type of skin tumor that produces skin lesions on the scalp, face, and upper trunk, may infect infants during the first year of life. It may then regress spontaneously. During the time the tumors are present, pressure in the eye may increase if bleeding occurs and blocks the trabecular meshwork. The baby's iris may also be affected by lesions. While the pressure is elevated, doctors treat the baby's eye with topical medication and with steroids, if necessary.

Trauma

Trauma to the eye may occur during birth, especially if forceps are used during delivery. Ophthalmologists may sometimes find it difficult to differentiate between congenital glaucoma and that caused by trauma. One way they identify trauma is by looking for other signs of forceps damage on an infant's forehead or cheeks. If trauma is suspected, treatment with medication is used to relieve the pressure in the infant's eye, and the traumatic event may resolve itself over a period of weeks or even several months. However, an affected infant's eyes should be monitored carefully during this period, and if primary infantile glaucoma is suspected, quick action will be needed to preserve the baby's sight (see page 41).

With the exception of secondary glaucomas caused by trauma and tumors, where the glaucoma may be transient, infantile glaucoma is a serious problem. With primary infantile glaucoma, the most prevalent type, early intervention within the first week or two of life increases the possibility that your baby will continue to have eyesight into adulthood. However, because the treatment approaches used today are only about thirty years old, we still do not know whether persons who undergo surgery for glaucoma in infancy may expect to retain their sight into their later years. With the congenital glaucomas associated with the various diseases mentioned in this section, the promise of continued sight depends on the severity of the problems in the eye caused by the disease. Fortunately, cases of all kinds of glaucoma in infants are rare.

JUVENILE GLAUCOMA

Glaucoma can occur at any age. In addition to infantile glaucoma—glaucoma that occurs within the first two years of life—and adult-onset glaucoma, there is also juvenile glaucoma, a subtype of primary open-angle glaucoma (POAG). This refers to glaucoma that is diagnosed during the period from early childhood through adolescence. At one time, the age period designated by this term stretched all the way to age thirty-five, but ophthalmologists today prefer an age range consistent with the common use of the word.

As with POAG, myopia apparently increases the risk of this disease, and African-Americans appear to be more susceptible than members of other ethnic groups. One study of thirteen infantile and juvenile glaucoma patients found that individuals with these conditions tended to have thickened trabecular meshworks. This thick, compact tissue may be related to immature development of the meshwork, and may account for a decreased outflow of fluid and resulting rise in intraocular pressure.

Genetics also plays a part. Building on research at The Glaucoma Foundation and subsequently at Duke University, the identification of a genetic defect on chromosome 1 linked to glaucoma has led to the discovery of a gene responsible for juvenile glaucoma (see page 15). The genetic basis of the condition may be the reason that people with juvenile glaucoma tend to be resistant to medication and laser treatment as the primary and initial therapy. If a child or adolescent develops glaucoma, it would be wise to request genetic testing to determine whether this defect is present.

Secondary juvenile glaucoma may result from any of the diseases discussed in Chapter 2 or from any of the congenital diseases mentioned earlier in this chapter. As with adults and babies, there is an array of conditions that can cause a rise in pressure resulting in secondary juvenile glaucoma. Conditions such as diabetes mellitus or pigmentary-dispersion syndrome can result in glaucoma during the childhood years. With diabetes, the problem is runaway blood vessels proliferating over the retina and trabecular meshwork causing blockage; with pigmentary-dispersion syndrome, flakes from pigment of the iris lodge in the trabecular meshwork. Inflammation of the eye associated with arthritis has also been diagnosed in juvenile glaucoma. The debris from the inflammation clogs up the trabecular meshwork.

Since nearsightedness is one of the conditions related to the development of glaucoma, research is ongoing into ways to delay the progression of myopia. One approach involves the use of rigid gas-permeable contact lenses to modify the curvature of the eye. Two others focus on the use of laser treatment to etch the surface of the cornea and on a corneal ring; both of these are designed to correct vision by altering the curvature of the cornea. Whether any of these treatments in the long run will reduce the incidence of glaucoma at a later age in life remains to be seen, but sight without glasses appears to be generally improved.

People with infantile and juvenile glaucomas make up a small percentage of the general glaucoma population. Unfortunately, they generally do not fare as well as people who get glaucoma when they are in their sixties or seventies. The reason for this lies in the nature of the disease. Glaucoma is, for the most part, a progressive disease. The earlier in life it develops, the greater the chances it will progress to the point that it impairs vision. In addition, glaucoma contracted in infancy or childhood is often related to some impairment in the structures of the eye. Any such problem, whether it is in the lens, iris, trabecular meshwork, retina, or anywhere else, has the effect of weakening the eye.

Nevertheless, medical and surgical management of glaucoma is important, and eye doctors are ever seeking out new and better methods for controlling intraocular pressure in patients of any age. Before proper treatment can begin, however, a precise diagnosis of the condition of the eye is required. In the following chapter, we will discuss some of the diagnostic procedures you can expect your doctor to perform.

CHAPTER 4

Diagnosis—
The Equilateral Triangle

Grief has limits, whereas apprehension has none. For we grieve only for what we know has happened, but we fear all that may possibly happen.

Pliny the Younger (First century A.D.)

For most of the people in our support group, the diagnosis of glaucoma came as a shock. After he had successfully repaired retinal tears, my ophthalmologist told me in a follow-up examination that I had glaucoma in my left eye. Rita's doctor diagnosed her glaucoma after she complained about a painful episode in which she awakened one morning to find she couldn't open her right eye. Dorothy had a persistent pain in her right eye and right ear, and thought she might be having sinus problems. All of us were informed by the ophthalmologists who evaluated our eyes that our intraocular pressures (IOPs) were above the normal range of 10 to 21 mm Hg.

Most often, however, the diagnosis that you have glaucoma follows a routine eye examination. William's ophthalmologist told him his eye pressures were several points above normal and that, because of his myopia (nearsightedness), he would have to be monitored for glaucoma. He developed the disease within a year. William's case is typical of how most people's glaucoma is discovered. Both optometrists and ophthalmologists routinely check their patients for the presence of glaucoma during eye examinations. There are also organizations such as Prevent Blindness America that conduct mass glaucoma screenings.

Diagnosis, both preliminary and ongoing, is a major feature of glaucoma management, for if you have glaucoma, your eye may undergo subtle changes that signal the need for either a change in the treatment schedule or additional treatment. Basically, the diagnosis of your eyes' condition consists of four parts: the routine eye examination plus three specialized evaluations—checking your pressure, examining your optic nerve, and measuring your visual field. We call these three tests the "equilateral triangle" because each carries equal weight in assessing your condition.

THE ROUTINE EYE EXAMINATION

Think of the eye examination as a physical for your eyes. In a routine eye examination, your doctor will want to check a number of things, including your visual acuity (how good is your distance and near vision?) and the condition of your cornea (is it clear, free of disease?), your pupil (does it respond by constricting when a bright light is shined on it?), and your iris (is it round, as it should be?). Your eye doctor will also view your eye through an instrument called a slit lamp. This device magnifies your eye and can be fitted with a number of attachments for various facets of your eye examination.

Visual Acuity Testing

Just about everyone is familiar with the Snellen chart. From early childhood on, we are asked to read letters on a chart placed twenty feet away. Your visual acuity is measured by how far down on the chart you can read. This tests your distance vision. If you can read the letters on the "30" line, your visual acuity is said to be 20/30—that is, you can read at twenty feet what the "normal" person (a person with 20/20 vision) can read at thirty feet. Each of your eyes is tested in turn. Your visual acuity may be approximately the same for both eyes, or there may be a noticeable difference between the two. Your doctor will have you look at the Snellen chart while he or she uses an instrument called a retinoscope to determine the degree of correction (if any) needed for each eye.

When tested with the Snellen chart, visual acuity depends upon the ability to separate the elements of the letters on the chart. Each letter is made up of parts. For example, "P" and "B" have vertical bars and circles. "G" has an opening in its circle that distinguishes it from "O." As the letters become smaller, it becomes harder to distinguish between letters with parts that closely resemble each other. When I try to read the 20/30 line, for example, I confuse "G" with "O" and sometimes "G" with "B." I also have trouble with "T" and "P," since I see a vertical bar and a horizontal bar for each. Possible reasons for losing fine detail include myopia that has reached a stage where it cannot be fully corrected, or the loss of some of the nerve cells responsible for seeing details, or a cataract that is impeding vision. From your history and the examination at hand, your eye doctor will be able to determine the cause.

On the other hand, you may see the letters on the Snellen chart quite clearly, but feel you are not seeing as well as you should when you travel about in the outside world. If you have glaucoma, glare can be a particular problem. Glare from certain types of bright light and especially from the sun can wipe out many features in your surroundings. When Dorothy goes out into bright sunlight, she sees a white fog and can make out only shadows of buildings. She grew up in Cleveland, where it rains a lot, and when she returns for a visit, she finds that the cloudy days offer her maximum vision. The reasons for the disparity between your score on the Snellen chart and what you see in your everyday life lies in the fact that your doctor's office offers the optimum situation for seeing in terms of light and contrast. The problem of contrast can be particularly irritating for public transactions involving computer displays, such as reading bus or train station schedule monitors, cash registers, traffic lights, and ATMs. For instance, I always have to ask the checker at the grocery store to tell me how much I owe, as it is difficult for me to read off the electronic display on the register.

Following the assessment of your distance vision, your eye doctor will want to check your *near-point accommodation,* or close vision, the type of vision used for reading. You will be handed a small chart containing different lines of words that diminish in size. How far down on the chart you can read determines your near visual acuity. To accommodate to close vision, the ciliary muscle contracts, thickening the lens and increasing its focusing power. Young children have the greatest ability to make this type of focusing adjustment, for their crystalline lenses are more soft and malleable than those of adults. With age, the lens hardens and accommodation becomes more difficult. This is why people over forty often need glasses for reading even though they see perfectly well at a distance. Nearsighted people are less likely to run into this problem, as their lenses are already fixed into a position for near-point accommodation.

Through the Slit Lamp

For the slit lamp examination you sit on what I have come to call the "eye throne." Each doctor's office is different, but usually you are seated in a comfortable chair from which the Snellen chart can be read and which can be spun around to face the slit lamp, the device the doctor uses to examine the inside of the eye.

The slit lamp is an instrument that projects a beam of light onto and into the front part (the anterior chamber) of the eye, enabling your doctor to examine the conjunctiva, sclera, cornea, iris, lens, and a portion of the vitreous. The image of the eye and its structures is magnified. An attachment to this basic tool permits the examination of the ciliary body, the retina, and the optic nerve, which is in the back of the eye. To view the critical drainage system—the area where the iris and cornea meet to form the angle, where the trabecular meshwork sits—your doctor will first anesthetize your eye with a topical drop, then place a special contact lens called a *goniolens* on your eye. This lens allows the doctor to view the angle and ascertain whether it is open or narrowed. Primarily, doctors evaluate this structure to determine the likelihood of an attack of angle-closure glaucoma. For your part, all you need to do is to place your chin in the chin rest and your head against the headrest, and follow your doctor's instructions when he or she asks you to look in various directions for specific examinations.

Your doctor will also check the health of the cornea by observing it through the slit lamp. The cornea should be smooth, clear, and shiny, and free of irregularities in size, clarity, and smoothness. A child's cornea should not exceed eleven millimeters in diameter. If a child's cornea is larger than this or bulbous in shape, this may be an indication of congenital glaucoma. The cornea is also normally free of blood vessels. If any are seen, disease may be present. A ground-glass appearance is characteristic of corneal edema (swelling due to fluid accumulation). Cloudiness or irregularity of the cornea may signal that you have one of the corneal problems described in Chapter 2.

Next, your doctor will want to assess the condition of your pupil. A healthy pupil is round and responds to light stimuli. When you are seated in a dim room, your pupil will automatically constrict if a beam of light is shined on it. If the beam of light hits only one eye, your other pupil will respond consensually, that is, it also will constrict. The pupils should be round and regular in shape, but in certain forms of glaucoma they may take on an irregular shape due to wasting away of the iris. In some cases, inflammation of the iris can cause the iris to adhere to the lens, in the process changing the shape of the pupil. People who take pupil-constricting medications such as pilocarpine or carbachol for long periods, as many of us with glaucoma do, often have pupils that no longer respond to light stimuli. If such a pupil is stretched to permit cataract surgery, it often remains at the width to which it has been stretched. I have two stretched pupils as a result of cataract surgery.

Progressing to the iris, your doctor will look for shape and regularity. Pigmentary-dispersion glaucoma can be detected by examining the iris; the loss of pigment from the iris that causes this disease leaves spindle-like shapes in the iris. Wasting away of the iris may indicate progressive iris atrophy (see Chapter 2). Inflammation is a sign of iritis.

Finally, the lens is examined for changes in its transparency. Both the cornea and the lens are composed of transparent tissues that allow light to enter the eye. If the lens becomes cloudy as a result of a cataract, it diminishes the amount of light reaching your retina, in turn dimihishing vision. In some very advanced cases of cataracts, the pupil may also look gray and opaque.

IOP: GAUGING YOUR PRESSURE

The first of the specialized evaluations your doctor will perform is the measurement of the pressure in your eye. Once thought to be the leading indicator of glaucoma, an elevated intraocular pressure (IOP) now forms only one leg of the triangle of diagnosis. However, a high IOP is a clear signal that glaucoma may be present, so if your IOP rises above the normal level of 10 to 21 mm Hg, it calls for attention on the part of you and your doctor.

> For ten years, Richard tolerated a pressure of 30 mm Hg while maintaining 20/20 vision. However, in his last visual field test, scotomas (defects) appeared in his peripheral vision, and although Richard still sees perfectly well, he now realizes that his high IOPs are affecting his optic nerves.

Ideal intraocular pressures vary. The normal range lies between 10 and 21 mm Hg. Eye doctors are happiest when pressure is in the low teens. Yet there are some people who apparently are able to withstand relatively high pressures, up to 30 mm Hg, without losing vision. On the other hand, there are some individuals whose pressures are at the low end, in the range of 12 to 14 mm Hg, and who lose vision regardless. These individuals have what is called normal-tension glaucoma. Extraordinarily low pressures may cause problems, too. Pressures between 0 and 5 mm Hg may lead to the lens becoming dislocated and touching the cornea. Pressures this low are extremely unusual, however. When they do occur, it is usually in special circumstances, such as immediately following surgery. In such cases, the eye usually returns to normal on its own in short order.

The ideal pressure for a person with glaucoma is based on whether or not the individual is losing sight. If your vision remains stable at, say, 15 mm Hg, then that may be your ideal pressure. But if you begin to lose vision at that pressure, your ophthalmologist will suggest medical or surgical interventions to lower your pressure.

Because IOP is such a potent indicator of glaucoma, eye doctors routinely measure pressure when you come in for an eye examination. This gives your doctor a fairly accurate reading of your pressure at that particular time of the day. It is conceivable, however, that your pressure may be different at different times of the day.

Evaluating the eye pressure is not new. Before the intricate instruments of today, doctors used digital pressure to determine the quality of resistance; they would simply press lightly on the closed eye with a forefinger. While the reliability of this method is questionable, there are those trained in the technique who claim they can discern gross differences in the rigidity of the eye. In fact, this method is still used in parts of the world where modern medical instruments are not readily available. And many glaucoma patients swear that they can measure their own pressures by touch. In the modern ophthalmologist's office, such methods have long since given way to more sophisticated technology.

Accuracy in Reporting—The Goldmann Tonometer

The Goldmann tonometer, which is attached to the slit lamp, is the instrument most commonly used by ophthalmologists to measure intraocular pressure, and is widely considered to be the most reliable. It measures the pressure of the eye through what is called the *applanation,* or flattening, method. In applanation tonometry, a probe pushes against your cornea and flattens it. The pressure in the eye is determined by measuring the amount of resistance to flattening.

To prepare you for the pressure test, your doctor instills an anesthetic drop and a drop of fluorescein (a substance that emits light when exposed to ultraviolet radiation) in the eye. You place your head in the chin rest and your forehead against the headrest of the slit lamp, and are asked to keep your eye wide open and look straight ahead (or at your doctor's ear). The doctor then focuses on your eye and directs a blue light at the tonometer probe. The instrument is brought forward until it touches your cornea. At the moment of contact you may see a bright yellow-green spot of light. A ring, called a fluorescent ring, is formed. The doctor then uses a control lever to push the tonometer probe against the cornea. As the cornea is flattened, the two halves of the fluorescent ring form a half-circle, at which point your ophthalmologist takes the reading of your IOP. If you wear contact lenses, you should remove them before this procedure because fluorescein may stain the lenses.

A Puff of Air—The Pneumotonometer

Since the introduction of the Goldmann tonometer, a number of other pressure-measuring alternatives have been developed that do not rely on direct contact with the eye. One of these is the *pneumotonometer.* You rest your head on this instrument, and it shoots a puff of warm air onto the eye to measure pressure. This instrument is primarily found in optometrist's offices and has been used for mass glaucoma screenings, since it does not involve making contact with the eye.

Some people who have had their pressure measured with the pneumotonometer prefer this instrument to the Goldmann tonometer. Others find the puff of air disturbing and tense up, which can affect the accuracy of the result and make repeat examinations difficult since in anticipation of the blast of air, examinees close their eyes. Contact lenses too will interfere with the accuracy of the measurement. Another problem that Prevent Blindness America has reported with the pneumotonometer is the number of false positives. Generally, if your reading on a pneumotonometer is above 22 mm Hg, you are referred to an ophthalmologist for more detailed evaluation with a standard tonometer.

However, for some people, such as those with sensitive corneas, the pneumotonometer may be better than the standard tonometer, although eye care professionals generally consider the pneumotonometer to give less accurate readings than the Goldmann. Prevent Blindness America found, based on thousands of screenings, that people who did not have glaucoma generally disliked the test, but people who did have glaucoma tended to prefer it over the Goldmann tonometer. Apparently, how you react to this machine depends upon your past experience with having your pressure taken.

Prevent Blindness America now uses a device called the Damato Campimeter for Glaucoma for its glaucoma screenings instead of the pneumotonometer. Like the pneumotonometer, the campimeter is noninvasive. Unlike the tonometer, it tests for signs of glaucoma-related damage, rather than intraocular pressure as such. It has been found to be accurate in determining glaucoma damage in the moderate-to-severe range and also in eliminating any patient discomfort.

The instrument is simplicity itself. It consists of a rectangular chart containing a diagram of fixation points and an occluder (cover) for the eye not being tested. You hold the chart at a reading distance from your eyes with one hand, and with the other hand you hold the occluder in place over the other eye. The examiner instructs you to locate a center dot on the chart. You are then required to focus on an asterisk and tell the examiner if you can see the center dot. You should not be able to, because the examiner is checking your blind spot (the area of your retina where your optic nerve exits your eye to connect with your brain). As you shift your focus from one numbered fixation point to another, you tell the examiner if you can still see the center dot and also the number, while the examiner records what you see.

There are three sizes of target points on the chart—small, medium, and large. The results are based on what you see and your age at the time of examination. At age sixty or less, any point you miss is considered abnormal; from age sixty to seventy, any medium-sized point you miss denotes damage; and after the age of seventy, any large point you miss suggests damage. Examiners report at least 79-percent accuracy in identifying existing glaucoma damage with this test. Unfortunately, it is not useful for early detection, when glaucoma damage is just beginning to reveal itself. Yet because it is easy to administer, it is useful for mass screenings, so more people may be reached and identified as having glaucoma, and perhaps saved from further vision loss if treatment is instituted.

Riding the Circadian Curve

Because your circadian rhythm dips and rises over a twenty-four-hour period, your intraocular pressure may follow a similar pattern. Both your diurnal (daytime) and nocturnal (nighttime) pressure may rise and fall. It may start out low in the morning and rise in the evening, or vice versa. As early as 1898, when the only means of measuring IOP was through digital pressure, eye specialists reported that pressure could vary depending on the time of day. There is no standard rhythm for this variation, and some people show more fluctuation than others. And variation may not be restricted to a twenty-four-hour period only; testing with a home tonometer reveals that over a five-day period, pressures can vary considerably, with the high point falling at different times of the day.

There are other factors that may affect your pressure as well. These include anxiety, holding your breath, certain medications, and your general physiological state—variations in your cardiovascular and respiratory systems may occur daily, weekly, or monthly, depending upon your age and whether you are male or female. Holding your breath while the measurement is being taken can give a higher reading. So can wearing a tight collar or any other restrictive clothing. You may have heard that the use of beta-blockers will lower your pressure. Some ophthalmologists believe that systemic beta-blockers (often prescribed for high blood pressure and other heart problems) have little effect on lowering intraocular pressure. What does concern them, however, is the cumulative effect of systemic and topical beta-blockers. If you are using both, you should have both your ophthalmologist and your general practitioner or cardiologist monitor you regularly.

Because of all these variables, some doctors like to hospitalize their patients for a day and a night to monitor their pressure. This practice is now less common than it once was, however. For some patients, being in the hospital caused anxiety, and doctors felt this might affect their IOPs. Also, the practice is expensive. As a substitute for overnight evaluation, your doctor may have you sit in the office for eight hours and take your pressure every few hours. Eye doctors believe that the greatest damage to the optic nerve occurs when the pressure is at its highest. Those with very little variation are therefore believed to be at less risk for nerve damage, provided that their eyes are responding to treatment.

Although we glaucoma patients worry every time our doctors take our pressures, it is best to remain as calm and relaxed as possible during the procedure. Breathe deeply and evenly, joke with your doctor—and, for goodness sake, wear nonrestrictive clothing.

Do It Yourself?

What glaucoma patient has not envisioned a home tonometer—an instrument that would allow you to take your own pressure at any time of day and make it possible to administer medication during the peak periods? But while a number of such devices have been developed, none has as yet gained wide acceptance. Obstacles to their use include needing someone at home trained in using the equipment and the expense of purchasing it in the first place. There is, however, one model, the Zeimer home tonometer, that is being clinically evaluated, and may be used in the future. It is designed to be used as an adjunct to a standard glaucoma examination; your doctor would train you to use it and then lend it to you for a week so that you can record your pressures five times daily.

OPTIC NERVE EVALUATION—HOLDING ON TO THE SAUCER

As soon as glaucoma is discovered, the optic nerve needs to be watched closely. Any changes that occur may require steps such as changing medication, adding another type of eye drop, laser treatment, or surgery.

A healthy optic nerve looks something like a white cup sitting on a red saucer (see Chapter 1). That saucer, the optic disk, is the object of intense scrutiny by your doctor. In a normal eye, the optic disk is a pink oval with a central depression (the cup). When damage occurs, the nerve fibers surrounding the cup die off, causing the tissues to appear pale or whitened. Eye doctors call this effect pallor. The dying off of nerve fibers widens the cup, an effect known as cupping. As the cup widens, the saucer narrows; the larger the cup-to-disk ratio, the more severe the damage—that is, the less of a rim your doctor sees, the greater the damage. Each case is individual. African-Americans and nearsighted persons normally have larger cups than other people. The disk size may be different in each of your eyes as well.

Your ophthalmologist will assess both the color of the disk and the size of the cup to establish glaucoma damage. Disk color is subject to individual variation. People with perfectly normal vision may have degrees of pink ranging from very deep to very light. Your doctor will need to recall from one examination to the next the color of your disks. This can be a problem if you visit a glaucoma clinic where a different doctor may do the workup each time you visit. Evaluation of your disk color will then be more subjective.

The examination is a simple procedure. First, your ophthalmologist will instill eye drops to dilate your pupil. For full dilation of the pupil, it may be necessary to place drops in your eyes several times during the half hour or so it takes for your pupil to expand. When your pupils are sufficiently wide, your doctor will be able to see your optic nerve clearly by looking into your eye through the slit lamp.

Following the examination, your eye will still be dilated for a period of time. Dilation can last from four to eight hours. During this time, bright lights or bright sunlight may cause discomfort, for your widened pupil is now letting in too much light. You may find yourself unsteady as a result of this unusual brightness. It is a good idea to have someone accompany you to the examination if you know that your eyes will be dilated.

Refining Optic Nerve Evaluation

Diagnosis of a physical condition is a combination of art and science. But as diagnostic tools become more sophisticated, art gives way to technology. The optic nerve is made up of bundles of nerve fibers. For years, ophthalmologists have believed that they would be able to detect glaucoma-related changes in these fibers if they had the right instruments. There are now several systems that employ a combination of laser technology, computers, and sophisticated photographic procedures for examining the optic nerve. These new tools are not yet in widespread use, but in the future they may provide doctors with a diagnostic window not previously open. Some of the more promising procedures include:

- *Polarimetry.* This is one of the newest technologies for assessing the condition of your retina and optic nerve. It utilizes a nerve fiber analyzer, which consists of a diode laser and a computer, to assess the thickness of the retinal nerve fiber layer. Light from the laser (which does not damage eye tissue) enters the eye and strikes the nerve fiber layer. As it strikes, the light waves change direction. The amount of change is directly proportional to the thickness of your nerve fiber layer; the thicker the layer of nerve tissue, the greater the change produced. The degree of change is analyzed by computer, which produces an image of the retina and a printout that establishes glaucoma-related damage. A thin nerve fiber layer indicates that cells have been lost. This technique promises to reveal information about the retina and optic nerve that a visual field test may miss. It may be especially useful in early detection of glaucoma and in identifying healthy areas in late-stage syndromes of the disease. The scan takes 1.5 seconds to perform.
- *Ultrasound biomicroscopy (UBM)* utilizes an instrument that can re-

veal structure as small as 50 microns in size (half the diameter of a human hair). This enables a doctor to monitor the iris, lens, ciliary body, and the angle where the cornea and iris meet. It is particularly useful in diagnosing narrow-angle glaucoma and predicting when medical or surgical intervention is necessary. The test is a simple procedure. You lie on a table while your eye is anesthetized and an eye cup placed over it. Then a pen-sized instrument is held close to the surface of the cornea for a few minutes.

- *Optical coherence tomography (OCT).* This technology, which makes possible a more precise evaluation of the condition of the retina and the optic nerve head, operates something like ultrasound, which uses sound waves to create images. However, OCT uses light waves, which travel much faster than sound waves do. The light from your retina and optical nerve is reflected and displayed by means of a video camera that produces a picture of these structures, allowing your doctor to determine the thickness of the nerve fiber layers (the thicker they are, the healthier the tissues). The OCT unit is compact, relatively low in cost, and is designed to be mounted on the slit lamp.

- *Photogrammetry.* This method involves taking a series of stereophotographs, which are then plotted on a stereoplotter and read by a trained photogrammetrist. It is used to evaluate the depth of the cup in the optic nerve. Knowing the depth of the cup, in addition to its width, should provide for a better understanding of optic nerve damage.

- *Computer analysis.* Computer technology can be used to produce a digital color image of the optic disc, and computer analysis used to assess its pallor (the degree of nerve-fiber loss). An ophthalmologist using this system would then need to determine whether the pallor is the result of glaucoma or some other eye condition, such as vascular damage, nutritional damage, or tumor. This method of assessing pallor may be useful in both early detection and in charting the course of glaucoma.

- *Fluorescein angiography.* This method involves injecting fluorescein, a dye, into a vein in the arm. Once the dye has traveled to the head by way of the blood circulation, photographs are taken of the blood circulation in the eye and analyzed by computer. This makes it possible to assess the health of blood pathways in the eye; glaucoma damage is associated with a decrease in the blood supply to the optic nerve. This is believed to be particularly true for people with normal-tension glaucoma.

- *Flowmeter testing.* A flowmeter merges the asssessment of the rate of blood flow and the perfusion, or filling, of the arteries, veins, and capillaries. An infrared diode laser scans the eye, and resulting information is analyzed by computer to generate an image that can be viewed on a monitor or a black-and-white or color printout. The scan itself takes no more than two seconds to perform.
- *Electrophysiology.* This is a technique for measuring damage to the optic nerve and the ganglia cells. It may have the potential for evaluating damage to these areas before such damage appears on the visual field tests. There are two tests, the electroretinogram (ERG) and the visual-evoked potential (VEP) test, that fall into this category. The (ERG) registers the electrical response of the retina to a brief pulse of light that illuminates the entire retina. People with glaucoma register less light. The VEP test uses electrical stimulation to probe the primary occipital visual areas located in the lower back of the brain. The VEP reveals information about the workings of the visual pathway.

Why this intense scrutiny directed at the optic disc and nerve fibers? Many ophthalmologists believe that the loss of nerve fibers in the optic disk precedes the detectable enlargement of the cup. Nerve fibers die when they are subjected to too much intraocular pressure. Unfortunately for us glaucoma patients, our visual field tests do not always show the existence of defects until we have lost at least 40 percent of the nerve fibers—and, with them, 40 percent of our vision.

There are other factors besides pressure that appear to contribute to nerve-fiber loss. For example, researchers have identified tiny hemorrhages in the capillaries of the eye that may precede nerve-fiber loss. Hemorrhages occur when blood-vessel structures become weakened, although it is not known just why this occurs.

The Importance of Optic Nerve Evaluation

Whether your eye doctor subscribes to some of the newer methods of detecting nerve-tissue damage or relies on visual observation, his or her goal is maintain a steady watch on the condition of your optic nerve. If any damage is detected, your eye doctor will take steps to stop, or at least slow down, the progression of nerve-fiber loss.

These measures may include additional medication, laser treatment, and/or surgery, if necessary. The purpose of all these therapies is to lower IOP, for it is believed that pressure is one of the primary factors in the loss of nerve fibers. These fibers are thin and delicate, and cannot withstand too much pressure. Exactly what level of pressure is too much appears to vary from person to person, so the goal is to maintain your IOP in the range that is right for you.

CHECKING THE PERIPHERIES—THE VISUAL FIELD

If you train your eyes on a fixed point, you can still see from side to side and up and down. This area of vision surrounding the fixed point is called the visual field, and includes your peripheral vision (the extremes of vision to the left, right, up, and down while the eyes are focusing straight ahead). When fixed on a central point, the normal eye can see up to 109 degrees on the temporal side (toward the side of the head); 65 degrees toward the nose; 60 degrees to the top; and 75 degrees to the bottom.

Ophthalmologists describe the visual field as an island or hill in a sea of blackness. At the top of the hill, plumb in the center, resides the macula, which provides you with near and distance vision that, ideally, is sharp and clear. Along the sides of the hill, in diminishing sensitivity, are the peripheral nerves. These areas are best suited to detecting sudden movement (a tiger leaping out of the bushes or a speeding car bearing down on you, for example). These nerves also accommodate your eyes to dim and dark surroundings.

Peripheral vision is made possible by the retina, the innermost layer of the eye, which is composed of blood vessels and nerve cells that are activated when light strikes them. There is a natural blind spot in the retina that lies 10 degrees to the temporal side of the eye. This is the area where the optic nerve exits the eye; and there are no light receptors in this region. People with perfectly healthy eyes may at times notice they fail to see something that is within the range of the blind spot.

Many of us with advanced glaucoma suffer defects in our peripheral vision. I am often unaware of a person approaching me from my side until that person is right next to me. I also find I bump my head on overhead kitchen cabinet doors. Members of our group complain that when they look straight ahead, they cannot see the sidewalk. The reason that glaucoma generally affects peripheral vision first lies in the fact that there are fewer cells in that part of the retina, so the loss of even a few can have an effect on sight. Yet some people with glaucoma also lose sight in their central vision, where the supply of nerve cells is the densest. This situation is considered more serious. Losing sight in the central area may hamper your ability to fixate— that is, to focus your eyes on a single point. It is also a sign that glaucoma is progressing rapidly. If you lose sight in your peripheral vision, you can still see about you by turning your head. If you lose sight in your central vision as well, seeing will become more difficult for you.

My first experience with a visual field examination was with a method called campimetry, a procedure in which my ophthalmologist moved a pointer around a large screen on the wall. I fixed each eye, in turn, on a dot in the middle of the screen, and answered affirmatively each time I caught a glimpse of the pointer. Eye doctors say that this system can still determine a person's field quite accurately, but it is time-consuming and also expensive, because it involves a lot of a doctor's time.

Dancing Lights

With the proliferation of medical technology in the past half-century, it is only logical that campimetry has largely given way to more sophisticated instruments for analyzing visual field defects. The visual field tests now used in this country and other Western nations rely on either computerized or manually driven instruments to record your eye's response to stimulation. There are currently three main instruments that eye doctors use to detect defects in the visual field. With all three instruments, a sort of floor plan, or chart, of your visual field is made, either drawn out on a preprinted chart by a trained technician, or recorded automatically by computer. The choice of instrument may depend upon how fast you are able to signal a reaction to seeing a spot of light, as well as on your doctor's assessment of which device will give the best reading for your condition. If you are a quick responder and do not tire easily, you will probably do well on the automated instruments. If you need more time and automation upsets you, the manually driven instrument may be more suitable.

Measurement of your visual field is based on what your rod and cone cells transmit when light stimuli, in the form of spots of light, reach them. When you see spots of light, you press a buzzer. Whichever type of system is used, you need to be as comfortable as possible while taking a visual field test, for you will be sitting immobile for twenty to thirty minutes. With a patch over the eye not being tested, you rest your forehead against the headrest and place your chin on the chin rest. In one hand you grasp the buzzer that you will use to register your responses. Depending upon the instrument, your examiner will sit either in back of or alongside the machine. Whether the machine is manually operated or automated, an examiner should be present to monitor your eye movements, for it is a great temptation to track the light movement or to search it out by shifting your eyes away from the designated fixation point. If you do not fixate on the center point, the test is invalid. I often think I'm doing a great job of keeping my eye focused on the central dot until I hear my examiner cautioning me to keep my eye fixated.

Gear-Shifting With the Goldmann

The first modern instrument for checking the visual field, the Goldmann Visual Field Analyzer, employs spots of light that are moved around manually from the periphery toward the center of a dome-shaped screen. When I take this test in my ophthalmologist's office, I am reminded of the shifting of gears in a sports car; every now and then, the technician creaks the machine into a different position.

To take the test, you fix each eye, in turn, on a black spot in the center of the screen, while the technician starts the light at the outer edge of your peripheral field and gradually brings it closer to your fixation point. When you see the spot of light, you press a buzzer. Your responses are recorded as lines on a chart representing your field of vision.

Because it is manually operated, the Goldmann allows the examiner the flexibility of giving you more time if your reaction time is slow, and of repeating sequences of spots of light if there is a suspicion that you may have given an incorrect response. Mistakes can happen. It is possible to become confused while taking the exam and think you see pinpricks of light, especially if you already have some eye damage and/or if you have cataracts. The pinpricks of light will appear dimmer and are sometimes more difficult to discern than the light the technician is moving. As with many manually driven instruments, the Goldmann may one day become obsolete, for doctors are gravitating toward the use of automated instruments in lieu of training technicians.

On Automated Drive

Hard on the heels of the Goldmann, a new approach called static perimetry was introduced for evaluating the visual field. In this method, the light stimulus remains in one position at a time but the brightness is increased until you perceive it. There are two main instruments utilizing this approach, the Humphrey and the Octopus.

Both the Humphrey and the Octopus rely on automated computer programming. They investigate the nature of light detection at threshold—that is, the very dimmest pinprick of light that you can see. A point of light is first presented at its dimmest and then progressively increased in brightness and size. If you have lost vision in a particular area, you will not see a point of light there, no matter whatever its size or brightness. The Humphrey, the more commonly used of the two, uses one of two programs: the 30-2 program, which tests seventy-four individual points within the center 30 degrees of the visual field, or the 24-2 program, which tests fifty-eight points. The 24-2 program eliminates some of the points where patients make the most errors, and is generally preferred by ophthalmologists.

These instruments are programmed to take into account the possibility that you may make errors such as buzzing at nonexistent lights. If this occurs, the machine will repeat a sequence. With both the Humphrey and the Octopus, the points of light succeed each other quite rapidly, and the speed can become rather disconcerting. In addition, while only fifty-eight points may be assessed, the machine will test each one four or five times, resulting in what can seem like an endless examination.

My first experience with the Octopus prompted me to write an impassioned letter to my ophthalmologist requesting that the program be replaced by one more suited to my condition—namely, one with brighter, larger lights. I assumed that since the information was computerized, it would be possible to examine me using lights that weren't so hard for me to see. If only my assumption had been correct! Unfortunately for me, the Octopus quite accurately detected areas in my visual field where I had lost sight.

With both of these machines, the examiner still needs to monitor you, although the recording of your exam is automatic. These tests take longer than examination with the Goldmann, and you may experience eye fatigue. If your examiner leaves the room while you are taking the test and you need to rest, you can stop most machines by pressing down on the buzzer (keep your thumb on the buzzer until you feel ready to continue). Releasing the buzzer will signal the machine to resume its progress.

Problems With Visual Field Testing

Taking a visual field test, especially for the first time, can be worrisome. First of all, you are anxious about what the test will reveal. Second, the testing process itself can induce anxiety. With both the Octopus and the Humphrey, a few seconds may elapse during which no points of light appear. Even though you understand that these intervals are built into the program, it can make you uneasy not to see anything. The reason for these lapses is to determine if you are buzzing randomly or actually responding to the light stimuli. Most examiners will tell you to press the buzzer if you think you see the light, but if you are too eager, you may make a lot of errors, which can jeopardize the validity of your test. I fell into that situation, and my doctor told me my test was invalid. I felt like I had received an "F" on a school paper. After that, my ophthalmologist tested me only with the Goldmann, which suits me fine, for I find I am less anxious with this instrument. Still, not all of the anxiety is eliminated this way.

In addition, assessing visual fields is not foolproof. Since there are millions of nerve cells in both the retina and the optic nerve head, it is impossible to locate all the scotomas (defects) in the average field. As a result, as much as 40 percent of your field of vision may be compromised before the defect shows up on your visual field test. Before this happens, you may very well notice on your own that you are not seeing as well as you once did. Researchers estimate that a truly thorough test of the visual field could conceivably last forty hours. Needless to say, such a test would hardly be feasible. What researchers have done instead is to develop a series of tracks following areas where scotomas are most likely to appear. The points of light are programmed along these tracks.

Additionally, problems may occur at the test site that result in faulty or inaccurate readings. For example, the room lighting must be stabilized. It is important to keep the room dark or dim in order to eliminate any light other than that on the screen. A patient's clothing, skin, or hair may absorb or reflect light, depending on color and style.

A sensitive examiner will adjust the level of light before the test to take account of these factors.

Persons with cataracts and/or pupils that are constricted because of the eye drops they are taking may not receive true reading. Some people have both cataracts and constricted pupils, which may make their fields appear to be more damaged than is actually the case. This condition dogs many of us in the glaucoma group, and we wonder how much more we could see if our eyes were freed of these handicaps. Nevertheless, a capable ophthalmologist can judge whether glaucoma is stable or progressing provided that they have a good record of past fields to use as a basis for comparison.

Other problems also interfere with obtaining a true visual field evaluation. Your reaction time—the amount of time that elapses between your sighting of the flash and your pressing the buzzer—varies with the length of the test and with your alertness. The automated tests (the Humphrey and the Octopus) take longer than the manually driven variety (the Goldmann), and your attention may wander. One examiner I know even found a woman had dozed off during the exam! Then, too, depending upon the retinal location being tested, your reaction time can vary, which may reduce the accuracy of the test. Kinetic testing (the Goldmann) depends upon the skill of the examiner, and human error may confound the results. For instance, the examiner must decide on the optimum speed of the test, based on his or her assessment of the patient's ability to respond. The examiner also must choose whether or not to repeat a sequence of light stimuli if he or she is uncertain whether you are actually seeing them. Finally, the examiner completes your chart by hand, drawing a line connecting all the points you saw in the exam.

With static perimetry (the Humphrey and the Octopus), the problem of examiner error is removed, but the timing problem remains. Some researchers maintain that the retina needs about two seconds to rest after registering a stimulus at the retina's threshold (the dimmest light it can register). Also, when a light gradually progresses in brightness to the point at which you can see it, your eye requires more light than it would if the light were presented as intermittent flashes, each one brighter than the last. What may be more important in taking the automated test, however, is your reaction time—pressing the buzzer the instant you see the spot of light. If you are older or tend to be nervous, you may need more time than the machine allows. Many older patients complain that the fast pacing of the test causes fatigue, which lowers their attentiveness. If you have trouble with this, you should know that some machines have a special control to adjust for speed. Encourage your technician to program a more comfortable speed for you if this is possible.

Your mental and physical state also contribute to the outcome of your visual field. For instance, Marion's visual field test indicated defects in the six-month period following the death of her daughter. Subsequent tests failed to reveal these defects. Stress, anxiety about going blind, fear of machines, inability to press the buzzer quickly enough (some people simply react more slowly than others), systemic medications such as tranquilizers or antihistamines, and even the design of the machine (large-breasted women have difficulty getting close to it) all may have an effect on your responsiveness. Constriction of the pupil and/or dimness of the lens due to cataracts can also derail a true reading. If you feel you did not do well due to personal circumstances, schedule another test. You and your doctor will want the most accurate reading possible, for if the results of the visual field test correlate with the degree of damage seen on the optic nerve head, your doctor will be better able to make an accurate diagnosis of your condition.

Corrective Measures

The visual field normally loses sensitivity with age. This is not usually noticeable in a person with normal vision, but age differences affecting the visual field are taken into account with the standard visual field testing methods. Myopia (nearsightedness) may also create a problem. Researchers have found that as the degree of myopia increases, visual sensitivy decreases. If you are myopic, you may find that during parts of the visual field test, you will look through a corrective lens; other times you will focus without optical help. The reason for this approach is to provide you with the optimum opportunity to have the light stimulus focus properly on your retina. Your ophthalmologist and/or trained technician will make this decision based on your prescription.

Some eye doctors say that they have seen patients who have done better in visual field exams once their IOPs were lowered. Others assert that field tests done before therapy to lower IOP, especially if cataracts were present and then surgically removed, simply did not accurately reflect what a glaucoma patient could actually see. I believe that this was the case for me. Following a combination cataract-filtration surgery, the eye I believed had suffered considerable field damage became my "good" eye—until I had a cataract removed from the other eye. After that, I could see quite well out of both eyes.

Researchers are still busy seeking better means of assessing the visual field. One approach, designed to take only six to eight minutes for each eye (as opposed to the fifteen to thirty minutes of current tests), involves looking through a monocle at a television screen. Humphrey has a newer model that uses color—blue lights against a yellow background, instead of the standard white-on-white of current tests—which may provide for greater accuracy in revealing progressive visual field loss in glaucomatous eyes.

One new method that may one day compete favorably with perimetry as a test of the visual field is called spatial-contrast sensitivity. In this test, you are presented with alternating light and dark wavelike bars and asked to respond when you see them. The spaces between the bars vary in shade, and the patterns of bars vary. Although still in the research stage, this test may be useful for separating people with glaucoma from those with normal vision.

DIAGNOSIS—THE CONTINUING STORY

In addition to the procedures discussed above, your eye doctor may perform or recommend additional diagnostic work to gain a complete understanding of the condition of your eyes. If a retinal problem is suspected, such as a tear in the retina or detachment of the retina, he or she may refer you to a retinologist, or retina specialist. This practitioner, using lenses optically designed for retinal examination, will evaluate the health of your retina. A retinologist will also determine the health of the macula and the fovea, the structures in the center of the retina that are crucial for sight.

If you have glaucoma, your doctor will regularly undertake what we have called the triangle of evaluation. This consists of a test of your intraocular pressure, examination of your optic nerve, and perimetry (the visual field test). When you have glaucoma, your eyes are always in the process of being diagnosed or evaluated. Glaucoma is not a static condition. Even though you may be taking medication, and may even have had other interventions such as laser treatment or surgery, you will still need to have your eyes constantly reevaluated. Depending on your condition, your ophthalmologist may recommend visual field tests every three months, twice a year, or yearly. Your pressure will be checked whenever you visit your ophthalmologist. Depending on the state of your glaucoma, your eye doctor may also want to examine your optic nerve each time you have a field test.

Unfortunately, even with the best of medical care available today, many of us continue to lose sight. I have lost some of my peripheral vision. Rita is in danger of losing her remaining operative eye. Some of us are luckier. Miriam has lost no sight, nor has Carl. What this means, of course, is that each of us is unique, and our conditions respond uniquely to the treatment we receive.

Researchers are seeking better tools to diagnose evidence of glaucoma defects at earlier and earlier stages. The medical community believes that if treatment is instituted early on, visual field loss may be stopped in its tracks. If tools for detecting early visual field loss can be developed and made part of the standard diagnostic workup, perhaps preventive measures at that point may curtail damage to the retina and the optic nerve. These measures would most likely involve earlier treatment with medications, which are considered the first line of defense in controlling glaucoma. In the next chapter, we will discuss the various medications that doctors prescribe for glaucoma. We will also take into account the effects that these medications have on general health and quality of life.

CHAPTER 5

Medication—The First Line of Defense

Better use medicines at the outset than at the last moment.

Publius Syrius (First century B.C.)

In the United States, a diagnosis of glaucoma usually means the immediate use of eye drops to lower intraocular pressure. Most of these drugs work by either reducing the secretion of aqueous humor or by contracting the ciliary muscles, which then acts on the trabecular meshwork by pulling open the spaces through which the aqueous humor flows out of the eye.

My first reaction to my glaucoma diagnosis was dismay that I would need to use eye drops for the rest of my life. Little did I know then what lay in store for me. Initially, I regarded the procedure of instilling the drops as a bit of a nuisance. But when I began to experience side effects, I started to take the medication more seriously.

Since my initial experience with the drops, I have learned a twofold lesson. First, eye drops can, indeed, be the first line of defense, and may halt or delay the advance of glaucoma. Second, eye drop medications are powerful. They can cause serious side effects and must therefore be used with care. I might add a third lesson as well—studies have shown that if they are instilled properly, eye drops can keep your intraocular pressure low enough to delay visual field damage to the eyes with progressive glaucoma.

HOW DO DROPS WORK?

All medications are designed to inhibit or to stimulate certain functions of the body's cells. For example, the class of drugs called beta-blockers act on the cells of the ciliary body, causing it to reduce its production of aqueous humor. When less fluid is produced, the chances of fluid buildup in the eye, and resulting high pressure, is lessened.

Various medications are commonly used to lower intraocular pressure. They fall into a number of basic categories, based on the way in which they act on the eye.

MEDICATIONS THAT ACT ON THE CILIARY MUSCLE

A group of substances called *cholinergic agents* are among the mainstays of the medical management of glaucoma. These agents work on the autonomic (involuntary) nervous system. What these drugs do is to act something like acetylcholine. Acetylcholine is a derivative of the amino acid choline that acts as a neurotransmitter in the body—that is, it plays a role in the transmission of nerve impulses. Like acetylcholine, the cholinergic agents cause the ciliary muscle (see page 4) to contract. This in turn stretches open the spaces in the trabecular meshwork and allows the aqueous humor to flow out more freely. Pilocarpine and carbachol, two of the most commonly prescribed glaucoma medications, are members of this family. These drugs are also known as miotics, a term used to describe substances that cause constriction of the pupil.

A related family of compounds that act primarily on the ciliary muscle are the *anticholinesterase* drugs. These medications also stimulate the parasympathetic nervous system, but they do so indirectly, by preventing the breakdown of acetylcholine rather than by simulating its action. They do this by binding to the enzymes acetylcholinesterase and butylcholinesterase, which normally break down acetylcholine in the body. This prevents the enzymes from doing their job, leaving more acetylcholine available to stimulate the nerve endings. When you apply any of these drops to your eyes, the ciliary muscle tightens. Demecarium (Humorsol), isoflurophate (Floropryl), and phospholine iodide (Echothiophate) are in the anticholinesterase drug family.

Pilocarpine

Pilocarpine is perhaps the oldest known drug for the management of glaucoma. Derived from the plant *Pilocarpus microphylus,* it was introduced to Western medicine in the mid-nineteenth century, when a Brazilian physician brought it to Paris after he noted that north Brazilian natives used it to induce sweating and salivation. The drug's properties were investigated by French and German physicians, who found that it reduced intraocular pressure. In the eye, it acts on both the ciliary muscle and the sphincter muscle that controls the widening and narrowing of the pupil. It causes the pupil to constrict and the ciliary muscle to tighten.

Pilocarpine is available in drop form in concentrations ranging from 0.25 to 10 percent, but is most commonly prescribed in doses ranging from 1 to 4 percent. The stronger solutions are recommended for patients with dark irises. Dark irises indicate heavy pigmentation, which makes it more difficult for the medicine to penetrate the eye. It can also be obtained in a 4-percent gel formulation, which is applied at night. As you sleep, the drug creeps up and into the eye because it is attracted to the film of tears covering the eye. Although this form lowered my pressure when I tried it, I hated it, for the stuck-together lids that resulted from applying the gel to the bottom lid made me uneasy. Other members of our support group have reported that they find the gel tolerable, a good trade-off, since the slow release of the gel frees them from the routine of using drops four times a day. Ocusert, a timed-release form of pilocarpine, is inserted in the eye and lasts for six to seven days. Younger patients seem to do better than older ones with this form of the drug. Ben, a member of our group, swears by it, glorying in the relief from the four-times-a-day schedule required for ordinary drops.

Common side effects of pilocarpine include decreased vision due to constriction of the pupil, which limits the amount of light reaching the retina. This problem is especially troubling in dimly lit rooms and at nighttime. I first became aware of this handicap once when I was on vacation and driving at night. I could not distinguish the side of the road, and had to ask my husband to take over immediately. Other problems experienced by those who use pilocarpine include myopia (nearsightedness), headaches centered around the eyes and forehead, and itchiness of the eyelids and conjunctiva. Less common side effects include retinal detachment, inflammation after eye surgery, cloudiness of the lens leading to cataracts, cysts on the iris, and precipitation of angle-closure glaucoma. This drug can also have systemic side effects, including nausea, vomiting, diarrhea, sweating, bronchial spasm, pulmonary edema, and slowing of the heartbeat.

Carbachol

Carbachol, first synthesized in 1932, is a stronger drug then pilocarpine, and it is not usually the first drug recommended for glaucoma patients because it does not permeate the cornea as easily as pilocarpine does. In order for a drug to be effective, it must permeate the cornea to reach the anterior chamber (the front part of the eye), where it can do its business. The action of carbachol is similar to that of pilocarpine; it stimulates the ciliary muscle and causes it to tense up. Carbachol also appears to increase the release of acetylcholine, giving the tensing up of the ciliary muscle an additional boost. I use carbachol because I was found to be allergic to all forms of pilocarpine.

Carbachol is more likely to cause side effects than pilocarpine is. It too causes constriction of the pupil and a consequent dimming of vision, headaches, and conjunctival hyperemia, better known as a bloodshot appearance. It permeates the blood vessels more readily than pilocarpine does, and should not be used if your eye is inflamed. Carbachol is not recommended for people with narrow-angle glaucoma. In addition, the systemic side effects of carbachol can be quite impressive. I discovered this when, after several years of casually administering the drug, I found myself going into cold sweats five minutes after I instilled the drops. Other members of our support group have reported other side effects, including increased salivation, increased stomach acidity, perspiration, vomiting, diarrhea, bradycardia (abnormally slow heartbeat), and bronchial constriction. People who have severe respiratory, cardiovascular, or gastrointestinal tract disease must use this drug with caution.

Anticholinesterase Drugs

The anticholinesterase agents demecarium (Humorsol), isoflurophate (Floropryl), and phospholine iodide (Echothiophate) have an interesting history. These medications were synthesized from chemicals that were used in World War II. After the war, some of these chemicals were converted into powerful insecticides, a number of which are still in use today. In the 1950s, scientists discovered that these agents had a strong effect on the parasympathetic nervous system (part of the autonomic nervous system), and reasoned that they might therefore be useful in lowering intraocular pressure.

Demecarium, available in concentrations of 0.125 and 0.25 percent, is the most stable of these drugs. Phospholine iodide is available in four strengths, 0.3, 0.6, 0.125, and 0.25 percent. Isoflurophate is rarely prescribed today, both because it degrades easily and because it is extremely sensitive to contamination. Getting a tiny bit of tear fluid on the tip of the applicator will spoil the entire bottle.

The side effects of these drugs can be severe. They include constriction of the pupil, the formation of cysts on the iris, and cataracts. The latter can occur because these drugs dehydrate the lens, which upsets the chemical balance of the lens so that it cannot process oxygen properly, causing it to become opaque. Other possible side effects include allergic skin reactions and retinal detachment. Systemic side effects can include vomiting, diarrhea, abdominal spasms, dizziness, and hypotension (low blood pressure). People with heart disease or bronchial problems are especially susceptible to side effects from these medications.

If you must take one of these drugs, it is a good idea to eat organic produce and steer clear of products containing pesticides. Since these drugs are derived from the same compounds as some of the pesticides used today, exposure to both may cause side effects to be more severe. These medications are usually reserved for people who have had cataracts removed, or who cannot tolerate pilocarpine or carbachol.

MEDICATIONS THAT ACT ON THE CILIARY BODY

Classes of drugs called *agonists* and *antagonists* lower intraocular pressure by affecting the activity of the ciliary body, the structure in the eye that secretes aqueous fluid. These drugs are a bit more mysterious than the cholinergic and anticholinesterase agents, for the whole picture of how they work is not fully understood. In the main, however, they interact with receptors—specialized cells or molecular structures located on the surfaces of the cells—that are designed to be influenced by substances such as hormones and neurotransmitters. Through their influence on receptors, these substances prompt, modify, or halt certain cellular activities. Many drugs work because their chemical structures permit them to link up with one or more of the receptors in the body, like pieces in a jigsaw puzzle. Generally, when drugs classed as agonists link up with receptors, they have the effect of modifying a cellular activity, either decreasing or increasing it. When an antagonist binds to a receptor, it blocks the receptor from interacting with the body chemicals designed to influence it, and so prevents a sequence of biological events that would otherwise take place.

Epinephrine

Epinephrine is the agonist drug used to control glaucoma. Some of the brand names it is sold under include Epifrin, Epinal, Epitrate, Eppy, and Glaucon. It is a nonselective medication because it acts on more than one area in the eye; it affects aqueous flow, trabecular outflow, and uveascleral outflow. Chemically, epinephrine is identical to the hormone adrenaline, which is secreted by the adrenal gland and is known to control glaucoma. Secretions of this fluid are extremely complex, and the mystery of its manufacture and diffusion still remain to be unraveled.

Epinephrine medications work well at reducing IOP, but may create one or two problems. After a period of use, or at times immediately after you instill the drop, your eye may become red. This is because epinephrine dilates the blood vessels in the eye. The redness is harmless, but most people object to walking around with a red eye. If your eye begins to itch and/or hurt, you may be having an allergic reaction to the medication.

Scientists have found that if epinephrine is combined with another drug, dipivefrin, better results can be obtained. This combination is sold under the brand name Propine. Because Propine penetrates the cornea and reaches the interior of the eye more rapidly, some of the troublesome effects of epinephrine are averted. But not for long. The body catches on and the reactions against the drug begin to reappear. Unlike the miotics, Propine dilates the pupil, which helps to counteract somewhat the pupil-constricting properties of the miotics such as pilocarpine and carbachol. It also constricts the blood vessels on the surface of the eye, which enhances the whiteness of your sclera, giving your eye a beautiful appearance.

Epinephrine can cause blurred vision if you wear soft contact lenses, because it stains the lenses. Propine is said to avert this problem, possibly because of its rapid penetration into the eye. People with heart problems and/or high blood pressure should use any drugs in the epinephrine family with caution, for systemic side effects can include acute hypertension (high blood pressure), arrhythmia (irregular heartbeat), and angina (chest pains). If you already have any of these problems, the drug can worsen them.

Apraclonidine

Apraclonidine (Iopidine) is another agonist drug used in the treatment of glaucoma. The mechanism of how it works is not completely established, but researchers believe it predominantly reduces the formation of aqueous humor. Originally, apraclonidine was used to counteract the temporary spikes in IOP that can occur directly following laser treatment. Heartened by its effect on intraocular pressure, ophthalmologists lobbied the U.S. Food and Drug Administration (FDA) to approve its use in the general treatment of glaucoma, and 1995, apraclonidine joined the list of medications prescribed for lowering IOP.

As with any medication, there can be side effects. Possible side effects of apraclonidine include dilation of the pupil, burning, discomfort, a foreign-body sensation, dryness, itching, blurred or dimmed vision, a generalized allergic response, and tiny hemorrhages in the conjunctiva. Systemically, it can cause abdominal pain, diarrhea, stomach discomfort, and vomiting. People with some forms of severe cardiovascular disease are advised against taking this medication because it lowers blood pressure. Some patients have complained of insomnia, dream disturbances, irritability, and decreased libido. Others have cited dry mouth, nasal burning or dryness, headache, heaviness or burning in the chest, clammy or sweaty palms, body heat, shortness of breath, fatigue, and pain in the extremities. In some patients, this drug apparently loses its effectiveness after several months' use.

I used apraclonidine for two weeks before I developed an allergic reaction to it. I was sorry to give it up because it did lower my IOP. Other members of our support group have been able to tolerate this medication well.

Brimonidine (Alphagan) is considered comparable to apraclonidine, but with fewer side effects. It is dispensed in a 0.2-percent solution and it is believed to reduce the flow of aqueous humor and increase uveoscleral outflow. Although it is considered less allergenic and less likely to cause adverse effects than apraclonidine, it nevertheless can cause side effects in susceptible individuals, among them dry mouth; eyes that are red, itchy, burning or stinging, and/or have a foreign-body sensation; headache; blurred vision; fatigue; drowsiness; and conjunctiva problems. Less common side effects include corneal erosion, sensitivity to light, sealing of the eyelid and/or conjunctiva, tearing, upper respiratory distress, eye ache, dizziness, redness and/or tenderness of the eyelids, gastrointestinal symptoms, weakness, blanching of the conjunctiva, abnormal vision, and muscular pain. This drug should not be used by anyone who takes monoamine oxidase (MAO) inhibitors, commonly prescribed for depression.

The Antagonists

Timolol (Timoptic), betaxolol (Betoptic), levobunolol (Betagan), and metipranolol (Optipranolol) are drugs in the antagonist family. These are the beta-blockers, so called because they bond to receptors called beta-adrenergic receptors in the body. The mechanism by which these medications lower IOP is not completely understood, but together with pilocarpine or carbachol, they are powerful tools for controlling open-angle glaucoma.

Timolol is the most widely used of the beta-blockers, but it can have major side effects. In people with cardiac or bronchial problems, it can cause hypotension and shortness of breath. It is potentially dangerous for persons with asthma and other diseases involving spasms of the airways because it can increase airway resistance. Some people report vague disturbances in both near and far vision with this drug, but this is usually experienced at the beginning of treatment and tends to disappear with continued use. Systemic side effects such as gastrointestinal distress, nausea, queasiness, and diarrhea do occur, but are usually temporary. Some men report that these drugs cause impotence, as systemic beta-blockers (often prescribed for high blood pressure) can do. If you do aerobic exercise, you may find that you cannot raise your pulse rate as you did before. I find this to be the case when I work out. Other members of our group report other symptoms. Yvette, who once almost sang professionally, no longer has the lung capacity for singing since she began using timolol, and Lillian swears that the drug is responsible for her frequent forgetfulness. Timolol may also have adverse effects on blood cholesterol, increasing the proportion of LDL ("bad cholesterol") and decreasing that of HDL ("good cholesterol"). If it causes dizziness, it may increase your chances of suffering a fall or other accident. Beware of using Timoptic if you have a heart problem. In rare cases, it can cause reduced blood flow that may be mistaken for clogged arteries. One woman I know was scheduled for open-heart surgery but was spared when an alert doctor thought to take her off Timoptic. Her blood flow returned to normal. Betaxolol appears to cause fewer side effects than timolol, but it is not as effective at lowering IOP. One of the newer medications, Timoptic XE, is taken once daily, preferably in the morning, as the flow of aqueous humor decreases naturally during the night.

The use of oral beta-blockers such as propranolol (Inderal), atenolol (Tenormin), or nadolol (Corgard) to lower high blood pressure may also act on IOP. If you take beta-blockers or calcium-channel blockers, you may need less beta-blocking eye medication. If you must take both forms of beta-blocker, it is a good idea to have your general practitioner or cardiologist confer with your ophthalmologist concerning your condition and medications.

Many side effects of both oral and topical medications appear to be idiosyncratic. You may do fine with your medication, experiencing at most a slight discomfort, while a neighbor taking the same medication may find it intolerable. Researchers are continually seeking to develop more effective mediations with fewer side effects. For example, studies are being done concerning an alternate form of timolol that may be able to produce the same results with fewer side effects.

MEDICATIONS THAT REDUCE THE FLOW OF AQUEOUS HUMOR

Acetazolamide (Diamox), methazolamide (Neptazane), and dichlorphenamide (Daranide, Oratrol) are oral drugs that have been used in the treatment of glaucoma for nearly forty years. They work by reducing the amount of fluid generated by the ciliary body. They belong to a family of substances called *carbonic anhydrase inhibitors*. Carbonic anhydrase is an enzyme found in the outer layer of the ciliary body whose function is to prompt the formation of bicarbonate from carbon dioxide and hydroxide. Bicarbonate is then neutralized by sodium to form aqueous humor. By inhibiting an enzyme needed for the process leading to the production of aqueous humor, carbonic anhydrase inhibitors reduce the production of fluid in the eye.

Until 1995, these drugs were available in oral form only. That year, much to relief of glaucoma patients, the eye drop Trusopt became available for glaucoma control. Trusopt is a liquid form of the drug dorzolamide, and it performs in the same way as the systemic carbonic anhydrase inhibitors do, curtailing the amount of aqueous humor the ciliary body produces.

Taken systemically, the carbonic anhydrase inhibitors may affect more than the eye, and organs such as the liver and kidneys may suffer. For this reason these drugs should not be taken by persons with kidney failure or liver disease. The same caution holds true for Trusopt, for while the eye drop form is more efficient in delivering the medication directly to the eye, many of the same side effects can occur with Trusopt that occur with the oral forms, especially in people who are sensitive to sulfa drugs (one of the components of Trusopt is a form of sulfa drug).

The systemic carbonic anhydrase inhibitors produce a mild metabolic acidosis, or an overly acidic state in the body. If it is severe enough, metabolic acidosis causes muscle weakness, diminished reflexes, and possibly paralysis. Most glaucoma patients who experience acidosis as a result of taking carbonic anhydrase inhibitors describe the condition as "acid stomach." Eating foods rich in potassium may counter this effect to some degree. Methazolamide does not have as great an effect on kidney function as the other drugs in this class. Dichlorphenamide can cause headaches and a loss of chloride and potassium through the urine, just as some diuretic drugs do.

Other possible side effects of these drugs include kidney stones, interference with the formation of new red blood cells, and psychological changes as agitation, confusion, and/or depression. If problems with blood-cell formation, such as aplastic anemia, occur, they are most likely to happen within the first two months of treatment. Stopping the medication may then reverse the condition, but not always. Other fairly common side effects of these drugs include decreased libido, either overgrowth or loss of hair, and loss of the sense of taste. A less common side effect is urolithiasis (urinary stones). These side effects are more apt to occur with acetazolamide than with methazolamide, although higher doses of methazolamide (200 or more milligrams daily) may cause them as well.

While some of the more systemic problems may not occur with the use of Trusopt, an additional set of side effects are possible. The drops may burn or sting when administered, and some patients complain of a bitter taste after they put in the drops. These effects are usually transient. Some patients have found their vision to be blurred; others have reported tearing, dryness, and photophobia (unusual intolerance to light). More rare are fatigue, skin rash, stones in the urinary tract, and inflammation of the ciliary body.

My own experience with Trusopt has gone well. It reduced my IOP about 4 points and I have had only minor side effects. Eliminating methazolamide from my drug routine has given me a new lease on life. I am restoring some of the weight I lost, am able to climb hills and stairs without gasping for breath, and my digestion is improved.

The carbonic anhydrase inhibitors, including Trusopt, are not recommended for pregnant women, since there have not been adequate or well-controlled studies to confirm their safety for the fetus. Likewise, although it is not known whether these drugs are excreted in human milk, many drugs are, and the use of these drugs while nursing may cause adverse reactions in nursing infants.

Before embarking on systemic drug therapy, if you find you cannot tolerate Trusopt, it is important for you to establish a baseline white-blood-cell count. At the same time, your body's electrolyte (mineral) balance should be established, especially the levels of chloride, potassium, and sodium.

BYPASSING THE TRABECULAR MESHWORK

Prostaglandins, naturally occurring substances synthesized from fatty acids in the body, regulate many physiological processes, including the flow of aqueous fluid across the iris, called the uveascleral route. A new drug, latanprost (Xalatan), a synthetic prostaglandin derivative, increases the transfer of fluid via the uveascleral route. This drug offers a different approach to glaucoma therapy, for it leaves intact the ciliary body and its production of fluid, and bypasses the trabecular meshwork, which may be blocked. One other effect that affects people with hazel eyes is a darkening of the iris caused by an increase in the amount of melanin (brown pigment) in the iris. However, at least according to one researcher, this may actually turn out to be beneficial, since melanin protects the eye by detoxifying free radicals and screening out harmful light rays.

Possible adverse reactions to latanprost include blurred vision; redness, burning, itching, or stinging of the eyes; foreign-body sensation; redness of the conjunctiva; dry eye; excessive tearing; eye pain; crusting, redness, swelling, and/or discomfort of the eyelid; and sensitivity to light. It may also make some people less resistant to infectious illnesses such as colds and flu. This drug does not have a long shelf life; once it is opened, the product is stable for only six weeks.

IN THE WINGS

The drug arsenal in the fight against glaucoma is constantly expanding, and there are a number of promising drugs that are still in the experimental stage, but that may soon be in regular use. In one two-center clinical trial study, a 2-percent solution of a carbonic anhydrase inhibitor called MK-926 decreased IOP by an average of 24.6 percent and 23.7 percent after six and eight hours, respectively. Two agonist drugs, called UK-14303-18 and B-Ht-920, respectively, have yielded reductions in IOP of up to 40 percent in animal studies. Researchers believe these drugs work by decreasing aqueous production.

Oxymetazoline, a component of many popular topical eye drops and nasal sprays, is also being evaluated as a potential drug for lowering IOP. Anisodoamine, an alkaloid derived from a Chinese plant of the *Solanaceae* family, has been shown in animal studies to significantly increase the flow of blood and delivery of oxygen to the retina, choroid, iris, and ciliary body. It also effectively reduced IOP and increased pupil diameter, with no significant alteration in heart rate or blood pressure.

Nitric acid is a compound that has numerous physiological effects on the body, including the relaxation of blood vessels and smooth muscles. It has also been found to lower intraocular pressure. Researchers speculate that nitric acid stimulates the outflow of aqueous fluid. Another group of compounds that may prove useful for the control of glaucoma are the glutamate antagonists. These work to reduce the accumulation of the amino acid glutamate on the nerve cells of the eye (glutamate is believed to be toxic in excess amounts).

Marijuana, best known as an illegal recreational drug, can lower IOP. In rare cases, patients whose glaucoma has not responded to standard therapy have been able to request and use marijuana legally. To receive marijuana on this basis requires a great deal of paperwork on the part of your ophthalmologist (although laws vary from state to state). Marijuana can also cause constriction of the blood vessels. Nevertheless, if other therapies have failed, it may be worth the attempt.

Calcium-channel blockers are compounds that are used primarily for the treatment of high blood pressure and other cardiovascular problems. They affect the resistance of the blood vessels, relaxing them and reducing the risk of spasms of the vessels. They may also help prevent damage to the optic nerve by promoting the unhampered flow of blood to the retina and optic nerve. These drugs may be especially useful for people with normal-tension glaucoma—people whose IOP is in the normal range (or lower) but who nevertheless continue to lose sight. However, calcium-channel blockers may be risky for some patients. Anyone considering using one of these drugs to control optic nerve damage should work with both a heart specialist and an ophthalmologist. These drugs are primarily supplied in oral form, although one, verapamil, is available as eye drops.

Finally, it may some day become possible to treat certain types of glaucoma by washing out debris clogging the trabecular meshwork. Research is focusing on the use of ethacrynic acid, a diuretic, which increases the outflow of fluid when placed in the eye. This compound appears to increase the trabecular meshwork's permeability by temporarily causing the cells in the meshwork to separate, which might make it possible to flush out any abnormal material from the meshwork and restore normal fluid outflow.

THE DELICATE BALANCE

Taking a drug is in no way a benign activity. Unfortunately, once you are in the grip of glaucoma, most often there is little choice; bypassing drug therapy may lead to blindness. The options available to people of African-American descent are, unfortunately, narrower than they for people of other ethnic backgrounds because glaucoma tends to occur earlier and progress more relentlessly in African-Americans. Two factors appear to play equal parts in this. The first is an inherited predisposition to the disorder, although the reason for this has yet to be identified. The second is the greater possibility of undertreatment. Some researchers say that because African-Americans tend to have thicker irises, medication does not penetrate as effectively. Based on this premise, some doctors prescribe stronger doses of medication—but not all of them do, raising the possibility of undertreatment.

Glaucoma patients who are using several different kinds of drops may feel that they are being overmedicated. They may be right. Studies suggest that there is a limit to the amount of medication that will affect a person's IOP. Adding medication after that point produces no gain. In addition, the medications themselves can cause problems. The long-term use of beta-blockers has been shown to cause a general low-level suppression of visual sensitivity. You may find that you have trouble detecting subtle contrasts between colors, or newspaper print may appear too light and therefore hard to read. Rita, who has visual sensitivity problems, can read information only if it is written in black magic marker. Both pilocarpine and epinephrine have been found to cause distinct changes in the cells of the cornea. The implications of these changes are not yet understood, but those of us who have been on long-term drug therapy may rightly wonder whether the subtle changes in the way we see and how our eyes feel are a result of drug-induced changes in the cellular structure of our corneas.

Indeed, it is difficult to tease apart glaucoma-related changes from the effects of glaucoma medication. For instance, many people who have glaucoma also get cataracts, and this problem, along with the side effects of glaucoma medications, may hide the exact nature of our visual sensitivity problems. I thought my eyes had been permanently affected by the medication I had been taking for more than fifteen years until I had my cataracts removed. I find my visual sensitivity much improved now.

Then, too, muscle mobility, including the mobility of the tiny ciliary muscle in the eye, generally declines with age. Animal studies suggest that the chronic use of pilocarpine may have a similar effect. The long-term use of pilocarpine has also been shown to irritate the conjunctiva. Irritated cells become inflamed, which damages cells and can lead to scarring and/or closure of a surgically created filter.

Given these problems, which many of us suffer and rail against, we might be tempted to dispense with the drops. But, as Shakespeare's Hamlet said, there's the rub. While the long-term damage to the eye that occurs with elevated pressure may not be the sole cause of glaucoma, it is, nevertheless, a potent factor, and ophthalmologists are convinced that keeping the pressure down is the way to preserve vision. So at this juncture, most of us would rather use medication than risk irrevocable damage to our eyes.

The National Eye Institute, realizing the need for more refined drug therapies, has funded studies directed at enhancing the vitality of the optic nerve, and correcting or delaying the onset of glaucoma. Hopefully, with the development of new, noninvasive diagnostic techniques, we may soon have a better understanding of how anti-glaucoma drugs affect aqueous production and ocular blood flow, and of the relationship between drug therapy and cell biology. New drugs may someday be developed that will preserve the function of nerve cells even in the presence of elevated IOP. These are vital issues, and researchers are working to provide answers that will affect those of us who have glaucoma.

DO IT RIGHT

When I was first diagnosed as having glaucoma, my doctor prescribed eye drops but did not instruct me in how to use them or tell me about their side effects. I soon began to experience side effects. Eventually I learned that a simple procedure called occlusion—pressing your index finger over your tear duct and holding it for three to five minutes after instilling the drops—can both eliminate some of the side effects and increase the effectiveness of the medication by keeping it in the eye, where it belongs. Fortunately, most (although still not all) ophthalmologists now routinely instruct their patients in the proper use of eyedrops.

The human eye holds approximately 10 microliters (about 5/100 teaspoon) of fluid. Commercial eyedroppers release drops ranging in size from 25 to 56 microliters. This means that your eye holds a total amount of fluid equal to about half of the amount contained in the smallest eye drop. Not surprisingly, therefore, many people deliver an excess of medication to their eyes. Where does this excess go? It travels into the nose and is absorbed by the body. The mucous membrane lining the nose sponges up the medication and passes it directly into the bloodstream. The effect of this mimics an intravenous shot more closely than it does swallowing a pill, for pills must go through the liver, where they are acted on before being delivered to your system, while drops absorbed through the nasal route do not.

Short of producing eyedroppers more in keeping with the amount of medication needed to keep intraocular pressure in line, some of the more disastrous side effects can be avoided by the technique of nasolacrimal duct occlusion. This method brings other benefits as well. Studies have shown that for some people, nasolacrimal duct occlusion reduces the need for stronger prescriptions; for others, it can delay the need for filtration surgery for several years.

To avoid or lessen systemic effects, and to increase the efficiency of your eye drops, here's how to do it (see Figure 5.1):

1. Gently pinch your lower eyelid to make a small lid pocket.
2. Tilt your head back.
3. Instill the drop in the pocket, close your eye, and gently press with your middle finger on the inside corner of the eye. This action occludes the nasolacrimal duct and keeps the medication in your eye. Keep your finger there for three to five minutes.
4. Remove your finger, straighten your head, and wipe or wash off any excess medication around your eye.
5. Repeat steps 1 through 4 with the other eye, if required.

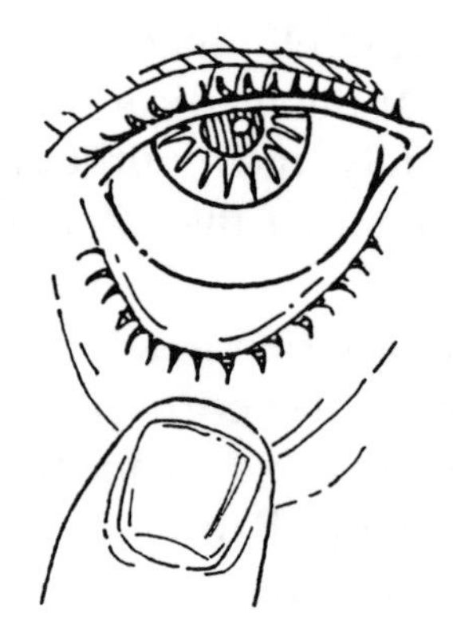

1. Pull down your lower eyelid to form a pocket.

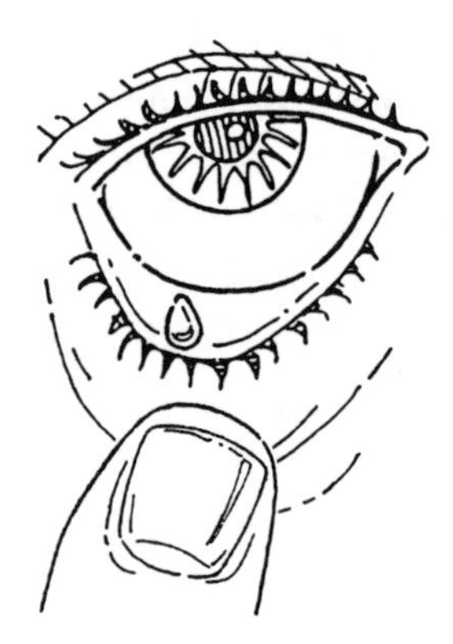

2. Instill the eye drop in the lid pocket.

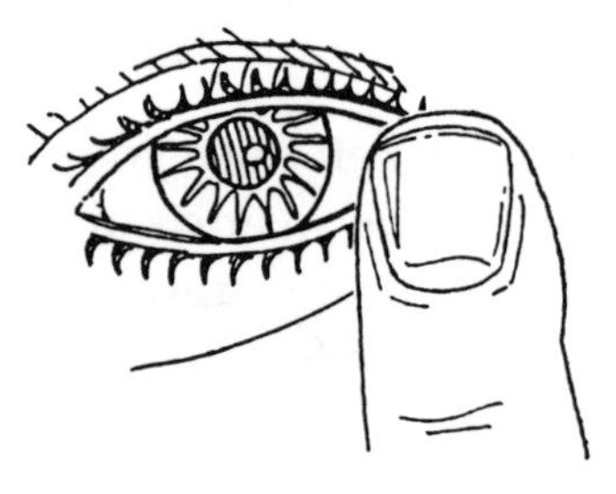

3. Gently press the inside corner of the eye to occlude the tear duct.

Figure 5.1 Instilling Eye Drops

A second method that some people find effective is to instill the drop as above, then to close the eye, without blinking, for three to five minutes. (Blinking causes the tear duct to open.)

Whichever method you find preferable, practice it with your eye doctor present to make sure that you are doing it right.

For glaucoma patients, medication is a fact of life. Much as we would like to be freed from using drops, we realize that the specter of blindness may await us if we allow our IOPs to rise. As new medications and reformulations of old medications reach the market, many of us may be relieved of the four-times-a-day schedule of eye drops—a problem that often interferes with social life. And as scientists develop more sophisticated medications that target specific sets of cells or tissues involved in glaucoma, we may find medications becoming an even more important ally in controlling our glaucoma than they are today. In addition, the time may soon come when we will be offered a choice of initial therapy strategies. In England and Europe, the usual treatment of glaucoma is surgery, followed by either laser therapy or medication if needed. A nationwide study sponsored by the National Eye Institute is currently underway that should give insight into which approach to treatment is preferable for patients with POAG, the most common form of glaucoma.

Meanwhile, for the present, we can eliminate some of the more serious side effects of medications we use by properly instilling our eye drops and by attending to our emotional needs. If drops fail to control IOP, glaucoma patients usually advance to the next step in glaucoma therapy—laser treatment. This will be the subject of the next chapter.

CHAPTER 6

The Healing Light

Science has always promised two things not necessarily related—an increase first in our powers, second in our happiness or wisdom, and we have come to realize that it is the first and less important of the two promises which it has kept most abundantly.

Joseph Wood Krutch (1929)

The term *laser* is an acronym for *l*ight *a*mplification by *s*timulated *e*mission of *r*adiation. Lasers work by channeling the energy in light. The basic unit of light energy is the photon. Light also has the property of color, which is determined by the length of the waves it travels in. For example, yellow light has a longer wavelength than blue. Sunlight, which is white light, is actually made up of all the colors of the spectrum together. In a laser, the atoms of substances such as crystals, gases, and dyes are excited to act on light of a single wavelength. A single wavelength represents a pure color. If an atom strikes a photon, the result is two photons, both with the same wavelength. In a laser, these multiplying photons are reflected back and forth in a mirrored chamber, and some of them escape the chamber through a lens to form a laser beam—a coherent, concentrated stream of light made up of photons all having the same wavelength. The powerful, concentrated light beams generated by lasers are capable of tasks as varied as cutting through steel and performing delicate surgical operations.

You may have experienced the power of light in the classic grade-school science experiment in which you use a mirror to focus sunlight on an object, and the concentrated beam of sunlight burns a hole in a piece of paper. Or you may recall the boys in *Lord of the Flies* using a pair of glasses to start a fire. While these examples are not true lasers, they do give you some idea of the power of a concentrated beam of light.

In ophthalmology, different types of lasers are used for different procedures. The most common are the argon laser; the neodymium: yttrium-aluminum garnet (Nd:YAG) laser; the diode laser; and the holmium laser. The beams created by these lasers interact with the tissues of the eye. The energy each delivers to the tissues determines whether the site will be burned, coagulated, or cut. For example, the argon laser used for trabeculoplasty places a series of burns on the trabecular meshwork. Where the burns occur, scar tissue forms, which improves drainage because it puts traction on the surrounding tissues, widening the spaces between the burns. It is also believed that an as-yet-unexplained chemical change takes place in the tissue as a result of the laser contact.

The tissues of the eye on which laser therapy works best are those that contain pigment, which is an absorber of laser light. Brown pigment deposited in the trabecular meshwork is a good heat absorber. With the wet form of macular degeneration (which accounts for 12 percent of cases), the retinal layer beneath the blood vessels is targeted. Laser treatment is also used to quell diabetic retinopathy.

Many people with advanced glaucoma have had one or more laser treatments. Yet the concept of using lasers in ophthalmology was just that—a concept—until two ophthalmologists, J.B. Wise and S.L. Witter, performed a pilot study using argon laser therapy for open-angle glaucoma in 1979. The news of this new treatment stimulated coveys of researchers to pursue the study of this fascinating new procedure, and within a few years, laser treatment gained ascendancy as an intermediate treatment between medication and filtration surgery. It seemed possible that laser treatment might not only delay the need for surgery, but in less serious cases might even control the glaucoma so that no further intervention would be required. Patients and physicians alike were enthralled with this new quick, bloodless procedure. Requiring only a topical anesthetic and taking no more than ten to twenty minutes, laser treatment required no expensive hospital stay and virtually eliminated postoperative trauma.

That laser treatment has become a remarkable tool for the management of glaucoma and other eye diseases is indisputable. Trabeculoplasty is the most common procedure for glaucoma patients, but there are other common laser treatments that many of us have had as well. Different conditions call for different procedures.

TRABECULOPLASTY

Trabeculoplasty is the most common laser treatment for controlling chronic open-angle glaucoma. In this procedure, a series of minute (about 1/128-inch long) burns are made around the periphery of the trabecular meshwork. These burns cause a shrinking of tissue that forces apart the tissues in the meshwork, creating openings through which the aqueous humor can flow. Areas of scarring develop from these burns, and these may cause the meshwork to bow inward and pull open the Schlemm's canal. Contradictorily, however, scarring may also make the trabecular tissue less porous, which may be why the positive effects of laser treatment often last only several years.

For this procedure, topical anesthesia is applied to the eye by means of eye drops, as it is before testing for intraocular pressure. The surgeon then places a special contact lens on the eye. This lens is equipped with mirrors that provide an enlarged view of the trabecular meshwork (this structure cannot ordinarily be seen through the slit lamp, which is the doctor's usual way of looking at the interior structures of the eye). During the procedure itself, which normally lasts no longer than ten minutes, you may see flashes of light with each application of the laser. Few people experience any pain. I myself experienced a sensation of pressure. Other people I know have reported experiencing very little discomfort at all. Perhaps the most unpleasant aspect of the procedure lies in having to keep your head pressed against the headrest and remain motionless.

Afterwards, most people experience no pain and little or no discomfort. In fact, as you sit in the waiting room for the two to three hours necessary before your doctor can test whether the treatment has increased your IOP (it can do that in some cases), you may be surprised at how well you feel. I remember the day following my first trabeculoplasty, when I walked into my ophthalmologists's office, he marveled at my chipper mood.

When laser trabeculoplasty was first introduced, 100 to 129 burns were made around the periphery of the meshwork. Later, ophthalmologists found they could get adequate control of glaucoma by making only 50 burns at first, treating only half the perimeter. If IOP rises again within a period of time—months to years—another 50 can be added. Some ophthalmologists have now reduced the number to 25 burns at a sitting.

While 50 or 100 burns may seem like a lot, the burns are infinitesimally small. They destroy only a negligible part of the trabecular meshwork, and the treated area looks no different from the untreated area. In fact, it is a good idea to ask your doctor for a record of which side was treated; if for any reason you should have to seek treatment from a different physician, you will want to be able to give your new doctor this information, since it is not considered advisable to treat the same area more than once.

If you have the form of glaucoma caused by Fuch's endothelial dystrophy (see Chapter 2), the corneal edema (swelling) that accompanies this condition may make trabeculoplasty difficult, for it obscures your ophthalmologist's view of the trabecular meshwork. I once experienced this problem, for I have corneas that are easily irritated. I am allergic to many of the topical medications and to the commonly used topical anesthetic. The problem became compounded by the contact lens placed on my anesthetized eye. The pressure of the lens together with the effect of the anesthetic drop produced edema, preventing my ophthalmologist from continuing with the laser treatment. Subsequently, my doctor found an anesthetic drop to which I was not allergic, and he was able to perform a trabeculoplasty.

After undergoing trabeculoplasty, the most common laser procedure for people with glaucoma, you should remain in the clinic or your doctor's office for one to three hours to have your intraocular pressure checked. You should also follow your ophthalmologist's instructions concerning follow-up care, which may require a visit on the following day and then one week later, with less frequent monitoring after that.

The idea of prophylactic (preventive) trabeculoplasty—that is, treatment done before the situation absolutely demands it—is gaining ground among some ophthalmologists, although it is not universally recommended. Many ophthalmologists feel there is no need for trabeculoplasty until there is some indication of visual field loss. Others, however, advocate prophylactic trabeculoplasty, reasoning that this treatment may be more effective in preventing loss of eyesight.

While laser treatment for open-angle glaucoma is still generally considered to be the second line of defense, to be used if medication fails to yield satisfactory results, some practitioners believe it should be considered for use as an initial treatment. A study funded by the National Eye Institute suggests that if patients with newly diagnosed primary open-angle glaucoma are treated with laser surgery, the need for treatment with medication may be delayed for two years or more, or, if medication is required, less of it may be necessary. In this study, more than 80 percent of the eyes that received initial laser surgery finished the first two years of follow-up with successful control of the glaucoma, with either no medication or just one eye drop.

IRIDECTOMY/IRIDOTOMY

Iridectomy, speculated about in the early 1900s and tinkered with during the 1950s and 1960s, has been the preferred treatment for the control of narrow-angle glaucoma for some years now. It is also used as a preventive measure in those whose angles are so narrow that an acute angle-closure attack is considered likely. The width of the angle is measured on a grading scale, I through IV. Normally, angles are open to grades III or IV, that is, 30 to 40 degrees. Grade II, a 20-degree angle, is considered "iffy," and needs to be monitored. Grade I, an angle of 10 degrees or less, may precipitate an acute glaucoma attack if the iris moves into the angle, something that can occur if the pupil simply becomes dilated.

In iridectomy, a small piece of the iris is removed, creating a hole that allows the aqueous humor to pass from the posterior chamber behind the iris into the anterior chamber in front of the iris. Laser iridotomy (using the laser to make a small hole in the iris) replaces surgical iridectomy, and reduces the danger of damage to the lens. Two types of laser are used for this procedure. The argon laser heats up the tissues of the iris, and as the pigment in the iris absorbs the laser energy, a hole is formed. This particular type of energy also coagulates blood vessels in the area, reducing the risk of bleeding. As an alternative to the argon laser, the Nd:YAG laser may be used. The Nd:YAG does not require multiple applications, as the argon laser does. Instead, with as little as one shot, a hole is made in the iris. There may be some bleeding, but this is temporary and normally resolves itself in minutes. The choice of which laser should be used lies between patient and doctor. Treatment with the argon laser is generally considered safer, since each burn is relatively weak. With the Nd:YAG laser, which makes one explosive shot, it is easier to do harm. However, if you have blue eyes, which have less light-absorbing pigment, the YAG may be best for you. Either laser can be used for brown eyes.

There are occasions (only 5 percent of cases) when an iridotomy may not provide relief. This is more likely to occur in persons with plateau iris (see page 19). Unfortunately, this condition is sometimes not diagnosed until an iridectomy reveals the problem. If plateau iris is diagnosed, a series of laser burns applied at low energy around the periphery of the iris usually succeeds in contracting the iris and moving it out of the angle.

Either iridectomy or iridotomy is the treatment of choice for a condition called pupillary block. This problem is a structural one, and it is caused by the aqueous humor building up behind the iris. To reach the anterior section (the front of the eye) from the posterior section (the back of the eye), the aqueous humor must squeeze through a channel formed by the lens and the iris. If this channel is blocked, aqueous humor builds up behind the iris and pupil, and pushes the iris into the angle. An iridotomy corrects this problem by creating a passageway for the aqueous humor to flow from the back of the eye into the front of the eye and be dispersed through the trabecular meshwork.

Another structural problem, pigmentary-dispersion syndrome (see page 20), is also yielding to early treatment with iridotomy. Unlike pupillary block, where the iris pushes forward, the iris here is pushed backward, a condition referred to as reverse pupillary block. Iridotomy equalizes the pressure between the two chambers, restoring equilibrium, and also flattens out the iris into a more normal position. Not everyone with pigment-dispersion syndrome needs to have this treatment, however. Most patients with this problem respond favorably to treatment with pilocarpine, which not only lowers the pressure but also stretches the iris taut, keeping it from sagging backwards and rubbing against the zonules. On the other hand, some patients with pigmentary dispersion require both pilocarpine and an iridotomy.

Can an iridotomy fail? In a way, yes. If your doctor is very cautious, he or she may not make an adequate hole and may need to re-treat your eye. But the overall success rate for this procedure is high—98 to 99 percent. With surgical iridectomy, scar tissue can form and block off the hole because the body, in its wisdom, wants to heal the wound. Laser treatment directed to the scar tissue that has formed usually succeeds in eliminating scar tissue from the opening, allowing the aqueous fluid to flow out freely again.

CYCLOPHOTOCOAGULATION/ CYCLOABLATION/CYCLOTHERAPY

Another laser treatment for open-angle glaucoma involves reducing the amount of aqueous humor in the eye by destroying part of the ciliary body, which produces the fluid. Prior to using lasers for this purpose, attempts were made using high-frequency radio signals (electrodiathermy) and freezing the ciliary tissue (cryotherapy). Neither of these attempts produced truly satisfactory results, as they tended to destroy too much tissue, leaving the eye without enough fluid to remain healthy. A type of laser treatment called *cyclophotocoagulation* (or sometimes, alternatively, *cycloablation* or *cyclotherapy*) appears to be safer and more precise because it produces less inflammation and a lesser degree of destruction.

There are two methods used for this procedure. If the eye can be sufficiently dilated (which may not be possible in persons who have been using miotic drugs such as pilocarpine or carbachol for a long time), the laser beam can enter the eye through the pupil. With a newer technique, the doctor uses a probe that is moved across the sclera and is positioned right above the ciliary body. The eye receives a local anesthetic that keeps the patient comfortable during the procedure. An endoscope at the end of the probe allows the doctor to view target areas on a television monitor. The heat of the laser coagulates or destroys a part of the ciliary tissue.

Nevertheless, even with this newer technique, there are problems. The ophthalmologist must decide just how much of the ciliary tissue should be destroyed. Too much, and the eye will fail to produce enough fluid (a condition called hypotony), which can ultimately cause the tissues of the eye to disintegrate. Too little, and the eye will continue to produce too much fluid, and the pressure will remain too high. For this reason cyclophotocoagulation is usually reserved for people whose IOPs cannot be controlled in any other way, and, especially if the IOP is abnormally high, causes pain as well as optic nerve damage. The success rate runs just under 70 percent.

A newer version of this treatment, called endocyclophotocoagulation, may increase the success of this procedure. This treatment can be performed during cataract surgery or as a single procedure. A tiny probe just one-twentieth of an inch in diameter that contains a minute laser and light camera system is advanced under the iris until the doctor can see the ciliary body. Half to three-quarters of the ciliary body can then be treated by laser. The treated areas no longer function, but because the ciliary body is composed of tiny hills and valleys, the laser energy does not reach all of the cells, leaving enough to produce the amount of aqueous fluid the eye needs. Either the Nd:YAG or the diode, a newer type of laser, can be used for most forms of cyclophotocoagulation.

SCLEROSTOMY

Sclerostomy is a procedure that involves the creation of a hole the size of a pencil tip in the sclera to serve as an outflow channel for the aqueous humor. It is performed by directing laser energy through a pencil-point probe that pierces the cornea at the edge, where it meets the sclera, in the 12:00 position on your eye. This hole creates a drainage passage through which the aqueous humor flows. Sclerostomy can be performed under local anesthesia. You may feel irritation, a slight stinging, or some other minor discomfort, but since the procedure is fast—ten to twenty minutes—the discomfort is limited.

A modification of the sclerostomy now being investigated involves directing laser light from inside the eye. The doctor bounces light off a mirror in a contact lens that is held on your eye during the procedure. The laser beam crosses the eye and treats the sclera from within, forming a hole from the inside out. Fluid then collects under the conjunctiva to form a sort of a blister, called a bleb, that acts to filter out the fluid. This version of the procedure is still considered experimental, however.

Sclerostomy was designed to replace trabeculectomy, the standard filtering operation (in which the doctor surgically creates a drainage hole), and it offers several advantages over conventional surgery. To begin with, it is quick and involves less bleeding. Also, since only the area of the hole receives the full brunt of the laser heat, the surrounding tissues do not suffer as much as in conventional surgery. Scar formation, the bugaboo of conventional surgery, may be less of a problem as well, because the infrared energy of the laser cauterizes the wound edges. But to date sclerostomy has yielded only a 50-percent success rate, compared with 85 to 95 percent for trabeculectomy. The holes often clog up and IOP rises again. Then, too, sclerostomy does not result in the creation of a flap to guard the drainage hole, which conventional surgery does. As a result, fluid may rush out too quickly, causing the anterior chamber to flatten.

When sclerostomy works, IOP may be successfully lowered to about 15 to 16 mm Hg. In some cases, patients still have to take medication. Yet sclerostomies do fail 50 percent of the time, so most doctors still prefer the surgical alternative.

PHOTOCOAGULATION OF BLOOD VESSELS

Neovascular diseases such as diabetic retinopathy, which are characterized by runaway blood vessels, are now yielding to a combination of medication and laser therapy. In a type of laser treatment called *panretinal photocoagulation,* a series of about 2,000 burns is placed around the periphery of the retina. The destruction of this tissue curtails the proliferation of blood vessels. This procedure results in the loss of the outer limits of peripheral vision, but the central and middle ranges (the area that is targeted when you take visual field tests) remains intact.

> Carlos, a member of our group who has diabetes, has had five laser treatments in each eye and has used Timoptic to bring down his IOP. The laser treatment successfully eliminated the runaway blood vessels that were causing his pressure to rise, and he hopes that the laser treatment will prevent future blood vessels from doing the same thing, although he understands that he may need to have more laser treatment in the future should new blood vessels proliferate. However, his ophthalmologist is hopeful that with close monitoring, Carlos can escape the devastating effect of blindness that once was the common fate of persons afflicted with diabetic retinopathy. Carlos, too, is optimistic about the future of his eyes. While he doesn't see as clearly as he once did, his vision is still quite good.

Photocoagulation can also be used for the form of macular degeneration that results from growth of blood vessels under the retina. The laser beam acts on the retinal layer beneath the blood vessels, causing the vessels to die. To treat this condition, an ophthalmologist anesthetizes the affected eye and then uses a special contact lens to view the part of the retina where the macula is located. This procedure is similar to other laser treatments of the eye. Patients experience some minor irritation, but unless there is an infection, they do not need to use antibiotic drops. However, unlike glaucoma (where most types do initially respond to laser treatment) macular degeneration is not always treatable, and in many cases continues its inevitable course.

ARGON-LASER SPHINCTEROTOMY

One side effect of the miotic medications is that the pupil becomes constricted after you have used the medication for a number of years. If your pupils are always tiny, less light falls on your retina, diminishing your sight in dim, hazy, or dark places. Furthermore, a tiny pupil makes it more difficult for a doctor to examine the back of the eye.

A technique using the argon laser can correct this problem. The doctor creates burns around the border of the pupil, causing the sphincter muscle around the iris to open. The result is a wider opening of the pupil. On rare occasions laser light reaches the retina during this procedure, causing some damage.

The size of the pupil does not affect chronic open-angle glaucoma one way or the other. Therefore, the decision to have this procedure rests upon you. Dorothy, who wanted to see better, had the treatment, and now she complains of excess glare, although this effect is not reported in the medical literature.

TREATMENT FOR NANOPHTHALMOS

Among the eyes most resistant to glaucoma therapy are those that fall into the category described by the word nanophthalmos (small eye). This is an eye that is smaller than average. Because of the small size of the eye, the angle formed by the iris and cornea is often narrower than the 30- to 40-degree opening common to the majority of eyes. This condition predisposes a small eye to narrow-angle glaucoma. To correct this problem, your doctor may recommend an iridotomy (see page 95), which is considered the first line of defense.

Because of the closeness of the internal structures in such eyes, extreme care needs to be taken if any type of intervention is made. In these eyes the sclera is thick, and when the eye is opened and pressure is released, fluid can pour into the choroid and be unable to escape through the thick sclera. To bypass this problem, doctors make a small opening in the sclera. You cannot tell if you have a smaller eye than usual just by looking, but if you are extremely far-sighted, this may be the case. Upon examination, your ophthalmologist can say for certain and inform you about the narrowness of your angle or other conditions that may be present.

PHOTOCOAGULATION OF THE RETINA

Photocoagulation of the retina is not used in glaucoma therapy as such, but is employed in the treatment of retinal holes and tears. By creating laser burns around the periphery of the hole, scar tissue is induced to form. This tissue acts like a dam that keeps the hole from getting larger. If a retinal hole is not contained, vitreous fluid can seep through, enlarging the hole and eventually causing the retina to detach. A detached retina is a serious condition and can lead to blindness or reduced vision if it cannot be put back in place either through surgery or laser treatment.

As with trabeculoplasty, a contact lens is first inserted in the anesthetized eye before this procedure. This lens enlarges the view of the retina, allowing the doctor to aim the light beam accurately. This procedure can last from fifteen to twenty minutes.

I had my first laser experience when I developed holes in both retinas. Before becoming aware that my retinas were in trouble, I had seen flashes of light, and I had read somewhere that these flashes of light might be symptoms of retinal damage. The treatment my ophthalmologist suggested was to use laser burns to seal the holes. To say the least, I was apprehensive about this new approach. While I experienced some discomfort and minor pain, I reacted, I now believe, more to the fear of the treatment than to the procedure itself. At the end of the treatment I found myself soaked with perspiration. Afterward, although I felt fine, I was advised not to read or do any close work that required rapid movement of my eye for a week. At the time, ophthalmologists believed that making these movements while the tissues were healing could result in detachment of the retina. Today, these restrictions no longer apply, since this theory was disproved. To prevent inflammation, my ophthalmologist had me use steroid drops, which may or may not have led to my glaucoma. Some ophthalmologists no longer prescribe steroid drops after laser treatment. Other drops, such as antibacterial drops, are used only if the contact lens contacts the eye. In some cases, ophthalmologists no longer prescribe drops at all.

HOW SAFE IS LASER TREATMENT?

No intervention into the biological processes of the body is without risk. Although laser therapy is regarded as essentially benign, it does produce subtle changes. It certainly is not as invasive as a scalpel, but a laser does destroy minute portions of tissue. Laser treatment is widely claimed to be painless, but most of the people I know who have experienced it speak of an unpleasant sensation. I'm convinced I felt a sizzle. Matthew said it stung. Penny felt pain. Each of the clinic patients Rita has worked with has reacted differently, but one common thread was that those who appeared to have the greatest difficulty were the ones who were most tense before and during surgery. Another cause of discomfort is the pressure of the contact lens on your eye. Your ophthalmologist holds this lens firmly against your eye to prevent it from making any movement during the procedure. If the iris moves, it can interfere with the doctor's ability to accurately target the area to be treated.

Your ophthalmologist is in the best position to advise you honestly of the benefit-to-risk ratio for any laser treatment. But it is important to realize that this treatment can cause changes in some people. There is also at least a theoretical possibility that laser treatment may lead to free-radical damage, for the powerful laser light does affect tissue. This might be comparable to the type of damage you would experience from bright sunlight. These rays of light cause free radicals to form in the cells of the lens and the retina, where the free radicals may cause degenerative changes. Some ophthalmologists believe that macular degeneration may be caused by exposure to ultraviolet light, whether natural or laser generated, although there is as yet no hard research to confirm or verify this theory.

Complications of laser surgery are not common, but they can include increased IOP, uveitis, adhesions—two structures of the eye sticking together—corneal burns, distortion of the pupil, and visual field loss. Bleeding is uncommon, but when it does occur it can be easily controlled. IOP can increase following laser treatment as a result of pigment being released in the process and settling into the trabecular meshwork. Ophthalmologists routinely use apraclonidine (Iopidine), a drug that reduces the formation of aqueous humor, to prevent this problem. Inflammation, which may be caused by the laser in some susceptible eyes, is controllable with corticosteroids. The risk of corneal burns and abrasions appears to be related to the skill of the doctor performing the procedure, so if you decide to have laser treatment, you should choose an ophthalmologist experienced with your particular condition if possible. These complications usually clear up within a week.

A word here about making holes in the eyes, for that is what these lasers do. Many of us react with horror that a part of our eyes, no matter how tiny, will be destroyed by the heat of a laser. We are right to be concerned, yet the alternative of watching our eyes deteriorate from the progression of our glaucoma is a far more frightful prospect. In general, the therapeutic use of lasers has been found to keep glaucoma at bay for many patients. Since laser treatments are such quick procedures, local anesthesia is routinely recommended rather than total anesthesia. Some of us might quiver at the idea of having something done to our eyes while we are fully alert. And if you are extremely nervous, you might want to be fully anesthetized. But as someone who has had a number of laser procedures performed under local anesthesia, I believe the feeling that you are participating in your own treatment outweighs most other considerations. Moreover, full anesthesia entails greater risk and produces much greater stress on your body as a whole.

GAUGING THE SUCCESSFUL OUTCOME

When I was first informed that I would need laser treatment, I responded to this information with shock and dismay. Since that time I have talked with many other glaucoma patients, and this response is by no means uncommon. After recovering from the news that I needed the intervention of trabeculoplasty, I wondered about the result. Would it prevent future vision loss? Would I need more interventions? When I joined the glaucoma support group, I found that everyone had these concerns.

Some people may not do as well as others with trabeculoplasty. For instance, there is some evidence to suggest that older people with pigmentary-dispersion glaucoma may experience an initial decrease in IOP, but that after nine months or so, the trabeculoplasty is no longer so successful. Some patients are convinced that their treatments fail because of their doctors' lack of skill. Ben, who had a first trabeculoplasty with one doctor and a second, in the same eye, with another doctor, achieved a satisfactory drop in IOP only after the second laser treatment. He may be correct in his assessment, or it may be that the second treatment would have been needed in any case. There is also evidence to suggest that trabeculoplasty yields poorer results in patients who have already experienced significant vision loss.

Age is a factor as well. Patients younger than forty do not do as well with trabeculoplasty as those seventy or older. Some studies indicate that persons who have had cataracts removed do less well than those whose eyes are intact. Other studies find no difference.

Exfoliative glaucoma, which appears to advance more rapidly than primary open-angle glaucoma, is thought by some researchers to respond well to trabeculoplasty in the first year. However, laser treatment for this condition is thought to lose its advantage within two years. Other studies find that exfoliative patients do best with trabeculoplasty over the long term and still others say that they do as well as primary open-angle patients. I have exfoliative glaucoma and I did poorly in one eye, but much better in the other eye. So go figure.

Long-term, success rates with laser treatment for persons of African-American descent are significantly different from those for whites. Only 32 percent of African-American patients, as against 62 percent of white patients, maintained a successful outcome after five years.

Some patients worry that the scar tissue formed from the laser burns may cause additional problems. If the burns are placed in the appropriate sites, future problems should not occur. But if the burns are placed too close to sensitive structures such as the fibers in front of Schlemm's canal, scarring can occur.

In short, not everyone responds in the same way to laser treatment. This should come as no surprise, since any intervention into the body's functions affects each individual according to his or her own physical and mental makeup. Added to the idiosyncratic reactions of individuals is the contradictory evidence from many studies. That can perhaps be accounted for by the small number of subjects from which the data is drawn, or the researchers' inability to take into account factors that can skew a study—particulars such as the participants' state of health, attitudes, and the duration of their glaucomas, to name but a few. What we report here should be considered as a broad guide. Is your trabeculoplasty working? Only your doctor can judge.

Laser treatment may or may not alter your medication routine; you may be required to take the same amount afterwards that you took before. For most people, laser treatment—specifically, trabeculoplasty—buys time. Most trabeculoplasties last no more than five to seven years. After that time, if your ophthalmologist determines that you have suffered vision loss, he or she will probably recommend a filtering operation. Filtration surgery is the subject of the next chapter.

CHAPTER 7

The Final Battalion

If anything is sacred, the human body is sacred.

Walt Whitman (1855–1881)

Surgery is generally considered the third and final step in the battle against glaucoma. Trabeculectomy, also known as filtration surgery, is the most commonly performed operation for the treatment of glaucoma, especially chronic open-angle glaucoma. In this procedure, the surgeon removes a small portion of the trabecular meshwork and constructs a bleb from a flap of scleral tissue. A bleb is a blister that acts to filter fluid from the eye.

The concept of using surgery to treat glaucoma dates back to the early 1800s, when William Mackensie, a Scottish physician and author of a textbook on eye diseases, performed a sclerotomy—a procedure that involved cutting a small piece out of the sclera to allow the fluid to flow out of the eye more freely. The results, although initially beneficial, were temporary. In 1857, George Critchett, an ophthalmologist practicing at the Moorfields Eye Hospital in London, expanded the sclerotomy slightly to include a small piece of the iris, and called the operation an "iridodesis." It was Louis De Wecker, who developed what he called a "filtering scar" in 1869, and Felix LaGrange, who in 1906 performed an iridectomy (see page 95) combined with a sclerostomy (see page 98), who finally succeeded in producing an operation that filtered the aqueous humor from the eye.

During the early to middle 1900s, various methods were devised for invading the sclera in such a way that it formed a bleb. Some of the methods used included removing part of the cornea, heating up the sclera, and other procedures that are no longer used. By 1968, doctors had developed the modern filtering operation. Since then, there have been many refinements, and doctors now claim a success rate as high as 85 to 90 percent. Your own individual chance of a successful outcome depends upon your age and race, and whether it is a first-time procedure for you. The odds of success are lower with repeated procedures and for patients who have ICE syndrome (see Chapter 2).

Interestingly, in Europe, filtration surgery is generally the first treatment recommended, rather than the last. They do use drops and laser treatment, but only after surgery shows signs of failure. They believe this approach ultimately costs less and better preserves quality of life—that patients are happier and do better with surgery as the primary intervention, because they need not contend with drops, pills, or laser treatment. They also maintain that trabeculectomy is much more likely to be successful if performed on a virgin eye—that is, an eye that has not been subjected to medication. American ophthalmologists argue that using medication as a first resort eliminates the possibility of irreversible side effects. Furthermore, for some people, medication in the form of one or two drops is sufficient to maintain ideal intraocular pressure, eliminating the need for either laser treatment or filtration surgery.

Nevertheless, eye specialists on both sides of the Atlantic are carefully examining the pros and cons of which treatment sequence—medication–laser–filtration surgery or filtration surgery–laser–medication—best preserves sight. The definitive answer may well come from a major study being sponsored by the National Eye Institute. In this study, called the Collaborative Initial Glaucoma Treatment Study, 600 open-angle glaucoma patients are divided into two groups, with one group receiving the American sequence and the other the European sequence. At the end of the study, which may take from five to ten years, researchers should be better able to determine whether the European or American approach should be considered the preferred protocol.

WHEN TO APPLY THE KNIFE

A number of considerations must be factored into the equation of whether (or when) to have a filtering operation. Some ophthalmologists advise having a trabeculectomy if they fear that continuing treatment with medications for much longer may cause changes in the tissues of the eye that will prevent a good bleb from forming. Early surgery is also likely to be recommended if you have a condition for which medication is not effective and laser treatment is not possible—for instance, if you have angle closure caused by the iris adhering to the cornea, a cloudy cornea caused by corneal disease, a type of juvenile or secondary glaucoma that is caused by the ciliary body pushing into the front of the eye, uveitis, or aniridia. It may also be recommended for patients who have trouble complying with the four-times-a-day drops regimen.

In persons with primary open-angle glaucoma, the decision to operate is usually prompted by a worsening visual field, an uncontrolled rise in pressure, and signs of damage to the optic nerve. The level at which pressure becomes high enough to demand surgery varies from person to person. When my pressure rose to 24 mm Hg, my ophthalmologist recommended filtration surgery. Jacquelyn, on the other hand, has normal-tension glaucoma (see Chapter 2), so she became a candidate for an operation when her pressure was just 12 mm Hg. Ophthalmologists agree that pressure is only part of the story of glaucoma, but it is still the yardstick they most commonly use, and it has proven to be a potent indicator for the majority of us on the state of our eyes' health. Of course, as with any surgical procedure, you may want to seek a second opinion before agreeing to undergo trabeculectomy.

GETTING READY FOR SURGERY

Once you have made the decision to have surgery, your doctor will advise you on steps you can take that should have a positive effect on the outcome. For example, there are certain medications that should not be taken within twenty-four hours before surgery. There are good reasons for this cautionary step. Pilocarpine users are often advised not to use these drops within twenty-four hours of surgery because this drug tends to promote inflammation and also the breakdown of the blood-aqueous barrier, a system of filtration that governs which materials in the blood are allowed to enter the aqueous humor. Pilocarpine may also aggravate a condition called pupillary block (see page 45), which affects most people with narrow-angle glaucoma to some degree. On the other hand, some doctors prefer that patients continue using pilocarpine, for the constriction of the pupil it causes acts to protect part of the eye.

Phospholine iodide (Echothiophate) should be discontinued two weeks before surgery because it inhibits the action of an enzyme that works to break down commonly used anesthetics. If the anesthetic is not broken down and eliminated from the body, serious problems may result. It is also advisable to stop using carbonic anhydrase inhibitors and beta-blockers (see Chapter 5) before and after surgery, because these drugs decrease the amount of aqueous fluid production. Decreasing the amount of fluid production is undesirable because a good flow of aqueous fluid helps in the formation of the bleb. Some doctors prescribe a regimen of antibiotic drops to be taken for a week before surgery to prevent infection.

Drugs not associated with glaucoma therapy may cause problems as well, and may have to be discontinued for a time before surgery. Some of these include anticoagulants (blood thinners), even aspirin, which promote bleeding. If you must take these drugs, the doctor who prescribed them can consult with your ophthalmologist to decide the best course for you.

The decision as to which drugs to stop before surgery may vary somewhat from patient to patient, however. In my case, my doctors had me continue taking the drugs I was on (carbachol, Timoptic, and Neptazane) right up to the time of surgery, because they felt if I stopped them, I might experience a sudden rise in IOP that would damage the optic nerve. They considered that this risk outweighed any possible negative effects from taking the drugs.

Another decision that will have to be made is whether to have the surgery on an inpatient or outpatient basis. Times are changing. When I had my first filtering operation, I had general anesthesia and remained in the hospital for five days. For my second filtering operation (combined with cataract surgery), I had local anesthesia and remained in the hospital overnight. In my third experience, another combined cataract and filtering operation (this time for my other eye), and again with local anesthesia, I stayed in a free-standing clinic for three hours and then went home.

On the other hand, Rita has been hospitalized for each of three surgeries, because of the severity of her glaucoma condition. For two filtering operations, she had local anesthesia and remained in the hospital for two days. For a third operation, a combined cataract and filtering operation, she had general anesthesia and remained in the hospital for eleven days while her ophthalmologist monitored her progress. Yvette, another member of our group who had a combined cataract and filtering operation, had local anesthesia and remained in the hospital for two days.

For the most part, surgeons now prefer to perform these operations in an outpatient setting if possible, given the patient's situation. Economically, this makes sense, for you avoid expensive hospital bills. And depending upon your personality, the outpatient setting may be more conducive to recovery than a hospital. I loved the idea that I could go home directly after surgery. However, some people may wish to have some nursing attention for a few days. Also, your doctor also may require that you spend several days in the hospital so that he or she can monitor your anterior chamber and be sure that your eye does not become infected. Ultimately, the decision as to whether or not to be hospitalized after surgery (and if so, for how long) should be made by you and your doctor, depending on your particular condition and preferences. Your insurance coverage may be a factor as well.

THE SURGICAL EXPERIENCE

What is it like to have a filtering operation? If you receive general anesthesia, you will go to sleep and wake up some time later with a patch over your eye. If you have local anesthesia, you may or may not first be given an anti-anxiety drug such as alprazolam (Xanax). Then, twenty minutes or so later, a local anesthetic will be injected into your eye. This causes a sharp pain, but it lasts no more than a few seconds. Once the operation begins, you should feel no discomfort, and you will be alert enough to talk to your doctor (I did). Depending on the condition of your glaucoma, the operation can take as little as half an hour to over an hour. A combined cataract and filtering operation usually takes no more than ninety minutes to perform.

Most doctors today prefer to use local anesthesia. However, if you have a complicated case, or if you are extremely nervous and fearful, your surgeon may suggest general anesthesia.

THE BLEB

The cornerstone of trabeculectomy is the construction of the filtering bleb. To perform this delicate operation, you doctor views your eye through a microscope placed several inches above the eye. The magnification gives your surgeon an excellent view of the structures of the eye. The first order of business is to open the eye. This is accomplished by opening the conjunctiva, which has the consistency of plastic wrap, to get to the sclera. The doctor then creates a flap by cutting a triangle or rectangle about three-eighths inch (or less) across into the sclera.

The flap hinges at the cornea, and it exposes the drainage area. A block of sclera is then cut out, revealing the iris and trabecular meshwork. An iridectomy is performed to prevent the iris from prolapsing (slipping) into the incision. A bit of trabecular meshwork is also excised to form a new channel to carry the aqueous fluid into the conjunctiva, where it is dispersed. The flap is then sutured, the conjunctiva closed, and the operation is complete.

You may hear filtering operations described as *partial-thickness* or *full-thickness.* These terms apply to the depth of the scleral flap. In partial-thickness surgery, the incision goes only through part of the sclera to form the flap, and results in a thinner bleb. A full-thickness procedure goes through the entire sclera and results in a thicker bleb. Most surgeons prefer to do partial-thickness operations, although with younger patients, some surgeons claim that full-thickness surgery is more effective.

Either directly before or after the operation, your doctor will administer a type of drug called an *antimetabolite.* There are two primary antimetabolite drugs in use: mitomycin-C and 5-fluorouracil. Mitomycin-C is administered before the eye is opened up; 5-fluorouracil is injected into the bleb once after surgery and again three to five times thereafter. The purpose of the antimetabolite is to prevent your body from summoning up its healing system, which would result in scarring that could render the bleb useless. The antimetabolites have shown good results in delaying wound healing. They may irritate the cornea and cause it to become cloudy, but this problem usually resolves itself once the drug is discontinued. A new drug under investigation, beta-aminopropionitrile (BAPN), which inhibits the action of an enzyme involved in scar tissue formation, may one day give additional support to efforts to keep the bleb open.

What you are battling in preserving a functioning bleb is the body's own defenses. When a wound is created, your body marshals its forces to promote healing. As a crucial part of this, clotting factors and platelets in the blood attract fibroblasts (cells from which connective collagen fibers develop) to the site of the trauma, and they replicate themselves there. The more fibroblasts are attracted to the wound area, the greater the amount of connective fiber formed. This is the basis of scar tissue formation.

There are some medications that interfere with this process. Atropine, an antispasmodic drug, normalizes the permeability of the blood-aqueous barrier (see page 107). Normally, this barrier becomes more permeable than normal in response to trauma (like a surgical incision) in the area; this allows more clotting factors and platelets to get through to the site of the injury quickly, promoting healing. Corticosteroids also reduce the permeability of capillaries and inhibit the body's attempts to recruit macrophages and neutrophils (the cellular cleanup crew) to the damaged area. Miotic drugs such as pilocarpine and carbachol, on the other hand, increase permeability of the blood-aqueous barrier and so are usually eliminated at this time.

The flow of aqueous humor fills the new space created by the corneal flap and causes it to rise and form the bleb, which resembles a sort of a blister. Directly after the operation, a diffuse bleb forms that may cover as much as a quarter of the eye, but within a week, the bleb contracts to three-eighths inch or so in size, and the anterior chamber stabilizes. As the bleb matures, it develops small cysts that are believed to aid in the outflow of fluid. The outcome of a successful filtering operation is a well-functioning bleb.

In addition to the antimetabolites, other drugs important for healing include the corticosteroids, which fight inflammation. After a filtering operation, you will probably be given prescriptions for antibiotic drugs and most probably an eye drop form of the steroid prednisolone, such as Pred Forte. Clinical studies have shown that corticosteroids, which fight inflammation, help to maintain good bleb formation. It may seem strange if your ophthalmologist prescribes a steroid, given the knowledge that steroids can cause IOP to rise. However, the positive effects of using steroid drops for a short period after surgery appear, in most cases, to outweigh the problem of a slight rise in IOP.

After the filtering operation, your surgeon will monitor your progress closely. Since the introduction of the antimetabolites in the late 1980s, outcomes for this operation have improved. Before the antimetabolites, results were uneven—a bleb might scar over in about a year (my first one did) or it could last ten years, as Leona's did. Older patients' blebs generally lasted longer because their healing mechanisms had slowed down, while younger patients especially frustrated their doctors with their efficient healing.

After my combined cataract and filtering operation, my surgeon gave me a videotape of the entire process. What impressed me most about the tape—aside from the knowledge that it was my eye that was being worked on—was the dexterity with which my surgeon manipulated microsurgical tools. His fingers never touched my eye, even when he was stitching up the bleb. The creation of the bleb took only half as long as the cataract operation did. The whole procedure lasted about an hour.

AFTER SURGERY

Immediately after surgery, your eye will be monitored to see how well the aqueous is flowing. Trabeculectomy got a boost when doctors discovered that they could use sutures (stitches) to close the incision. Sutures give the ophthalmologist a measure of control over the postoperative flow of aqueous humor. If the eye achieves optimal pressure after surgery, the ophthalmologist does nothing. If, however, the pressure rises, the ophthalmologist can lyse (cut) one or more stitches using a laser. This opens the wound more widely, allowing a greater flow of aqueous and reducing pressure. For the best results, this procedure is done in the first few weeks following surgery.

Should postoperative leakage, or too great a flow of aqueous fluid, occur, your surgeon may elect to place a device called a Simmons shell on your bleb. Too great a flow can occur if the opening is too large. The Simmons shell is made from transparent plastic. It is dome-shaped and about three-quarters inch in diameter. It creates pressure on the bleb, stemming the flow of aqueous fluid. If the aqueous fluid flows out too quickly, the anterior chamber can become flat, a sitaution that can result in parts of the eye, such as the iris and the cornea, adhering to each other. Or a surgeon may decide to reopen the eye and restitch the flap. After Rita's last operation, her surgeon did just that.

In some cases, a doctor may want to force more fluid through the bleb, and will advise massage to keep the bleb open. This should be performed only under a doctor's advice and direction. Both Rita and I have been advised to massage our eyes after filtering surgery. Once, when I was vigorously massaging my eye, I caught a look of bewilderment on a child's face, and I heard her whisper to her mother, "What is that lady doing?" I realized at that point that it would be better to do my massaging in private.

Before you return home, you will be advised of certain physical restrictions—to avoid stooping and lifting heavy objects, for instance, and to wear the rigid eye-protective shield that your doctor will give you. This perforated metal shield fits over the entire eye and should be worn during the day when necessary and certainly at night. You tape it to your face with special tape your doctor provides.

It is a good idea to increase your intake of (nonalcoholic) fluids, and discontinue use of your regular eyedrops. It is also a good idea to reduce eye movement in both eyes. Be sure to follow your doctor's instructions in using special medications correctly. It may seem like a nuisance to put two or three sets of drops into your eyes three or four times a day, but the healing of your eye and the prevention of infection are paramount at this stage. Most likely you will be using a steroid drop. Steroids must be tapered off gradually, rather than stopped abruptly, and are usually the last medication to be discontinued.

In most cases, your ophthalmologist will give you a printed list of instructions following eye surgery, or advise you verbally what steps to take. But it is a good idea to know in advance what you should expect. The following are some commonly recommended precautions for the postoperative period:

- Do not engage in any strenuous activity. Keep your head elevated, and do not bend from the waist.
- Discuss the issue of painkillers with your doctor. If you have any discomfort, ophthalmologists usually recommend acetaminophen (Tylenol or the equivalent) instead of aspirin, because aspirin can promote bleeding. If the recommended dose of acetaminophen does not adequately control pain, do not increase the dosage, but consult your doctor.
- If your eye feels "sandy," as if you have something in it, close both eyes and lie quietly in a darkened room.
- If the patch is removed on the day of surgery, wear the protective shield during sleeping hours. Keep using the shield until your doctor instructs you to discontinue.
- You may find your eye sensitive to bright light or sunshine. Sunglasses can relieve this problem.
- Avoid straining when you go to the bathroom. A stool softener such as docusate sodium (available as Colace and other products) can be prescribed to soften stool if necessary. It should be taken daily for two weeks.

Finally, from preparing for surgery through recovery, you need to keep in mind that you are more than an eye. Your entire being is involved in the successful outcome of this operation. Psychologically and spiritually, your attitude toward the operation and your postoperative frame of mind are crucial to the healing process. I have now undergone three glaucoma operations, two of which were combined with cataract extraction. For the last two, I had a much more positive attitude about how effective the operation would be. My postoperative success has not proved me wrong. Rita too found that with a change in attitude, her healing time was reduced.

EVALUATING THE SUCCESS OF FILTRATION SURGERY

A successful trabeculectomy is one that results in lowering intraocular pressure through the creation of a well-functioning filtering bleb. The overall success rate for this type of surgery may be as high as 85 to 90 percent. Yet within that overall rate, there are considerable individual variations in outcome. Some patients, especially those over sixty-five or those with chronic diseases that affect healing, tend to have more widespread blebs that filter more efficiently. This success may be attributed to their bodies' slower than normal healing response. African-Americans tend to develop heavier scars, and before the use of antimetabolites did not do as well with filtration surgery as people of other ethnic backgrounds. Now the success rate for African-Americans is roughly equal to that of people of other races.

People who have neovascular glaucoma are at great risk of bleb failure because their runaway blood vessels tend to scar down the flap, although they do somewhat better if they have retinal laser treatments (see page 98) before undergoing trabeculectomy. In persons with uveitis (inflammation of the uvea), a filtering operation may cause more inflammation and result in scarring at the site of the bleb opening that blocks the new filtration site.

Surgery tends to be less successful on eyes that have undergone cataract surgery. Some surgeons report a 69-percent success rate, while others claim better results. This gloomy outlook appears to be changing, however, with current techniques for cataract removal (more about this in Chapter 8). Furthermore, more and more eye surgeons are now electing to perform combined cataract and filtration surgery and reporting greater success with this operation both in controlling glaucoma and in restoring vision formerly clouded by cataracts.

It should be noted, though, that even with surgery that is considered successful by medical standards, many patients complain they do not see as well after filtration surgery as they did before. One study reviewed the charts of forty-five patients who had undergone trabeculectomy without the use of antimetabolite treatment (which may cause some blurring of vision). This study showed that at three, six, and twelve months following surgery, 89 percent of the patients lost one or two lines on the Snellen chart (see Chapter 4) as compared with their vision before surgery—a relatively small but measurable loss of acuity. My own experience was similar. After my first trabeculectomy, the vision in my eye went from 20/30 to 20/40 vision. Some doctors claim, however, that with most patients, the preoperative vision ultimately returns.

Other postoperative effects have been noted as well. Rita and Lori, an associate of hers, both had trabeculectomies the same week in the same hospital. Both were in their early thirties. Their operations were successful in lowering their IOPs, but later—although they had different types of glaucoma—they both experienced pain in the eyes that had been operated on just before their menstrual periods, and the pressure in those eyes went up, causing a slight impairment of vision. While cooking, standing over a pot of boiling water, their eyes hurt as if they were blistered. In addition, both Rita and Lori found it difficult to see in bright sunlight. However, when they talked to their doctors about these problems, they were advised that it was unlikely that their symptoms were related to the surgery.

COMPLICATIONS

As with any type of surgery, complications are a possibility with trabeculectomy. Some of these are more serious; others are less so. And for some people, filtration surgery ultimately does not work.

Guarding against complications and failure of the procedure requires intensive postoperative care on the part of both patient and surgeon. The following are some of the problems that may occur:

- *Repeated surgery.* If a first operation fails, a second or third may be performed, but with each new intervention, the odds of success drop.
- *Conjunctival buttonhole.* This is a tear on the conjunctiva that may occur during surgery. It must be attended to immediately, for, if left untreated, it can cause excessive runoff of aqueous fluid and a bleb may fail to form.
- *Scleral flap disinsertion.* This is a situation in which part of the scleral flap guarding the opening is torn off during the procedure. This must be corrected to insure proper filtration.

- *Vitreous loss.* Eyes that are highly myopic (nearsighted); enlarged, with a thin sclera; or aphakic (without their natural lens) may experience leakage of vitreous humor at the operated site. A surgeon must take care to clean up the vitreous, or it may plug the hole. This is not usually a problem with standard filtration surgery.

- *Bleeding.* People with high blood pressure and blood clotting disorders (either hereditary or drug-induced) may be predisposed to bleeding. When a filtering operation is performed, there is some inevitable bleeding when the sclera is cut into. This bleeding usually stops spontaneously. However, in cases such as those mentioned above, if there is continual bleeding, the surgeon usually will coagulate the problem area.

- *Hemorrhage.* Two different kinds of hemorrhage (excessive bleeding) may occur. One is in the highly vascular tissue, called the choroid, within the eye; the other is in the orbit of the eye (the eye socket). Both of these conditions are correctable when caught in time and treated with the utmost dispatch. If the hemorrhage occurs in the choroid, the patient may feel pain even if he or she has been given a local anesthetic. This problem is treated by immediate closure of the incision and intravenous administration of acetazolamide (Diamox) and mannitol to lower IOP. With this treatment, the eye eventually stops bleeding. Immediate action is the key here, for if the bleeding is not controlled quickly, vision loss may follow. Orbital hemorrhage may occur after injection of the local anesthetic. The eyeball becomes tense and the optic nerve may be compressed. This is also treated with mannitol to lower IOP, and the filtering surgery is postponed until the hemorrhage resolves, usually within two to three weeks. General anesthesia may be recommended for the subsequent operation.

- *Malignant glaucoma.* Between 2 and 4 percent of patients operated on for angle-closure glaucoma develop a condition known as malignant glaucoma. Despite the name, this is not related to cancer. Rather, it is a form of angle-closure glaucoma in which the ciliary body rotates and blocks off the flow of aqueous fluid, causing the pressure to rise sharply. This condition can occur hours, days, or weeks after filtering surgery. It may also occur after cataract extraction, miotic therapy, spasm and swelling of the ciliary body, and after treatment with miotics following filtration surgery. It is sometimes confused with pupillary block (see page 45), but while pupillary block can be relieved with an iridotomy, control of malignant glaucoma involves either medication or laser treatment. Atropine and cyclopentolate are the drugs of choice. Carbonic anhydrase inhibitors and beta-blockers (see Chapter 5) are also prescribed to control this problem.

- *Hypotony and flat chamber.* Hypotony is the medical term for a flat anterior chamber caused by leakage from the wound. Flat chamber is the same condition caused by the fluid draining too rapidly through the newly created drainage channel. If hypotony occurs, a doctor will take corrective measures. In the case of flat chamber the situation usually resolves itself in a few days. Surgeons describe flat chambers on a scale of 1 to 3. Grade 1 flat chambers usually re-form spontaneously. Grade 2 chambers need to be watched carefully, and sometimes may need to be re-formed. Grade 3 chambers always require re-formation. Several methods may be used to reform the anterior chamber. Leaks or tears may be repaired, if necessary, and sodium hyaluronate injected into the eye to deepen the anterior chamber. A balanced salt solution can also be used for this purpose.

- *Infection.* An infection is a medical emergency. If infection occurs, treatment will probably involve both topical and oral antibiotics. Steroids may be added to the treatment as well. While it has been beneficial for bleb formation, the use of mitomycin-C has increased the incidence of infection.

- *Superciliary effusions.* This condition, which sometimes follows filtration surgery, is believed to occur when a drop in pressure causes the choroid to swell. As a result, aqueous fluid collects under the ciliary body, disturbing the balance of fluids between the front and back of the eye. Steroid drugs sometimes reduce the swelling of the choroid and normalize the fluid balance.

- *Cataract formation.* Younger patients with clear lenses do not usually develop cataracts, but other patients sometimes do. The reasons that cataracts form after filtration surgery vary. A nick from one of the surgical tools can damage the lens. Or, if too much fluid is lost and the anterior chamber flattens, the lens may move forward and touch the cornea, causing damage. Topical steroids may also cause cataract development, although the combination of topical and systemic steroids is more likely to be the cause.

- *Corneal dellen.* In this condition, the area adjacent to the bleb dries out. It is not considered a serious problem. When treated with a topical lubricant, most dellens gradually clear. If the problem becomes serious and affects the bleb, it may be necessary to recreate the opening.

- *Internal sclerostomy blockage.* This occurs when the iris or a membrane in the area blocks the opening internally. When this problem occurs, laser treatment is used to open the site.

- *Wipe-out.* This is the most feared result of filtration surgery. Although IOP is lowered, visual field loss and loss of central vision continue to occur. When this happens, there is considerable visual field loss, especially if this loss affects fixation, the ability to focus on a given spot. This is a kind of glaucoma that is extremely difficult to control, and definitive answers as to why it happens are not yet available.

While complications can occur, and sometimes surgery does not succeed, it is important to remember that most of the problems that arise can be treated, and most people who reach the point of needing surgery do benefit from the procedure. With any type of medical treatment, there are individual differences. My first trabeculectomy lasted one year before scar tissue covered the drainage hole. Rita's lasted six months. Several members of our support group have had the good fortune of more than a ten-year mileage on their surgeries.

With my first combined procedure, my bleb lasted three years. However, with medication, my IOP is in an acceptable range and my ophthalmologist sees no need for further intervention. With my second combined operation, which is more recent and where the ophthalmologist used phacoemulsification, to remove the cataract, and mitomycin-C, I have not as yet had to use medication for the bleb is functioning very well. Yvette also had both of her eyes operated on. The first eye underwent two separate operations, whereas the other eye underwent a combined procedure (although not using phacoemulsification). She is now using medication in both eyes to control her IOP and her ophthalmologist sees no further need for surgical intervention. How your eye will respond to surgical treatment appears to depend on two factors: the skill of your ophthalmologist and your particular condition.

It may come as a great disappointment if you discover that you still have to use medication after filtration surgery, whether you have two separate procedures or a single combined procedure. Rita recently had combined surgery, then after that, a seton implant (more about this later in this chapter) because her bleb scarred over. Even with all the interventions, she still has to use a full complement of medications. While many people who have had filtration surgery never need to use another drop of medication again, there are those of us who may not escape using medication for the rest of our lives, even though we have had filtering operations.

CORRECTIVE MEASURES: REOPENING THE BLEB

Once you have had a trabeculectomy, you hope your glaucoma problem is solved. As we have seen, however, that is not always the case. Scar tissue may form around the opening that has been made, for the body wants to heal the wound and sometimes succeeds in doing so. If this situation occurs, the filtering opening is no longer patent, or open.

Ophthalmologists have had some success in vaporizing the scar tissue, if it is internal. Another method used is called needling—the doctor introduces a needle under the conjunctiva and reopens the bleb. After this procedure, massage may be prescribed to encourage the fluid to flow out of the opening again. Erika, whose filtration surgery failed after two years, is pleased with the results of the reopening of her bleb. Her IOP has dropped low enough that she was able to stop using timolol in that eye. Topical steroids are routinely prescribed after this procedure.

OTHER TYPES OF GLAUCOMA SURGERY

While trabeculectomy is the most commonly performed operation for glaucoma, there are other surgical procedures that are used as well, either for different types of the disorder or in cases where the standard procedures fail to yield good results. For infantile and juvenile glaucoma, surgery is often the first-line treatment.

Surgery for Congenital Glaucoma

There are two operations designed specifically for the treatment of infantile glaucoma. These are goniotomy (surgical parting of the trabecular meshwork fibers) and trabeculotomy (creation of a hole in the trabecular meshwork). Both require that the surgeon make an incision beneath the iris and into the trabecular meshwork. The methods differ slightly (in goniotomy, the incision is made through the cornea, whereas in trabeculotomy, it is made through the sclera), but the result is the same; these operations allow the aqueous humor to flow out through the normal channels. Currently, some ophthalmologists feel that goniotomy is more suitable for children with a degenerated trabecular meshwork and for infants with such conditions such as Sturge-Weber syndrome, aniridia, Axenfeld's syndrome, congenital rubella, and Lowe's syndrome (see Chapter 3). Children three and over whose glaucoma has not stabilized may profit more from a trabeculotomy.

Ophthalmologists prefer to perform corrective surgery within days of an affected child's birth, because delay can result in severely impaired vision or blindness in the affected eye. At this very early stage in a baby's development, the trabecular meshwork is at its most receptive to correction and is also most vulnerable to permanent impairment. Also, if action is not taken, because of the elasticity of the sclera from infancy to two years, a baby's eye can stretch as a result of pressure, resulting in poor vision, scarring, and possibly leading to amblyopia, or lazy eye (an eye with decreased vision that cannot be corrected with glasses). If the outflow system is corrected early on, a baby's eye will have a drainage channel available when it begins to produce its full complement of fluid.

After the operation, a child may favor the untreated eye and not use the operated eye. This situation can lead to amblyopia. If the child does not use his or her treated eye, the visual pathways to the brain from that eye—although corrected for seeing—will not develop normally. Thus, the link between eye and brain that is necessary for processing what is seen will be absent, and the child will ultimately be blind in that eye. To prevent this, an ophthalmologist will usually patch the untreated eye, forcing your child to use the treated eye.

Early treatment has been found to be successful in saving vision about 90 percent of the time in cases of congenital glaucoma. However, the glaucoma itself may not be cured, and the child will need lifelong monitoring. At present, evaluation of the long-term effectiveness of such treatment is still under study, since the first generation of patients who underwent goniotomy as infants are now only in their late twenties or early thirties.

Microprostheses

When glaucoma cannot be controlled by filtration surgery combined with medication, ophthalmologists turn to the surgical installation of what is called a *seton,* a tiny prosthesis through which the aqueous fluid can drain. A seton may be a tube, valve, or shunt that is implanted in the anterior chamber of the eye and terminates on the surface of the sclera. The purpose of a seton is to whisk away fluid according to the simple law of physics.

Statistics in the medical literature report that valve implants can account for as high as 82-percent control of IOP in persons who have primary open-angle glaucoma. However, with any implant, problems can occur. Scarring or cell debris from inside the eye may clog the opening. Infection may develop. The anterior chamber may flatten if too much aqueous leaves the eye, causing parts of the eye such as the iris and cornea to stick together. If the tube is not securely anchored, the conjunctiva may erode, and if the tube is improperly placed, the cornea may be damaged.

Rita, unfortunately, experienced trauma with her first seton. At the time of her operation, she was taking the systemic corticosteroid prednisone. Her face swelled up due to the large dose of the steroid, and she became hyperactive and unable to sleep—a problem that led to depression. A month after the tube was inserted, she was scheduled for another corneal transplant and the removal of her implanted intraocular lens, which, she was informed, had tilted because of excess scarring caused by the surgery. In Rita's case, scar tissue builds up rapidly after surgery. At the time of the removal of the lens, her ophthalmologist also cleaned out the tube, which had become clogged with scar tissue. Four weeks after this complicated operation, her eye collapsed. Rita was never given an explanation for the failure, but she theorizes it may have been because that eye had undergone thirteen operations. It is well known that the greater number of surgeries in an eye, the lower the odds of a successful outcome. After this experience, Rita needed eight months of emotional healing before she could accept the encouragement of her doctors to obtain a scleral shell, which is like a contact lens and fits over the entire eye, giving it a normal appearance. The day that she decided on this prosthesis, her spirits lifted. Once she started wearing it, she again began to take an interest in her appearance and she began the long road to recovery.

Research into more effective implants is being conducted in various places. New designs and materials are currently being tested and, so far, results have been promising, so perhaps this intervention may prove more free of problems in the future.

Daily, it seems, scientists are penetrating the mysteries surrounding the once intractable disease that is glaucoma. Biomolecular research is revealing how cells interact and influence each other. Ever more sophisticated technology for viewing body structures are revealing how these parts of the eye function. One day, scientists may finally unlock the riddle of the glaucomas, giving us precise knowledge of how to treat them, especially the more intractable cases, such as Rita's, and the other glaucomas that cause blindness. Meanwhile, treatment for glaucoma continues to improve, as newer drugs are brought on the market and laser therapy and filtration surgery are further refined. The key to glaucoma control for the vast majority of us who have this condition is to work with our ophthalmologists on keeping our IOPs within acceptable ranges and to see to it that we also work in other ways towards physical and emotional health.

CHAPTER 8

The Cataract Connection

The wish for healing has ever been the half of health.

Seneca (First century A.D.)

When the hole in the needle escapes your probings; when your rose-colored towels start to take on a beige cast; when you cannot tell a brown suit from a black one; when the sky looks gray on a clear day—you are seeing the effects of a cataract, and you may start thinking about having it removed.

Cataracts form when the fibers of the lens become opaque. Unfortunately for long-term glaucoma patients, cataracts do form. Long-term glaucoma patients as a group fall into the demographic category most prone to cataracts—persons aged sixty-five or older—although younger persons also can develop cataracts, especially if they get too much exposure to ultraviolet (UV) radiation. In addition to being in the age group most likely to develop cataracts, people with glaucoma are even more susceptible because filtration surgery and the medications used to control glaucoma may cause injury to the lens. When the lens is injured, cataracts develop.

Eye doctors believe that 90 percent of all cataracts are age related. Therefore, we who suffer from long-term glaucoma can expect to develop cataracts, both from the aging process and from interventions such as filtration surgery. Cataracts have been known to develop within the first few weeks after filtration surgery. If a small cataract is present before surgery, the cataract may worsen. Often a cataract begins to develop two to three years after the operation. Operation-related cataracts are thought to be a result of too much fluid flowing out of the eye. In addition, the various instruments used to open the eye may injure the lens. If there is direct injury to the lens during this procedure, for example, a cataract forms immediately. However, even the risk of postoperative cataracts appears to be age related; with younger patients, the incidence of cataracts following operations is lower than it is with those over sixty-five.

Of course, these are just statistics. We all have our own stories to tell. I developed my first cataract three years after I had filtration surgery in my left eye. My right eye, which had not had filtration surgery but was being treated with carbachol and timolol, also developed a cataract, but not until twelve years later. Rita developed cataracts in both of her eyes within weeks of her filtration surgery. She had her first corneal transplant and then had to go right back into the operating room for cataract removal. She wonders if her cataract developed so rapidly at least in part due to the corneal transplant, as well as the stress she experienced as a result of needing and then of having the surgery.

Other members of our group have had varying experiences with cataract formation. Both of the cataracts in Yvette's eyes developed before she had her filtering operations, but she had previously taken steroids for a cancer problem, and had also been on pilocarpine and timolol for her glaucoma. Dorothy, whose narrow-angle glaucoma and pigmentary dispersion have left her with little remaining sight, has been told by several specialists that her cataracts are insignificant, and that removing them would give her little relief.

A CASE OF ASSAULT

Why do cataracts form? The reason may lie in the unique position of the eye. It is buffeted by many different environmental stresses—ultraviolet radiation from the sun; injury; and, possibly, pollution. It is also subject to physical manipulation (as in surgery) and medical tampering from the drugs we take, such as corticosteroids, for example. Free radicals—destructive molecules, ions, and atoms that bedevil all the cells of the body—also circulate in the eye and may damage the tissues there.

That the eye survives as well as it does in most cases is indeed remarkable. Each part of the eye is composed of several thin layers of cells that form tissues. The lens is no exception. Less than half an inch in diameter, convex on both sides, and suspended behind the pupil by fine fibers (zonules), the lens is a part of the eye that is extremely vulnerable to insult, especially from ultraviolet rays. And UV exposure is cumulative, which may explain why cataracts become more common with age.

If the hole in the earth's ozone layer continues to widen, the incidence of cataract formation in the general population may skyrocket because of increased exposure to UV radiation. The major hole in the ozone layer is situated over the continent of Antarctica, and is already affecting the eyes of both people and animals in Patagonia, a region of South America. Researchers have reported blindness in animals living there. Other environmental considerations, such as the increased use of personal computers, photocopying machines, and the like, all of which emit light radiation, may also play a role, although there is as yet no definitive evidence linking them to cataracts.

In infants, cataracts may be due to an inborn metabolic error. Unfortunately, cataracts in infancy are usually accompanied by other problems, including developmental disabilities, kidney disorders, and Fanconi syndrome, a syndrome of congenital anemia that leads to stunted growth and rickets. The prognosis for infants born with these disorders is not good. They usually do not survive to adulthood.

Although rare, a condition known as galactosemia can be a cause of early cataracts in infants. People with galactosemia lack the enzyme necessary to break down galactose, a substance formed in the gastrointestinal tract by the digestion of lactose (milk sugar). If the level of galactose in the blood becomes too high, it accumulates in certain tissues, including the lens, where it is converted into a substance that draws water into the lens. The increased water causes the lens to become opaque.

WHEN IS CATARACT SURGERY NEEDED?

If getting stronger glasses is enough to correct the loss of visual acuity caused by a cataract, most doctors will advise you to leave it alone. Removal of a cataract becomes necessary only if the loss of sight it causes interferes with your daily activities. Yvette had her cataract removed when she could no longer read the street signs. I decided to have my cataract operation when I discovered I would need a second filtering operation; I opted for a combined filtration-cataract procedure.

Your eye doctor can advise you as to how necessary a cataract procedure may be when he or she charts your acuity on the Snellen chart (see Chapter 4). As you see only larger and larger letters, you begin to realize how much your cataract is interfering with your vision. That information, together with your general sense of how well you are coping with your daily activities, is your key to determining the most opportune time for cataract removal.

With infants, ophthalmologists judge the degree to which cataracts are interfering with vision through several different techniques. These include preferential viewing (seeing how the baby responds to a set of objects) and possibly by measuring electric responses of the visual cortex (the part of the brain responsible for seeing) to light stimulation. This system is called visual evoked potential, or VEP. Responses by the infant both to viewing objects and to VEP gives the ophthalmologist information on how well the child is seeing.

You may believe you have lost a great deal of sight from the progression of your glaucoma. This impression may be caused by the chronic use of miotic drops such as pilocarpine or carbachol, which constrict the pupil and limit the amount of light reaching the retina. While it identifies areas of vision loss, a visual field test does not always determine what you will be able to see once your cataract is removed. Evaluation with something called a the *p*otential *a*cuity *m*eter (PAM) test can, to some extent, measure your visual acuity, and may be more useful for determining your prospects after cataract surgery.

The cataract in my right eye had become so thick that I believed I would never see well enough to drive again. Yet my PAM test indicated that I had about 20/50 vision, which I considered not too bad. When I had my cataracts removed, I was astounded and gratified to find that I had still had a lot of good, clear vision left—enough to make me regret that I had let my driver's license lapse. You really don't know just how much you will be able to see when your cataract is removed until you experience it. Fortunately, for many of us, glaucoma damage usually occurs in the peripheral areas of the visual field, leaving intact the central areas, where we do most of our seeing.

Color vision especially can be affected by cataracts. Harold had forgotten what blue looked like until a cataract was removed from his left eye. The brilliance of the color then astounded him. Other colors have become clearer for him as well, and he can now distinguish between subtle shades of color. Now when he scans his suits he can tell the difference between his dark brown suit and his black one.

CATARACT REMOVAL

In its simplest terms, cataract removal involves extracting the clouded lens and replacing it with a man-made substitute, an intraocular lens implant, that functions in place of the natural lens. The implants are usually made of silicone or plastic. There are two basic types of cataract surgery, termed *intracapsular* and *extracapsular* cataract extraction, respectively.

The lens is enclosed in a capsule, like a pillow inside a pillowcase. With intracapsular extraction, an iridectomy is performed (see page 95), and then the lens and capsule are removed in one piece. Doing the procedure in this order makes it less likely that pupillary block (see page 45) will occur. This operation also removes the posterior capsule and the zonules, the fibers that suspend the lens in place. An intraocular lens implant is then placed in the eye, braced in the anterior chamber with haptics, tiny extensions on the sides of the lens.

In the extracapsular procedure, the front of the lens capsule is removed to allow the surgeon to get at the lens. The back of the lens capsule is left intact and the lens is removed. A viscoelastic solution is injected into the eye to keep it firm, and, with the capsule still in place, the intraocular lens can then be slid into it. If a silicone implant is used, the incision need only be widened to one-tenth of an inch, for the implant can be folded like a taco and inserted. A plastic lens cannot be folded and requires a larger incision. Haptics extend from the implant, which is half the size of the normal lens, to hold the lens in place. The viscoelastic solution is then drained from your eye and replaced with a fluid that is virtually identical to the aqueous humor.

Phacoemulsification is now a commonly performed type of extracapsular extraction. With phacoemulsification, ultrasonic vibrations are used to fragment the lens. The fragments are then sucked out with a special instrument through such a tiny incision that stitches may not be needed. This procedure has been called the "no-stitch" cataract procedure.

Many glaucoma patients and their surgeons prefer extracapsular surgery along with phacoemulsification. With this method, there may be less opportunity for pupillary block, in which fluid builds up behind the iris and pushes the iris into the angle. Intracapsular surgery, which was routinely used from the 1950s to the 1970s, today is recommended only for special cases, such as situations in which the back of the lens capsule cannot be used to support the implant. Phacoemulsification has become the procedure of choice for one out of five surgeons. Until the early 1990s, many glaucoma patients were unable to take advantage of this procedure because it could not be used on people with constricted pupils—the result of long-term use of miotics such as pilocarpine and carbachol. Today, surgeons overcome this problem by using special clips to pull open a constricted pupil and performing a sphincterotomy (an incision in the sphincter, the circular muscle responsible for the action of the pupil) to gain access to the lens. The enlargement of the pupil may remain permanent, but this does not pose any problems other than some photosensitivity.

There are some cases in which cataract surgery is not recommended. For example, placing intraocular lens implants in a child's eyes may not be appropriate. Children's eyes need to be evaluated on a case-by-case basis. Secondary glaucoma complicated by the presence of cataracts must also be judged on a case-by-case basis. Uveitis (inflammation of the uvea) poses a special problem. People with this condition are often advised to avoid cataract surgery because the implanted lens can cause greater inflammation in the eye, although there are some surgeons who claim success in such cases.

UNDERGOING CATARACT SURGERY

When you schedule a cataract operation, your surgeon may require that you have a medical workup first. Since these operations are now commonly performed in an outpatient setting, your general practitioner can order the necessary tests. The whole operation procedure, either cataract surgery alone or a combined cataract and filtering operation, can take ninety minutes to perform if the case is uncomplicated. Depending on your condition and the surgeon's preference, you may stay overnight in the hospital or you may go home after the operation.

During the operation, if you are having local anesthesia, your surgeon will inject the anesthetic around your eye. It may hurt, but the discomfort will last for only a few seconds. The surgeon will then perform the cataract surgery. If you are having glaucoma surgery at the same time, that will be done immediately after the intraocular lens implant has been put in place.

After the operation, your eye will be bandaged overnight. In the morning, your eye will be checked by your surgeon and your IOP measured. You will most likely be advised to take an assortment of drops, including antibiotics to prevent infection and steroids to reduce inflammation. You will also be given an eye shield, a perforated plastic oval to fit over your eye, to protect your eye when you sleep, and you will be advised not to bend your head, lift anything heavy, or strain during bowel movements (a stool softener can be used if necessary to prevent this problem). Otherwise, you can assume your daily activities. Some surgeons say you can shower (mine did); others advise against it. I discovered that as a result of going into a squatting position instead of bending my head to pick things up (amazing how many things fall to the floor!) I received a bonus—my thigh muscles became stronger.

Within four to five weeks, depending on how quickly your eye stabilizes, you may then be fitted with glasses. Yes, glasses. Many ophthalmologists prefer to implant lenses that make the eye slightly myopic and then correct distance vision with eyeglasses or contact lenses, especially with patients who are already nearsighted. They have found that people who are accustomed to viewing the world myopically don't adapt well if their vision is fully corrected.

The decision as to what strength lens implant to use is based on a combination of measurements, including the curvature of the cornea, the depth of the anterior chamber, and the dimensions of the eye itself. You have something to say about the strength of the intraocular lens as well. You are entitled to discuss in advance with your doctor what you feel will be most comfortable for you. At this stage, unfortunately, bifocal intraocular lenses are not available, so you may decide on a reading-strength intraocular lens with additional correction (glasses or contact lenses) for distance. This combination (my preference) feels familiar to most nearsighted people. Some doctors and patients have opted to have one eye fitted with a reading-strength lens and the other with a distance lens. While this arrangement is convenient and eliminates the need for glasses, it makes it impossible for the eyes to converge and work together properly, which is important for close work and depth perception.

POSSIBLE PROBLEMS

As with any type of surgery, complications can arise with cataract removal, and people with glaucoma may be more likely than others to experience some problems. Pupillary block is uncommon, but it may occur as a complication of cataract surgery. In this condition, the aqueous fluid is unable to squeeze through the space between the lens and the iris, and pressure builds up, pushing the iris forward to block the drainage channel. This can cause a dramatic increase in intraocular pressure. Pupillary block can be corrected with an iridectomy or iridotomy (see page 95). Studies indicate that there are fewer cases of pupillary block if extracapsular extraction is used.

Another difficulty may occur if the intraocular pressure decreases to a critical stage. While we who have glaucoma want to have low intraocular pressures, too-low pressure may result if the aqueous fluid passes from the anterior chamber too rapidly, causing the chamber to flatten. When the chamber is flat, parts of the eye like the iris and cornea, which are normally kept apart by the fluid, can touch and stick together—and that is a decidedly undesirable event. An IOP under 5 mm Hg may be an indication that this is happening.

Bleeding may also be a problem. Any intervention into your eye (or any other part of your body, for that matter) can cause the disruption of blood vessels. Most often these bleeding vessels can be cauterized or will seal themselves, but in some cases it may take a day or so for such a situation to resolve. In most cases it does resolve, but until the blood clears away your vision will be blurry.

If you have a fragile cornea, something called corneal decompensation may occur. In this condition, the cornea begins to lose cells and is unable to regain its former shape and consistency. This problem occurs if your cornea has a scarcity of cells, which may result from laser treatment or the use of medication. Glaucoma patients are more prone to this effect.

Your eye may also react to the implanted lens material by forming adhesions at the lens's points of contact. If the lens is improperly positioned, chronic iritis (inflammation of the iris) may result. If there is recurrent bleeding, neovascularization may develop, promoting a condition similar to the neovascular glaucomas (see Chapter 2). In some cases, a cataract operation can also precipitate an attack of narrow-angle glaucoma, for with this operation there can be a slight shifting of the parts in the eye, and these—the pupil, the ciliary body, or even trapped air—can block the angle through which the aqueous fluid flows.

Postoperative clouding of the capsule holding the lens in place may occur in as many as 35 percent of cases or more. This condition occurs in both glaucoma patients and people without glaucoma. It is treated with a procedure called a *capsulotomy.* Using the Nd:YAG laser, the ophthalmologist makes a hole in the capsule, allowing light to penetrate through to the retina. It is a quick and relatively painless procedure. Rare problems with this procedure can result in *cystoid macular edema* and retinal detachment. Cystoid macular edema, a swelling of the macula with fluid, can cause reduced vision if it cannot be corrected with steroid therapy. Retinal detachment may respond to laser therapy.

Longer-term complications of cataract surgery are also possible, though not common. One of these is glaucoma. Thanks to the new techniques for removing cataracts, this is no longer a frequent occurrence, but it does happen to some people. When the eye is operated on, it becomes inflamed. Steroids are commonly prescribed to tame the inflammation. These drugs, as well as complications such as bleeding, the release of lens particles, a phenomenon called "ghost cells" (see Chapter 2), and vitreous humor moving from the back of the eye into the front of the eye can cause glaucoma.

> Some years ago, Jan discovered that she had developed glaucoma—a result, she was told, of a successful cataract operation. She did not know which method of cataract extraction had been used in her case, but it might have been intracapsular extraction, which poses a greater likelihood of postcataract glaucoma.

Finally, if you have glaucoma and your ophthalmologist has already performed a filtering operation to control it, a cataract operation may, in effect, undo that operation. The cataract operation can cause scarring of the operated area. The bleb may even close altogether, necessitating additional interventions.

WHAT TO EXPECT AFTER SURGERY

After cataract surgery, normal sight does not return immediately. It can take days, even weeks. I had both standard extracapsular extraction and phacoemulsification, one in each eye. Both were combined operations. With the first operation, my sight did not come in for six weeks. I worried that I had lost whatever sight I had had in that eye permanently until one day when I discovered I could read the newspaper. Thereafter, good sight returned in that eye. With the second operation, done by phacoemulsification, I had full sight recovery within a week. My regular ophthalmologist, who sent me to the surgeon performing phacoemulsification, says that other patients he referred for phacoemulsification had similar experiences. People with narrow and open angles do equally well with the procedure.

Most people with glaucoma find that their IOPs are much the same after cataract surgery as they were before. Studies have shown that fewer than 10 percent of glaucoma patients who undergo cataract surgery with intraocular lens implants have greater difficulty in controlling glaucoma afterwards than they did before. At the same time, vision often improves markedly. One study of forty glaucoma patients who had extracapsular surgery for cataracts revealed that over 90 percent of them reported improved vision, results comparable to those for cataract patients without glaucoma. Intraocular pressure increased an average of only 2 mm Hg, and additional glaucoma medication was needed in only 20 percent of the cases. In another study, 70 percent of people who had IOPs over 21 mm Hg before cataract surgery were found to have pressures *under* 21 mm Hg a year after surgery.

Believe me, having a cataract removed can make a world of difference. I know, for I had mine extracted from an eye that I had thought had lost a good deal of sight. Now I no longer make embarrassing mistakes like walking into the men's room and startling a dignified gentleman engaged in the act of zipping up his trousers. Nor do I lose my husband in a crowd. All tall men once looked the same to me. Now I don't have to make excuses—like the time I sent a handmade white sweater to a dear friend as a gift and she told a mutual acquaintance she couldn't understand why I had sent her this old sweater full of pale yellow spots.

OPTIONS

In patients who have both glaucoma and cataracts, some ophthalmologists favor correcting glaucoma through a filtering operation first and then, some months later, performing a cataract operation. Yvette's physician recommended this sequential method, and she has been pleased with the result. Other ophthalmologists prefer to do a combined operation, starting with cataract removal and concluding with a filtering procedure. They argue that once the eye is surgically opened up, it makes more sense to do both operations at the same time. Not long ago, this was considered too risky for the average glaucoma patient. It was believed that a combined procedure would be too traumatic for their fragile eyes. However, with refined techniques, and in the hands of a practiced surgeon, the combined operation is gaining wider acceptance and may soon be the preferred model when both operations are needed.

There is still a belief among some ophthalmologists that control of glaucoma is usually more effective with the two-stage process than with combination surgery because a well-functioning bleb may eliminate the need for medication in some patients. In a combined procedure, it may be harder to produce a good filtering bleb and the use of medication (usually the beta-blocker timolol) may still be necessary. In an early study of seventy-five eyes that were subjected to the combined operation, only 20 percent of patients had a filtering bleb at the end of twelve months. However, with the use of antimetabolites that prevent scarring, the situation may be corrected. Nevertheless, in the long run, the decision on what is best for you will probably depend upon your surgeon's evaluation of the condition of your eye. And as surgeons refine their techniques the promise of successful surgeries is sure to increase.

I cannot end this chapter without talking about the wonder of new sight following a cataract operation. The lushness of colors—a limpid blue sky, a magenta evening against which the sharp outlines of buildings stand in stark relief, the subtle contrasts of white and beige, the bloom in a child's cheeks—all become accessible once again. And with this restored vision comes a returning sense of joy and thankfulness for this extraordinary reprieve from a formerly dim and colorless environment.

CHAPTER 9

Complementary Therapies

It was a sign of health that he was willing to be cured.

—Seneca (249 A.D.)

Americans spend some $10 billion a year on alternative therapies. The National Institutes of Health (NIH) has opened an Office of Alternative Medicine. In Seattle, a publicly funded clinic was established to offer both conventional and alternative therapies to low-income patients. It seems that ancient and so-called new-age therapies are finally suiting up to take their place in the pantheon of healing practices. The NIH Office of Alternative Medicine has made grant awards for study in a variety of different fields, including diet and nutrition/lifestyle changes, mind-body control, herbal medicine, and manual healing. While none of the awards applies directly to research on eye health, the findings may stimulate further investigation into this area.

But no matter how basic research is channeled into investigating complementary therapies, the number of self-help therapies currently available, and the supply of alternative publications on the shelves of local bookstores and health food outlets, is soaring. The message is clear. The public—you and I—want to take charge of our health. According to eminent journalist Bill Moyers, who hosted a public television series called *Healing the Mind—The Art of Healing,* there are those among us who believe we are on the cusp of a revolution in medicine that will combine ancient wisdom with modern medicine.

Before I investigated complementary therapies, I looked in the mirror and contemplated the possibility that I might one day lose most of my sight. I no longer feel this way. Rita, too, who already had lost one eye to a particularly difficult form of glaucoma, began to investigate complementary therapies to help save her remaining eye. Although neither Rita nor I have given up conventional medical treatment, we have found that by incorporating complementary therapies into our lives, we have gained better control of our conditions, and are, by and large, healthier. For both of us, the outlook now appears to be more promising than what we had once believed. In other words, we have transformed ourselves from medically dependent to *respant*—a term Bernie Siegel, M.D., author of *Love, Medicine and Miracles* and other books on self-healing, coined by combining the words *patient* and *responsibility*. A respant, according to Dr. Siegel, is an individual who takes responsibility for his or her own treatment.

THE PRINCIPLE OF SELF-HEALING

Many of us take better care of our cars than we do of ourselves. We see to it that the spark plugs are cleaned, the motor tuned up, the brake fluid replenished when necessary, and so forth. In order to drive our cars, we know we must provide them with the proper fuel. Just as a car won't function without gas and care, your body will eventually feel the effects of neglect if you cease to pay attention to keeping it healthy. By exploring techniques of self-healing and complementary therapies, in combination with healthy nutrition and exercise, you can take charge of your own health.

The principle underlying self-healing is the connection between the mind and the body. Many practitioners feel that this connection is so powerful that the two cannot be separated. That is, what happens in the mind is reflected in the body—a basic concept taught in introductory college courses on anatomy and physiology. The theory of the mind-body connection is hardly a revolutionary idea. Buddhist philosophers have taught this principle for centuries.

Much of self-healing relies on the actions of the immune system. The immune system comprises a set of organs, substances, and processes that interact in ways so complex that researchers are constantly discovering new facets of its activity. From these discoveries have come tantalizing clues to ways to control and eradicate disease. As most of us learned in high school science class, our bodies are vessels containing thousands and thousands of different chemicals. Scientists are now identifying many of these chemicals, and finding that some of them are as powerful as any medicine prescribed by your doctor. For example, certain white blood cells called neutrophils contain a substance with natural antibiotic activity rivaling that of penicillin. These neutrophils attack bacteria by making their cell membranes so leaky that they die.

The complexity of the human body almost defies the imagination. It contains about 50 trillion cells—a universe within a single body. On each cell's wall are receptors, chemicals designed to capture materials the cell needs to maintain its stability and perform its designated functions. Not only that, but these receptors change their molecular shapes in response to instructions from the cell. Enclosed within each cell is a swirling mixture of water and other chemicals. In the center of the cell is the nucleus, which contains the spiral twists of DNA. Each cell in the body has its own specific function. Cells in the kidney maintain the balance of water and waste products, and regulate the levels of electrolytes (mineral salts) in the body. Cells in the ciliary body manufacture aqueous humor, the substance that nourishes your eyes. With the exception of the cells in the nervous system, all of the cells in the body, including those of the bones, are in a constant state of renewal and regrowth.

Evidence that our bodies are designed to heal—that nature has supplied us with all the materials necessary for this process—is apparent every day of our lives. Cuts scab over, bones knit, tissues regrow. Most of the ailments that afflict us are self-limiting. It is only when diseases overwhelm our defense mechanisms that serious breakdown occurs. And it is here that both traditional and complementary therapies are directed.

THE NATURE OF ILLNESS

Why do we get diseases? Is this our genetic destiny? Is it the environment we live in? The food we eat? Our lifestyle? The stress of modern living? The way we think? Or can it be a combination of some or all of the above? These questions are still being explored—by scientists, environmentalists, and holistic practitioners.

There is a theory that if it is necessary to maintain life, the body will sacrifice a non-vital organ. If your heart or lungs are diseased, you may die, but if the eyes, ears, uterus, breasts, colon, or a kidney breaks down, your body can still function with the loss or partial loss of these organs. Another theory holds that disease will strike at an organ that is genetically weakened. Still other theories point to lifestyle factors that are detrimental to health. Dr. Deepak Chopra, noted lecturer and author of over fifteen books on self-healing, has observed that people who have survived heart attacks often say they brought their illness on themselves through stress, neglect of hypertension, and bad diet.

When I review how I spent my youth and middle age, I find I cannot separate my lifestyle from my condition. Looking back, I now believe I actually invited glaucoma into my life. Louise L. Hay, an author, counselor, teacher, and lecturer, suggests that pressure from long-standing hurts may result in "stony unforgiveness," which she equates with glaucoma. In my own case, in retrospect, I could see why my awareness of the hurts I experienced, combined with my drive to be "superwoman" (though before this became a cliché) led me to say, when I developed retinal holes, that "my eyes popped." Beneath the good humor I displayed at the time, I realized I had seethed with resentment because I felt that none of the people around me seemed to care very much about the overload I was dealing with, both at work and at home. Yet only in retirement could I recognize this, and only then did I finally find the space that I had denied myself, to pursue self-healing and self-expression.

The common thread that binds self-healing therapies together is they enable you to become your own healer. Through your belief in the power of God, mysticism, vitamins, laughter, or anything else that you choose to try, healing your sick body becomes possible. And there is some scientific evidence that changes do take place in the body in response to self-healing practices. An August 7, 1996, article in *The New York Times* cited transcendental medication (TM) as being twice as effective overall in lowering blood pressure as progressive muscle relaxation, which in turn was more effective than simple instruction in healthy lifestyle habits. The National Institutes of Health has allocated $3 million for two further studies of the long-term effects of TM in reducing blood pressure, stress, and heart disease in African-Americans.

CONSIDERING ALTERNATIVE APPROACHES

Compared to the tools of modern medical technology, which at times defy comprehension, the modalities of self-healing are deceptively simple. What they do require is time, commitment, and belief in the process. The self-healing therapies we wish to share here are those we have personally found to be beneficial. We also will touch upon some of the techniques practiced by individuals we know of who have, through their own efforts, found ways to heal themselves or to better their vision.

Choosing an alternative therapy or lifestyle that meets your needs can be daunting, in light of the number of therapies available. You may find yourself grazing among such therapies as acupuncture, aromatherapy, Ayurveda, biofeedback, chiropractic, exercise, faith healing, homeopathy, meditation, naturopathy, macrobiotics, nutrition, psychic surgery, psychotherapy, self-massage (or other forms of massage therapy), and yoga, to name a few. The list of self-healing and ancient practices seems to go on forever, and many of them may sound exotic and unfamiliar.

You may prefer to design your own eclectic routine, drawing from those therapies that best meet your needs. In choosing your own therapies, always remember that common sense should be your guide. Rita realized this when talking to a chiropractor about her disappointment in standard medical treatment. He asked whether she would choose to go to a chiropractor or to a doctor to reset a broken bone. There and then Rita realized that complementary therapies and standard medical practices can function together. Learning about what foods are best for you, how correct breathing can enhance your health, and what exercise can do for you, together with tapping into your inner spiritual resources, can lead to developing self-healing routines that may benefit your condition.

We must emphasize that none of the therapies we have investigated is a *cure* for glaucoma. And the only evidence that exists as to whether intraocular pressure can be lowered by one alternative therapy or another is what the scientific community calls "anecdotal"—that is, it consists of individual people's stories, not laboratory or clinical experiments. Yet both Rita and I have experienced real results from our complementary therapies. I have been able to reduce the amount of medication I take, and Rita has lowered her IOP by an average of 5 points. But the biggest change is that we no longer feel that glaucoma is controlling us.

EASE OFF ON YOUR MIND—MEDITATE

"I think, therefore I am," said René Descartes in the seventeenth century. His writings on mathematics, philosophy, and psychology set the stage for a rational and scientific approach to understanding the phenomena of life. In Western societies, the rigor of scientific discipline has dominated medical practice ever since. Not until the

1960s was there a re-emergence of the notion of connectedness between body and mind, and with that, the idea that age-old remedies might indeed be beneficial.

One of the methods used in alternative healing that has steadily gained in both popularity and acceptance among medical practitioners is meditation. Meditation is now part of programs for stress reduction at mainstream medical establishments, notably at the University of Massachusetts Medical Center in Worcester, Massachusetts; the Deaconess Hospital in Boston; and New York University Medical Center's Cardiac Wellness Unit and New York Cornell Medical Center, to name a few. Many patients who go to these clinics report relief from symptoms, and many are able to decrease the amount of medicine they take.

How does meditation affect eye pressure? We have different stories to tell. Rita practices a form of Buddhist meditation. She includes a combination of meditation and diet in her daily routine, and it has brought about a lowering of her IOP. Through her spiritual practice she has also learned about herself—how she thinks, relates, and acts on problems. By constantly working to become responsible for her actions, she has gained more control of her life.

I too use meditation. Since I have begun meditating, I have become aware of a change in myself. My drive to meet the demands and obligations of the day is not diminished, but it is now tempered by an awareness of my own needs. In the act of allowing myself a portion of the day to meditate and exercise, I release my tensions and am better able to cope with whatever the day may throw my way.

Meditation can take a number of different forms, but all are routes to the same place. Since meditation was introduced into Western cultures, various schools and forms of meditation have sprung up. You can learn to meditate by taking a course or workshop, by working directly with a teacher, by following instructions in a book, or by trying to find the way by yourself.

There are two basic types of meditation: active, or physical, and inactive, or nonphysical. The quiet stillness and central focusing of inactive meditation clears the mind of extraneous thoughts, allowing the deeper regions of the mind to emerge. The active form (yoga, chanting, and Tai Chi are types of active meditation) achieve the same purpose. With both forms, practitioners state that they feel good and are refreshed afterward. Some practitioners say they reach a state of bliss. Others claim they feel relaxed. Still others use meditation to clear away negative thoughts.

For both Rita and me, an initiation ceremony followed by several months of practice sessions led into dedicated meditation. Nonmeditators may wonder how sitting quietly for twenty to thirty minutes twice a day can produce any kind of beneficial effect, but we can tell you that deep relaxation serves a very important function. Meditation lies at the heart and soul of any of the self-help therapies, and there is research in peer-reviewed medical journals crediting meditation with better health and longer lives in individuals who practice it regularly.

PRACTICE RELAXATION

Few of us can get through the day without feeling twinges of anxiety, stress, or tension. Inner and outer influences have a way of stirring up the adrenaline (the "fight-or-flight" response), whether we're in a fast-paced job, managing a home, conducting a business, retired, or anything else. Meditation is one way to remove yourself from the tensions and to recenter, or regenerate your energy. Relaxation is another. Meditation and relaxation are not the same thing. In meditation, you work for a more focused and more centered you by emptying your mind of conscious thought. With deep relaxation, you use your mind to direct responses in your body. Whereas active meditation can be characterized as a state of active body/passive mind, and inactive meditation as passive body/passive mind, deep relaxation would be described as passive body/active mind.

Initially, deep relaxation can be achieved by using an instructor or an appropriate audiotape. Many tapes are now available at bookstores and specialty outlets such as East-West stores. For the purposes of eye care, you may want to make your own tape incorporating the instructions we have found beneficial outlined below. Once you learn this technique, practice it whenever you feel the need for soothing and relaxation. Doing this while going home after an exhausting day teaching emotionally disturbed children, I found I could turn a boring subway ride into a relaxing therapeutic period.

This exercise should take from fifteen to twenty minutes. Turn on your answering machine or turn off the ringer on your telephone. Wear comfortable clothes. Lie or sit in an easy position and keep your eyes closed throughout the experience. Perform the following thirteen steps:

1. Become aware of your breathing. Draw air in through your nose from your diaphragm. Feel the air enter your body. Now feel it leave your body by exhaling it from your mouth. Take six slow, deep breaths. Inhale. Exhale. Feel the passage of air into and out of your body. Keep this pace of breathing throughout all thirteen steps.

2. Feel your toes. Curl them. Then consciously relax them. Focus your attention on your calves. Tense them. Relax them. Sense your thighs. Tighten and relax your thigh muscles. Now tighten and then relax each whole leg at a time. Repeat the sequence until your legs feel warm and relaxed.

3. Allow the relaxation to move up your body and into your pelvic region. Allow your muscles to tighten and completely relax. Feel the warmth of the relaxation spreading throughout your body.

4. Allow the relaxation to move into your digestive region. Feel your stomach relax, then feel your intestines, your liver, and your gallbladder relax. Your whole lower body now should feel warm and relaxed. Be aware of feeling safe and secure.

5. Let this feeling move into your chest. Feel your diaphragm relax with each deep exhalation. Be aware of your lungs expanding and contracting. Allow a feeling of complete freedom to come into your lungs.

6. Focus on your heart. Let the awareness of the strength of your heart come to you. Let feelings of joy, beauty, and happiness emerge. Stay with your heart for a moment.

7. Breathe through your mouth and make any sounds you wish. You may want to yawn or sigh. Enjoy the feeling of contentment as relaxation moves into your throat.

8. Relax your jaw, your lips, your tongue. Be aware of the increased flow of energy coursing through your body—energy that is now freed up.

9. Let the energy move—let this warm, free feeling of expansion accompany the energy into your eyes. Focus on your eyes. Keep your body relaxed and feeling safe and warm. Breathe in and out with your eyes. Feel that you are incorporating only the most positive energy from outside of yourself into your body. Gently

draw this energy in. Keep your eyes soft and relaxed. Make no demands on them. Don't try to force anything to happen.

10. Now feel your aqueous humor being secreted from your ciliary body. Give yourself permission to feel this vital process. Make friends with your aqueous humor. Know it is the nourishing fluid that feeds your eyes and controls the moisture inside your eyes. Let yourself feel any pressure, but do not be alarmed. Trust that your eyes know the process of healing.

11. Feel the aqueous humor seeping through the porous tissues of your trabecular meshwork and into the outflow channels. Feel the pressure in your eyes subsiding.

12. Now move your awareness to the back of your eyes. Focus on your optic nerve. Be aware of axons carrying messages to the optic nerve. Trust that your optic nerve is stable. Trust that blood is flowing into the region to nourish it.

13. Experience total relaxation throughout every part of your body. If tears come, let them. If angry feelings want to emerge, don't stop them. Let your body do the work of healing.

Be aware: If you faithfully perform relaxation exercises, you may develop symptoms of inner peace! Some of these include enjoyment of each moment, less worrying, feelings of connectedness with others and nature, a tendency to smile, the ability to let things happen, and a deepening and extending of feelings of love.

CONSCIOUSLY RECLAIM YOUR VISION

The word *disease* consists of the prefix *dis*, meaning "not," and the word *ease*, meaning "comfortable." In essence, then, when you have a disease, the affected part of the body is not comfortable.

> No matter how badly off you are, or how disabled you may be, there is a strong power within you that can always heal you—or at the least make your situation better. No matter how you feel, your higher self is always there to be your best friend. Knowing this, you need not feel isolated, fearful, or helpless. Our power of healing exists in every muscle of our bodies, in every brain cell, nerve fiber, every blood vessel. We are born with the power of healing within ourselves, and we need only to redis-

> cover it. Finding this power is like opening a closet and finding what you have been looking for everywhere. It was there all the time, but you didn't see it.

These are the words of Meir Schneider, who was born with glaucoma, astigmatism, nystagmus, and cataracts—in other words, blind. He now sees 20/70, a recovery brought about by his own intensive efforts to restore his sight. He drives a car, enjoys watching the ocean spray the beach, reads, and lives a sighted life. His faith in his body's ability to heal itself is no different from that of Norman Cousins, who cured himself of the crippling disease of ankylosing spondylitis through a combination of laughter and intravenous vitamin C, or Nancy Maris, a writer who daily challenges the debilitating effects of multiple sclerosis, or countless others who have defied the "odds" assigned to them by the medical community. No part of the body is immune to self-healing. For those of us who have steadfastly refused to accept the medical diagnosis for our condition, but decided instead to consciously reclaim our sight, this belief has become a reality.

The Myopia Connection

Myopia, one of the risk factors associated with glaucoma, usually strikes in childhood, often at eight or nine years of age. This is about the time when children are beginning to use their eyes for close work for extended periods on a daily basis. They are in the classroom for six or more hours a day, five days a week. Homework, television, and computers and video games add to the eyes' burden. According to some theorists, this stress on the eyes—together with a genetic predisposition to myopia—is behind the increasing incidence of myopia in developed countries, where reading is a priority.

From the early nineteenth century on, there has been a lively interest in how near-point accommodation and convergence (focusing the eyes on a near object), maintained repeatedly for more than two hours at a time, leads to a change in the shape of the eyeball. Researchers have observed that close reading over a period of time causes a rise in IOP, and the eyeball lengthens to compensate for this rise. In people with myopia, the eyeballs gradually become more elongated, causing the light entering the eye to fall short of the retina and resulting in blurred vision.

Some studies correlate high scholastic achievement with myopia. Other research has found correspondences between faulty near-point convergence (the inability to focus properly) and elevated intraocular pressure. If placing unnatural demands on the ciliary muscles, which are responsible for regulating near- and-far point vision, can provoke myopia, then perhaps it may be possible to reverse this process.

The Optometric Extension Program Foundation, the College of Optometrists and Vision Development, and a small organization called the Optometric Training Institute specialize in training people to focus their eyes properly and to learn to use better whatever vision they have. They use a variety of methods, including biofeedback, to help glaucoma patients. One practitioner, Dr. Joseph Trachtman, an investigative researcher, optometrist, and author, has found vision training to be helpful in lowering the IOP of some glaucoma patients.

One of the earliest pioneers who sought a cure for myopia was Dr. W.H. Bates, who published a book entitled *Perfect Sight Without Glasses* in 1920. This seminal work still influences practitioners today. I first learned about Dr. Bates' method in my early twenties, when I met an optometrist named Charles Rothman. Crippled by polio at an early age, Rothman overheard a physician tell his mother that he would never walk and would be better off institutionalized. He went on to defy this prognosis, teaching himself not only to walk but to ride a bicycle. He also sailed through his studies and applied for and entered optometry school—notwithstanding the howls of protest of advisors, friends, and family members who claimed he was too frail to withstand the rigors of the profession. Using his success as an example, he set about working with patients, helping them improve their eyesight through exercises based on Dr. Bates' treatment plan.

I have to say that although I worked diligently with Rothman, I never got the desired effect of the Bates method. Others have, however. The writer Aldous Huxley, facing the risk of losing his sight when afflicted with chronic retinitis at the age of seventeen, adapted the Bates method to his own needs and maintained some sight throughout his life. More recently, Dr. Deborah Banker, an ophthalmologist who has developed a kit on self-help vision care, and John Selby, author of *The Visual Handbook: A Guide to Seeing More Clearly* (Element Books, 1987) have also adapted Bates' method, as well as developing some of their own techniques for curing myopia. And in Japan, Mashiro Oki, author of *Practical Yoga: A Pictorial Approach* (Japan Publications, 1970) has taught a method he conceived to correct his myopia. Dr. Banker, Oki, and Selby claim that their eyeballs have returned from the elongated shape characteristic of myopia to a normal, round shape.

Dr. Banker stresses that the exercises for the eyes need to be maintained, or the eye will slip back into its old form. What knits these inspiring stories together is these individuals' commitment to a change of lifestyle that includes a belief in the possibility of self-healing.

Stimulate Your Perception

Stimulating perception is one of the most effective methods of improving eyesight. It makes sense. Although your eyes respond to light and images, and send these signals to your brain, it is your brain that ultimately decides what you see of the world around you. It is the information stored in your brain—the features and/or images familiar to the memories encoded in your brain—that is reactivated by what you see.

Using magnetic resonance imaging (MRI) and advanced computer programs to map specific areas of the brain, scientists have been able to observe both what happens to the signals the optic nerve sends to the visual cortex and how the cortex interprets them. It turns out that the more information you possess about the visual world, the more adept your brain is at interpreting what the eyes see from even a minimum of clues. For instance, you can recognize a person you know well from nothing more than the sight of a familiar tilt of the head, a slope of a shoulder, the curve of a chin, a hairdo, or a bald spot.

The basis for recognizing other persons and objects begins in infancy, when a baby learns to know its mother as separate from self. Forever after, the things a person knows and learns influence how he or she experiences different objects. Recently my husband and I traveled to India. At the Taj Mahal, we marveled at the lacy script rendered in black marble embedded in the white marble that framed the portals of the building. To our eyes, the script was a beautiful element of the building's design. To Muslims, however, it was a meaningful message from the Koran. What we know determines how we see an object. Seeing becomes perception only through knowledge of the object.

Unfortunately, if you have glaucoma, the drops, the cataracts, and the decreased vision often corrode your desire to examine objects carefully. You may find you have little interest in examining the features of a person's face, looking in store windows, or studying architectural details, for example. Yet developing your perceptual powers can actually help you to overcome the debilitating effects of glaucoma and its treatments. Perception-sharpening exercises like those outlined below can help. These exercises are adapted from the work of W.H. Bates, Meir Schneider, John Selby, and Deborah Banker.

Before undertaking any of these exercises, take a few minutes to practice breathing. Breathe in from your diaphragm or stomach, through your nose; breathe out through your mouth. Keep your breathing slow and steady. Then begin the exercises. For the following perceptual exercises, pretend that you are an artist or a writer and that you must render or describe details.

1. Look at a building. Observe the brickwork, the inset of the windows, the door frame, the roof. If you can read the building address, look at each number individually. Keep your eyes traveling over the surface of the building. Do not stare at one spot.

2. Take a partner. Look at your partner's face—the eyebrows, eyelashes, nose, cheeks, mouth. Pretend you are going to draw the face and you want to represent each feature.

3. Look at a tree. Now look at the bark, a twig, a leaf, the veins in the leaf, and so on.

4. Blink a lot. Blinking is nature's way of lubricating your eyes.

5. Slowly open and close your eyes, one at a time. Move your head back and forth with your eyes closed, then, for a fraction of a second, open each eye slowly. By opening each eye very slowly, you can eventually blink with only one eye at a time.

6. Draw a large **E** in black magic marker on a sheet of paper. Look first at the lower bar, then at the upper bar, the vertical bar, and the center bar. Picture the E in your mind. Then step five feet away from the E. Blink slowly a few times. Look at the E again, then blink slowly again a few more times. Never stare. If you can see the E, move back a few feet. Repeat this sequence until you can no longer see the E.

7. Stimulate the cells responsible for peripheral vision. Extend your arms out to each side. Wiggle your fingers. Can you see the motion? If not, bring your arms closer to your body until you just glimpse your wiggling fingers.

8. Close your eyes. Visualize a large circle. Pretend there is a pencil affixed to your nose. Trace around the circle. Squeeze it into an

oval. Trace around the oval. Make it into a figure-eight. Trace around the figure-eight. Write your name, tracing each letter.

9. Tape a piece of paper over the bridge of your nose. Hold your index fingers in front of you and move them first clockwise, then counterclockwise, then have one finger go clockwise and the other counterclockwise. Follow the motions with your eyes.

10. When reading, sit where you can see a wall calendar or some other item with large type. If you can find a Snellen chart, hang it on the wall. Raise your eyes occasionally to look at it. If you read in daylight, look out the window after every five or six pages. Focus on a distant object when you do so.

11. Pause occasionally in your reading and remember the last word you read. Visualize the whiteness around the word. Think of the blackness of the letters. Look at the word again. Remember to avoid staring. Move your eyes around the object. When you think of it, shift your eyes. You see best when your eyes make saccadic movements, that is, tiny automatic movements that your eyes make to fixate on objects. Your eyes will experience the least fatigue when viewing an object consisting of words or letters with quick glances.

In addition to perceptual exercises, there are a number of tension-relieving exercises that may be helpful:

1. Massage your jaw. Yawn. Allow yourself to make noises. This releases facial tension.

2. Feel the sternocleidomastoid muscle—the muscle that runs from behind your ear, down the side of your neck, and into your shoulders. Place four fingers on each side of the muscle and massage the muscle, checking along the whole area for tension and sore spots. Massage twenty times.

3. Do shoulder rotations, ten times with each shoulder.

4. Move your head loosely around in a circle, first clockwise, then counterclockwise, ten times each.

These exercises should help to relieve tensed-up muscles and promote healthy circulation. Many of us become tensed up when we concentrate on an activity. Tension in the body restricts blood flow, and restricted blood flow to the optic nerve is implicated in glaucoma.

TRY ACUPRESSURE OR SHIATSU

In China, grade-school children are taught to massage around their eyes, because it is believed that this simple exercise—based on the ancient tradition of acupuncture—will alleviate eyestrain and thwart myopia. Acupuncture, the practice of therapeutically inserting small, sharp needles into specific points of the body, has gained respectful attention in the Western medical community. This practice is best known for its effects on the nervous system. Acupuncture appears to release body chemicals known as endorphins and enkephalins, which are the body's natural painkillers.

Acupuncture is based on the ancient Chinese philosophic principle of yin and yang. In this philosophy, the earth is represented by the female principle, the yin. The heavens are represented by the male principle, the yang. When the natural universe is in harmony, yin and yang are in balance. The body too contains yin and yang, and when these forces are out of balance, sickness and disease occur. To correct the imbalance, points along twelve meridians, or lines, that run along the body are stimulated, enabling *chi* (vital energy, or the life force) to flow more freely. Various points along the meridians correspond to different organs and parts of the body.

Can acupuncture cure glaucoma? Neither acupuncturists in China nor those in this country make such claims, but they do say that treatment can help relieve some of the symptoms. Many of us would prefer not to explore an "iffy" situation or a situation that we are unfamiliar with. What we can do, however—and what both Rita and I have found to be effective in our own lives—is to practice shiatsu, a type of massage or body work. Shiatsu acts on the same points along the meridians prescribed in acupuncture for the health of the eyes. When these points are massaged, energy flows more freely, balancing the body's various systems. The exercises below take no more than ten to fifteen minutes, depending upon the length of your massage:

1. With your thumbs on your temples and your index fingers bent against your brow, massage the exact center of your eyebrows fifty times. Now move your thumbs about an inch to the right. Massage fifty times. Return to center and move your thumbs an inch to the left. Massage fifty times.

2. Massage your lower eye socket, just beneath the pupil, fifty times.
3. Place your index fingers in the upper inner corners of your eyes. You will feel a tender spot. Massage that area gently in a rotary motion fifty times.
4. Place your index fingers on the outer corners of your eyes. Massage that area in a rotary motion fifty times.
5. Place your fingers on the area just below the tear duct. Massage that area in a rotary motion fifty times.
6. Press your thumbs into the hollows of your temples. Massage these areas fifty times.
7. Feel the hollows just above the center of your eyebrows. Massage fifty times.
8. Press your thumbs on your upper forehead, near the hairline. Massage fifty times.
9. Place your index finger and middle finger directly below your nose. Remove your middle finger. With your index finger, press and push upwards towards your eyes. Repeat this exercise fifty times.
10. Place your index fingers just below your earlobes. Feel the hollow. Massage upwards fifty times.
11. Place your thumbs just beneath the bony structure at the back of your head, where your neck meets your head. You will feel hollows and possibly tenderness. Massage fifty times.
12. Do a circular massage starting with your eye sockets and increasing the range of your massage until you take in your whole face.
13. With your thumbs, find the hollows in the back of your head, just below the top of your scalp. They should feel like the soft spots on a baby's head. Massage fifty times. Then massage the back of your scalp fifty times.

When doing the massage, use pressure that is firm but not uncomfortable. Apply pressure for ten seconds or so, then release for a few seconds before applying pressure again. While the pressure should be firm enough to stimulate the point in question, it should not be acutely painful. If it is, either decrease the pressure or discontinue the massage.

GIVE YOUR EYES A BREAK—PALM

Perhaps the single most important thing you can do for your eyes is to palm. Dr. W.H. Bates introduced palming as a method to give the eyes complete rest. While you may believe your eyes are at rest during sleep, we now know that during REM sleep, the period of sleep during which we dream, our eyes are actively engaged in following dream sequences.

To palm, close your eyes, then cup your hands slightly and place them over your eyes, with your fingers crossed on your forehead. Think black. Palm for at least twenty minutes. Do not press on your eyelids. Some people combine palming and meditation. After palming for ten to fifteen minutes, you will feel your eyes resting and losing tension. When you withdraw your hands, your eyes will feel refreshed.

EXERCISE!

Those who say they have improved or overcome their myopia and/or glaucoma often speak of the trinity of spirituality, exercise, and diet. Many persons with glaucoma say that exercise does help. And there is good evidence in the literature that vigorous exercise, such as bicycling or running, can lower eye pressure. For example, subjects in one study experienced an average reduction in IOP of 4.6 mm Hg after three months of aerobic exercise training. When the exercise program was discontinued, original IOP levels returned. Brisk walks, yoga, stretching, and even weight-lifting are all beneficial for general health, bone strength, and improved circulation, and are an important consideration for managing glaucoma. Rita dances to fast music an hour a day. I walk one to six miles a day, and lift weights and garden in the summer. One member of our glaucoma support group has found a lowering of eye pressure in the practice of yoga.

To get the greatest benefit from exercise, establish a daily routine. Whatever series of exercises you fashion for yourself, keep in mind that exercise should be pleasurable—fun to do. Anxiety about performing a particular exercise only feeds negative impulses in your body, and this is something that should be avoided. If you have pigmentary-dispersion or exfoliative glaucoma, be aware that high-impact exercise may cause a release of pigment. Consult with your health care provider before beginning any exercise program.

INVESTIGATE HERBAL APPROACHES

The use of medicinal herbs is one of the fastest growing areas of alternative therapy today. Actually, herbal medicine has a close historical relationship to conventional medicine. Although many of our medicines are synthesized in laboratories, plants grown for medicinal purposes and gathered from the far reaches of the globe, especially in tropical rain forests, still form the foundation of our pharmacy. Treatments that cover a wide range of diseases, including glaucoma, were first observed by anthropologists, explorers, and other people working with indigenous populations. From early times, shamans, purportedly the oldest professionals in the evolution of the human healing practices, used a wide variety of plants, some of which are still effective today in the management of glaucoma.

Plants of the order *Solanaceae,* including nightshade, henbane, jimsonweed, and mandrake, are all poisonous in their natural state. Yet they contain atropine, an antagonist to acetylcholine. Used in the eye, the drug belladonna, which is derived from nightshade, blocks the action of the pupillary sphincter and causes the eye to dilate. In the nineteenth century, scientists reasoned that if there was a substance that could cause the pupil to dilate, there must certainly be a substance that would create the opposite result—constriction of the pupil. In 1863 a substance named *physostigmine,* purified from the fruit of the calabar bean, was found to cause sedation of the spinal cord—and, in overdose, paralysis. Further refined to reserpine, it was found to indeed constrict the pupil, but at the expense of vision; it caused shortsightedness. Enter pilocarpine, a derivative of the plant jaborandi, brought out of Brazil and found in 1876 by researchers to have therapeutic effects on a number of diseases. One of its actions is to lower pressure in glaucomatous eyes.

There are other plants that have been shown to reduce eye pressure as well. For example, smoking the leaves of *Cannibas sativa* (better known as marijuana) is known to decrease IOP. In a scientific study conducted in 1980, the eighteen participants showed a decrease in their IOPs within sixty to ninety minutes. However, they also experienced the other well-known effect of marijuana—they became loopy. In 1981, in a small study of eight people, researchers found a reduction of IOP could be achieved by isolating one of a group of substances known as cannabinoids from the marijuana plant and instilling it in 0.1-percent or 0.05-percent solution. At the 0.05-percent level, an average reduction in IOP of 5 mm Hg lasted for eight to nine hours; at the 0.1-percent level, the reduction lasted as long as ten hours. And indeed, there is an eye drop called Cannibol that is produced in Jamaica, West Indies, and has been used for roughly twenty years for the treatment of glaucoma. The manufacturers of the medication claim that it reduces IOP about 5 percent in the first fifteen minutes. However, this drug is not available in the United States.

With the exception of eyebright, which is available in health food stores and which some members of our support group use, most herbal treatments for glaucoma come from countries other than the United States. Compresses made from eyebright (*Euphrasia officinalis*) are said to relieve redness, swelling, visual disturbances, acute and subacute inflammations, conjunctivitis, and blepharitis. Some other remedies include:

- Pasque flower (*Anemone pulsatilla*). In Europe, the whole herb or an abstract of it is taken internally for eye conditions such as iritis, retinal problems, cataracts, and glaucoma.
- Silver ragwort (*Cineria maritima* or *senecto cinceraria*), which grows wild in Mediterranean regions and is a member of the daisy family, is a popular potted plant. Its juice is said to be useful for conjunctivitis.
- Barberry (*Berberis vulgaris*) contains an alkaloid, berberine, that has been found useful as a stimulant for hypersensitive eyes, inflamed lids, and chronic allergic conjunctivitis.
- Bilberry (*Vaccinium myrtillus*), a member of the *Ericaceae* family, has been used as an eye remedy in Europe and South America for hundreds of years. The active constituents of the bilberry fruit, which is similar to our blueberry, are anthocyanidins, a type of flavonoid, and are antioxidants. Essentially, these substances help to strengthen the tiny capillaries that deliver nutrients to the muscles and nerves of the eye by decreasing their permeability, thereby limiting damage to these vessels. It also accelerates the regeneration of retinal purple (rhodopsin), a pigment the rod cells in the eye need to adapt to dim light, thus heightening your perception in twilight or at nighttime. In addition, this powerful shrub acts as a free radical

destroyer. Bilberry is available in health food stores. If you decide to use bilberry, look for a product that specifies a content of 25 percent anthocyanosides. Dosages may be in the 40- to 60-milligram range. If you plan to take more than 120 milligrams a day, consult a health care practitioner.

- Ginko (*Ginkgo biloba*), an herb derived from the ginkgo tree, is an antioxidant and is useful in repairing free radical damage. Furthermore, the flavonoids it contains become concentrated in the lens of the eye. Ginkgo relaxes the blood vessels, especially the small arteries, and has been found to be helpful in increasing the blood supply to the brain and extremities. Taking ginkgo extract has been found to yield improvements in memory, intellectual function, depression, dizziness, and headache. Although its effect on glaucoma has not been evaluated, it does help other problems linked to impaired circulation, and impaired circulation has been cited as one of the reasons for damage to the optic nerve. If you decide to take ginkgo, look for a product that specifies a 24-percent flavonoid content. Dosages may be in the 40- to 60-milligram range. If you plan to take more than 120 milligrams a day, consult a health practitioner.

At the very least, these herbal preparations are soothing for inflammatory conditions. Bilberry and ginkgo biloba may have a more direct effect on the health of your eyes. Filtered sea water, available in health food stores, has also been reported to be effective in lowering IOP. Make sure, however, that the water is sterile and free from toxic metals.

In China, many diseases are treated with a combination of traditional and Western medicine. The Chinese have been using herbal products for over 5,000 years, and have identified a number of them that are helpful for maintaining the health of the eyes. Clinical studies have found positive results from *Radix salviae multiorrhize* (RSM, the root of a species of salvia); *Fructus ligustri licidi* (FLL); *Thizoma ligustici Chuanxiong*; and *Radix astragli sue hedysari* (RASH, the root of a species of astragalus known as milk vetch). All of these appear to stimulate microcirculation, which may improve the supply of blood to the optic nerve and retina. Improvements in visual acuity and in visual field exams have also been reported. If you wish to pursue Chinese herbal medicine, we suggest you consult a qualified herbalist.

The ancient Indian practice of Ayurveda also includes the use of medicinal herbs. In this practice, specific herbs are used for specific physical ailments. The preparations generally used for eye problems include ashwangandha, guggul, and forskolin. Ashwangandha, from the nightshade family, contains compounds that stimulate the immune system. It is a more generalized treatment, and is used for sexual debility, nerve exhaustion, old-age problems, memory loss, muscular weakness, insomnia, weak eyes, skin diseases, cough, malaise, and problems with the glands. Resin from the guggul plant apparently has a positive effect on cholesterol, and may be beneficial for arteriosclerosis. Forskolin, which is derived from a species of coleus, strengthens the heartbeat, lowers blood pressure, inhibits blood clotting, stimulates hormone production, and stimulates the regeneration of nerves after injury. It has also been found to be effective in reducing IOP. Nature's Way, one of the larger U.S. herbal suppliers, has a product called Forskohlii that contains forskolin.

While your doctor will attend to the medical and surgical aspects of helping you to retain your sight, there is much you can do that will improve the outcome of your glaucoma therapy. By making time for meditation, massage, exercise, and the other suggestions we have proposed in this chapter, you will begin to feel that you too have some control over what happens to your eyes. No one knows all of the answers as to why our eyes behave as they do, but by drawing on some of the ancient and more modern healing practices, we may find some of these answers for ourselves.

CHAPTER 10

Eating for Healthy Eyes

People who shut their eyes to reality simply invite their own destruction, and anyone who insists on remaining in a state of innocence long after that innocence is dead turns himself into a monster.

—James Baldwin (1955)

"Do you eat like your mother?" Miriam's doctor asked, when Miriam worried that she too might develop glaucoma. Now, twenty-five years later, Miriam is free of glaucoma, although she falls into two high-risk categories—she has both a family history of the disease and exfoliation syndrome. She believes that her nutritional lifestyle—vegetarianism—is responsible for her continuing eye health.

Diet is commonly associated with cancer, heart disease, and other degenerative diseases. There is good reason to believe that nutrition plays a major role in maintaining the health of the eyes as well.

WHAT IS A GOOD DIET?

Choosing what you put into your body, deciding upon a particular lifestyle, selecting an article of clothing, or making any of the numerous other decisions that affect your life boils down, in the final analysis, to your commitment, interest, and pleasure. However good it may be for you, a diet that gives you no pleasure may cleanse your arteries but depress you. I reached my present level of near-vegetarianism in small increments over some six or seven years. I began by eliminating wheat, milk, and eggs following a comprehensive test for allergens. My headaches diminished, my skin cleared, and the morning eyelid puffiness that had plagued me disappeared. More recently, since I have taken to eating more raw vegetables, whole grains, and very limited amounts of fish and chicken, my energy level outlasts that of my contemporaries—and that of many persons twenty to thirty years my junior.

Rita had been studying nutrition since the age of eighteen and, although she knew a great deal about it, she still had problems with body swelling, a chronic yeast infection, bad skin, and poor reading concentration. In 1988, she consulted a nutritionist for a diet that might affect her glaucoma. Gradually, her nutritionist encouraged her to eat natural foods and eliminate additives. The first time she cheated on her diet with a can of diet soda, she experienced pains in both of her forearms. She queried her nutritionist, who told her that the discomfort would disappear within two days, and indeed it did. Now adhering strictly to the diet, Rita has seen an improvement in her IOP. Within three months, her pressure went down by 5 points. A year later, her diet interrupted by a vacation, she found her pressure had risen 5 points. Rita immediately resumed her diet and on her subsequent checkup, just three weeks later, her pressure had again dropped the 5 points. People often compliment her on her complexion. Her chronic yeast infection is under control. The swelling in her hands, face, and feet is gone.

WILL A DIET REALLY AFFECT MY EYES?

There is a theory that says our diseases migrate to the weakest areas in our bodies. In modern developed countries, unfortunately, the eyes are vulnerable to disease. We are exposed to environmental factors such as pollution, ultraviolet rays, and toxins in the foods we eat. It is much more difficult today to eat a proper diet than ever before. In the last several decades, the proliferation of fast foods, junk foods, foods containing dyes and additives, processed foods, and pesticide-contaminated foods has grown exponentially. Now, to avoid the hazards, we must read labels before we buy. We need to look for the amount of fat different foods contain, the various forms of sugar, and other elements that are combined with the foods found on the supermarket shelf.

A good diet does appear to have beneficial results on the health of our eyes. As with Miriam, who despite her risk factors has not developed glaucoma. I believe that my glaucoma has stabilized since I changed my diet. Dr. Ben C. Lane, an optometrist and nutritionist, and director of the Nutritional Optometry Institute, tells the story of his mother, who had begun to develop cataracts. The cataracts disappeared when Dr. Lane reconstructed the entire family's diet. In their book *Vision—A Holistic Guide to Healing the Eyesight* (Japan Publications, 1985), Joanne Roitee and Kojo Yamamoto write about Masahiro Uki, who improved his vision (he was myopic) through diet and other forms of holistic therapy.

For those of us who want a magic bullet, the pace of health changes based on diet can be maddeningly slow. Do not despair. It took a long time for a diet that failed to provide you with the proper nutrients and that contained substances toxic to your system to rob your body of its vital energy. Repairing the body is an ongoing process, and results are achieved in extremely small increments. But you will probably find, as I did, that by eliminating foods that you are sensitive to, decreasing the amount of processed foods you eat, avoiding white flour and sugar, and eating the freshest vegetables you can find—and, in essence, following the newest guidelines recommended by the U.S. Department of Agriculture—you will provide your body with the nourishment necessary to rebuild and maintain its cells and tissues.

Good health is your responsibility. Your physician can patch you up when something goes wrong. But that's really what it is—patching. Operations and medicines all have side effects. Certainly, medical intervention has its place and is often beneficial. My cataract operation, for instance, added to my quality of life. But I would no doubt have been much happier if I had never needed a cataract operation, or if I had never developed glaucoma in the first place.

When a part of the body breaks down, it is a signal to you that your body has reached its limit of tolerance to your particular way of living and eating, and that the time is right for change.

FREE RADICALS

The idea that nutrition is important for the eyes is supported by the growing evidence of the danger of free radicals. What are free radicals? They are molecules or fragments of molecules that are highly reactive—that is, they readily enter into chemical reactions with other substances—because they have unpaired electrons spinning in their orbit. These electrons seek out other electrons to counterbalance them, and they may snatch an electron from an adjacent molecule or donate an unmatched electron from their own structures, in the process destabilizing the hapless compound that is their target. Many molecules and fragments of molecules may behave in this fashion, but the most dangerous are different forms of oxygen. When an oxygen molecule encounters another substance and snaps up or sheds one of its electrons, the resulting compound is said to be *oxidized.* You see oxidation all about you. When metal rusts, when cut apples turn brown, when paint deteriorates or varnish or finish degenerates, you are witnessing oxidation.

There is a positive side to free radicals. The reaction that allows the blood to carry oxygen to all of the body's cells involves free radicals. Because of free radicals, food is transformed—the formation of crust on toast and the lovely sear on a barbecued steak are two examples. Free radicals are responsible for the immune system's ability to squelch pathogens; for the digestive system's ability to break down the food we eat; and for the nervous system's ability to fire up muscles, thoughts, and feelings. However, if there are more free radicals than the body can control, they may begin to attack the cells and cause serious damage.

The free radical theory is not new. In the 1960s, Dr. Denham Harmon associated free radicals with degenerative diseases. The medical establishment turned a blind eye to his findings, however—until, in the flowering of biomolecular research, respected laboratories confirmed his early findings and assumptions. There is now evidence that free radicals are generated in the course of various metabolic actions, such as the conversion of glucose (simple sugar) into cellular energy. The majority of the free radicals formed in this way are well contained and either reused or eliminated, but some of them escape, and researchers believe that these escaped free radicals may cause cellular damage.

Natural and man-made free radicals constantly bombard us. Radiation from the sun, electronic equipment, and other sources contribute to free radicals. So do peroxidized fats—cooking oils, both saturated and unsaturated, especially if they are heated or if there is even a hint of rancidity. Ozone, alcohol, tobacco smoke, and chlorine and aluminum from tap water and cooking pots are everyday sources of free radicals. Our own metabolic processes add to free-radical activity, as does an inadequate supply of oxygen, which can occur if we habitually breathe too shallowly.

Free radicals are also generated when iron, copper, and/or other naturally occurring metals react with oxygen. Normally, your body protects you from excesses of these elements, especially iron, by storing this element within the hemoglobin in red blood cells or by supplying a protein to ferry it from one place to another. But if something goes wrong with this system, or if there is simply too much of certain metals for the body to deal with, a chain reaction is set up that contributes to the production of free radicals that oxidize fats. Oxidized fats are the type most likely to accumulate in the blood vessels, causing arterial damage.

It is possible that many diseases are a result of free radical damage. Type II (adult-onset) diabetes and Parkinson's disease fall into this category. Certain cancers may be caused by reactions between free radicals and DNA that pave the way for uncontrolled replication of cells. Free radicals may also be behind joint pains by diminishing the quantity of lubricant in the joints or interfering with the elasticity of the tendons.

A free radical is an accident looking for a place to happen, and the eyes are not exempt. Cataracts, which are a bane for many of us, may be partially caused by free radical activity in the lens of the eye. Glaucoma researchers have begun to examine the relationship between free radical activity and the destruction of nerve tissue in the eyes. There is some evidence that if oxidation is counteracted by antioxidants (free radical scavengers), visual field loss due to glaucoma may be decreased.

THE BODY FIGHTS BACK

Information about free radical damage would be depressing if we did not know that the body wages war against the enemy. We are equipped with a number of important enzymes that scavenge and destroy free radicals, including superoxide dismutase (SOD), catalase, and glutathione peroxidase. There are also enzymes that repair DNA that has suffered free radical damage. These include endonuclease, exonuclease, and polymerase. Scientists estimate that each cell endures some 10,000 free radicals assaults every day, but that most of the damage is repaired almost immediately.

To bolster the activity of antioxidant enzymes, an army of vitamins must chug up to the front lines. These are extracted from the food we eat, and can also be taken in supplement form. Antioxidant nutrients known for their ability to mop up free radicals include vitamin A, beta-carotene, vitamin E, and vitamin C. Minerals such as selenium and compounds like bioflavonoids and phenolics, plus fiber and even compounds found in herbs such as rosemary, green tea, and turmeric, also function as antioxidants.

EYEING THE ANTIOXIDANT VITAMINS

From research on the eyes, there appears to be little doubt that free radicals take their toll. Exactly how the antioxidant vitamins work in the eyes still remains to be charted, but there is evidence that they do have some effect. Researchers are trying to determine if taking antioxidants by mouth results in enough of these substances getting into into the eyes, or if the development of antioxidant eyedrops would be more effective.

Vitamin C

Vitamin C (ascorbic acid), the most widely acclaimed of the antioxidant nutrients, has also been the most extensively researched. Vitamin C is found in high concentrations in the aqueous humor and also in the trabecular meshwork, where it may influence cell metabolism. Studies in which high doses of vitamin C have been given to people with glaucoma have shown promising results, but have also pointed to some possible side effects. Dr. Gary Todd, a holistic ophthalmologist, cited a case in which one of his patients, unable to tolerate glaucoma medications, did well on ten grams of ascorbic acid for a year, until this treatment, too, became intolerable for her.

Doctors in Europe and Asia use vitamin C as a treatment for eye disorders. It has been shown to lower IOP, but it must be taken in high doses to yield this effect. An experimental study in 1966 indicated that a single dose of 500 milligrams of vitamin C per kilogram (2.2 pounds) of body weight reduced intraocular pressure by an average of 14 mm Hg, but usually also caused gastrointestinal symptoms. It is believed to reduce the production of aqueous humor at least in part by causing acidosis (overacidity) of the tissues. It may also increase outflow facility, through some as-yet-unidentified mechanism.

Acidosis can be a problem accompanying high doses of vitamin C, causing acid stomach and other symptoms (see page 82). The chances of developing acidosis may depend on how vitamin C is administered. When test subjects took 100 to 250 milligrams per kilogram of body weight divided into three to five doses daily, they did not suffer acidosis. In individuals who have sickle cell anemia and who are using acetazolamide (Diamox) for glaucoma, the acetazolamide raises the level of vitamin C in the aqueous humor and thus increases the sickling of cells. People with this problem should ask their doctors about the possibility of switching to methazolamide (Neptazane) instead of acetazolamide.

Vitamin C also appears to play a role in maintaining the strength and proper dilation of blood vessels. Dilation of the blood vessels, especially the capillary system, is important for keeping the optic nerve healthy. Vitamin C may also inhibit the development of some cataracts. A health study that examined the nutrient intake of over 50,000 women found that women who consumed the highest amounts of vitamin C, vitamin E, and the carotenoids were 40 percent less likely to develop cataracts than the women with a low antioxidant intake.

In the concentrations normally found in the aqueous humor, vitamin C decreases the efficiency of fibroblasts, the cells that rush in to repair damage by creating scar tissue. It thus helps to inhibit wound healing after filtering operations. Another finding worth noting is that, in laboratory cultures, trabecular cells have been stimulated by ascorbate (vitamin C) to grow new cells.

Of course, we need to view studies carefully, since the results are often contradictory. Some studies show significant effects on IOP; others do not. We can only hope that further research will be done to closely investigate the role of this important vitamin in protecting eye structures.

Good food sources of vitamin C include beets, red peppers, citrus fruits, broccoli, cauliflower, papaya, kale, strawberries, asparagus, cantaloupe, spinach, tomatoes, and mangoes. Most fresh, ripe fruits and vegetables contain some amount of vitamin C.

Bioflavonoids, a recommended companion to vitamin C, are biologically active compounds found mostly in the peels of fruits and vegetables, especially in the white pulp and core of citrus fruits. Like vitamin C, bioflavonoids prevent clumping of red blood cells and help maintain the blood vessels. Bioflavonoids also enhance the absorption of vitamin C.

One bioflavonoid, rutin, is also helpful in preventing bleeding, especially recurrent bleeding from weakened blood vessels, because it strengthens the walls of blood vessels. As far back as 1939, an experimental study involving people with chronic open-angle glaucoma found that the addition of rutin to the diet could reduce IOP by 15 percent or better, and also improve response to miotic drugs such as pilocarpine and carbachol. Rutin is found in many plants, but most abundantly in buckwheat, and is also available in supplement form. Quercetin, which is similar to rutin, may be substituted.

Dr. Ben Lane of the Nutritional Optometry Institute cautions against taking vitamin C three times a day, as this may block the absorption of copper, chromium, calcium, and other minerals. He recommends a total dose of no more than 2,500 milligrams of supplemental vitamin C daily, preferably taken in the morning and evening. If you have a sensitive stomach, calcium ascorbate may be the best formulation.

Vitamin A and the Carotenoids

Vitamin A, a powerful antioxidant, is known primarily for its effect on the retina, especially that of improving night vision. The body converts vitamin A, found in animal tissues, to the fat-soluble compound retinol for storage in the liver. Once vitamin A is stored in the liver, zinc is needed to liberate it for transport to the eyes as needed.

Vitamin A is found in fish, fish liver oil, eggs, and liver. It is possible to use beta-carotene, one of a class of substances known as carotenoids, as a substitute for vitamin A, because beta-carotene is a precursor of vitamin A and is converted into retinol in the liver. Dr. Gary Todd has found that taking supplemental vitamin A palmitate in combination with manganese has been helpful to some people with glaucoma.

Beta-carotene sources in food vary immensely. Sweet potatoes top the list; raw carrots follow. At the low end are apples. In between lie a host of fruits and vegetables, including purslane (best known as a common weed, but now also grown commercially for use in salads), butternut and hubbard squash, mangoes, dandelion greens, kale, turnip greens, beet greens, red pepper, papaya, cantaloupe, Swiss chard, fresh or dried apricots, bok choy, mustard greens, collards, tomatoes (also sauces and juices), broccoli, nectarines, prunes, tangerines, asparagus, romaine lettuce, avocados, plantains, Savoy cabbage, Brussels sprouts, green peas, endive, peaches, oranges, and bananas. In natural sources, you not only get beta-carotene, but all the carotenoids as well—alpha-carotene, beta-carotene, zeta-carotene, cryptoxanthin, lycopene, lutein, zeaxanthin—plus a host of other compounds probably necessary for health. People who have diabetes may lose their ability to convert beta-carotene to retinol, and so must take vitamin A in its fat-soluble form. Fat-soluble vitamin A is found in fish liver oil, eggs, and liver. Air pollution, nitrates, nitrites (commonly used in fertilizers), and cooking and canning destroy or weaken vitamin A's effectiveness.

The carotenoids, of which beta-carotene is only one, are gaining ground among natural ways of achieving eye health. In addition to beta-carotene, two carotenoids that relate directly to eye health are lutein, which is present in spinach, marigolds, sunflowers, and kale, and lycopene, which is found in tomatoes.

Lutein has received considerable attention, especially for the problem of macular degeneration. Studies suggest that a high intake of foods rich in lutein and zeaxanthin, another carotenoid, may protect the retina from oxidative damage leading to degeneration of the macula. Such super foods include kale, spinach, collard greens, broccoli, Brussels sprouts, leaf lettuce, green peas, and summer squash. Foods that contain a moderate amount of lutein include cabbage, carrots, corn, green beans, and tomatoes. And you might pop a marigold into your salad for color and nourishment. Lutein is also available in supplement form, either by itself or as part of one of the eye therapy supplementations. However, lutein and beta-carotene should not be taken together at the same time because they compete for absorption in your gut. Therefore it is better to take your beta-carotene, say, at breakfast and your lutein with your dinner, especially if you're having a salad dressed with olive oil. Both lutein and beta-carotene are more readily absorbed with a bit of fat.

Vitamin E

Vitamin E, the third powerful antioxidant vitamin, is best known for its positive effects in delaying or protecting against the development of cataracts. A Johns Hopkins University and National Institute on Aging study found that persons with a moderate to high intake of vitamin E developed fewer cataracts than those with a low intake. Since vitamin E slows oxidative destruction, it has become an adjunctive therapy for a variety of degenerative diseases, including arthritis, heart disease, some types of cancer, atherosclerosis, and in some cases, tardive dyskinesia, diabetes, and Parkinson's disease.

Dr. Gary Todd has found that his patients heal faster following cataract surgery if they take supplements of vitamin E plus the minerals selenium and zinc. He also found that visual acuity improved in those persons taking vitamin E.

Fresh green, leafy vegetables, eaten raw or with a minimum amount of cooking, can provide vitamin E. This vitamin is concentrated in human milk but is not present in cow's milk. Other foods that contain vitamin E include wheat germ oil; cold-pressed corn, soy, and cottonseed oils and products made from these oils; fortified cereals; poultry; and seafood. Wheat germ has the highest amount. Fortified cereals such as Total and Product 19 also contain high amounts of supplemental vitamin E.

OTHER ANTIOXIDANTS THAT MAKE A DIFFERENCE

With ongoing research into the vast array of substances present in food and plants, the range of known antioxidants is widening. Herbs such as bilberry and ginkgo biloba (see Chapter 9) have antioxidant properties. Certain flavonoids derived from purple grapes, blueberries, bilberries, the white part of oranges, and other fruits are considered impressive antioxidants as well.

Coenzyme Q_{10}, which is chemically known as ubiquinone, is essential in the production of cellular energy in all organisms that utilize oxygen. A coenzyme is a substance that combines with another substance to create an active enzyme, one of the over 1,000 complex proteins in the body that cause necessary chemical reactions and other transformations to take place. There are twelve types of coenzyme Q, but the human body manufactures only one type—coenzyme Q_{10} (or CoQ_{10}), named for its molecular structure, which resembles a head with a tail consisting of ten repeated units. Coenzyme Q_{10} facilitates the conversion of food into energy and works to neutralize free radicals during the process of energy transport.

Although there are no studies establishing a specific effect of CoQ_{10} on glaucoma, this substance's antioxidant activity makes it worth considering for eye health. Foods that are a good sources include bran and wheat germ, soybeans and other legumes, meat, fish, and vegetable oils. However, refining and processing may remove much of the CoQ_{10} that is naturally present in foods. Supplements are also available.

Glutathione is a compound composed of the amino acids cysteine, glutamic acid, and glycine that has been found to have antioxidant activity. Research has shown that both glutathione and its constituent amino acids can protect the retina from injury due to free radicals. Furthermore, studies suggest glutathione levels in the retinas of people over the age of sixty-five—the group most prone to glaucoma—are lower than in those of younger people. Glutathione has another important function—that of supporting the mechanisms by which vitamins C and E detoxify free radicals.

Glutathione is available in supplement form, but retinal cells apparently do not take up added glutathione. In other words, glutathione from supplements won't get into your eyes. Instead, glutathione levels may be raised by increasing the amount of cysteine, glutamic acid, and glycine available for glutathione synthesis. Plant foods are good sources of these amino acids.

MORE IMPORTANT VITAMINS

While the antioxidant vitamins are busy mopping up free radicals in your system, that is not the whole story. There are a number of other vitamins that are necessary for good health and that can affect the health and optimum functioning of your eyes.

Vitamin D

This vitamin is vital for the metabolism of calcium and regulates the absorption of calcium and phosphorus from the intestinal tract. A deficiency of vitamin D results in rickets in young children; irritability, weakness, and softening of the bones in adults; and underutilization of calcium and phosphorus in bone and tooth formation in people of any age. Vitamin D may have a direct effect on the eyes, and it is vital for maintaining overall good health.

The body can usually produce all the vitamin D it needs; in the presence of sunlight, two cholesterol-related compounds in the skin are converted into vitamin D. Food sources of vitamin D include butter, egg yolk, fish liver oils, fatty fish such as salmon, tuna, herring, sardines, and liver and oysters. Supplements are available, but rarely necessary or even advisable, as vitamin D is one of the few vitamins that you can overdose on.

The B Vitamins

The "B-Team" can have a profound effect on the health of the eyes. The B vitamins act as coenzymes (see page 166). They are the fellows that see to it that oxidation reactions essential to cell growth and carbohydrate metabolism occur as they should. The B vitamin family is a large one.

Vitamin B1 (Thiamine)

This member of the B group is important in the metabolism of carbohydrates; energy production; the synthesis of RNA, niacin, and fatty acids; and the transmission of nerve impulses. In the body, thiamine is used in the production of an enzyme, cocarboxylase, that is a natural cholinesterase inhibitor (cholinesterase inhibitors lower IOP).

A deficiency of thiamine can lead to impaired vision and damaged nerves. A study conducted in Guyana found that among a group of people who ate a diet deficient in the B vitamins, there was a preponderance of open-angle glaucoma, while there was no glaucoma among those who ate a more balanced diet. Food sources of thiamine include brewer's yeast, peas, wheat germ, pasta, peanuts, whole grains, beans, liver, and pork.

Vitamin B_2 (Riboflavin)

This vitamin is involved in the breakdown of dietary fat, the synthesis of fatty acids, the activation of vitamin B_6 and folic acid, and the synthesis of corticosteroids, red blood cells, and glycogen, the form in which energy-supplying glucose is stored in the muscles and liver. A deficiency of riboflavin can affect the mucous membranes and moist tissues in the eyes and nose. It also maintains the supply of glutathione, a major antioxidant, in the lens of the eye. Dietary sources of riboflavin include brewer's yeast, broccoli, wheat germ, almonds, milk, cottage cheese, yogurt, pasta, kidney, liver, and heart. Processing foods destroys this vitamin, and pasteurization of milk products depletes it.

Vitamin B_3 (Niacin, Niacinamide)

Vitamin B_3 occurs in two forms, niacin and niacinamide. Niacin is often used to lower blood pressure, because it dilates blood vessels, and is also helpful for lowering the level of cholesterol in the blood. Because of its effect on blood vessels, some ophthalmologists consider it useful for increasing the flow of blood to the optic nerve.

Food sources of niacin include brewer's yeast, peanuts, soybeans, and whole grains, as well as high-quality protein foods such as eggs, milk, poultry, fish, meat, and liver. Cooking depletes foods of niacin, and alcohol destroys it. If taken in supplement form, niacin can cause a temporary flush shortly after ingestion, and if taken in excess doses over prolonged periods of time, it may cause liver damage. Niacinamide is not believed to have these effects, however, it is not considered as effective at lowering cholesterol or increasing circulation. The body can make niacin from the amino acid tryptophan, but thiamine, riboflavin, and vitamin B_6 are needed for this process.

Vitamin B_6 (Pyridoxine)

Vitamin B_6 is involved in many metabolic processes, including the breakdown of amino acids (important for protein formation), fats, and carbohydrates; the release of glycogen from the liver to supply energy; and the synthesis of antibodies, red blood cells, DNA, and elastin. Food sources of vitamin B_6 include soybeans, lima beans, legumes in general, avocados, bananas, walnuts, filberts, buckwheat (kasha), peanuts, chicken, steak, tuna, kidney, beef, pork, veal, and salmon. Oral contraceptives and other drugs may deplete this vitamin, and older people often have deficiencies.

Vitamin B_{12}

Vitamin B_{12} is necessary, along with folic acid, for the synthesis of RNA and DNA; helps to maintain nerve tissue; and is active in glucose metabolism. A 1958 study of the effect of vitamin B_{12} on optic nerve tissue revealed that it increases the strength of the tissues in new cases of glaucoma, but is not effective for long-standing cases. A later study, in 1969, confirmed that it is beneficial for optic neuropathy provided the treatment is started within six months of visual deterioration. In a 1976 study on laboratory monkeys, scientists produced severe vitamin B_{12} deficiency in the animals, and five of them developed gross visual impairments. Autopsies of the deficient animals showed degeneration of the peripheral visual pathway. No abnormalities were found in a B_{12}-supplemented control animal.

Food sources of vitamin B_{12} include liver, oysters, poultry, fish, clams, salmon, and eggs. Since this vitamin is found mainly in animal foods, strict vegetarians may need to take supplements, as may older people, people who consume alcohol, and women who take birth control pills, who may have trouble absorbing B_{12} from foods. The authors of the first study cited above recommended taking 100 to 250 micrograms of supplemental vitamin B_{12} daily.

Folic Acid

Folic acid, another of the B vitamins, prevents anemia, is important for new cell growth, and is vital in the early months of fetal development (a deficiency has been linked to spina bifida). Drs. Ben Lane and Gary Todd have both found that some patients with visual problems improve when folic acid is added to their diet.

It is easy to get enough folic acid if you eat a lot of raw green, leafy vegetables and fresh, ripe raw fruits. Folic acid is also present in liver, eggs, asparagus, endive, bean sprouts, garbanzo beans, whole wheat, and salmon. Cooking destroys folic acid.

Pantothenic Acid

Pantothenic acid might be called a brain chemical. A deficiency may result in nerve and optic degeneration. Pantothenic acid is important for energy production and the synthesis of red blood cells, cholesterol, and steroids. It also stimulates antibodies and intestinal absorption. Major sources of pantothenic acid include liver, kidney, heart, brewer's yeast, sunflower seeds, peanuts, buckwheat flour, royal bee jelly, egg yolk, bran, fish, and whole-grain cereals. Before modern food processing, deficiencies of this nutrient were uncommon. However, growing foods in sterilized soils and fumigating stored foods with methyl bromide greatly reduces the amount of the vitamin in foods.

Biotin

Biotin is an energy metabolizer and a synthesizer of antibodies, niacin, and digestive enzymes. Dr. Gary Todd has found that a daily supplement of 1,000 micrograms of biotin lowers blood sugar levels in diabetics, and a similar dose has been effective in lowering IOP in some patients.

Biotin is normally produced by the bacteria in the intestines. As a result, it is possible to become deficient in biotin if you must take heavy doses of antibiotics. Food sources of biotin include liver, kidney, egg yolk, milk, yeast, whole grains, cauliflower, active culture yogurt, nuts, legumes, and fish. If you are interested in experimenting with biotin supplementation, seek the cooperation of your doctor.

Choline

Choline, also called a brain chemical, is synthesized with the aid of pantothenic acid and acetylcholine, that trusty chemical messenger so important in the management of glaucoma (see page 74). It is also a major component of lecithin (the other is inositol), an important compound for controlling the buildup of plaque in the arteries. Healthy individuals normally produce choline. Unprocessed foods, egg yolks, soybeans, fish, cereal, legumes, lecithin, and liver are also rich sources of choline. Most fatty foods contain choline, but cannot, unfortunately, be recommended because of all the other negative effects they may have.

Para-Aminobenzoic Acid (PABA)

You have probably seen PABA listed as the active ingredient in your favorite sunblock. In the body, it is involved in protein metabolism and the synthesis of folic acid, and stimulates pantothenic acid to do its job. PABA may inhibit the effectiveness of sulfa drugs. Therefore, if you usually take supplements containing PABA but need to take sulfa drugs, eliminate the PABA for as long as you must take the medication.

Vitamin K

Vitamin K is a fat-soluble vitamin that is necessary for blood clotting and the proper uptake of calcium. Vitamin K is synthesized by the "friendly" bacteria in the intestines, and most people produce all they need. However, the supply of vitamin K can be diminished by long-term use of antibiotics, because these drugs destroy both harmful and beneficial bacteria. Green and yellow vegetables are good food sources of vitamin K.

MINERALS—THE SALTS THAT BUILD AND KEEP US HEALTHY

Minerals are inorganic substances that are nevertheless important for all bodily processes. In the best of times, supplementation of minerals would not be necessary, for you would get those you need from your drinking water and from the foods you eat. However, much of the food sold in this country is grown in soils depleted of essential minerals.

Minerals influence virtually all the chemical reactions in the body, including some of the vital processes necessary for eye health. They may be divided into three classes, based on their functions and the amounts required by the human body: structural minerals; lesser minerals; and trace elements.

The Structural Minerals

The structural minerals include calcium, phosphorus, magnesium, potassium, sodium, chlorine, and sulfur. You may need to ingest several grams of each of these minerals daily.

Calcium

Calcium might be called the most essential of all minerals, for without it many of your bodily functions would deteriorate. Calcium is necessary for the formation of bones and teeth; is involved in growth, blood-clotting, muscle contraction, nerve-impulse transmission, and cell permeability; and is a catalyst in many physical reactions. Good food sources of calcium include dairy products, collards, turnip greens, broccoli, kale, figs, tempeh, tofu, and canned salmon and sardines (with the bones). Hard water supplies a goodly amount. Calcium is also widely available in supplement form. However, it is probably best absorbed from foods.

Magnesium

This important mineral plays a necessary role as a catalyst in many reactions, including the transmission of nerve impulses, muscle relaxation, and cellular energy production. The formation of tooth enamel and bone depend on it. It also helps you adapt to cold. Magnesium deficiency is associated with a loss of calcium and potassium, and may aggravate diabetic cataracts. To maintain your body's magnesium level, eat soybeans, shrimp, wheat germ, whole grains, molasses, clams, cornmeal, spinach, baked potatoes, oysters, crab, peas, liver, beef, green vegetables, and nuts. If you grow your own food, try adding some magnesium sulfate to the soil. Bathing in Epsom salts also adds a bit of magnesium to your system.

Phosphorus

Phosphorus is an energy producer. It is important for the absorption and transport of nutrients, the synthesis of DNA and RNA, and maintenance of the proper acid-alkaline balance in the body. Ideally, your intake of phosphorus should be equal to that of calcium, however, many people get far more than they need. An excess of phosphorus can result in a syndrome called *hyperparathyroidism,* a condition that causes the sclera to distend, allowing for more rapid development of myopia and other refraction changes. If you drink a lot of carbonated soft drinks or eat a lot of foods like sardines, whole eggs, whole-wheat bread, tuna, sirloin steak, trout, wheat germ, chicken, mackerel, or wheat bran, without also consuming high-calcium foods, you may be getting too much phosphorus. Foods low in phosphorus but rich in calcium include cheese, string beans, cow's milk, zucchini, and broccoli. Neutral foods include grapefruit, chicory, and watermelon.

Potassium

Potassium is involved in the regulation of the body's fluid balance and in nerve-impulse transmission, muscle relaxation, and insulin release, and, together with sodium, governs your body's electrolyte activity. Those of us who have to take acetazolamide (Diamox) or methazolamide (Neptazane) to control our eye pressures may experience potassium deficiency due to the diuretic action of these drugs, which depletes the body of potassium. Foods rich in potassium can easily be worked into your diet. Most fruits and vegetables are good sources of potassium, including bananas, cantaloupes, mangoes, lima beans, potatoes, avocados, broccoli, apricots, figs, liver, milk, peanuts, and citrus fruits and juices.

Sodium

Sodium is necessary for the integrity of cell membranes, and is found in the fluids of the body (serum, blood, and lymph) and in the tissues. It maintains a proper balance between calcium and potassium, which is necessary for normal heart action and the biochemical equilibrium of the body. It also prevents excessive loss of water from the tissues.

Unfortunately, as with phosphorus, most of us get too much sodium rather than too little, especially if we eat a lot of processed foods. Excessive sodium intake has been linked to high blood pressure, which may have an effect on the blood vessels in the eyes (see Chapter 2). However, people who adhere to strict low-sodium diets and/or take diuretic medications may indeed be deficient in sodium. I found myself with that problem when a dietitian I was working with ordered a series of blood tests, and found my sodium level out of sync with my potassium level. A proper balance between sodium and potassium is essential. If you are on Diamox or Neptazane, you may find that this balance is disrupted. This can be determined by a blood test. A deficiency of sodium can result in weakness, nerve disorders, weight loss, and disturbed digestion.

The Lesser Minerals

The lesser minerals are needed only in milligram amounts daily. These include iron, manganese, copper, and zinc. Unlike the structural minerals, which are readily available in foods, the lesser minerals may not be supplied in sufficient amounts in the diet, because much of our food is grown in mineral-depleted soil.

Copper

The level of copper in the body must be carefully balanced—too much is toxic; too little can cause hypothyroidism, which some eye specialists interested in nutrition speculate affects intraocular pressure. Copper is important for the absorption of iron, and works with iron in red blood cell formation. It is an energy releaser and is essential for the synthesis of collagen, elastin, and melanin.

Most people are not deficient in copper because it is widely distributed in foods and drinking water. It can also enter the body through the skin if worn on the body. Major sources include shellfish, liver, cherries, nuts, cocoa, and gelatin, as well as drinking water (it leaches into the water from copper water pipes). Copper supplements should be taken with caution, since too much copper can result in the production of free radicals and can also cause nausea and vomiting.

Iron

Iron is essential to life. Plants require it to manufacture chlorophyll, and animals require it for the formation of hemoglobin, the protein responsible for delivering oxygen to the tissues through the bloodstream. We need only 1 to 4 milligrams of iron daily to sustain hemoglobin activity, but since iron is poorly absorbed from the food we eat, we need to consume foods containing 15 to 30 milligrams (the higher number if you are a menstruating woman, the lower if you are a senior citizen) to ensure a sufficient supply. Iron should be taken in supplement form only under the direction of a physician, as the presence of too much iron in the system is unhealthy. High iron levels have been linked to heart disease. Too much iron also leads to a free-radical explosion in the body, and can cause chromium to be depleted. Older people may have an excess of iron in their systems. For such individuals, donating blood a few times a year not only stands to save lives, but should also bring iron levels back to normal.

For those who need to increase their iron consumption, vitamin C and acidic foods such as citrus fruits aid in the absorption of iron. Using iron pots for cooking also adds iron to your diet, as does eating apricots, peaches, prunes, raisins, figs, brewer's yeast, turnip and beet greens, spinach, alfalfa, liver, clams, meat, chicken, fish, asparagus, and cream of wheat. Persons who may need additional iron include menstruating women and persons recovering from injury or surgery.

Manganese

Manganese acts in conjunction with vitamin C and is also a major element in the enzyme superoxide dismutase, an important scavenger of free radicals. Dr. Gary Todd found that IOP was lowered in a group of glaucoma patients after six weeks of treatment with 40 milligrams of manganese daily. Not all were affected equally by the treatment; some responded at half the dose. Manganese deficiency may manifest itself in flabby muscle tone, diabetes, and heart disease. This vital trace mineral is found in rice and wheat bran, corn germ, whole grain cereals, green vegetables, nuts, dried legumes, tea, ginger, clover, blueberries, citrus fruits and juices, seaweed, and alfalfa. Supplemental manganese should not be taken in doses over 20 milligrams daily except at the direction of a doctor.

Zinc

Zinc plays many vital roles in the body. It is a cofactor in some twenty different enzymes, assists in protein synthesis, and is essential to the development and maintenance of the immune system.

In recent years, dietary zinc has gained considerable attention and respect in the medical community. The effect of zinc on the body is widespread—among other things, it has an impact on fertility, skin growth, healing, taste, protein digestion, carbon dioxide removal, disease resistance, and the processing of alcohol. It also activates vitamin A. Zinc is essential for DNA and RNA production. Research now also associates zinc deficiency with some forms of macular degeneration. Dr. Gary Todd found that a daily dose of 20 milligrams of zinc reversed the formation of some cataracts in certain patients.

Dietary sources of zinc include eggs, oatmeal, liver, nuts, beef, lamb, peas, carrots, milk, oysters, herring, clams, wheat germ, bran, and green leafy vegetables. Zinc may be lacking in commercially grown vegetables, however, because agribusiness farmers usually do not add zinc to their soil. And if you eat foods such as tuna or swordfish, which contain mercury, your zinc supply may be further diminished, since the mercury causes zinc to be leached out of the body. If you take zinc supplements, preferred formulations are zinc picolinate, zinc orotate, zinc gluconate, or chelated zinc.

The Power of Trace Elements

While you need only a tiny bit—just micrograms—of the trace elements, they are essential for the proper functioning of the body. To understand how little is required, consider that a teaspoon would contain 4.5 *million* micrograms. Yet many of these elements have been identified as essential for a number of bodily processes, among them iodine for the health of the thyroid gland, chromium to regulate insulin production, and molybdenum for carbohydrate metabolism.

Chromium

In recent years, chromium supplementation has been touted in supplement ads as a way to increase strength, lose weight, and even help treat diabetes. Research has not validated the first two, but the relationship between chromium and diabetes is well known. Chromium acts in conjunction with insulin, and in several studies, people taking 200 micrograms of chromium a day were better able to shed excess blood sugar from their bodies than a control group who took a placebo. Blood sugar control is the cornerstone of diabetes management, and diabetics are among the people most likely to go blind from glaucoma or diabetic retinopathy (see Chapter 2).

An observation study linked a deficiency of chromium with a high IOP in persons with open-angle glaucoma. Dr. Ben Lane of the Nutritional Optometry Institute found that the level of chromium in the red blood cells of both open-angle glaucoma and diabetic patients is lower than in healthy individuals. Specifically, he found that persons with a chromium level less than 150 nanograms per milliliter (ng/ml) were more likely to have IOPs greater than 22 mm Hg. Confirming Dr. Lane's hypothesis, another study found that persons with healthy eyes had an average blood chromium level of 279.25 ng/ml, while those with open-angle glaucoma had an average level of only 118.05 ng/ml. Dr. Lane suggests that chromium's interaction with insulin may be one of the factors that sustains strong ciliary-muscle eye-focusing activity—the ability to read fine print. An adequate chromium intake may thus help to prevent the stretching of the eyeball that results from prolonged close work (see page 144).

Good sources of chromium include sweet fruits, starchy vegetables, whole grains, egg yolks, molasses, liver, brewer's yeast, red meat, cheese, butterfat, legumes, peas, broccoli (one of the best-absorbed sources), black pepper, and even red wine. Eating refined sugar leaches chromium from the blood. The mineral vanadium may counteract the action of chromium. Therefore, sea vegetables and/or large quantities of mushrooms, which are rich in vanadium, should be somewhat restricted in the diet.

Iodine

Iodine regulates the body's energy by acting on the thyroid hormone thyroxine. The average person's diet is not likely to be deficient in iodine. There is some interest in exploring the relevance of thyroid function with eye health. Dr. Gary Todd believes that persons with underactive thyroid glands may be more susceptible to glaucoma.

Molybdenum

Molybdenum is involved in the mobilization of iron from storage in the liver, the excretion of uric acid, and carbohydrate metabolism. The official recommended daily allowance (RDA) is between 150 and 500 micrograms daily. If you eat whole foods such as whole-grain cereals, brown rice, millet, buckwheat, legumes, alfalfa, and brewer's yeast, you should be getting your daily requirement of this important mineral.

Selenium

Selenium is an important antioxidant that works in conjunction with vitamin E. It vacuums up free radicals and protects against heavy metals such as cadmium, mercury, and arsenic. It is also a component of the enzyme glutathione peroxidase, another powerful antioxidant, which has been found to be less active in persons who develop cataracts (see page 161). Foods such as whole grains grown in selenium-rich soil are a good source of this mineral, as are tuna, seafoods, and meat.

Silicon

Silicon is highly concentrated in the cornea, sclera, and vitreous. There is not a great deal of research, however, on its relationship to glaucoma. We do know that silicon stimulates the growth of collagen, which is vital for the health of the connective tissues, including those of the eye. A diet rich in whole grains, vegetables, and fruits should provide sufficient silicon for eye health.

Sulfur

Sulfur is necessary for the synthesis of body proteins such as collagen, and so is essential for healthy hair, skin, and nails. It aids in blood clotting and acts as a detoxifier. It is also one of the ingredients in the medication dorzolamide (Trusopt), which decreases the production of aqueous fluid. Radishes, turnips, onions, celery, horseradish, string beans, watercress, soybeans, meat, garlic, asparagus, and egg yolks are all good sources of dietary sulfur.

ESSENTIAL FATTY ACIDS

We have all heard a lot about the need to lower our intake of fats. However, if we eliminate all fat, we may find ourselves deficient in the essential fatty acids. We do need some fat in our bodies, but it should be the right kind—unsaturated fats, not hydrogenated fats (in margarine and shortening) or saturated fats (in meat, dairy products, and refined coconut and palm oils). We need fat for the formation of cell walls, brain tissue, hormones, and enzymes, and for the utilization of vitamins A, D, E, and K. Fat protects our internal organs and keeps skin healthy, and it functions as a building block in the membranes of every cell in our bodies—including the cells of the eye.

Unsaturated fats are sources of essential fatty acids. They are called essential because the body cannot produce them, but must obtain them through the diet. Essential fatty acids are divided into two families: omega-3 (linolenic acid) and omega-6 (linoleic and arachidonic acids). Both linolenic and linoleic acids help to fight inflammation by promoting the production of anti-inflammatory prostaglandins (see page 83). Cold water fish such as salmon, tuna, sardines, mackerel, and herring, cod liver oil, flaxseed, walnuts, and pumpkin seeds are good sources of linolenic acid. Linoleic acid can be obtained from soybeans, lecithin, and safflower, sunflower, corn, soy, walnut, sesame, pumpkinseed, and Brazil nut oils. Arachidonic acid is plentiful in peanuts.

AMINO ACIDS

Amino acids are the building blocks of proteins, necessary for the growth and maintenance of body weight, heat, and energy, and essential for growth and repair of tissue. There are over twenty different amino acids that are important to the body. Of these, there are two that may have a particular impact on eye health: glutamate (also called glutamic acid) and glutamine.

Research has found that excessive amounts of glutamate in the eye may be associated with a deterioration of the ganglion nerve cells, which carry messages from the eyes to the brain. However, there is preliminary evidence to suggest that supplementation with L-glutamine may be helpful in correcting this situation.

TO SUPPLEMENT OR NOT TO SUPPLEMENT?

Our ancestors did quite well without supplementation. They gathered their fruits, nuts, seeds, tubers, leaves, and ate their kill, and obviously lived productively, for their DNA lives on in all of us. Even today, in pockets of the world where modern dietary practices have not penetrated, there are healthy individuals free of disease who have never heard of supplements. Then why take them? Mainly because we cannot be certain that we extract from the foods we eat all the vitamins and minerals our bodies need for healthy maintenance. As we age, our bodies become less efficient at absorbing nutrients from foods. Moreover, many medications affect nutrient absorption. Research suggests that people over sixty may need more supplementation than those who are younger. Seniors who live alone may be most in need of supplementation, for they often pay little heed to what they eat.

In 1994, nutritional supplements constituted a $4-billion industry. I take them. Rita takes them. Nobel-Prize-winning chemist Linus Pauling took them. The case to be made for taking nutritional supplements stems first from the recognition that the way we grow, handle, and prepare our foods may rob us of essential nutrients. Modern agricultural methods, which involve growing a single crop and adding to depleted soils high-growth chemicals such as phosphorus and nitrogen, yield grains and vegetables low in minerals. Add to this the fact that long-distance transport and storage of foods destroys their vitamin content. Then cooking and serving—especially long cooking, boiling in water, and delays between cooking and serving—further compound the problem.

Taking supplemental vitamins has been promoted by nutritionists and health care advocates for many years, and studies published in peer-reviewed medical journals confirm that supplementation produces positive results. A Canadian study of persons sixty-five years and older found that those who took a modest daily amount of a broad spectrum of vitamins and minerals had markedly fewer infections and a stronger immune response than those fed a dummy pill. Researchers in Boston reported, based on studies involving more than 120,000 men and women, that taking a daily supplement of 100 or more units of vitamin E reduced the risk of coronary disease.

Some people prefer to take organic vitamin supplements. Others feel that synthetics are equally effective. Claims can be confusing. If you decide to take nutritional supplements, choose a brand recommended by your doctor, nutritionist, or other health care provider.

Vitamin E supplements can be particularly confusing. Different vitamin E supplements are designated as "d-tocopherol," "dl-tocopherol," and other things. The "dl-" forms (dl-tocopherol) are syn-

Should I Take "Eye Vitamins"?

Just several years ago, there were only a few products advertised as "eye vitamins" on the market. Now there are more than twenty-two. The vitamin industry has obviously realized that consumers are desperately seeking to maintain the health of their eyes. So should you take one of these products? It depends.

If you are supplementing your diet already with an array of vitamins plus the herbs bilberry and ginkgo biloba, you may already be ingesting all the ingredients found in an "eye vitamin." However, you may find it more convenient to take a single supplement rather than multiple tablets and capsules.

If you do decide to take a vitamin especially formulated for the eyes, choose one that contains a good supply of antioxidants (beta-carotene, vitamin C, vitamin E, selenium, quercetin, citrus bioflavonoids, bilberry, ginkgo biloba), the B vitamins, plus the amino acids L-glutamine, L-glutathione, L-cysteine, and N-acetylcysteine. You probably won't find a formula that contains all of these ingredients, but there are some formulas that come close, including Bright Eyes from Futurebiotics; Cata-RX from Vision Research Laboratories; Eye Formula from KAL; Eye Power from Nature's Herbs; Ocucare from Nature's Plus; OcuDyne from Allergy Research; and Oxi-Freeda from Freeda Vitamins. Before buying any vitamin product, check the ingredients list for the product's purity.

Ideally, your vitamin supplement intake should complement your diet. If you eat wisely—lots and lots of green leafy vegetables, the cruciferous vegetables (broccoli, cauliflower, and others), yellow pigmented vegetables and fruits (carrots, sweet potatoes, cantaloupe, and others) and whole grains, and if the food is organically grown, you are probably ingesting your vitamins and minerals in the most absorbable form. Furthermore, whole foods contain hundreds of substances called phytochemicals that have healing powers. However, if your diet is lacking sufficient quantities of any of these components, try to choose a vitamin formula that supplies the particular nutrients you may be missing.

thetic. In addition, vitamin E is actually a family of related compounds. Alpha- beta-, delta-, and gamma-tocopherol are four primary forms found in nature. "Mixed tocopheròls" denotes a compound in which alpha, beta, delta, and gamma are included, and most closely resembles vitamin E as found in foods.

Vitamin A also is available in a number of different forms, including preformed vitamin A and beta-carotene, which the body converts into vitamin A as needed. We recommend that, unless you suffer from diabetes and/or anorexia, you use beta-carotene as a source of vitamin A because it also acts as an antioxidant, .

Many of us who decide to start a program of nutritional supplementation are put off by the need to take pills or capsules, because we just can't seem to get those pills and capsules down. If you have trouble taking supplements in pill or capsule form, try this technique. Place a tablet on your tongue and take two successive gulps of liquid without pausing. On the first gulp, swallow some liquid. This action causes the epiglottis to fold down and cover your larynx. On the second gulp, swallow the tablet with some liquid. The tablet will slide down before the unsuspecting epiglottis can take up its sentry position again.

WHY EAT ORGANIC?

There is a movement in this country attempting to turn back the clock to a time when food was free of dyes, added chemicals, radiation, and dubious enhancements such as the growth hormone given to dairy cows to increase the production of milk. At the same time, recent years have seen outbreaks of "mad cow disease" in Great Britain, large-scale food-poisoning outbreaks from tainted hamburger, and bacterial contamination of the water supply in some of our large cities. In 1994, according to the U.S. Centers for Disease Control and Prevention, some 7 million Americans became ill and 9,000 died from acute food poisoning. Clean food may well become a consumer battle cry in the next decade, as Americans become aware of the possibility of *E. coli*-poisoned meat, *Salmonella*-infected chicken and eggs, chemical-contaminated seafood, pesticide-laden fruits and vegetables, and a new wave of genetically altered foods.

Our agriculture, our methods of farming, our chemical manufacturing, and the defense and other industries that spread across this nation spew toxins into the land we live on, the water we drink, and the air we breathe. By 1996, total pesticide use in the United States came to over 100 million pounds. More than 900,000 farms and about

69 million households in this country use some type of pesticide. On farms, a combination of herbicides, insecticides, and fungicides make up the deadly brew. According to the U.S. Environmental Protection Agency, industry releases billions of pounds of chemical waste into the environment *every year*. And the problem is worldwide. You can't escape it.

Pesticides are concentrated chemicals designed to kill living creatures. In fact, some of the pesticides used today were first developed for chemical warfare. Phosphine, for one, used today to produce chemical herbicides and insecticides, was the agent involved in almost all deaths due to poison gas in World War II. Zykon-B, another modern pesticide, is the substance the Nazis used in their infamous gas chambers. Other widely used pesticides, including malathion and parathion, are members of the nerve gas family.

Pesticides affect more than the creatures they are designed to kill. A pesticide sprayed on a corn plant, for instance, may kill the corn borers that would threaten the crop, but when the corn is later fed to chickens or hogs, these animals ingest pesticide residues along with the corn. Pesticides accumulate in the tissues and cells of animals and, as one organism consumes another, the pesticide residues in their bodies become more and more concentrated. Thus, the higher up you are on the food chain, the more concentrated the pesticides. Since humans sit at the top of the chain, eating animal foods and animal products, our exposure to pesticide residues increases.

What Toxic Chemicals Lace What Foods?

How pesticides and toxic chemicals are used in our environment can be bewildering. Some are used to control insects, others to kill weeds. There are chemicals that regulate the growth of fruit on the trees, and there are chemicals (fungicides) to prevent fungus from attacking foods in the field or in storage, such as fruits, grains, and vegetables.

Some of the most prevalent chemicals that show up in our foods include the following:

- *Daminozide* (Alar), a growth regulator used on apples, peanuts, cherries, peaches, grapes, tomatoes, and pears.
- *Alachlior* (Lasso), a pesticide used on corn and peanuts. Residues are found in crops, animal products, ground water, and soil.
- *Inorganic arsenicals,* including growth regulators used on grapefruit,

fungicides on grapes, and herbicides on golf courses. These chemicals are also acutely toxic.

- *2, 3 dichloropropene* (Telone), a multipurpose pesticide used on potatoes, sugar beets, and other vegetables and grain crops. It is classified by the EPA as a probable human carcinogen.
- *Ethylene oxide (ETO),* which is applied to coconuts, black walnuts, and spices to kill bacteria.
- *Aldicarbs* (Temik), which is found in imported foods such as bananas and coffee. Traces also are present in ground water in a number of states. It is extremely toxic to humans and wildlife.
- *Cyanazine* (Bladex), an herbicide used primarily on corn, sorghum, and wheat. It has been found to cause birth defects in laboratory animals.
- *Chloral-isopropyl N-(3-Chlorophenyl) carbonate (CIPC)* and *maleic hydrazide,* agents used on potatoes to inhibit sprout growth. CIPC, which is the more commonly used of the two, is mildly toxic to animals. Maleic hydrazide is highly toxic. Practically all of the residue from these chemicals is concentrated in the skin of the potato.
- *Dinocap* (Karathane, Mildex, Dikar), a fungicide found on a variety of fruits and vegetables, primarily apples. This chemical causes birth defects in animals.

In addition to all these, there are many others. Unfortunately, when you buy produce that has not been grown organically, there is no way to tell which chemical or chemicals may have been used on it.

How to Beat the Toxic Chemical Problem

Eating organic foods—foods produced without the use of pesticides, herbicides, or artificial fertilizers or growth-stimulators—is one way to reduce your exposure to these chemicals in foods. Once available only in health food stores and through food co-ops, organic produce can now be found in many supermarkets. As of 1995, twenty-seven states had passed laws pertaining to organic labeling. In some states, for instance, the "organic" label not only means that a given food has been produced organically, but that the land it was grown on has not been treated with certain chemicals for a specified number of years.

But just sixteen states (Colorado, Florida, Idaho, Kentucky, Maryland, Minnesota, New Hampshire, New Mexico, Oklahoma, Oregon, Rhode Island, South Dakota, Texas, Virginia, Washington, and Wisconsin) require certification of organic farms. Some states, including Massachusetts and Vermont, have state-run or state-sanctioned programs in place to certify organically raised foods. In the remaining states, there may be independent regional grower organizations that perform these functions, or there may be no regulations at all. The passage of the Organic Foods Production Act of 1990, which came into effect in 1996, mandates that the U.S. Department of Agriculture establish a national definition for organically grown foods, fix certification guidelines, regulate labeling, ensure that food labels come from certified farms or processors, and create a national board to develop standards.

Aside from the problem of noxious chemicals, is there any difference in quality between food grown organically and that produced by the farming methods most commonly used today? According to an article published in *The Journal of Applied Nutrition*, organically grown foods contain higher levels of important minerals than conventionally grown foods. The levels of selenium, an important mineral that acts as an antioxidant, can be nearly four times higher in organically grown foods as compared with conventionally grown produce. Levels of magnesium, manganese, and zinc are also significantly higher.

If, however, it is not possible or feasible to purchase only organically grown produce (or to grow your own), you can minimize your exposure to various chemicals with a number of simple precautions:

- Wash bananas, corn, grapefruit, melons, lemons, and oranges before peeling them. Avoid using orange or lemon peel unless it is from organically grown fruit.
- Thoroughly wash cabbage, cucumbers, eggplants, peppers, and tomatoes. Discard the outer leaves of lettuce and cabbage.
- Peel cucumbers and other fruits and vegetables if they have been waxed. Eggplants, peppers, and apples are often waxed to give them a shiny appearance. Wax is hard to remove. Scrub any suspect fruits or vegetables well or use a wax remover, obtainable in many health food stores.
- Wash the following very well: cauliflower, cherries, grapes, green beans, lettuce, potatoes, and strawberries. Dr. Ben Lane of the

Nutritional Optometry Institute suggests using kosher soap when washing vegetables. It is so pure you can eat it, for it is made from coconut oil. It is labeled "kosher" and can be found in supermarkets.

- Peel potatoes, cut away any green areas, and scoop out the eyes before boiling or steaming them. Baking is acceptable, since dry heat inhibits some of the migration of the toxins.
- If apples are not certified organic, peel them.
- Place broccoli or spinach (unless organically raised) in a bowl of water with a drop of liquid dishwashing detergent (or swish kosher soap into the water) and agitate, then rinse thoroughly.
- Peel carrots, peaches, and pears before eating them.
- Trim the leaves off celery.
- Canned tomatoes or tomato sauces from the United States contain lower concentrations of pesticide residues. Imported produce is more likely to have larger amounts of pesticide residues. About one third of the fresh and frozen foods we eat comes from imported vegetables and fruits. It is not always possible to tell the origin of produce, however, it is fair to assume that out-of-season fruits and vegetables may be imported.
- Beans and peas register low levels of pesticide residues, while apples receive more chemicals per acre than any other major crop in the United States. A small battle-scarred apple may be a better choice than the large, shiny red beauty. Just think—if worms shun the fruit, why should you eat it? Those fantastic-looking fruits most likely have received heavy doses of pesticides.
- Buy cold-pressed vegetable oils processed without chemicals and without preservatives, and store them in dark bottles in your refrigerator.

Some people claim that there cannot be totally organic produce because some pesticides drift from neighboring farms, or chemicals already present in the water or soil, prevent the growing of a totally organic product. Nevertheless, the more of these contaminants you can avoid by eating organic produce, the more you reduce the pesticide load on your body.

THE ADDITIVE CONUNDRUM

In addition to worrying about toxic chemicals such as pesticides, we have to be concerned about all the chemicals that are intentionally added to food for various reasons. What do we do about all the additives found in our foods today? Are they safe? Can they cause illness? Whatever food product we purchase—candy bars, soda, meat, crackers, flour, sweeteners—we can be almost certain that one or more additives are present. The following is a quick overview of some of the most commonly encountered food additives.

The Sweet Ones

Many of us may be lulled into complacency by thinking we can ingest an artificial sweetener when we want to avoid consuming sugar. But while we may not put on the pounds, we may be inviting health problems. Here is some information on some of the better known sweeteners found on your grocer's shelves.

Acesulfame-K, sold under the brand names Sunette or Sweet One, is synthesized from ketones and oxocarbonic acid. Each serving contains less than 4 calories and is equal in sweetness to two teaspoons of sugar, and it can be used in baking. Acesulfame-K is used in chewing gum, dry beverage mixes, confections, canned fruit, gelatins, puddings, and custards, in addition to being a table-top sweetener. The FDA does not report any toxic effect, but the Center for Science in the Public Interest reported that in two separate animal studies, animals fed acesulfame-K were more likely to develop tumors than those in a control group.

Aspartame (NutraSweet or Equal) is derived from two amino acids, aspartic acid and phenylalanine. It is found in over 6,000 products, including soft drinks, desserts, baked goods, gelatins, gum, frozen desserts, juices, cereals, vitamins, and pharmaceuticals, and is also used as a table sweetener. Persons with phenylketonuria (PKU) must avoid this product, as they lack the enzyme necessary to break down phenylalanine; the accumulation of phenylalanine in the brain can cause mental retardation in children as well as other adverse effects. There have been reports of dizziness, headaches, and epileptic-like episodes linked to the ingestion of aspartame, and at higher than normal temperatures, aspartame may break down to yield methyl alcohol, which produces formaldehyde when oxidized. Dr. Deborah Banker, ophthalmologist and author of *Self Help Vision Care,* claims that aspartame oxidizes to formaldehyde when ingested. It has also been implicated in dry eye syndrome. If you are diabetic, you should consult your physician before using this product.

Saccharin (Sweet 'N Low, Sugar Twin) has been in use since 1879. In 1977, the FDA announced it would ban the use of saccharin in foods, based on Canadian studies that linked it to bladder cancer in laboratory animals. At the time, Americans consumed 5 million pounds of saccharin yearly, 74 percent in diet soda, 14 percent in dietetic food, and 12 percent as a tabletop sweetener. The Calorie Control Council, an organization comprising commercial producers and users of saccharin, howled in protest, and the FDA, urged by Congress, delayed the ban, although warning labels were instituted. Britain banned saccharin in 1979 for uses other than as a tabletop sweetener. France has outlawed its use except in nonprescription drugs, and Germany restricts its use in certain foods and beverages.

The Colorings

Food colorings have also received their share of scrutiny, and a number of them have been withdrawn for use in food. Those that remain, although they may still be of questionable safety, are classified by the FDA as GRAS—*g*enerally *r*ecognized *a*s *s*afe—and are still allowed for use in food products.

USFD&C Red Dye #3 has been banned from cosmetics and some foods because it has been termed a carcinogen, but it is still on the market. Some 180,000 pounds of it were used in 1990, in products including maraschino cherries and red pistachio nuts. Red #3 can cause seizures and menstrual problems, and has been found to increase the risk of brain tumors in rats.

USFD&C Blue #2 (triphenylmethane, a coal-tar derivative), is approved for use in both foods and drugs. It can be found in bottled soft drinks, bakery products, cereals, candy, confections, powdered drink mixes, mint-flavored jelly, frozen desserts, and rinses, and is used as a dye for kidney tests and testing milk. Blue #2 has produced malignant skin tumors in laboratory animals. USFD&C Blue #4, approved for use in drugs and cosmetics, also needs further study.

USFD&C Yellow #5 (tartrazine, another coal-tar derivative) is approved for use in foods, drugs, and cosmetics. It is found in prepared breakfast cereals, imitation strawberry jelly, bottled soft drinks, gelatin desserts, ice cream, sherbets, powdered drink mixes, candy, confections, baked products, spaghetti, and puddings. It is also used in hair colorings, rinses, hair-waving fluids, bath salts, and many over-the-counter and prescription drugs. It may cause allergic reactions in susceptible people, including hives, stuffy nose, and, occasionally, severe breathing difficulties. Persons sensitive to aspirin may also be sensitive to this dye.

The Food and Nutrition Act of 1994 mandates that color additives must be listed on the labels of foods and other products. For Yellow #5, additional information is required on the label regarding possible allergic responses.

The Preservers

Since ancient times, people have sought means to preserve foods from spoiling. Pickling, salting, drying, and jellying have been traditional means, but these methods, while extending the time in which the food can be eaten, also transform foods. Modern methods aim to preserve foods while leaving them closer to their original forms, but they may cause some health problems as well.

Butylated hydroxyanisole (BHA) and butylated hydroxytoluene (BHT) prevent oxidation and retard rancidity when added to foods containing oil. However, animal studies suggest that BHA may be carcinogenic. Studies on BHT are divided. Some say it causes cancers, others that it prevents them. Although BHT is currently classified as GRAS, the FDA is pursuing further studies on this additive. It is prohibited as a food additive in England.

That lovely red color in corned beef, ham, and hot dogs is due to the presence of potassium nitrates. While nitrate inhibits the growth of botulism-causing bacteria and it is in itself harmless, bacteria found in foods and in the blood easily convert it to nitrite, which combines with natural stomach and food chemicals to form nitrosamine, a cancer-causing substance. The high temperatures at which many of these foods, especially bacon, are cooked, can cause this transformation to occur. Bacon and other meats cured with ascorbic acid or erythorbic acid, which inhibits the formation of nitrosamines, are safer—but they still contain dangerous saturated fats.

Like the vivid color of dried fruits? It's sulfites that keep them glowing. There are six sulfites currently classified as GRAS: sulfur dioxide, sodium sulfate, sodium and potassium bisulfite, and sodium and potassium metabisulfite. The use of these substances is extremely common in processed foods, but they must be listed on the label. They are not supposed to be used on fresh foods sold in supermarkets and restaurants. Nevertheless, sulfite dioxide fumigation is still used on such products as table grapes. Sulfites are now suspect for a number of allergic problems. They can cause acute asthma attacks, loss of consciousness, anaphylactic shock, diarrhea, and nausea in susceptible individuals.

The Substitutes and Other Additives

In addition to sweeteners, colorings, and preservatives, there are many other additives found in food products. There are flavor-enhancers, emulsifiers, stabilizers, and numerous "substitute" ingredients.

Simplesse is a fat substitute made from whey (a byproduct of cheese) that is dried and broken down into microparticles with the same texture and particle size of fat. It can be used in any food product that requires fat, although in baking, recipes need to be adjusted to maintain the proper balance between liquid and dry ingredients. Simplesse is generally considered safe because it is a food product.

Olestra is a synthetic fat substitute that can be used at high temperatures. Its safety has been questioned by the Center for Science in the Public Interest, among others. It may lead to depletion of the fat-soluble vitamins (A, E, D, and K) because these vitamins may dissolve in Olestra and be eliminated from the body. Because it is not digested or assimilated by the body, it can also cause digestive problems. In the manufacturer's own studies, a third of the volunteers got diarrhea when they ate 20 grams of Olestra a day, about the amount in a single two-ounce serving of potato chips. It can also cause anal leakage resulting in greasy feces and stained underwear, and may cause liver problems.

Monosodium glutamate (MSG) is the monosodium salt of glutamic acid, one of the amino acids, and it is used to enhance flavor in a wide variety of food. It is found in Asian takeout food, many processed foods, hydrolyzed vegetable protein, bouillon cubes, and lots of flavor-enhanced foods. In addition to being high in sodium, MSG can cause symptoms of sensitivity in susceptible people, including headaches, chest tightness, and a burning sensation along the forearms or in the back of the neck. It is known to cause brain damage and reproductive dysfunction in both male and female lab animals. There are some studies in the literature indicating that an excess of glutamates may be responsible for the death of cells in the eye. While no direct connection has been established between MSG and eye damage, for glaucoma patients, it is probably a good idea to limit or avoid foods containing MSG.

Carrageenan is a carbohydrate derived from seaweed that is used as a stabilizer and emulsifier in oils, cosmetics, and foods. You will probably find it listed as one of the ingredients in chocolate flavored drinks, pressure-dispensed whipped cream, ice cream, frozen custard, sherbets, ices, cheese spreads, salad dressings, artificially sweetened jam, and jellies. While it is generally considered to be relatively safe, its use as a food additive is still being studied.

AND NOW FOR CAFFEINE

Many of us can give up red meat but refuse to part with our morning coffee, even though we know it can cause nervousness, stomach distress, and insomnia, and may aggravate fibrocystic disease. Coffee is one of the substances that can cause your system to become overly acidic. Some practitioners advise glaucoma patients to avoid coffee and other foods, such as tea and chocolate, that contain caffeine, but studies on its effects are inconclusive. Neither Rita nor I drink coffee. We believe that it is probably a good idea to minimize your intake of caffeine.

WHAT ABOUT ALCOHOL?

You may have heard that liquor lowers intraocular pressure. This is true to some extent—a drink or two does lower IOP in some people. However, the effect wears off, even as it gives you a false sense that you have your IOP under control. Also, the breakdown of alcohol in the body generates harmful free radicals. Some experts therefore advise that people with glaucoma limit their intake of alcohol. It is best to be on the safe side and imbibe hard drinks sparingly, if at all.

PLANNING YOUR MEALS

Now that you know the importance of your diet for the health of your eyes, and, of course, your entire body, what do you eat? The best general advice we can give is to adapt the U.S. Department of Agriculture's daily recommendations—six to eleven servings of bread, cereal, rice, and pasta; three to five servings of vegetables; two to four servings of fruit; two to three servings of milk, yogurt, or cheese; and two to three servings of meat, poultry, fish, or legumes—bearing in mind that the less processed a food is and the fewer additives it contains, the better it is for you. Thus, whole wheat products are healthier than refined wheat products; brown rice is preferable to white rice. Organic is better than nonorganic. Sugar and other sweeteners should be used in the tiniest amounts possible or not at all.

For breakfast, instead of having processed breakfast cereals such as corn flakes, crisp rice cereal, oat flakes, and the like, try hot oatmeal, corn grits, millet, quinoa, or teff. With your bread, cereal, rice, and pasta, think whole-grain, low-sugar. Your vegetables and beans can do for lunch and act as side dishes to your main meal. Try to buy fresh produce and either cook and eat it immediately or eat it raw. When cooking dried beans, simmer them only until they are tender, not mushy.

With fruit, fresh is better than canned. Fresh-squeezed juices have a somewhat higher vitamin content and taste better than pasteurized or reconstituted juices. Eat fruits in season, and watch out for imported fruits. They may contain a load of pesticides and other chemicals.

Some nutritionists believe that milk products can cause or contribute to a variety of illnesses. Many nutritionists state that consuming any type of dairy products causes mucus production, and they advise eating these foods occasionally or not at all. In addition, many adults, especially African-Americans, Asian-Americans, and some people of Mediterranean ancestry, tend to be lactose intolerant. This condition is caused by a lack of sufficient lactase, an enzyme necessary to digest milk sugar. If you are lactose intolerant, skip the dairy products and seek other dietary sources of calcium, such as dark green leafy vegetables and/or sardines or salmon with the bones. Yogurt may be palatable, especially if it is made with active bacteria (*Lactobacillus bulgaricus, Streptococcus thermophilus, L. yugurti, L. acidophilus,* or *L. bifidus*). These helpful bacteria are normally found in the intestines and are important for proper digestion.

For needed protein and minerals, nonvegetarians might opt to eat one or two servings daily of fish, chicken, or turkey. (Note that the standard serving size is three ounces, which is less than what many people think of as a serving of meat or poultry.) Chicken or turkey should be skinned and the fat trimmed away. When purchasing fish, the smaller, the better. Fresh sardines are good. Big fish should be eaten rarely because toxic chemicals such as mercury may accumulate in their tissues. Red meat and pork—if you must have them at all—can be used *occasionally* to diversify your diet, if they are trimmed of all fat.

Nuts and eggs might substitute for fish or meat occasionally.

According to Dr. Ben Lane of the Nutritional Optometry Institute, if eggs are cooked gently, just to the soft stage, they are a good whole food, and if you do not have a cholesterol problem, you can enjoy an egg a day. Egg yolks contain many valuable nutrients, among them chromium and sulfur. Nuts are high in protein, but are also high in fat, so they should not be eaten every day. Almonds and nuts containing essential fatty acids—peanuts, walnuts, Brazil nuts—are best.

Dr. Lane also recommends that the best way to be sure you get all the necessary amino acids, vitamin C, vitamin E, chromium, and magnesium is to eat the following minimally processed foods: sprouted or pre-soaked whole grains and legumes; almonds, Brazil nuts, walnuts, and sunflower seeds; raw milk cheeses and seed cheeses made from sunflower seeds and wheat berries; homemade yogurt and buttermilk; and melon with lettuce or celery. He advises against eating a heavy protein diet and eating hydrogenated fats such as margarine and shortening. Hydrogenated fats contain a kind of mutated fatty acids called trans fatty acids. In a study he conducted of 400 patients, including 52 with ocular hypertension and/or glaucoma, Dr. Lane found that pigmentary-dispersion and exfoliative glaucomas were strongly associated with excessive protein and trans fatty acid intake. Excessive consumption of protein is common among Americans because we eat too much of foods like meat, poultry, fish, cheese, and eggs. A high-animal-protein diet also causes the loss of calcium and other minerals through excretion in the urine.

What about all those other mouth-watering foods we all love? Well, you can eat them sometimes. Salad dressing, condiments, ice milk, ice cream, sour cream, cream cheese, peanut butter, various chips, potato salad, fried potatoes, cookies, cake, white rice, and fast foods, to name some of the most popular, fall into the "sometimes" category.

WHAT ABOUT WATER?

In addition to eating a healthy diet, nutritionists generally advise drinking eight glasses of water a day. Yet many of us have heard that excessive water-drinking raises IOP. Is this true? Well, yes and no. If you drink a quart of water in the space of thirty minutes—as suggested in some dietary programs—you may indeed raise your IOP. Spacing your water intake out over an entire day should pose no problem.

Generally speaking, if you drink up to eight ounces of water each time, you should not run into problems with IOP, provided each glass is taken one to two hours after the preceding one. The benefits of water cannot be overemphasized. Water removes toxins from your system and lubricates your body. It is the principal chemical component of the body, comprising 65 percent of body weight for males, 55 percent for females. It is indispensable for metabolic activity within your cells, and it is the medium in which the chemical reactions in your body can take place. Outside of the cells, it is the principal way that substances are transported throughout your body. So drink up—it's important to your health.

Eating healthfully is not a new concept. The history of healthful food collection and preparation dates back to the ancient cultures of China, India, and Japan. Napoleon observed that an army travels on its stomach. Our forefathers coined "three squares a day," a maxim that still survives today. So what happened? Unfortunately, for many of us the food picture has changed. While we are fortunate to have a plentiful supply of food, the way in which foods are grown and processed in this country may contribute to the illnesses we have. The foods we eat may contain questionable additives and other substances, or they simply may not provide our bodies with enough of the essential vitamins and nutrients. Or we may not be eating enough of the right foods.

Interest in how food and supplements can fend off the ravages of glaucoma has waxed and waned since the 1940s, but with the explosion of supplements now on the market, new knowledge about how free radical activity may damage such vital areas of the eye as the optic nerve, and anecdotal evidence from complementary therapists of the benefits of supplements, interest in these subjects is now quickening among practitioners of traditional medicine. There have been a number of long-range studies that shed light on the effect of nutrition on the eyes. For example, a study done in Beaver Dam, Colorado, found that people who took multiple vitamin supplements had a 40-percent lower chance of developing cataracts than those not taking supplements, even taking into account such factors as drinking and smoking habits. Further, they found that people who ate foods containing saturated fat and cholesterol were more likely to develop macular degeneration than other people. The same researchers are now looking at patients with glaucoma, but have not yet come up with data to support a particular diet or intake of nutrients.

A good diet and supplementation with vitamins and minerals may not only help to reduce intraocular pressure, but may, in fact, contribute to the health of the optic nerve. Scientists now consider this to be an important factor—perhaps the most important factor—in preventing the loss of vision due to glaucoma. Most important, eating for eye health need not wait for confirming studies. Both Rita and I have profited from a change in our diets and the use of supplements. Taking charge of what and how you eat is but another rung on the ladder of becoming a respant, a person responsible for his or her own treatment.

CHAPTER 11

Grab the Reins of Responsibility

The fault, dear Brutus, is not in our stars, but in ourselves, that we are underlings.

William Shakespeare (*Julius Caesar*)

Consumers Union recently surveyed 70,000 readers and found that about one fourth of them were dissatisfied with their health care. About 29 percent of all the readers were unhappy that their doctors never sought their opinions about their medical conditions, and the same number complained that they were never told how they might improve their health with lifestyle changes. Some 21 percent resented being kept waiting.

The very nature of glaucoma can create problems in our relationships with our doctors. First, it is a chronic, and often progressive, disease, so treatment is never finished. Then, too, especially in the early stages, we are asked to use medications that reduce our vision and/or make us feel ill (or at the very least under par), even though we are not experiencing any pain or loss of sight. Under these circumstances, possible long-term gains may not appear to be worth the discomfort of the treatment.

Over thirty years ago, at an annual meeting of the Pacific Coast Ophthalmological Society in California, one of the speakers described three basic types of doctor-patient relationships:

1. Active–passive. A passive patient is acted on by the doctor. Most often this relationship is confined to infants, people with severe injuries, and comatose individuals.

2. Guidance–cooperative. The patient comes to the doctor seeking

help and expects to follow his or her directions. In essence, this relationship is not unlike the relationship between parent and child. This relationship is the most common of the three types.

3. Mutual participation. An adult-to-adult cooperative relationship, this is the best type of relationship for a person with a chronic disease, such as glaucoma, to have with his or her physician. Management of such diseases depends upon the full cooperation of the patient, including consultation with the doctor at established intervals.

So what has happened to the doctor-patient relationship in the past thirty years? Do we now have more democratic, adult-to-adult relationships with our doctors? To hear members of our support group talk about it, the answer is a resounding no. Rita recalled a sick sense of identification after viewing a television program in which self-healing advocate Dr. Bernie Siegel showed drawings that patients made of themselves with their doctors. Some of these, astoundingly, were very much like the drawings small children make. In children's drawings, parents or other adults often appear as enormous figures, towering over the small child. In these drawings, the patients lay on examining tables while monster-sized doctors hovered over them.

Some members of our group tell of following their doctors' instructions and finding their conditions worsening. Others relate stories of being rebuffed when they made attempts to establish more mature, equal relationships with their physicians. In some teaching hospital environments, people complain that they see a doctor for only a few moments—and that only after a technician, resident fellow, or assistant has completed the preliminary examination.

Are doctors uncaring, unfeeling, out of touch with their patients' needs? Perhaps. Yet the majority of doctors I and others have known have rejoiced with us when we held our own and were saddened when the glaucoma progressed. Then where does the problem lie? Are these isolated incidences, or is this a widespread problem?

The suspicion that many doctors are insensitive to the needs of patients is being addressed nationwide. Hospitals are incorporating sensitivity training sessions into their residency programs for doctors. In these programs, medical students and residents assume the role of patient. They may wear blurred contact lenses, walk around with joint-restricting splints, listen to actors impersonating elderly and/or ill persons, and/or spend the night in a hospital bed in traction or with

IVs in their arms, to name but a few of the techniques used. Reports from the institutions that have used this type of training are encouraging. Many of the doctors who have been through such programs say that the experience changed the way they look at their patients.

In the long run, this is good news. But for the immediate future, it may not solve the problems that patients complain about. Ultimately, it is up to each of us to choose his or her doctor wisely, and work to establish a responsible adult-to-adult relationship with that practitioner.

CHOOSING A DOCTOR

The first step in developing a satisfactory doctor-patient relationship, obviously, involves your choice of doctor. In this age of specialization, it is probably wise to seek out a glaucomatologist, if your case is complicated and if this is possible in your locality. Your family physician, the American Optometric Association, a glaucoma support group, and possibly friends and acquaintances who have similar problems can all be helpful in locating people with the qualifications you are looking for. The Glaucoma Foundation can supply a list of glaucoma specialists in your area as well.

The next step is to select a practitioner from among those you are considering. How do you know when a doctor is the right one for you? For most of us, intuition or a feeling of rapport clues us in. A first impression is often the most accurate, for that is when your antennae are alerted. Signs you may pick up include the condition of the office, the lighting, and the availability of appropriate reading materials, such as booklets and pamphlets describing your condition. Noting how patients respond to the doctor can also affect your judgment. Finally, your insurance coverage may be a factor in your decision.

Set the tone for your relationship on your first visit to the doctor. Supply your doctor with your medical history. Inform your doctor if there is a family history of glaucoma, and keep your doctor abreast of any other health problems you may have as well as any new medications you may need to take for them. Write down in advance any questions you would like to ask so that you will not forget any of them while you're in the office (for lists of suggested questions, see What to Ask the Doctor, page 198). If you find you have trouble remembering what the doctor tells you when you get home, bring

What to Ask the Doctor

Being an active partner in the management of your glaucoma means, first of all, being informed. A good doctor should discuss all aspects of your condition and its treatment with you, and should be willing to answer any questions you have. Some of the questions you will want to know the answers to are outlined below.

If you have just been diagnosed:

- What type of glaucoma do I have?
- How does this type differ from other glaucomas?
- Could lifestyle factors such as caffeine, alcohol, or smoking affect my prognosis?

If your doctor prescribes medication:

- Are there any other treatment options?
- What effect will the medication prescribed have on my vision?
- What is the prognosis, if I take the medication faithfully, that my glaucoma will not worsen?
- Are there risks in taking the medication?
- What are the benefits from taking the medication?
- Would not taking the medication cause a loss of sight?
- Is there an alternative to taking medication?
- How do I put the drops in my eyes?
- What side effects might I expect from this medication?
- Would you take this medication if you were me?

Once you are in treatment:

- What is the state of my intraocular pressure?
- What was the result of my last visual field test?

- If my condition worsens, should I seek a second opinion?
- Are there other diagnostic tests that might give a more accurate diagnosis of my condition and, if so, what would I have to do to have these tests done?
- What problems or warning signs should I be on the lookout for?
- Should I bring someone else along for routine follow-up visits?

If either laser treatment or filtration surgery is recommended:

- Would it be wise to seek a second opinion?
- What will the procedure be like?
- Will I experience pain or discomfort?
- What are the typical success rates for this procedure for people with my condition?
- How many times have you performed this procedure?
- Do I have a choice between inpatient and outpatient treatment and, if so, which setting would be best for me and why?
- What precautions should I take after the procedure?
- How do people usually feel after this procedure?
- What do I need to do to insure that my recovery is safe and effective?
- Should someone accompany me when I go for the procedure?
- What should I do to prepare myself for the procedure?
- Is there a choice between having local or general anesthesia? If so, which is recommended and why?
- Will the procedure stop the progression of my glaucoma?
- Will I need to use medication after the procedure?
- How long will it be before I can resume my normal activities?
- If antibacterial and/or cortisone drops are prescribed, how long after the procedure will I have to take them?

If your vision worsens:

- When should I be referred to a low-vision specialist?
- Can you assist me in seeking help from my state authority?

If you have narrow-angle glaucoma:

- What should I do if I have an acute glaucoma attack?
- What are the pros and cons of having prophylactic laser treatment?

Armed with the answers to these questions, and any others that arise in your mind, you will be better able to truly work with your doctor to maximize your sight and your health.

along a spouse or friend who can verify the information, or invest in a pocket tape recorder to record your doctor's words.

Once the relationship is established, you can expect your doctor to:

- Tell you the state of your eye condition—your intraocular pressure, your visual field, the condition of your optic nerve, and any other relevant information.
- Answer all of your questions about your condition.
- Explain the use of all medications prescribed, including what they will do, how much should be taken (and when), and the proper method for taking them.
- Tell you what procedures to follow if you get a glaucoma attack.
- If laser treatment or surgery is required, discuss with you all post-operative procedures and precautions.
- Refer you to a low-vision specialist if your condition worsens.

In this adult-adult relationship, you are responsible for:

- Complying with your doctor's instructions.

- Keeping your appointments or, if you cannot, giving your doctor twelve to twenty-four hours' notice of cancellation.
- Informing your doctor immediately if you have an allergic or other adverse reaction to medication.
- Promptly bringing to your doctor's attention any of the following alarm signals: red eye(s), pain in the head or eye that persists even after you have taken an analgesic, sudden loss of sight, or swollen eye(s).

The relationship between you and your doctor is such a sensitive one, and your health and well-being depend upon both your doctor's care and your self-care. Many people find that establishing a credo that explicitly lays out how they prefer to be treated by their doctors helps them to crystallize their thoughts about dealing with this disease. You can use this sample to develop your own:

This I know:

I have glaucoma.

I know that I can lose my sight if I do not participate in a management program.

I know that drugs and surgical procedures involve risks.

I am aware that many people become severely visually impaired or go blind.

Therefore:

Do not frighten me with dire prognoses.

Extend good thoughts, advice, and encouragement, and especially hope.

Tell me what I need to know to help myself.

Don't discourage complementary therapies if I think they will help.

Please understand: I rely on you to help in a positive way. I am not against good medicine if it has been shown to be a means toward prolonging my eyesight. I believe in the body's mental powers and immunological activities as well as its spiritual capabilities. I need all the help I can get from these sources. So when I talk about them, don't dismiss them as nonsense. I will do whatever I can to maintain and retain my sight.

I have read about people who have fought back, and know of people who claim they have been able to avoid a diagnosis of glaucoma, and I am encouraged by these reports.

Once you have developed your own credo, you can look at it from time to time, as you need to, to help you keep your focus and perspective.

COPING WITH GLAUCOMA THERAPY

Whether you are a newly diagnosed patient or a long-time veteran of glaucoma, you will probably find yourself in the position of having to cope with the available therapies for your disease, from the instillation of eye drops to laser treatment to various surgical procedures. Each of these treatments carries with it a burden of individual responsibility. Of the three, medication is the most pervasive, for just about all of us are on some form of medication for our glaucoma. Some of us also must take medications for other short- or long-term diseases, and these too may affect the condition of the eyes, especially with narrow-angle glaucoma.

Make Friends With Your Eye Drops

Some of us regard our drugs as two-faced—we are pleased when they stem the tide of the glaucoma but, at the same time, we bemoan the effect they have on our bodies, especially if they diminish what we see or if they irritate our eyes. Understanding the properties of different drugs can, at times, help in learning to better tolerate a drug that is useful in controlling intraocular pressure.

Your physician's primary consideration in deciding to prescribe any medication is that he or she considers it to be the most effective for controlling your condition. If you have faith in your physician's judgment, then you should have faith that the medication will do its job. It is wise to have your prescriptions filled by a pharmacist who keeps a record of all the medications you take so that he or she can advise you of possible drug interactions. A responsible pharmacist will perform this service. A pharmacist can also tell you about any side effects you may experience. Some side effects are minor, while others may be cause for concern. Some medication side effects are caused by preservatives or other additives, rather than by the active components. If you experience any unusual symptoms when you start taking a prescription medication, report this to your physician immediately.

The National Eye Institute states that one quarter of glaucoma patients who are prescribed timolol (Timoptic) and one third of glaucoma patients who are prescribed pilocarpine are negligent in the use of these medications. They use up to 25 percent less than their prescribed doses. If you are supposed to use prescription medication, follow your doctor's instructions exactly. Don't cheat on your eyes.

Always take your medications on time. If your doctor tells you to take your medication four times a day, that is easily broken down to taking it when you wake up in the morning; at lunchtime; at dinnertime; and before you go to bed. A prescription for three times a day translates to taking medication every eight hours; twice a day is every twelve hours. If you need more sleep than usual, taking your medication one hour earlier or later is not a cause for alarm. However, if you miss a dose, do not double up on the next dose. Simply resume your regimen with the next regularly scheduled dose. If your physician does not give you instructions on instilling your eye drops, or if you are not sure about how to do this for best effect, refer to page 87 for a discussion of how to do it properly.

Be aware also of other factors, such as diet, that may affect your medications. Some medications work best when taken on an empty stomach. Others are most effective if taken with food. Still others are fine in combination with some foods but not others. Food interactions are not generally a problem with topical medications such as eye drops, but some oral medications can cause problems if mixed with certain foods. Ask your doctor or pharmacist about any recommendations or precautions regarding food interactions.

If you take more than one medication, keep a record of everything you need to know about each one, including the name, address, and phone number of the doctor or doctors who prescribed it; where the prescription was filled; precautions regarding interactions with other medicines, foods, alcohol, and/or tobacco; directions for taking it; and the date for refills. Let someone else in your household know where this record is kept. If you live alone, let a friend or family member know. If you have trouble remembering when to take what—which can happen if you have to take more than one drug—using medication charts can be helpful.

Medication charts are useful aids for remembering which drugs to take at which times. Such charts can usually be obtained from doctors or eye clinics, or you can create a simple chart yourself. Use a separate chart for each medication. Follow the example in Figure 11.1 (see page 204), listing the days of the week and the times you are supposed to take the medication in question. Post the charts inside the cabinet

Figure 11.1 Sample Medications Chart

Day	Time 1 6:00 a.m.	Time 2 12:00 noon	Time 3 6:00 p.m.	Time 4 12:00 mid
Sunday		✓	✓	✓
Monday	✓	✓	✓	✓
Tuesday	✓	✓		
Wednesday				
Thursday				
Friday				
Saturday				

where you store your medications and after you take each dose, place a check in the appropriate box.

Running out of medication can be disastrous to your eyes. Always have a spare bottle of drops on hand and enough tablets to last a month.

If you are pursuing alternative therapies and think you are doing well and may be able to dispense with medication, wait until you see your doctor for confirmation before you discontinue your medication. We all touch our eyeballs from time to time, hoping to assess the state of our pressure. While a practiced physician can sometimes determine the condition of your IOP this way, only a tonometer can give an accurate reading.

Take Care of Your Medications

Once, during an unusually hot, humid spell, my Neptazane tablets, stored in the medicine cabinet in my bathroom, grew beards. Subsequently I discovered that the medicine cabinet is the worst place to store medicines. In that moist, warm environment, many medical preparations can undergo subtle (or not so subtle) changes, lose strength, or actually become toxic. A cool closet is a better place for storage.

When you travel, your medicines may be subject to changes in temperature that can destroy their effectiveness. In summer, the temperature can reach well into the hundreds of degrees inside a parked car, on a picnic table, or even in your pocket. Such extremes of heat can have a particularly negative effect. For example, timolol (Timoptic) loses 20 percent of its potency at 212°F, and at approximately 250°F, its shelf life is shortened to thirty-five weeks. However, it can be frozen and thawed and not lose its effectiveness. After being heated to 219°F, dorzolamide (Trusopt) remains useful for only one week; if the temperature is raised to 250°F, this drops to three days—compared with two years if kept at 54°F. One of our group members carries his eye drops in a small vacuum bottle that has been stored overnight in the refrigerator.

For virtually all medications, the buildup of heat is to be avoided. If you order medication by mail, be sure to get it into a cool place as soon as it is delivered. If you are away during the day, arrange to have a neighbor pick up packages rather than risk having them bask in the sun in a mailbox or on a doorstep. Always be on the lookout for signs of medicine deterioration. Epinephrine, for example, oxidizes and needs to be kept cold. If a medication containing epinephrine becomes discolored, this may be a sign of oxidation, and the bottle should be replaced with a new prescription. Similarly, if a medication gives off an unusual odor, consult your pharmacist.

Transferring medication to other containers is not advisable. Those snappy little pill boxes, unfortunately, do not provide for proper storage or identification of medication. If you need to carry medication with you while away from home, it is better to use an old container from an earlier prescription that you have saved for this purpose. That way, you will have the proper identification and instructions for the drug.

When taking your medications, always cast light on the subject. Taking medication in the dark can lead to wrong applications. Sometimes it's difficult to tell one bottle from another, especially if they are both the same size. However, glaucoma medications come with color-coded containers and/or caps. Most of us take more than one eye drop. The color codes help us to differentiate between the medications and remember the times we are supposed to take them. In good light it is easier to see the color coding of your medications.

Never use any medication after its indicated expiration date. Discard out-of-date medications, whether prescription or over-the-counter. If you have sample pills that were given to you some time ago on a trial basis and you don't know the expiration date, don't risk using them. They may have outlived their safety zone.

Similarly, never use medication that was prescribed for someone else, even if they swear to the medication's effectiveness. And do not assume that an over-the-counter medication will be safe for you just because it requires no prescription. These products too can cause drug interactions. There are numerous medications on the market that specifically should *not* be taken by persons with glaucoma, especially narrow-angle glaucoma. The key word for medications that can aggravate glaucoma is *anticholinergic.* Any drug that has this property should be avoided. (*See* pages 207 through 210 for more information on medications to avoid.)

Beware of Polypharmacy

How many medicines do you take a day? A week? A month? Michael, who discovered that he had glaucoma following a cataract operation, worried that the Timoptic added to his medical routine would cause serious breathing problems, for he already took medication to control asthma and heart disease. Michael is an aware consumer who reads all the available information on drugs carefully before taking them, so he knew that beta-blockers such as Timoptic can sometimes have undesirable effects on people with asthma. Yet many among us are not that well informed, and unthinkingly swallow multiple pills and elixirs, with little regard for the possibility that they may combine to produce negative effects.

Polypharmacy is just that—taking two or more prescription medications simultaneously, whether for the same disorder or for different ailments. This is sometimes unavoidable, but it can pose hazards to the unaware consumer. Senior citizens, the group most likely to have glaucoma, are also the most likely to be taking multiple medications. Although seniors make up only 13 percent of the population, they take 30 percent of all prescription drugs.

In this era in which there is medication for every problem, some medications may precipitate a major glaucoma attack in a person with narrow-angle glaucoma. These include the sulfa drugs, which cause the lens of the eye to swell, narrowing the angle and possibly closing it altogether. Certain antidepressants, antispasmodics, antihistamines, anti-Parkinsonian agents dilate the pupils, which too may cause narrowing of the angles. Persons with nanophthalmos, or small eye (see page 100), may be especially vulnerable to a glaucoma attack as a result of the effects of these drugs, for if the pupil of such an eye dilates, the chances are greater than normal that the iris may move into the drainage channel and cause blockage.

Some types of drugs that may cause problems for glaucoma patients include the following:

- *Alpha-chymotrypsin*. This enzyme, used in cataract extraction to lyse (cut) the ligaments holding the cataractous lens in place, can cause IOP to rise. In addition, the cut ligaments may get into the trabecular meshwork. Other drugs used in cataract surgery, *hyaluronic acid* and *sodium chondroitin sulfate*, which protect the cornea during the placement of the lens implant, can increase the viscosity of the fluid in the eye, making it harder for the fluid to exit. Washing these substances out of the eye at the end of surgery may prevent a rise in IOP as a result.

- *Analgesics*. Many over-the-counter painkillers carry FDA warnings cautioning people with glaucoma to consult their physicians before using them. Orphenadrine citrate (Norgesic) has been reported to cause problems for glaucoma. Aspirin, that old standby for treating aches, pains, and whatever, may be dangerous for people who have narrow-angle glaucoma, for it can cause lens swelling, myopia, a shallowing of the anterior chamber, and a rise in pressure. If you experience blurred vision after taking aspirin, you should count yourself among the susceptible and avoid this drug in the future.

- *Anesthetic agents*. For the most part, drugs used for general anesthesia lower intraocular pressure. However, a rise in pressure has been documented with the anesthetic agents succinylcholine, ketamine, nitrous oxide, and chloral hydrate. Since these drugs are administered by anesthesiologists, if you must undergo a surgical procedure, have the anesthesiologist check with your glaucomatologist on the best anesthetic approach.

- *Anti-arthritis drugs*. Chloroquine (Aralen) may cause retinal changes.

- *Antidepressants*. Amitriptyline (Elavil), phenelzine (Nardil), and tranylcypromine (Parnate) can all aggravate glaucoma.

- *Antihypertensive agents*. Certain drugs prescribed for high blood pressure can be dangerous. Clonidine (Catapres) may precipitate an attack of angle closure in susceptible patients. Other blood pressure drugs, including chlorothiazide (Diuril and others); hydrochlorothiazide (Esidrix, Hydro-Diuril, Oretic, and others); polythiazide (Renese and others); chlorthalidone (Biogroton, Hygroton, and others); hydralazine (Apresoline); spironolactone (Aldactone and others); and trichlormethiazide have been documented to cause the lens to swell, putting these drugs out of bounds for the patient with narrow-angle glaucoma.

- *Antinausea drugs.* Scopolamine (Donnagel, Transderm Scōp) may cause a rise in intraocular pressure. Use dimenhydrinate (Dramamine) instead for motion sickness.

- *Anti-Parkinsonian agents.* Trihexyphenidyl (Artane) is an anticholinergic agent (see page 206), and may precipitate an attack of angle-closure glaucoma.

- *Antipsychotic agents.* Perphenazine (Trilafon) and fluphenazine (Prolixin), which are used to treat psychological disorders, belong to a class of drugs associated with the deposition of pigment in the eye. They also have anticholinergic effects.

- *Antispasmodic agents.* Propantheline (Pro-Banthine) and dicyclomine (Bentyl), used in the treatment of peptic ulcers and to treat irritable bowel syndrome, respectively, are both contraindicated in glaucoma.

- *Cardiac agents.* Disopyramide (Norpace), which is used to combat arrhythmia (irregular heart rhythm), is an anticholinergic agent.

- *Cocaine.* In addition to its many other harmful effects, this drug dilates the pupils and can cause angle closure. Persons with open-angle glaucoma also should avoid the use of this drug.

- *Hormones.* The sex hormones estrogen and progesterone, present in oral contraceptives and in drugs used for hormone replacement therapy, may affect IOP because it rises and falls with hormonal rhythms. Rita discovered that her IOP rose and fell in a consistent pattern with her menstrual cycle. Her doctor dismissed the idea, but a friend who also has glaucoma and is the same age concurred with Rita's observation of a rise in pressure during the menstrual period. Changes in IOP during the menstrual cycle have been noted by other ophthalmologists. I suspect that my glaucoma, or at the least my visual field and optic changes, might be due partly to the oral contraceptives I took during my thirties. And there is a small study in the literature that establishes this effect—that younger women who suffer acute angle-closure attacks do so during their menstrual periods. Paradoxically, however, some researchers claim that women with open-angle glaucoma who take an estrogen-progesterone combination experience a lowering of their IOPs. Clearly, more research is needed in this area.

- *Parasympatholytic agents.* Cyclopentolate (Cyologyl), tropicamide (Mydriacyl), hydroxyamphetamine (Paredrine), atropine (Atropisol, Homatro, Hydrobromide), and scopolamine (Hyoscine), used to dilate the pupil before certain diagnostic procedures, all produce adverse effects in patients with open-angle glaucoma because these drugs raise IOP. The people who are at greatest risk are those who do not know they have glaucoma.
- *Parasympathomimetic agents.* These include the old standbys, pilocarpine and carbachol, which are important in the treatment of open-angle glaucoma and in breaking attacks of angle-closure. But they can precipitate angle closure in patients with narrow angles if they are used for therapy. Pilocarpine can also aggravate glaucoma in patients with uveitis, malignant glaucoma, neovascular glaucoma, or pupillary block glaucoma. In addition, some practitioners caution against using these agents in conjunction with certain other glaucoma drugs, including phospholine iodide (Echothiophate), Demecarium (Humorsol), and disopropyl fluorophosphate (DPF, or Floropryl).
- *Sulfa drugs.* Drugs belonging to this class of antibiotic may be associated with swelling of the lens in some people.
- *Sympathomimetic agents.* Drugs in the epinephrine family are generally used to lower IOP, but in some people these drugs may cause a rise in pressure and dilation of the pupil. They may also precipitate an acute angle-closure attack in people with narrow-angle glaucoma. The phenylephrine family, which includes drugs used as inhalers for asthma or treatment of hemorrhoids, can worsen or even precipitate a glaucoma attack in sensitive patients with repeated usage.
- *Tobacco.* Here is yet another reason to give up smoking. In a study of 100 glaucoma patients, 25 who stopped smoking experienced an

average drop in pressure of 2 to 7 mm Hg after they quit. Seventy-five diehards showed no change. A study involving cataract development found, through statistical analysis of a large group of American male physicians and female nurses, that people who smoked twenty or more cigarettes a day had twice the risk of developing cataracts of people who had never smoked.

- *Vasodilators.* Nitroglycerin, sold under many brand names for the treatment of angina (a type of cardiovascular disease that causes chest pain as the primary symptom), has produced transient partial blackout of vision, but this may be because it causes a fall in blood pressure. It also causes the pupils to dilate, but no cases of glaucoma have been reported as a result. Although there may be questions about the effects of these drugs on glaucoma patients, vasodilators are considered safe for normal patients with narrow-angle glaucoma and for people with open-angle glaucoma.

It is vitally important that any physician you visit be informed about all the medications you are taking, whether they relate to your current complaint or not. For example, most of the drugs described above are likely to be prescribed by a general practitioner or internist, not the ophthalmologist who treats you for glaucoma. That doctor probably will not know about your glaucoma medications unless you mention it. It is therefore always a good idea to raise the subject of other drugs you are taking whenever a doctor prescribes or recommends any medication.

IF SURGERY IS NECESSARY

If medication fails to control your glaucoma, your doctor may recommend a filtering operation. Today, this type of surgery is usually performed on an outpatient basis and you are discharged in a matter of hours. However, if you have a particularly difficult case, your doctor may recommend at least an overnight stay, or a one- to two-day recovery period in the hospital.

A hospital stay should not be a tug-of-war between you and your caretakers. Often, however, there are slip-ups in communication between the nursing staff and the surgeon that can create problems. For example, even though you know what your medication routine should be, your nurse must follow your doctor's instructions. It is a good idea to review with your doctor the instructions for the eye not operated on when you enter the hospital.

I learned this lesson during one of my stays in the hospital for a filtering operation. After surgery, the pressure in my unoperated eye climbed to 35 mm Hg, and I realized that I should have discussed the care for that eye with my doctor. Several years later, with another filtering operation that required only an overnight stay, I again ran into a problem. When the time came, I attempted to put the prescribed drops in my unoperated eye, and the nurse, who had instructions that I needed drops three times a day instead of four, tried to stop me. This taught me to get all of my doctor's instructions in writing before entering the hospital. It is also a good idea to write down any questions you wish to ask of your doctor. This simple activity may save you a lot of grief.

Any time you need care in a hospital, you should take as active a role as possible, and be aware of your rights and responsibilities (see Patients' Rights and Responsibilities, page 212). How easy is it to assert your rights as a patient when you are in the hospital undergoing an operation? Some members of our support group report it has gone "without a hitch." Others have sorry stories to tell. The importance of knowing your rights is perhaps best illustrated by Sara's experience. She was scheduled for cataract removal with a doctor she had confidence in, but found, to her dismay, that two other physicians had been assigned to her case. She was not aware that, because the operation was not an emergency, she could reschedule it to another day, when her chosen physician would be available. So she submitted to the change in plans. Unfortunately, the surgery did not turn out well, and she was left with virtually no sight in that eye.

Remember, *you do have rights.* Whether your hospital bill is paid through Medicare, an HMO plan, a form of Medicaid, or some other insurance provider, your care is being paid for. Furthermore, if you receive less than adequate care and courtesy from any staff member in the hospital, you have a right to bring this to the attention of the hospital authorities. Many hospitals have a patient ombudsman or advocate who will help you untangle any problems with the hospital. In some states, such as New York, Massachusetts, and New Jersey, patients are also entitled to a written discharge plan describing how their health care needs will be met when they leave the hospital.

EVERYDAY EYE SAFETY

One thing we do *not* want is to complicate our lives with eye injuries on top of our glaucoma. Prevent Blindness America has developed

Patients' Rights and Responsibilities

If you need surgery, you should know in advance what you have a right to expect from those engaged in your health care. You should also know what they can realistically expect from you. As a patient, you are entitled to certain basic rights:

- The right to receive all necessary care.
- The right to be discharged when your doctor determines you are ready. Your discharge date must be determined solely by your medical needs, not by your Medicare, your insurance company, or any other payment system.
- The right to be fully informed about decisions affecting your insurance coverage or payment for your hospital stay and any necessary post-hospital care.
- The right to considerate and respectful care.
- The right to give consent for treatment.
- The right to refuse treatment, and to be informed of the medical consequences of such a refusal.
- The right to privacy and confidentiality.
- The right to know the rules and regulations that apply to you as a patient.
- The right to know what other institutions, if any, will be involved in your care.
- The right to know if the hospital proposes to engage in research that affects you.
- The right to reasonable continuity of care and to attentive monitoring of your case from start to finish.
- The right to appeal any written notices you receive from the hospital or your insurance provider stating that you should be discharged, or that your insurance provider or other health care organizations will no longer pay for your hospital care.

- The right to receive an explanation of your bill.

As a patient, you are responsible for:

- Providing, to the best of your knowledge, accurate and complete information about your medical history; reporting any unexpected changes in your condition; and making it clear that you understand what is expected of you.
- Following the treatment plan set up by the practitioner responsible for your care. This may include following instructions of the team of nurses and other health personnel who are charged with coordinating the plan of care. You are responsible for keeping your appointments, arriving on time, and notifying whoever is in charge of your plan if you have to change your schedule.
- Taking responsibility for the outcome if you do not follow the plan of care.
- Meeting the financial obligations of your care as promptly as possible.
- Abiding by hospital rules and regulations affecting your care and conduct.
- Showing consideration for the rights of other patients and hospital personnel in such areas as noise control, smoking, loud conversation, and the number of visitors.
- Showing respect for the property of all other persons (patients and staff) of the hospital.

In many hospitals, you can also count on support from the institution's patient advocate, whose job is to guarantee that patients receive good care while hospitalized.

Adapted from *Lifetimes,* a publication of the American Federation of Teachers.

guidelines for good eye safety practices. One of the most important of these is to wear appropriate eye protection while engaging in potentially eye-endangering activities.

Appropriate eye protection—safety glasses—should be worn by

all persons who work in factories where they may be exposed to flying objects and/or chemicals. At home, safety glasses should be worn for activities such as mowing the lawn, applying fertilizer or pesticides, using hand or power tools, using cleaning agents, or working on the car. In school, students, teachers, visitors, and anyone else exposed to eye hazards in shop and science classes should wear approved eye protection. In school sports, the greatest number of eye injuries are associated with baseball, which suggests that goggles should be worn for that sport, especially by batters and catchers. Of the 2.4 million eye injuries that require emergency-room treatment in the United States each year, some 43,000 are related to sports and recreational activities. An eye injury in youth can lead to glaucoma at a later date.

When choosing eye protection, you should be aware that safety glasses should have the monogram "Z87" on the bridge of the glasses, plus the manufacturer's logo on each temple. Goggles can be purchased at hardware stores, home care centers, and safety equipment suppliers.

What about sunglasses? There are sunglasses and there are sunglasses. You might opt for designer sunglasses or a pair of glasses from a low-vision center, or order a pair out of a catalog provided by one of the low-vision organizations. Whatever you do, be sure that your glasses protect your eyes from the threat posed by ultraviolet (UV) rays, both UVA and UVB. You might want to consider a type of lens that meets the standards of Prevent Blindness America, the American Optometric Association, and the American Academy of Ophthalmology.

Sight-Proof Your Living Quarters

Anyone who has brought up a child knows what it means to childproof your living quarters. A simple low-hanging tablecloth can spell disaster if tugged on by a toddler. Objects placed on a table can tumble on a child, causing bodily injury or, at the very least, a nasty fright. An alert parent safety-checks the home to avoid such mishaps.

The same care that goes into reducing household hazards to young children should be exercised in homes where a person with visual problems lives, especially an older and/or disabled person. At least 40 percent of all accidents occur in the home. The following are pointers to help you avoid household accidents:

- *Light your way to safety.* With age or deteriorating vision, you need more light, as much as two to three times the amount a healthy teenager needs to see the same object. Use fluorescent lights in the kitchen and bathroom. For close work, investigate bulbs and lamps especially designed for persons with low vision. Dorothy, a member of our glaucoma support group, places a yellow acetate cover over her fluorescent desk lamp. This softens the light and increases contrast. (See Chapter 14 for more information on visual aids.)

- *Use color to your advantage.* Falls can be prevented by choosing single-color carpeting rather than floral and other types of patterns, which can be visually confusing and may cause missteps. Call attention to such hazards as floor heights that differ from one room to another by laying down strips of colored tape at the intersections or by using different-colored floor coverings. To aid in the kitchen and dining room, choose tableware and dishes that contrast with your tablecloths and/or place mats. Light-colored plates display food better than dark plates do. Andrea, another member of our support group, gave her floral-patterned dishes to her niece and bought new ones that were solid white. Now she doesn't mistake a pattern for food. Joseph painted everything white and installed light-colored carpeting and white ceramic kitchen counters. He reported that he saw an invasive ant the other day—something he would have missed before.

- *Be aware of your visual limitations.* One problem associated with progressive glaucoma is the loss of peripheral vision. When you can no longer see your toes when standing up straight, you can be sure that you are missing objects in your path.

- *Learn your home environment well, and keep things organized.* Never leave objects on stairs or in travel pathways, and ask family members to help out by keeping objects in familiar places. During the repainting of our apartment, I fell over a floor fan that had been placed in a normally unobstructed path. Rita's husband, who is blind, sat down on what he expected to be sofa and landed on the floor—she had moved the sofa without informing him. Getting about can become a problem if your vision deteriorates. To gain confidence, reconstruct your home in your mind's eye, noting the placement of each object. Once you have learned the territory you can move about easily.

Sign Up for Medic Alert Services

You can be assured that your ophthalmologic needs will be taken into account if you should need medical attention in an emergency if you enroll with Medic Alert. This can be particularly reassuring if you live alone. For a small fee, this organization will keep a record of your allergies, medical conditions, medications, and special needs, and will provide you with a wallet card and bracelet or necklace giving an 800 phone number to be called in case of an emergency, so that medical personnel can be guided to administer the right treatment and notify the appropriate parties. We strongly advise that any person with a chronic medical problem enroll in this service.

Learn to Work Around Your Limitations

Many of us experience difficulty walking through an unfamiliar place. A new street might have a pothole, a depression, or a bump. Sidewalks may have low, medium, or high curbs. Any of these things, if undetected, can cause a fall and injury. To overcome walking problems, wear solid walking shoes and exercise to build your upper and lower body strength.

A few years back, my orthopedist suggested that I teach myself how to fall, for I confessed that I often fell, flat on my face. I thought he was crazy. How can you "learn" to fall? Later, however, I decided to do some weight-lifting exercises, raising weights above my head and to strengthen my arms, and I discovered that not only did the muscles in my arms rebuild, but the muscles in my torso strengthened. And to my astonishment, when I tripped, I often recovered without falling. If I fell, instead of landing on my face, I would land on a knee and hand, and be able to recover quickly. Another exercise that helped was assuming a sitting posture with my back against the wall to strengthen my thighs. Maintaining this position for three minutes can do wonders for your balance. Rita concentrates on sit-ups. Heel-toe walking also contributes to a good sense of balance and helps to eliminate tripping.

Glare and contrast sensitivity can interfere with your ability to see and to distinguish objects. These problems result from the loss of nerve cells in the eye. Glare can create a veiling haze that reduces the distinction between various degrees of brightness. This condition in turn leads to impaired contrast sensitivity. Glare can affect you in a number of ways. For example, if you are driving with a dirty windshield into a setting sun, light hitting the dirt particles scatters and creates vision problems. Your doctor can given you a test called a BAT (brightness acuity test) to determine the severity of your glare problem. To correct it, try out sunglasses of different tints until you find a pair that eliminates the glare. I have found that sunglasses with side shields, plus a brimmed hat, give me the best vision.

Contrast sensitivity is the ability to see well under conditions of reduced lighting or contrast. The loss of contrast sensitivity can affect you when you climb stairs; the flat part of the stair is usually brighter than the vertical, so to see the stair properly, you need to be able to distinguish between brightness levels. When driving, you need to be able to distinguish the features on the side of the road, and obstacles that might lie in your path. Contrast sensitivity is especially difficult in dimly lit rooms. Yvonne, who works in real estate, finds showing apartments to prospective clients treacherous if the halls are not well lit. And I cannot count the number of times I have bumped my shins on a ledge or the first stair tread, which I did not see because of reduced contrast sensitivity. To check your contrast sensitivity, your doctor can give you a contrast gradient visual acuity test. Wearing lightly tinted glasses may help to increase contrast sensitivity, but if you are in dark quarters, only better lighting will do.

Tips for General Eye Care

All of us need to take care of our eyes. But we who have glaucoma need to be especially vigilant about how we treat our eyes in our everyday activities. Taking some simple precautions may extend the life of your eyes.

Love that tan? Take care to wear goggles whenever you step into the sun. The sun's ultraviolet rays can cause serious eye damage. Closing your eyes is *not* an effective shield. The lenses and retinas are especially vulnerable to sun and light exposure. A recent study found that UV radiation accelerates aging of the photoreceptors in your eyes. Cumulative exposure ages the lens, leading to the formation of cataracts and possibly the retinal changes responsible for macular degeneration. The younger you are, the more UV radiation you absorb. And if you have had a cataract removed and your implanted lens is not treated to absorb UV radiation, you will receive fifty to several thousand times more UV radiation exposure than someone with intact lenses.

Keep your distance from the television set. Cuddling up to the TV screen can cause eye damage. Keeping a distance equivalent to five times the width of the screen is a good rule of thumb to follow.

Windy and/or snowy days may dry your eyes. Try using protective goggles.

Daily-care contact lenses are preferable to the extended-wear variety. This decreases the chance of infection. You can use eye drops along with contact lenses provided you are on a twice-daily eye drop medication schedule. Simply apply your eye drop before putting in your lens in the morning and after removing your lens at night. Over-the-counter eye drops designed to eliminate redness should be avoided. These drops may interact with other medications and irritate the eye.

The Importance of Looking Your Best

When we look good, we feel good, and when we feel good, our bodies respond by becoming healthier. Concern about looking your best is not frivolous, but a genuine part of well-being. For many women, this means not only paying attention to dress, but also the use of cosmetics. Women whose sight becomes limited sometimes stop even trying to apply makeup because they can no longer tell if they have put it on correctly. If this has happened to you, take heart, for there are ways to see to it that you still put forward your best appearance.

Take the advice of Lois Rigsbee, a chemist who worked for a number of leading cosmetic companies. She was diagnosed with glaucoma at the age of seventeen, and later developed retinal detachments and cataracts. She subsequently carved out a niche for herself in skin care for persons with low vision.

If you have sufficient sight to use a mirror, a super-magnifying (3X) mirror is essential. When it comes to applying cosmetics, using temperature contrast in conjunction with a magnifying mirror can be helpful. If you chill such items as cream blush and lipstick (but not powder or eyebrow pencil) in the refrigerator for one hour before applying them, you will feel the cold makeup against your skin, and this should enable you to place your cosmetics in the right areas.

When cleansing your skin, do your eyes first. Saturate a cotton pad with a water-based makeup remover and wipe it over your closed eyes, one at a time. Gently draw the pad under the lashes first with the eye closed, then with the eye open. Use a new pad for every step.

Then gently cleanse the rest of your face. If you use a toner to remove the last traces of cleanser and tighten the pores, apply it with a bit of sterile cotton and keep the toner away from the eye area. If you use masks or scrubs for deep cleansing, be sure to avoid the area around your eyes, and rinse your face very thoroughly afterward, to avoid the possibility that grit or other substances may get in your eyes. If you use more than one type of moisturizing cream, code the backs of the jars by applying drops of glue and allowing them to dry. For example, you might give your day cream one drop, your night cream two drops. This will allow you to differentiate among different products by touch.

Regarding makeup, apply foundation as usual. To place blush correctly, apply it on the "apple" of your cheek (the point of cheekbone nearest the nose) and smooth it towards the joint near the ear. With your finger or a short brush, apply eye shadow under (or over) the browbone. If you feel you must use mascara, apply it by resting your hand against your chin and, very slowly, applying the mascara to your lashes. I would note, though, that both Rita and I have stopped using mascara because we feel that flakes get into our eyes.

Different-color lipsticks can be distinguished from each other by wrapping the inner tube in transparent (not cellophane) tape, and applying a certain number of glue drops to identify each color. To apply your lipstick, use magnification for a better view. Chilling the lipstick in advance will also help you to sense the contour of your lips. Whatever cosmetics you use, be sure to replace them every four to six months to decrease the chance of bacteria entering your eyes.

When choosing shampoos, soaps, and other personal hygiene products, keep in mind that many brands contain a detergent known as sodium lauryl sulfate (SLS), which is rapidly taken up in the eye. SLS can be retained in eye tissues for up to five days, and can cause changes in some of the proteins of the eye tissues and retard the healing time of the cornea. Younger eyes are more susceptible to this effect. It may be difficult to find products that do not contain sodium lauryl sulfate. Castile soap, such as Dr. Bronner's pure Castile soap, is a good alternative. This product can be found in health food stores. It comes in a variety of scents, including peppermint, almond, and lavender. Castile soap can be used for just about everything. I use the peppermint for dishwashing, the almond for my hair, and the lavender for my bath. When shampooing, you might try wearing swimmer's goggles to protect your eyes.

DRIVING AND YOU

Some of us with glaucoma are fortunate enough to be able to continue to drive. Depending upon the state you live in, the following requirements may apply: You may be able to obtain a restricted license with as little as 20/70 vision in a single corrected good eye. For an unrestricted license, your best corrected distance acuity must be generally 20/40 or better. If your vision is between 20/40 and 20/70 and you have a visual field of not less than 104 degrees, you may be issued a restricted license that carries special restrictions such as a shorter than normal renewal period, permission to drive only in daytime, special mirror requirements, or limitations on highway driving. If your visual acuity is less than 20/70 but better than 20/100, you may be permitted to drive if you wear bioptic telescopes (see page 229) and can see 20/40 through this equipment and have a 140-degree visual field. Driving with bioptic telescopes requires practice, and you cannot apply for a license until you have undergone specific training.

Medication can sometimes affect your driving ability. Be especially careful when driving at night. Low light may impair your ability to track a moving object, navigate your automobile down the road, and discern objects from their backgrounds, any of which can produce hazardous conditions when piloting a moving vehicle.

If driving is part of your lifestyle, practicing a few essential safety precautions can help you to avoid problems and stay on the road. The following recommendations come from the American Optometric Association:

1. Use proper glasses for both day and night driving.
2. Avoid the use of sunglasses or tinted lenses for night driving.
3. Wear good-quality sunglasses in sunlight.
4. Avoid driving at dusk or at night if possible.
5. Clean your glasses regularly.
6. Choose narrow-temple eyeglass frames. Wide temples interfere with side vision.
7. Be an alert driver. Watch the road ahead, and check each side for vehicles, children, animals, or other hazards. Keep your head and eyes moving, and glance frequently in the rear view mirror and at the instrument panel.

8. Pace yourself to the flow of traffic.
9. Opt for a car with a clear windshield.
10. Maintain your headlights (adjusted properly) and taillights, and keep your windshield clean.
11. Always wear your seat belt. Air bags are good for additional safety, but remember that an air bag does not take the place of your seat belt.

The American Automobile Association (AAA) has published a booklet entitled *Rx for Safe Driving*. For a free copy, write to AAA Corporate Communications, 1000 AAA Drive, Heathrow, FL 32746–5063.

You may not have a choice about having glaucoma, but how you handle the "slings and arrows" of dealing with glaucoma is up to you. Whether your glaucoma is relatively minor or causes a major handicap, you owe it to yourself to take an active part in your treatment. By learning all that you can about the particular form of glaucoma you have, and by understanding the effects of medication and surgical interventions, you will find yourself in a position to discuss your course of treatment with your doctor intelligently. Always remember, you have a right to disagree with your doctor if you are in a nonemergency situation. You have a right to seek a second opinion and even a third if you so desire. By the same token, if you do not follow your doctor's recommendations, you need to understand that you are responsible for any harm that results.

Having an eye condition that diminishes your sight does not diminish you. It should not keep you from participating in activities you enjoy, provided you learn some simple ways of adapting. In the following chapter we will discuss some of the devices and equipment that can help to counter low-vision difficulties, as well as support services that aid you in coping with your condition.

CHAPTER 12

Support Services—There's Help Out There

Kick away the ladder and one's feet are left dangling.

Malay proverb

My first inkling that I might be traveling on the low road to disaster came not when I was diagnosed with glaucoma, but several years later, when I started to lose some sight. Then I found myself surreptitiously practicing being blind—trying to identify a favorite pen by feel, replacing toilet tissue in a dark bathroom, lightly passing my hand over a surface to feel if it was clean of grit—in other words, using my sense of touch to determine things I once could see at a glance. Only then did I become interested in support groups and visual aids. To my amazement, I found there is a lot of help out there—if you know where to seek it.

Rita, on the other hand, had a very different experience. She lost part of her sight quickly, and was constantly in great pain due to her rare type of glaucoma. No one in her life supported her during her time of crisis. When she did turn to social workers and medical staff for help, she found they did not understand visual impairment and were therefore helpless to offer her assistance and direction. After two frustrating years, she finally found—by sheer accident—the phone number of the New York Glaucoma Support Group. Through the coordinator's compassion and constant encouragement, Rita at last received support and understanding.

LOSE A LITTLE, GAIN A LITTLE

Sometimes we find ourselves having to give up some sight in the present with the hope of preserving vision over the long term. That is, the eye drops and surgical procedures prescribed to lower intraocular pressure can have the effect of decreasing vision. With a filtering operation, for example, you can lose one or more lines on the Snellen chart (see page 52), become subject to cataract formation, and develop light sensitivity. The various drops can cause innumerable side effects, ranging from increased myopia to cataracts.

Unfortunately, many eye doctors, although intent on preserving your sight, do not take the trouble to learn about the readily available resources that can make your life easier, help you to read or adjust, assist in looking for new employment or in retaining your current job with some modification—and, in general, lead you back into the productive life that is your true style. Rita realized this when, depressed by her condition, she met a librarian from the Library for the Blind and Physically Handicapped, who asked her to wiggle her fingers and then her toes. The librarian asked if Rita's fingers and toes still worked, and Rita admitted they did. At that moment, she understood that her inner self was still the same, despite her visual handicap; she had only to learn to live her life a bit differently. Soon after, Rita became an ophthalmic professional exploring services for the visually impaired. She also became a staunch supporter of these services and actively works to promote them among ophthalmic practitioners and patients.

While employed in ophthalmology, Rita found that many of the medical personnel she encountered resisted becoming involved in planning strategies to help their patients cope with problems caused by visual impairment. This may be, in part, because of the overwhelming amount of paperwork needed to fulfill insurance and other requirements. Or it may reflect a deeper problem—the kind of unfair treatment that has dogged disabled people throughout history.

COMING TO TERMS WITH VISUAL DISABILITY

James Garrett, a contributor to *Vocational Rehabilitation of the Disabled: An Overview* (NewYork University Press, 1969), traces the evolution of human attitudes toward illness. In early times, disease and illness were believed to be caused by divine or supernatural intervention. Although few people today would actually say they believe this, the concept that people with handicapping or debilitating conditions are somehow "less than human" weaves a sorry trail throughout history. Only very recently, with the passage of the Americans With Disabilities

Act of 1990, were disabled people in this country given the legal right to equal opportunity in the marketplace.

More remains to be done if we are to ensure that equality of opportunity in employment and in quality of life is available to all people. Liaison services with low-vision centers among clinics, doctors, and other medical personnel need to be firmly established. In addition, we need to redefine terms such as "legal blindness," often used to determine whether an individual qualifies for certain types of assistance or not. The criteria for legal blindness currently are 20/200 vision or lower in both eyes and/or a visual field of less than 20 degrees. However, this definition fails to take into account the array of conditions caused by glaucoma. Before a person with glaucoma reaches the stage of legal blindness, he or she may be plagued with diminished sight due to glare, loss of contrast sensitivity, and side effects of medications that may diminish sight, leading to falls and other injuries, and in other ways disrupting and limiting that person's lifestyle and competence. Yet under current laws, such an individual—while desperately in need of them—would be denied the various services available to the legally blind and left either to finance his or her own care or, as happens too often, sink into a quagmire of isolation and despair. This is clearly an issue that needs to be addressed.

Meanwhile, we glaucoma patients are left with the need to learn to cope with our own situations, both physically and psychologically. Emotionally, the loss of sight is experienced as a personal disaster. According to Mindy Levine, psychologist and counselor with the National Association for the Visually Handicapped, persons losing their sight go through stages of loss similar to the stages of grief described by Dr. Elisabeth Kübler-Ross in her famous work *On Death and Dying* (Simon & Schuster, 1970). Persons losing their sight go first through a state of denial and isolation that produces shock and disbelief. They refuse to admit to any limitations, but insist they can do everything they once did. To avoid realizing that they are unequal to their former selves, they may withdraw from social contacts and resist seeking help from professionals and agencies equipped to assist them.

In the second stage, denial may turn to anger: "Why me? Why am I being punished?" Anger may be turned on the medical provider, or on family and friends. Interestingly, studies indicate that a person who loses all vision at this point is in a better position to adjust than one who continues to lose vision gradually. This observation extends to children as well. Partially sighted children tend to have greater difficulty adjusting to their problems than totally blind children do, and parents of partially sighted children are apparently less understanding of their children's needs than parents of blind children are.

Bargaining ushers in the third stage. "Let me stay right where I am," we say. "I'll do everything right, take my medicine, eat the right foods, but please, God, let me keep whatever sight I have." When it becomes clear that denial, anger, and bargaining are no longer working, the fourth stage—depression—begins. Feelings of fear, anger, and sadness become overwhelming. We may find that family, friends, and services do not (and perhaps cannot) meet our expectations. For some people, this increases their sense of isolation. Others respond by beginning to fight for their rights and to seek out professional help that will help them to live with their reduced vision.

LOW-VISION SERVICES

When you experience problems with your eyesight, you may not fully comprehend the difference between low vision and going blind. They are not the same thing. Many people with low vision have some usable sight, and they become confused when they are termed legally blind. Low vision can best be described as insufficient vision to do some of the things you may want to do, whereas legal blindness is a specifically defined set of visual parameters (see below). You still may find yourself categorized as legally blind, and this is important, for when your condition progresses to this level you may take advantage of the services offered by your government for the blind and physically handicapped.

The following advice applies to all individuals with diminished sight:

- Ask for help if you begin to have difficulty with vision.
- Know your visual acuity and what services you are entitled to.
- If your vision is 20/200 in both eyes (corrected) and/or your peripheral vision is no more than 20 degrees, be aware that you are entitled to services for the legally blind.
- If you fall into the legally blind category, have your doctor fill out any paperwork necessary to enable you to receive assistance. In many states, there is a mandatory form for this. Many of these forms must be signed by a doctor and sent in by the doctor's office or clinic. The state then forwards the sender a registration number. Be

aware that you must ask your doctor to complete this paperwork. These may be mandatory state forms, but many physicians are unaware of their existence. As a result, many visually impaired people are subjected to a life without any supportive services. Avoid this pitfall. The services that you can obtain may help you save your job, prevent accidents, and possibly even save your life. (Be aware, however, that the process of receiving state registration can take several months or more.) If your doctor's staff is unaware of such forms, suggest that they call state agencies that deal with the blind for information and supplies.

- If you have become seriously visually impaired, insist that someone in the government or the doctor's office help you obtain emergency services from your state Trying to get to your doctor's office—or anyplace, for that matter—with poor vision can be dangerous to life and limb. Rita, unfortunately, experienced this problem firsthand. Leaving the hospital after a surgical procedure, she was hit by a truck and fell to the ground, and the truck's tire passed over her ankle. Thankfully, because her body was still in a relaxed state (the effect of the anesthesia), she was not seriously injured, but the accident left her fearful of going out alone afterward. If she had known her rights as a visually impaired person and understood her entitlement to support services, she might have avoided the accident.

- Services for people with low vision are available, but state laws do not always consider visual problems arising from glaucoma. Montana is one of the few states with a law that encompasses low-vision problems. If your state's definition of low vision excludes your particular problem, make a fuss. Write your state legislators and Congressional representative. Write letters to your local newspaper.

- If you are having visual problems, have another person escort you and assist you in making and recording your appointments with your doctor and other care providers. If need be, you can often hire a private escort service for this purpose.

- If you are undergoing any type of medical or surgical procedure, bring someone with you.

- If your doctor's office is located in a clinic or hospital and if you are having visual problems, speak to a nurse or other staff member who can help you obtain ambulette services. (Note that charges for such transportation may be paid by private insurance or Medicaid, or you may have to pay them out of pocket.)

Depending upon the funds and the organizations, both public and private, in your community, you can expect to find different services when you enroll in a low-vision program. In many cases, federal funds are allocated to pay for these services, but you must apply for them and be prepared to wait for your application to be approved. Most organizations that serve the blind and visually handicapped advise that you seek help when your vision first begins to fade, rather than waiting until the problem becomes more severe.

Just about every state has a commission for the blind and physically impaired or the equivalent. The services these organizations provide are generally in the areas of education, vocational rehabilitation, independent living, eye health, consumer advocacy, aids and appliances, consumer complaints, reduced-fare transportation, community-based programs and services, and even such amenities as theater passes. You can usually locate the address of the service by consulting your local telephone directory or by checking with directory assistance. Another good source of information concerning low-vision services available in your area is *The Directory of Services for the Blind and Visually Impaired in the United States and Canada,* published by the American Foundation for the Blind (see the References section at the end of this book).

The following are some of the services you can expect:

- Computer training.
- Rehabilitative services.
- Job modification.
- Adapted vacations.
- Transportation. If there is public transportation in your community and it does not provide access for the disabled, they are required to provide para-transit, which may be achieved with vans or taxis.
- Training in independent living skills.
- Occupational therapy.
- Mobility training.

- The services of social workers and other specialists equipped to handle government forms for low vision services in your area.

Much remains to be accomplished in the area of access to services. Services provided by state commissions for the blind and physically impaired may take months to crank up. Communication between your doctor's office and the organization that should provide you with these services may be nonexistent, or it may move at a snail's pace. If you find yourself in this position, don't despair. Be persistent. Positive action on your part can do much to unsnarl any red tape preventing you from taking advantage of the services you are entitled to. If the services you need are not available, you may be able to muster up political and community support to make these services available.

VISUAL AIDS

Captain Bligh, move over. You too can explore the hinterlands with a telescope—a telescope mounted right on your glasses. This device is only one of the many visual aids currently on the market that may enhance and broaden what you see. Especially designed for persons with low vision, these products range from inexpensive magnifying glasses to sophisticated telescopes. For a full range of options, you may wish to consult with a low-vision specialist. The American Optometric Association's Low Vision Section provides a nationwide listing of optometrists who offer these services (see the Resources section at the end of this book).

Telescopes and Special Lenses

Telescopes are becoming smaller and smaller, and can really benefit certain people with low vision. There is one unit that forms a bar or bridge across the top of your glasses, and is practically unobtrusive. You can also have telescopic lenses inserted into eyeglass frames, although this is expensive. In addition, there are sunglasses that cut glare, sharpen contrast, and change colors according to the amount of available light.

If you have lost some peripheral vision but still have decent central vision, specially designed eyeglasses may enhance your ability to see. An organization called Inwave Optics (see the References section at the end of this book) manufactures two lens designs that may be prescribed for a wide range of visual field losses. Essentially, what these lenses do is expand your vision, or make the best use of the vision you have. When I tried them on, they made me feel as if my vision had stretched out. Your optometrist or ophthalmologist may be able to supply these lenses, or you may need a referral to a low-vision specialist.

The Low-Vision Enhancement System

Exciting developments in technology to enhance vision are on the rise. Two of these are known to produce reasonably good results for some people. The first, the Low-Vision Imaging System (LVIS), was originally a product of a research and development program involving NASA, the U.S. Department of Veterans' Affairs, and the Wilmer Eye Institute at Johns Hopkins University. It is now manufactured, sold, and distributed by Visionic Corporation. The second system, V-Max, is manufactured by Enhanced Vision Systems.

Both of these instruments sit on your head and have a video camera mounted on the visor and one or two video monitors for your eyes. They provide for magnification for reading, distance, and contrast control. LVIS provides only black-and-white images, but it is easier to use because it allows for variable focus and can be tilted down as much as 45 degrees. V-Max gives color images and better distance viewing, but the camera cannot tilt, so you are forced to hold reading material up at what may be an uncomfortable angle. However, V-Max does have the added feature of adapting to closed circuit television. Both systems compensate for changing light conditions, such as when you move from bright outdoor light into dim indoor light, and for the visual requirements of different tasks.

The cost for either of these systems is substantial (between three and five thousand dollars) and some training is required, ranging from three hours to a couple of days. Those whose vision falls between 20/100 and 20/800 will most likely benefit from these systems, although highly motivated individuals with vision above 20/2800 might still want to consider them. Some states have allowed Medicare payments for these devices, and if you are legally blind your state commission for the blind and visually impaired might finance the system. However, with the present and future cutbacks in medical spending, the prospect of such funding is not bright. There are currently over sixty centers in the United States that offer these programs.

Lighting

The older we get, the more light we need to see well. This is true for everyone, and it is certainly the case for persons with low vision. In general, the greater the loss of sight, the more necessary it is to have the proper light. Of course, not all people's needs are the same. Dorothy cannot bear brightly lit rooms, and strong sunlight completely washes out her remaining sight. Unshielded overhead fluorescents, such as those found in supermarkets, drive me wild. On the other hand, Marion lights every room in her house brightly whenever she's home. She cannot tolerate even a hint of darkness.

Fortunately, the market is brimming with lamps and bulbs of every stripe to help you make your home into a comfortable place no matter what your particular needs. There are lamps that give off a glow that is close to natural light; lamps that combine magnification with light; reflector lamps; optically designed lamps that concentrate penetrating light with no heat buildup; and, of course, fluorescents. Many of these are available at lamp stores or by mail order. One good source is the National Association for the Visually Handicapped (see the References section at the end of this book), an organization that carries a complete line of items that can make your life easier.

Large-Print Items

One of the first accommodations to diminished vision that you may find yourself making is seeking out materials in large print. Although intended primarily for the visually impaired, these materials provide for easier reading for anyone who is losing the ability to read fine print without reading glasses—a group that includes most people over forty.

In addition to large-print books, magazines, and other reading material, you can find many everyday items with enlarged numbers, including watches, timers, clocks, thermometers, telephones, playing cards, bingo cards, crossword puzzles—you name it, and someone manufactures it.

Books on Tape

The Library of Congress provides a wide selection of recorded books and other materials and the machines to play them on—all of which will be sent to you free of charge. Many local public libraries now also make books on tape available. Some even have established low-vision centers. While I was recovering from my combined cataract and filtering operation, I found my neighborhood library a valuable resource for these tapes.

Helpful Household Products

If you are at the point where enlargement no longer serves your purpose, try using objects that offer tactile (touch) cues. For recreation, checkers, backgammon, chess, and tic-tac-toe are a few of the items that can keep you happily engaged. Need to know where your next trip will take you, or exactly where your daughter is moving to? A tactile map of the United States will give you this information. If you're a do-it-yourselfer, there are specially adapted measuring tools that will give you the precision needed for your projects.

Other products that can make your life easier include letter- or check-writing guides that provide templates—plastic sheets with openings corresponding to standard line spacing for writing or, for checks, appropriate spacing for the name, amount, and other blanks you have to fill in. There are bold black writing pens that provide for good contrast; voice-activated telephones that dial the number when you speak a name; and television screen enlargers, screens you place over your television to enlarge the picture.

In the kitchen, you may want to take advantage of a slicing guide. This is a knife set in an adjustable frame that allows you to make slices of varying thickness of bread, fruit, vegetables, meat, or cheese. Other useful household helpers include folding dustpans that fold up to make a funnel-like pouring spout; pie starters (aluminum wedges that you bake in a pie to give easy access to the first piece); jar openers that attach to the underside of a table, counter, cabinet, or shelf; small electric food choppers that eliminate the need to use a knife for small processing tasks; pot strainers for straining and rinsing foods; simmer rings that are useful if you find it hard to judge the height of a gas flame; egg rings for containing fried or poached eggs; egg separators for separating the yolks from the whites; and spaghetti measures, which allow you to measure how much uncooked pasta you want to dump into your boiling water. Need a little verbal reinforcement? There are clocks and watches that literally tell you the time, and calculators that pair a voice with the numbers you punch.

Do you like to sew, but are frustrated because you can no longer thread needles? Don't despair. There are spread-eye needles—you pull the needle apart, insert your thread, and release. Give a slight tug, and your thread is locked in. There are also needle threaders—you drop the needle into a funnel, lay the thread across the groove, press a button, and the needle is threaded—and self-threading needles, for both hand and machine sewing. A sewing gauge can help you space stitches for hems, scallops, or embroidery patterns, and be used for general measuring.

Taking your medicine can become challenging if you have more than one medical problem and your sight is not what it once was. For people with diabetes, there are click-count insulin syringes—each click on the syringe is equal to two units of insulin. There is also a device called the "Mani-Build" Becton-Dickinson Scale Magnifier and needle guide that magnifies the entire length of the syringe scale, simplifies mixing insulin, and helps you to locate bubbles in the syringe. These are but a sampling of the many items available.

MOBILITY TRAINING

If your vision deteriorates to the point that you fear going into the street without a companion or escort, you will want to consider mobility training. This is one of the first services offered by organizations that serve the blind and visually handicapped. Mobility training consists of training in the use of a cane to "sweep" in front of you to detect obstructions, potholes, crevices, or other obstacles in your path. This system is called the touch technique. The cane used has a pencil tip that the user taps in the area just in front of the trailing foot.

There is also another system, although not widely used, that may offer a more secure walk. This system includes a cane equipped with a ball-bearing-mounted rolling tip. The rolling action allows the user to make contact with the ground at all times, making for greater stability. It also reduces the chances of the tip getting stuck in cracks (a situation that can result in a nasty stomach poke when your cane comes to an abrupt halt, causing your body to lurch forward).

THE USES OF COMPUTERS

It may not be able to replace your seeing-eye dog on your trips to the supermarket, but if you have joined the ranks of those with low vision, your personal computer can nevertheless transform your lifestyle from dependent to freewheeling. Computers can enlarge print so that you can read it. If you are unable to read at even the highest magnification, they can read to you—anything from a newspaper to a bound book. You can write letters, documents, or novels on a computer, and the machine will read what you have written back to you—and even question your spelling, grammar, and sentence structure. There is a growing supply of computer software specifically developed for persons with disabilities, assuring that you will not be left dangling when your sight weakens. Perhaps best of all, the computer can be a means of connecting with the outside world. You can subscribe to services such as Prodigy, CompuServe, or America Online to take advantage of the multitude of services these programs offer, such as bulletin boards, access to libraries, electronic mail, shopping, communication with other people in the network, and so on, as well as access to the Internet.

I must confess I am still living in the Ice Age, for I don't have a computer, although I toy with obtaining one every six months or so. Rita does have a computer, and finds it indispensable. She is able to write, keep track of business and personal correspondence, and do many other things efficiently and easily.

Reading Programs

Some computers come with screen magnification programs that allow you to enlarge the display for easier reading. If you do not already have such a program, you can add one. There are a variety of programs available, and cost varies.

If you have passed the point of needing large print and need to have your computer read back to you, you will need a speech system. These consist of two parts, a synthesizer program and a screen access program. Prices vary, but generally the higher end systems give you the best speech. You need at least a 486-level personal computer to install a speech system.

The computer industry has also produced a number of reading machines that can be used either with or without a computer. All of these systems are supposed to do a reasonably good job of reading typewritten and printed documents. Manufacturers include Kurzweil Computer Products, C-Tech, Xerox, and Arkensone. These companies all produce both computers and reading machines. They recommend that if you wish to choose the product with the most accurate reading, you should assemble a set of documents and try them out for yourself on the various machines. There are differences among products in terms of the type of commands you give the computer, the speed of recognition, special features, and cost. If you are planning to purchase either computer software or a reading machine, be sure to try it out on the type of material you read most often, so that you match your needs with the machine's capabilities.

Computer Training

You can teach yourself to use a computer—Rita did—but to get the most out of computer technology and learn to use the Internet to your best advantage, specialized training may be advisable. Many colleges and other organizations offer training in computer skills. The American Foundation for the Blind (see the Resources directory at the end of this book) has a technological center that reviews all available computer technologies, and they also provide training. Baruch College, part of the City University of New York, has a unique program for the blind and visually handicapped.

If you plan to use the computer for work or educational purposes, your best bet is to start with your state commission for the blind and physically impaired. If you simply wish to use the computer to upgrade your quality of life generally, you may need to pay for training services, but your state commission should be able to direct you to appropriate training providers in any case.

Online Access

The Internet (also called the electronic superhighway) is a network of computer networks sharing data, software, and hardware devices. To gain access to the Internet, you must have a computer plus a modem, a device that converts information from your computer into electronic signals that can be transmitted over telephone lines. You must also establish an account with an Internet access provider, much as you must have an account with a telephone company in order to use your telephone. With access to the Internet, you can research in depth virtually any subject, including glaucoma (yes, both the Glaucoma Research Foundation (http://www.glaucoma.org) and the Glaucoma Foundation (http://www.glaucoma-foundation.org/info) have World Wide Web sites). Or you can just have fun browsing through the World Wide Web for things that interest you. You can send and receive E-mail, "chat" with other users, play games, or whatever. If your computer has multimedia capability, you can access sites that provide sound, whether in the form of speech or music.

America Online, CompuServe, and Prodigy are all commercial services that charge a monthly fee (plus, in some cases, hourly access charges) for access to the Internet and to their own services. Their usefulness for any given individual may vary because they are based on different types of software, and your own software must be compatible. Prodigy, for instance, uses a proprietary graphical format that is not accessible to blind users. CompuServe provides both DOS-based and Windows-based access, but they have announced plans to begin phasing out DOS-based access. America Online (AOL) uses Microsoft Windows, and can be used with Windows-based synthetic speech programs. This is the most popular commercial service. It uses a lot of graphics and is good on leisure activities. However, if you use a speech synthesizer, it will be able to translate only text material.

Some visually impaired people find UNIX shell accounts, offered by many Internet providers, to be the most appealing. You need to know something about using a computer for this system, but it tends to be the least expensive. It functions in the text mode, which means that if you need a speech synthesizer, the program is equipped to handle this technology.

If you know how to use a computer but cannot afford to buy one, check with your public library. Many public libraries now have computers available for patrons to use, either for free or for a nominal charge. Some even offer Internet services. When the New York Public Library started offering Internet access in eighty-seven libraries throughout the city, they found the response to be overwhelming.

Eye Protection for Computer Users

As wonderful and liberating as they are, computers may cause some problems if you fail to take certain commonsense precautions. When using the computer, keep the following suggestions in mind:

- Try not to stare at the screen for longer than five to ten minutes at a time. Raise your eyes, look around. After every fifteen minutes, walk around.

- Clean your computer screen once a week with a soft cloth to eliminate dust on the screen that can interfere with your vision.

- Remember to blink. Working in front of a computer screen slows down your blink rate. Reduced blinking can result in dry, tired eyes.

- Place the screen in such a way that you are looking down at a 15-degree angle. This reduces the amount of eye surface exposed to the computer environment.

- Reduce overhead lighting. Illuminate your desktop with lighting focused directly on your task.

- Don't have your monitor face a window. Light coming in a window interferes with the light on the monitor, especially if you have contrast problems.
- Use a monitor filter to reduce glare.
- Extensive testing in government and private research laboratories has not produced scientific evidence that radiation emitted by video display terminals is harmful, but to be on the safe side, keep a distance of at least two feet from the monitor.
- Have the keyboard at a height of twenty-eight to thirty-one inches. Be sure your chair is equipped with a backrest that can be adjusted to provide adequate mid-back support.

Many of the items discussed in this chapter, as well as many others that may be helpful to those with low vision, are available by mail order. Addresses of companies that provide computers and reading machines, as well as of other recommended suppliers, are listed in the Resources section at the end of this book.

BECOME AN ADVOCATE

Advocacy should be a very important component of any visually impaired person's agenda. Though our society now offers many aids and services for the visually impaired, many people do not take advantage of these resources. Persons who are unable to read regular print and who are not informed of the educational, recreational, or informational materials available are often unaware of their rights. Furthermore, materials available for the sighted are often censored for visually impaired and blind. For example, in 1986, the organization responsible for issuing braille materials decided that the material in *Playboy* was pornographic and not fit for blind users, and refused to publish it. *Playboy* had to take the case to court on the basis of the First Amendment, which guarantees the right to free speech, before the braille edition of the magazine was returned to the market.

Not long ago, no circulating library for the blind and physically handicapped existed in New York City. Rita and her husband, along with 400 librarians, started a movement that included petitioning the state government to create such a library. Three years of determined advocacy resulting in the issuance of a $16-million bond issue finally brought their effort to a successful conclusion. The New York City library is one of two circulating libraries in the state for the blind and physically handicapped. The other is located in Albany.

These are but two examples of the effect advocacy can have. If you find that the services you need to help you achieve a more productive and meaningful life are nonexistent in your community, you can make a difference through advocacy. Indeed, much of the important legislation protecting individual rights began as grass-roots movements. If you don't like the way things are going—get out there and fight to make a change. Our support group did just that several years ago. Many of us travel by bus, and we wrote letters to our state representatives and to the Metropolitan Transit Authority urging that bus operators be required to announce the street location of bus stops. Ultimately, this simple courtesy became the norm, benefiting not only the visually handicapped but tourists and other passengers as well.

BUILD A SUPPORT GROUP

The defining moment that turned me from a "glaucoma complainer" into a glaucoma activist occurred when I joined our glaucoma support group. Until that time, I alternated between denial and self-pity. Only when I met other people with similar conditions—some worse than mine, some better—did I begin to take stock of my situation, an appraisal that led me to the remaking of my life and the writing of this book.

Being visually impaired demands a new lifestyle that may require an overhaul of your previous life. The threats, real and imagined, loom large, especially if you are just entering your most productive years. This is what happened with Rita. Here, amid the encouragement of group members, Rita discovered that her energies could be focused on what she loved to do best—helping other people. She brought what she learned at the group to a hospital, first volunteering in their glaucoma clinic and then taking on a job as an ophthalmic assistant. When she found she needed certification for that job, she enrolled in school, and much to her gratification, achieved certification within two years. Her experience working directly with patients led her to become a valuable partner in working with me on this book. Presently Rita is working full time in advocating for better services for visually handicapped persons who may or may not be legally blind. From seeking these services for herself and for others in our group, Rita has learned that many needs are unmet, especially at the crucial moment when sight first deteriorates to the point where reading and traveling can no longer be achieved without assistance.

What a Support Group Can Do for You

A support group can help you learn about your condition, information you might not ordinarily hear from your own doctor. First of all, you will have the opportunity to interact with other people and discuss similar problems. Second, by inviting ophthalmologists and other practitioners in the field to address your group (they usually come in as a free service), you can learn about eye health, proper management of your condition, legal issues, complementary treatments, the various forms of glaucoma, operations and laser treatments, the latest research, and much more.

If your group is so inclined, you may want to develop a counseling service to help those in need overcome the hurdles they face when their vision deteriorates. Or your group might wish to advocate for more money either for glaucoma research or for access to services. You might want to settle on a single issue—better lighting on restroom doors, street announcements by bus drivers, elevators that tell the floor, having bottom steps in public places painted yellow, switching to good-contrast street signs located in places where you can see them, large-print menus and/or better lighting in restaurants, large-print programs in theaters and concert halls, and so on. The list of potential causes is endless. You know what drives you up a wall.

How to Start a Support Group

The clinic or the eye doctor you see can be an excellent starting place. There you will meet other people with glaucoma who have problems similar to your own—and, in many cases, who are baffled by their condition. They can form the nucleus of your group.

Try to enlist an eye doctor (one in a teaching hospital might be the most receptive) to sponsor your group. Or you might want to suggest to a local organization interested in eye care that your group is worth supporting. If you are lucky enough to find a sponsor, you can expect help in logistical matters such as finding a place to meet, sending out meeting notices, and maintaining a file of members. If you cannot find a sponsor, call around to local churches, synagogues, schools, your public library, or other local organizations that may be able to provide you with meeting space at no (or minimal) cost.

With your core of group members assembled, determine your goals. Do you want to have a group meeting occasionally for supportive discussion and let that be the extent of your program? Or do you want to educate yourselves about glaucoma? Do you want to take on an advocacy role? All of these are important issues, and the success of the group will depend upon the goals you set and your commitment to maintaining them.

There are organizations that can help you get started. Check to see if there is a self-help clearinghouse in your state. These organizations maintain records of self-help groups in different areas, and also supply technical assistance for those who wish to start their own groups. The National Center for Vision and Aging, sponsored by The Lighthouse, Inc. (see the resource directory at the end of this book), focuses on vision problems for the aging and also helps people to start support groups. Other organizations that may help with either technical assistance or with more concrete support, such as financing meeting notices, include the Foundation for Glaucoma Research and Prevent Blindness America. The New York Glaucoma Support and Education Group also is prepared to offer technical assistance. This is the organization Rita and I belong to. You can write to us in care of Prevent Blindness America, 160 East 56th Street, New York, NY 10022.

Management of glaucoma is a lifetime process—one we're sure you never bargained for. It affects the quality of your life in a variety of ways. A survey conducted by the Glaucoma Research Foundation found the following:

- That glaucoma has an impact on self and identity.
- That patients fear blindness.
- That the doctor-patient relationship is important.
- That the patient's relationships with family, friends, and acquaintances often suffer, both from the patient's sense of his or her own shortcomings and from the other party's lack of understanding of the glaucoma patient's erratic eyesight.

Physicians are well aware that the quality of life can diminish dramatically in some cases of glaucoma. An estimated 15 million Americans may have glaucoma, and 1.6 million of that number have visual field damage. Those of us who have glaucoma know only too well that it is not only a chronic but a progressive disease. Cell by cell, glaucoma takes its toll. During the time we researched and wrote this book, four members of the Glaucoma Support Group have lost considerable vision, among them Rita. Two lost the sight of one eye and another went blind. Rita suffered two glaucoma attacks that left her remaining eye with much reduced vision. She is now in the "legally blind" category. In seeking out such support services as transport, homemaking, mobility training, and job retraining, these individuals have experienced some of the indignities visited upon people with visual disabilities—being asked to sign papers that they could not read and that were not read to them, for instance. The fact that people may be made to experience further stress when they are already in one of the most stressful periods of their lives needs to be addressed. Rita, having learned the ropes the hard way, is now working to make life easier for other low-vision patients.

It helps to keep in mind that the medical community does want to manage glaucoma more effectively, and that researchers are hard at work seeking better treatments that will not affect your vision or create numbing side effects but will, in fact, protect your vision. Various organizations are funding research grants into such areas as the genetic bases of the various glaucomas, better understanding of intraocular pressure, restoration of the optic nerve, and many more. Much remains to be accomplished, but the seeds of basic research that will affect our glaucoma treatment have been firmly planted.

However, as glaucoma patients, we cannot sit back and wait for the "miracle cure" to happen. We need to examine our day-to-day activities to assure that we create the best of all conditions for the successful management of our glaucoma. Having confidence in your doctor's ability to treat your condition is one thing that can help to reduce anxiety. Knowing about the medications you need to take, and the probable outcomes of laser treatment and filtration surgery, puts you in an ideal position to discuss with your doctor the benefits or disadvantages of a treatment plan. Working in partnership with your doctor and adopting some of the self-help strategies recommended in this book should help you maintain a satisfactory quality of life.

We owe it to ourselves to examine our lifestyles—to discover how we can moderate stressful activities and toxic thoughts, improve our diets, and take responsibility for our health. We can support ourselves emotionally and with knowledge by joining with and/or forming support groups, and we can diligently seek out those services designed to accommodate our needs. Those of us who have been able to do this are often able also to climb out of the chaos that declining sight produces on one's psyche. Nobody ever promised us a free ride on this planet, but we can do much to make the road less bumpy, and help ourselves enjoy the trip.

References

Chapter 1
The Engineering Miracle

Blakeslee, Sandra. "Newfound Pathways Between Eye and Brain." *The New York Times*, 13 August 1991.

Brandt, James D., M.S. "Glaucoma Research Leading Scientists to New Treatments." *Matrix*, a publication of the University of California-Davis School of Medicine and Medical Center, Volume 2 No. 4, April 1995.

Bresson-Dumont, E., M.D., and A. Bechetoille, M.D. "Blood Pressure Variability as a Risk Factor for Progression of Glaucomatous Damage." Ophthalmologie Centre Hospitalier Universitaire, Angiers, France. Presentation at ARVO Conference, Fort Lauderdale, FL, 1996.

deKater, Annelies W., Ph.D., Aliakbar Shahsafaei, and David L. Epstein, M.D. "Localization of Smooth Muscle and Nonmuscle Action Isoforms in the Human Aqueous Outflow Pathway." *Investigative Ophthalmology and Visual Science* 33 (2) (February 1992).

deKater, Annelies W., Ph.D., Sandra J. Spurr-Michaud, and Ilene K. Gipson. "Localization of Smooth Muscle Myosin-Containing Cells in the Aqueous Outflow Pathway." *Investigative Ophthalmology and Visual Science* 31 (2) (February 1990).

deKater, Annelies W., Ph.D., Shlomo Melamed, M.D., and David L. Epstein, M.D. "Patterns of Aqueous Humor Outflow in Glaucomatous and Nonglaucomatous Eyes." *Archives of Ophthalmology* 107 (April 1989).

"Doctor, I Have a Question," 2nd edition. New York: The Glaucoma Foundation.

Freeze, Arthur S. "Glaucoma: Diagnosis, Treatment, Prevention." Public Affairs Pamphlet No. 568, February 1979.

"Gamut of Glaucoma Research Showcased." *GLEAMS*, a publication of The Glaucoma Research Foundation, Vol. 10 No. 2, Summer 1990.

Hayreh, Sohan Singh, M.D. "Role of Nocturnal Hypotension in Glaucoma and Anterior Ischemic Optic Neuropathy." Presentation at Science Writers Seminar in Ophthalmology, sponsored by Research to Prevent Blindness, Universal City, CA, April 1993.

Iwach, Andrew, M.D. "Glaucoma and Genetics." *GLEAMS,* a publication of The Foundation for Glaucoma Research, Vol. 10 No. 2, 1992.

Jonas, J.B., Xn Nguyen, and Go Naumann. "Parapupillary Retinal Vessel Diameter in Normal and Glaucoma Eyes. I mophometric data." *Investigative Ophthalmology & Visual Science* 30 (7) (1989): 1599–1603.

Kaufman, Paul L., M.D. "Pressure-Dependent Outflow." In *The Glaucomas,* ed. Robert Ritch, M.D., M. Bruce Shields, M.D., and Theodore Krupin, M.D. St. Louis, MO: C.V. Mosby Co., 1989.

Morrison, John C., M.D., F. Michael Van Buskirk, M.D., and Thomas F. Freddo, M.D. "Anatomy, Microcirculation, and Ultrastructure of the Ciliary Body." In *The Glaucomas,* ed. Robert Ritch, M.D., M. Bruce Shields, M.D., and Theodore Krupin, M.D. St. Louis, MO: C.V. Mosby Co., 1989.

Nelson, K.A., and G. Dimitrova. "Severe Visual Impairment in the United States and in Each State, 1990." Statistical brief 36, *Journal of Visual Impairment and Blindness,* March 1993, 80–85.

Pflugenfelder, Stephen C., M.D. "Capturing the Essence of Tears—At Last." Presentation at Science Writers Seminar in Ophthalmology, sponsored by Research to Prevent Blindness, Universal City, CA, April 1993.

"Reading Problems Tied to Defect of Timing in Visual Pathways." *The New York Times,* 13 April 1993, C3.

Research to Prevent Blindness. Annual Report, 1993.

Stone, Edwin M., M.D. "Mapping a Glaucoma Gene." Presentation at Science Writers Seminar in Ophthalmology, sponsored by Research to Prevent Blindness, Universal City, CA, April 1993.

"Study May Explain How Eye Achieves Link With Brain." *The New York Times,* 11 February 1992.

Tripathi, Brenda, M.D. "Interview With an Expert—Trabecular Meshwork." *GLEAMS,* a publication of The Glaucoma Research Foundation, Vol. 8 No. 3, Fall 1990.

"Vision Research, A National Plan 1994–1998." A report of the National Advisory Eye Council. Bethesda, MD: National Institutes of Health.

Chapter 2
Shedding Light on the Glaucomas

Aiello, Lloyd Paul, M.D. "Suppressing Abnormal Growth of Retinal Blood Vessels: Potential New Treatments for Neovascular Ocular Disease." Presentation at Science Writers Seminar in Ophthalmology, sponsored by Research to Prevent Blindness, Orlando, FL, October 1995.

Appiah, Aaron P., M.D., and Kevin C. Greenridge, M.D. "Factors Associated With Retinal-Vein Occlusion in Hispanics." *Annals of Ophthalmology* 12 (1987): 307–312.

Campbell, David G., M.D., M. Bruce Shields, M.D., and Jeffrey M. Liebman. "Ghost Cell Glaucoma." In *The Glaucomas*, ed. Robert Ritch, M.D., M. Bruce Shields, M.D., and Theodore Krupin, M.D. St. Louis, MO: C.V. Mosby Co., 1989.

"Diabetes and Glaucoma." *GLEAMS*, a publication of The Glaucoma Research Foundation, Fall 1983, Vol. 2 No. 2.

"Diabetes Increases Risk of Blindness." *Prevent Blindness News*, Winter 1994.

Farrar, S.M., M.D., M.B. Shields, M.D., K.N. Miller, M.D., and C.M. Stoup, M.D. "Risk Factors for the Development and Severity of Glaucoma in the Pigment Dispersion Syndrome." *American Journal of Ophthalmology* 108 (3) (14 September 1989): 233–251.

Fourman, Stuart, M.D. "Diagnosing Acute Angle-Closure Glaucoma." *Clinical Signs in Ophthalmology* Vol. X113, No. 1.

Fransen, Stephen R., M.D. "Screening for Diabetic Retinopathy Via the Internet." Presentation at Science Writers Seminar in Ophthalmology, sponsored by Research to Prevent Blindness, Orlando, FL, October 1995.

Greenidge, Kevin C., M.D., and Monica Dweck, M.D. "Glaucoma in the Black Population: A Problem of Blindness." *Journal of the National Medical Association* 80 (12) (1988): 1305–1307.

Hatchell, Diane L., Ph.D. "New Light on Origin/Treatment of Diabetic Retinopathy." Presentation at Science Writers Seminar in Ophthalmology, sponsored by Research to Prevent Blindness, Orlando, FL, October 1995.

Hwang, David G., M.D., and Ge Ming Lui, Pharm.D. "Corneal Cell Transplants and Gene Therapy: New Strategies for the Treatment of Corneal Disease." Presentation at Science Writers Seminar in Ophthalmology, sponsored by Research to Prevent Blindness, Orlando, FL, October 1995.

Karickhoff, John R., M.D. "Pigmentary Dispersion Syndrome and Pigmentary Glaucoma: A New Mechanism Concept, a New Treatment, and a New Technique." *Ophthalmic Surgery* 23 (4) (April 1992): 269–277.

Kass, Michael A., M.D., and Tim Johnson, M.D. "Corticosteroid-Induced Glaucoma." In *The Glaucomas*, ed. Robert Ritch, M.D., M. Bruce Shields, M.D., and Theodore Krupin, M.D. St. Louis, MO: C.V. Mosby Co., 1989.

Krupin, Theodore, M.D., and David E. Shoch, M.D. "Trumpeting the Perils of Glaucoma." Presentation at Science Writers Seminar in Ophthalmology, sponsored by Research to Prevent Blindness, Orlando, FL, October 1995.

Krupin, Theodore, M.D., and Marianne F. Feitl, M.D. "Glaucoma Associated With Uveitis." In The Glaucomas, ed. Robert Ritch, M.D., M. Bruce Shields, M.D., and Theodore Krupin, M.D. St. Louis, MO: C.V. Mosby Co., 1989.

Layden, William E., M.D. "Exfoliation Syndrome." In *The Glaucomas,* ed. Robert Ritch, M.D., M. Bruce Shields, M.D., and Theodore Krupin, M.D. St. Louis, MO: C.V. Mosby Co., 1989.

Layden, William E., M.D., and Robert N. Shaffer, M.D. "Exfoliation Syndrome." *American Journal of Ophthalmology* 78 (5) (November 1974): 835-841.

Leary, Warren F. "Blindness with AIDS Prevented by Drug." *The New York Times,* 25 April 1995, C5.

Lichter, Paul R., M.D., and Robert N. Shaffer, M.D. "Diagnostic and Prognostic Signs in Pigmentary Glaucoma." Paper presented at the 74th Annual Session of the American Academy of Ophthalmology and Otolaryngology, Chicago, October 1969.

Lowe, Robert F., M.D., and Robert Ritch, M.D. "Angle-Closure Glaucoma, Mechanisms and Epidemiology." In *The Glaucomas,* ed. Robert Ritch, M.D., M. Bruce Shields, M.D., and Theodore Krupin, M.D. St. Louis, MO: C.V. Mosby Co., 1989.

"Low-Tension Glaucoma Study Underway." *GLEAMS,* a publication of The Glaucoma Research Foundation, Winter-Spring 1987, Vol. 5 Nos. 1 and 2.

Migliazzo, Carl V., M.D., Robert N. Shaffer, M.D., Raisa Nykin, M.D., and Scott Magee, M.S. "Long-Term Analysis of Pigmentary Dispersion Syndrome and Pigmentary Glaucoma." *Ophthalmology* 93 (12) (December 1986): 1528–1536.

Miyake, K., M.D., K. Meisuda, and M. Inaba, M.D. "Corneal Endothelial Changes in Pseudoexfoliation Syndrome." *American Journal of Ophthalmology* 108 (1) (15 July 1989): 519–521.

Olsen, Randall J., M.D., Julie S. Lee, M.D., and Thom J. Zimmerman, M.D. "Glaucoma Associated With Penetrating Keratoplasty." In *The Glaucomas,* ed. Robert Ritch, M.D., M. Bruce Shields, M.D., and Theodore Krupin, M.D. St. Louis, MO: C.V. Mosby Co., 1989.

Prince, Andres M., M.D. "Glaucoma Associated With Retinal Disorders." In *The Glaucomas,* ed. Robert Ritch, M.D., M. Bruce Shields, M.D., and Theodore Krupin, M.D. St. Louis, MO: C.V. Mosby Co., 1989.

Richardson, Thomas M., "Pigmentary Glaucoma." In *The Glaucomas,* ed. Robert Ritch, M.D., M. Bruce Shields, M.D., and Theodore Krupin, M.D. St. Louis, MO: C.V. Mosby Co., 1989.

Schlotzer-Schrehardt, U., M.D., M. Kuchle, M.D., and G.O. Neumann, M.D. "Electron-Microscope Identification of Pseudoexfoliation Material in Extrabulbar Tissue." *Archives of Ophthalmology* 109 (4) (April 1991): 565–570.

Shields, M. Bruce, M.D. "Glaucomas Associated With Primary Disorders of the Corneal Endothelium." In *The Glaucomas,* ed. Robert Ritch, M.D., M. Bruce Shields, M.D., and Theodore Krupin, M.D. St. Louis, MO: C.V. Mosby Co., 1989.

Simmons, Richard J., M.D., John V. Thomas, M.D., and Moustafa K. Yaqub, M.D. "Malignant Glaucoma." In *The Glaucomas,* ed. Robert Ritch, M.D., M. Bruce Shields, M.D., and Theodore Krupin, M.D. St. Louis, MO: C.V. Mosby Co., 1989.

Streeten, B.D., M.D., A.J. Dark, M.D., R.N. Wallace, M.D., Li Zy, M.D., and J.A. Hoepner, M.D. "Pseudoexfoliative Fibrilopathy in the Skin of Patients With Ocular Pseudoexfoliation." *American Journal of Ophthalmology* 110 (5) (15 November 1990): 490–491.

Ward, Martin, M.D. "Neovascular Glaucoma." In *The Glaucomas,* ed. Robert Ritch, M.D., M. Bruce Shields, M.D., and Theodore Krupin, M.D. St. Louis, MO: C.V. Mosby Co., 1989.

Werner, Elliot B., M.D. "Low-Tension Glaucoma." In *The Glaucomas,* ed. Robert Ritch, M.D., M. Bruce Shields, M.D., and Theodore Krupin, M.D. St. Louis, MO: C.V. Mosby Co., 1989.

Chapter 3
Wrong Signals—Glaucoma in Infants and Children

"When a Child Has Glaucoma." *Glaucoma Watch,* a publication of Otsuka America Pharmaceutical, Inc., Vol. 2 No. 2.

Alward, William A.M., M.D. *Eye to Eye,* the newsletter of the Glaucoma Foundation, Vol 6 No. 1, Winter 1995.

Baker, Pam. "Alternative Therapy to Radial Keratotomy." National Eye Research Foundation, 910 Skokie Boulevard, Northbrook, IL 60062–4013.

Cantor, Louis B., M.D. "Glaucomas Associated With Developmental Disorders." In *The Glaucomas,* ed. Robert Ritch, M.D., M. Bruce Shields, M.D., and Theodore Krupin, M.D. St. Louis, MO: C.V. Mosby Co., 1989.

Dickens, Christopher J., M.D., and H. Dunbar Hoskins, M.D. "Epidemiology and Pathophysiology of Congenital Glaucoma." In *The Glaucomas,* ed. Robert Ritch, M.D., M. Bruce Shields, M.D., and Theodore Krupin, M.D. St. Louis, MO: C.V. Mosby Co., 1989.

Gramer, F., T. Nippold, M. Tausch, and C. Kraemer. "Visual Outcome After Goniotomy in Primary Congenital Glaucoma." Poster presentation at ARVO Conference, Fort Lauderdale, FL, 1996.

Hannon, Florence. "Contacts: An Rx for Myopic Kids?" *Contact Lenses,* June 1994.

Harris, A., Ph.D., G.L. Spaeth, M.D., R.C. Sergott, M.D., L.J. Katz, M.D., Louis B. Cantor, M.D., and B.J. Martin, Ph.D. "Retrobulbar Arterial Hemodynamic Effects of Betaxolol and Timolol in Normal-Tension Glaucoma." *American Journal of*

Ophthalmology Vol. 120 (1995):168–175.

Hoskins, H. Dunbar, Jr., M.D., and John Hetherington, Jr., M.D. "The Developmental Glaucomas." Proceedings of the New Orleans Academy of Medicine Glaucoma Symposium. St. Louis, MO: C.V. Mosby, 1980.

Hoskins, H. Dunbar, Jr., M.D., Ribert N., Shaffer, M.D., and John Hetherington, M.D. "Anatomical Classification of the Developmental Glaucomas." *Archives of Ophthalmology* 102 (September 1984): 1331–1336.

Hoskins, H. Dunbar, Jr., M.D., Robert N. Shaffer, M.D., and John Hetherington, M.D. "Goniotomy vs. Trabeculotomy." *Journal of Pediatric Ophthalmology and Strabismus* 21 (4) (1984): 143–158.

Iwach, Andrew, M.D. "Sturge-Weber Syndrome: Glaucoma Study Results Encouraging." *GLEAMS,* a publication of The Glaucoma Research Foundation, Vol. 7 No. 3, Fall 1989.

Kanski, Jack J., M.D., and James A. McAllister, M.D. "Primary Congenital Glaucoma." In *Glaucoma, A Color Manual of Diagnosis and Treatment.* London, England: Butterworth & Company, 1989.

Lotufo, David, M.D., Robert Ritch, M.D., Lucian Szmyd, Jr., M.D., and James E. Burris, M.D. "Juvenile Glaucoma, Race, and Refraction." *Journal of the American Medical Association* 261 (2) (13 January 1989): 249–252.

Luntz, Maurice H., M.D., and Raymond Harrison, M.D. "Surgery for Congenital Glaucoma." In *The Glaucomas,* ed. Robert Ritch, M.D., M. Bruce Shields, M.D., and Theodore Krupin, M.D. St. Louis, MO: C.V. Mosby Co., 1989.

Pillunat, Lutz E., M.D., Gerhard K. Lang, M.D., and Alon Harris, Ph.D. "The Visual Response to Increased Ocular Blood Flow in Normal-Pressure Glaucoma." Survey of Ophthalmology Vol 38, supplement (May 1994): S139–S148.

Shaffer, Robert N., M.D., and Robert L. Tour, M.D. "A Comparative Study of Gonioscopic Methods." *Transactions of the American Ophthalmological Society 1956.* First presented at the 91st annual meeting of the American Ophthalmological Society, White Sulphur Springs, West Virginia, June 1955.

Stein, Judith. "Study Confirms Value of Treatment to Prevent Blindness in Premature Babies." National Eye Institute, 14 April 1996.

Stoilov, Ivaylo, A. Nurten Akarsu, and Mansoor Sarfarazi. "Identification of Three Different Truncating Mutations in Cytochrome P4501B1 (CYP1B1) as the Principal Cause of Primary Congenital Glaucome (Buphthalmos) in Families Linked to the GLC3A Locus on Chromosome 2p21." *Human Molecular Genetics* 66 (4) (1997):641–648.

Tawara, Akihiko, M.D., and Hajime Inomata, M.D. "Congenital Abnormalities of the Trabecular Meshwork in Primary Glaucoma With

Open Angle." *Glaucoma* 9 (1) (1987): 28–34.

Vogel, Gretchen. "Glaucoma Gene Provides Light at the End of the Tunnel." *Science,* 31 January 1997.

Chapter 4
Diagnosis: The Equilateral Triangle

Airaksinen, P. Johani, M.D., Anja Toulonen, M.D., and Elliot B. Berner, M.D. "Clinical Evaluation of the Optic Nerve Fiber Layer." In *The Glaucomas,* ed. Robert Ritch, M.D., M. Bruce Shields, M.D., and Theodore Krupin, M.D. St. Louis, MO: C.V. Mosby Co., 1989.

Becker, Bernard, M.D. "Glaucoma Detection at the Earliest Possible Moment." National Glaucoma Research Report, Summer 1986.

Bretton, Michael E., M.D., and Bruce A. Drum, M.D. In *The Glaucomas,* ed. Robert Ritch, M.D., M. Bruce Shields, M.D., and Theodore Krupin, M.D. St. Louis, MO: C.V. Mosby Co., 1989.

Brody, Jane E. "Human Eye Found Doing Second Job." *The New York Times,* 3 January 1995.

Caprioli, Joseph, M.D. "Quantitative Measurements of the Optic Nerve Head." In *The Glaucomas,* ed. Robert Ritch, M.D., M. Bruce Shields, M.D., and Theodore Krupin, M.D. St. Louis, MO: C.V. Mosby Co., 1989.

Chauhan, Balwantray C., Ph.D., Raymond P. LeBlanc, M.D., Terry A. McCormick, and Jamie B. Rogers, M.D. "Test-Retest Variability of Topographic Measurements With Confocal Scanning Laser Tomography in Patients with Glaucoma and Control Subjects." *American Journal of Ophthalmology* 118 (4) (1994): 9–15.

Cyrlin, Marshall N., M.D. "Automated Perimetry." In *The Glaucomas,* ed. Robert Ritch, M.D., M. Bruce Shields, M.D., and Theodore Krupin, M.D. St. Louis, MO: C.V. Mosby Co., 1989.

"Damato Campimeter for Glaucoma, The." Chicago, IL: Prevent Blindness America.

Danyluk, Andrew W., M.D., and David Paton, M.D. "Diagnosis and Management of Glaucoma." *Clinical Symposia* Vol 43 (4), Ciba-Geigy Corporation, 1991.

"Disk Changes Can Be Detected Objectively." Interview with Bernard D. Schwartz, M.D. *Ophthalmology Times* 14 (4) (1989): 1, 34–35

San Leandro, CA: "Field Analyzer Primer, The." Manufacturer's product literature. San Leandro, CA: Humphrey Instruments, Inc.

"Fundus Topography by Laser Scanning Tomography." Manufacturer's literature on the Heidelberg Retina Tomograph. Carlsbad, CA: Heidelberg Engineering, Inc.

Harris, A., Ph.D., R.C. Sergott, M.D., G.L. Spaeth, M.D., J.L. Katz, M.D., B.A. Shoemaker, M.D., and B.J. Martin, Ph.D. "Color Doppler Analysis of Ocular Blood Velocity in Normal-Tension Glaucoma."

American Journal of Ophthalmology Vol. 118 (November 1994): 642–649.

Hayreh, Schan Songh, M.D. "Blood Supply of the Anterior Optic Nerve." In *The Glaucomas,* ed. Robert Ritch, M.D., M. Bruce Shields, M.D., and Theodore Krupin, M.D. St. Louis, MO: C.V. Mosby Co., 1989.

Hernandez, M. Rosario, M.D., and Arthur H. Neufeld, M.D. "The Extracellular Matrix of the Trabecular Meshwork and the Optic Nerve Head." In *The Glaucomas,* ed. Robert Ritch, M.D., M. Bruce Shields, M.D., and Theodore Krupin, M.D. St. Louis, MO: C.V. Mosby Co., 1989.

Hoskins, H. Dunbar, M.D., Scott D. Magee, M.D., Michael V. Drake, M.D., and Martin N. Kidd, M.D. "Confidence Intervals for Changes in Automated Visual Fields." *British Journal of Ophthalmology* 72 (8) (1988): 591–597.

"Humphrey Field Analyzer II." Manufacturer's product literature. San Leandro, CA: Humphrey Instruments.

Lynn, John R., M.D., Ronald L. Fellman, M.D., and Richard J. Starita, M.D. "Exploring the Normal Visual Field." In *The Glaucomas,* ed. Robert Ritch, M.D., M. Bruce Shields, M.D., and Theodore Krupin, M.D. St. Louis, MO: C.V. Mosby Co., 1989.

March, Wayne F., M.D. "A New Window on the Eye...and the Body." Presentation at Science Writers Seminar in Ophthalmology, sponsored by Research to Prevent Blindness, Orlando, FL, October 1995.

McDermott, John A., M.D. "Tomography." In *The Glaucomas,* ed. Robert Ritch, M.D., M. Bruce Shields, M.D., and Theodore Krupin, M.D. St. Louis, MO: C.V. Mosby Co., 1989.

Michelson, G., M.D., M.J. Langhans, M.D., and M.J.M. Groh, M.D. "Perfusion of the Juxtapapillary Retina and the Neuroretinal Rim Area in Primary Open Angle Glaucoma." *Journal of Glaucoma* 5 (2) (1996): 91-98.

Mikelberg, Frederick S., M.D., Craig M. Parfitt, B.A.Sc., Nicholas V. Swindale, D.Phil., Stuart L. Graham, M.B.B.S., Stephen M. Drance, M.D., and Ray Gosine, Ph.D. "Ability of the Heidelberg Tomograph to Detect Early Glaucomatous Visual Field Loss." *Journal of Glaucoma* 4 (4) (1995): 242–247.

Palmberg, Paul, M.D. "Gonioscopy." In *The Glaucomas,* ed. Robert Ritch, M.D., M. Bruce Shields, M.D., and Theodore Krupin, M.D. St. Louis, MO: C.V. Mosby Co., 1989.

Puliafito, Carmen A., M.D., Michael R. Hee, M.S., Joel S. Schuman, M.D., and James G. Fujimoto, Ph.D. "Optical Coherence Tomography: A New Eye on the Retina." Presentation at Science Writers Seminar in Ophthalmology, sponsored by Research to Prevent Blindness, Orlando, FL, October 1995.

Radius, Ronald L, M.D. "Anatomy

and Pathophysiology of the Retina and Optic Nerve." In *The Glaucomas,* ed. Robert Ritch, M.D., M. Bruce Shields, M.D., and Theodore Krupin, M.D. St. Louis, MO: C.V. Mosby Co., 1989.

Ritch, Robert, M.D. "Ultrasound Biomicroscope Promises to Revolutionize the Diagnosis and Management of Glaucoma." *Eye to Eye,* the newsletter of the Glaucoma Foundation, Vol. 5 No. 3, Summer 1994.

Rosenberg, Lisa F., M.D. "Glaucoma: Early Detection and Therapy for Prevention of Vision Loss." *American Family Physician, Eye and Eye Disorders* 52 (8) (1995): 2289–2298.

Schwartz, Bernard D., M.D. "New Knowledge Obtained by Modern Methods of Studying the Glaucomatous Optic Disc." *Ophthalmologie* 5 (1991): 116–125.

Schwartz, Bernard D., M.D., Takenori Takamoto, Ph.D., and Paul Nagin, Ph.D. "Photogrammetry and Image Analysis of Optic Disc, Retinal Nerve Fiber Layer, and Retinal Circulation in Glaucoma." *Ophthalmology Clinics of North America* 4 (4) (1991): 733–745.

Tsai, Clark S., M.D., Linda Zangwill, Ph.D., Casimiro Gonzalez, M.D., Ino Irak, M.D., Valerie Garden, M.D., Rivak Hoffman, B.A., and Weinreb, Robert N., M.D. "Ethnic Differences in Optic Nerve Head Topography." *Journal of Glaucoma* 4 (4) (1995): 248–257.

Williams, Ruth, M.D. "Visual field Research." *GLEAMS,* a publication of The Glaucoma Research Foundation, Fall 1991, Vol 9 No. 3.

Zeimer, Ran C., M.D. "Circadian Variations in Intraocular Pressure." In *The Glaucomas,* ed. Robert Ritch, M.D., M. Bruce Shields, M.D., and Theodore Krupin, M.D. St. Louis, MO: C.V. Mosby Co., 1989.

Zinser, Gerhard. "Tomographic Measurements at the Fundus with the Heidelberg Retina Tomography." In *Scanning Laser Ophthalmoscopy, Tomography, and Microscopy,* ed. A.E. Elsner. New York: Plenum Press, 1992.

Chapter 5
Medication: The First Line of Defense

American Association of Retired Persons. *AARP Pharmacy Service Prescription Drug Handbook* 2nd Ed. New York: Harper Perennial, 1992.

Bijlefeld, Marjolijn. "What's New in Glaucoma Drugs." *Eyecare Techology* January/February 1995.

Caputo, Brian J., M.D., and Jay L. Katz, M.D. "The Quality of Life of the Glaucoma Patient in Light of Treatment Modalities." *Current Opinion in Ophthalmology* 5 (11) (1994): 10–15.

"Despite Marijuana Furor, 8 Users Get Drugs From the Goverment." *The New York Times,* 1 December 1996, 33.

Dreyer, Evan Benjamin, M.D. "Glutamate 'Excitotoxicity' and Glaucoma." Presentation at Science Writers Seminar in Ophthalmology, sponsored by Research to Prevent Blindness, Orlando, FL, October 1995.

Epstein, David L, M.D. "The Search for a Rational Treatment for Glaucoma: A Trabecular Diuretic." Presentation at Science Writers Seminar in Ophthalmology, sponsored by Research to Prevent Blindness, Universal City, CA, April 1993.

Everitt, Daniel E., M.D., and Jerry Avorn, M.D. "Systemic Effects of Medications Used to Treat Glaucoma." *Annals of Internal Medicine* 112 (2) (1990): 120–125.

Feldman, Miriam K. "Prostaglandin for Glaucoma Will Expand Treatment Possibilities." *Review of Optometry,* 15 April 1995

Friedland, Beth R., M.D., and Thomas H. Maren, M.D. "Carbonic Anhydrase Inhibitors." In *The Glaucomas,* ed. Robert Ritch, M.D., M. Bruce Shields, M.D., and Theodore Krupin, M.D. St. Louis, MO: C.V. Mosby Co., 1989.

Greenfield, David S., M.D. "New Directions in Glaucoma Treatment." *Eye to Eye,* the newsletter of the Glaucoma Foundation, Vol. 7 No. 4 , 1996.

Gross, Jonathan, M.D., Robert W. Daly, M.D., Carl B. Camras, M.D., and Maurice H. Luntz, M.D. "A Current Approach to Medical Therapy of the Glaucomas." New York: The National Glaucoma Trust, Inc., 1991.

Hartenbaum, David, M.D., Michael Stek, M.D., Brian Haggert, M.S., Dan Holder, Ph.D., John Earle, Ph.D., Alice Wysocki, M.S., and Bernard Schwartz, M.D. "Quantitative and Cost Evaluation of Three Antiglaucoma Beta-Blocker Agents: Timoptic-XE vs. Two Generic Levobunolol Products." *The American Journal of Managed Care* Vol. 2 No. 2 (1996): 157–162.

Hilts, Philip J. "Cause of Blindness in Glaucoma May Be Nerve Toxin, Not Fluids." *The New York Times,* 20 March 1996.

Hoskins, H. Dunbar, Jr., M.D., John Hetherington, Jr., M.D., Scott D. Magee, M.S., Raisa Naykhin, M.D., and Carl V. Migliazzo, M.D. "Clinical Experience With Timolol in Childhood Glaucoma." *Archives of Ophthalmology* 103 (1985): 1163–1165.

Hosoda, Motohiro, M.D., Shigeki Yamabayashi, M.D., Masaschi Furuta, M.D., and Shigeo Tsukahara, M.D. "Do Glaucoma Patients Use Eye Drops Correctly?" *Journal of Glaucoma* 4 (3) (1995).

Hyman, Barry N., M.D. "Calcium Channel Blockers Cause Controversy." *OWN,* September 1995, 15.

Liberman, Ellen, Ph.D. "Glaucoma Research: What's Next." *Review of Ophthalmology,* June 1994.

Lustgarten, J.D., M.D., and S.M. Podos, M.D. "Topical Timolol and the Nursing Mother." *Archives of Ophthalmology* 101 (9) (1983): 1381–1382.

McMahon, Charles D., M.D., Robert N. Shaffer, M.D., H. Dunbar Hoskins, Jr., M.D., and John Hetherington, Jr., M.D. "Adverse Effects Experienced by Patients Taking Timolol." *American Journal of Ophthalmology* 88 (1979): 736–738.

Mittag, Thomas W., M.D. "Adrenergic and Dopaminergic Drugs in Glaucoma." In *The Glaucomas,* ed. Robert Ritch, M.D., M. Bruce Shields, M.D., and Theodore Krupin, M.D. St. Louis, MO: C.V. Mosby Co., 1989.

Nardin, George F., M.D., Thom J. Zimmerman, M.D., Alan H. Zalta, M.D., and Kathy Felts, M.D. "Ocular Cholinergic Agents." In *The Glaucomas,* ed. Robert Ritch, M.D., M. Bruce Shields, M.D., and Theodore Krupin, M.D. St. Louis, MO: C.V. Mosby Co., 1989.

Netland, Peter A., M.D. "Glaucoma Therapy from the Heart: Calcium Channel Blockers." Presentation at Science Writers Seminar in Ophthalmology, sponsored by Research to Prevent Blindness, Orlando, FL, October 1995.

O'Connor, Tom. "New Drug to Improve Care of Glaucoma Patients." Omaha, NE: University of Nebraska Medical Center Department of Public Affairs, 24 January 1996.

Rácz, Peter, M.D., Mária R. Ruzsonyi, M.D., Zoltán Nagy, M.D., and Laszlo Z. Bito, Ph.D. "Maintained Intraocular Pressure Reduction With Once-a-Day Application of a New Prostaglandin, F2oe Analogue (PhXA41)." *Archives of Ophthalmology* Vol. 111 (May 1993): 657–661.

Rácz, Peter, M.D., Mária R. Ruzsonyi, M.D., Zoltán Nagy, M.D., Zsuzsanna Gagyi, M.D., and Laszlo Z. Bito, Ph.D. "Around-the-Clock Intraocular Pressure Reduction With Once-Daily Application of a Latanprost by Itself or in Combination With Timolol." *Archives of Ophthalmology* Vol. 114 (March 1996): 268–273.

Schwartz, Michal, Ph.D., Eti Yoles, Ph.D., Arieh Solomon, M.D., and Michael Belkin, M.D. "Potential Therapy of Glaucomatous Neuropathy: Neuroprotection and Neuroregeneration." Paper to be published in the *Journal of Glaucoma.*

Steinberger, David A. "Doctor, I Have a Question." *Eye to Eye,* the newsletter of the Glaucoma Foundation. Vol 5 No. 3, 1995.

"Trusopt." Formulary information monograph. West Point, PA: Merck & Co., Inc., 1994.

White, Manley F., professor of pharmacology, faculty of medical sciences, University of West Indies, Kingston, Jamaica. Telephone conversation regarding drug made from marijuana to treat glaucoma.

Wilson, M. Roy, M.D., and Michael V. Drake, M.D. "Glaucoma in Blacks: Epidemiology and Management." *Clinical Signs,* a publication of Alcon Laboratories, Fort Worth, TX, 13 (2) (1992): 2–15.

Zimmerman, Thom J., M.D. "How to Apply Eye Drops Properly and Why It Is Important." *Eye to Eye,* the newsletter of the Glaucoma Foundation, Vol 5 No. 3, 1995.

Chapter 6
The Healing Light

Ah-Fat, Frank G., M.D., and Christopher R. Canning, M.D. "A Comparison of the Efficacy of Holmium Laser Sclerostomy ab externo versus Trabeculectomy in the Treatment of Glaucoma." *Eye,* a publication of the Ophthalmological Society of the United Kingdom, 8 (1994): 402–405.

Allingham, R. Rand, M.D., Annelies W. deKater, Ph.D., A. Robert Bellows, M.D., and Joseph Hsu. "Probe Placement and Power Levels in Contact Trans-Scleral Neodymium:YAG Cyclophotocoagulation." *Archives of Ophthalmology* 108 (1990): 738–742.

Bachman, J.A., M.D., and J.E. Conto, M.D. "Postoperative Complications of Subconjunctival THC-YAG (Holmium) Laser Sclerostomy." *Journal of the American Optometry Association* 65 (5) (1994): 311–320.

Bellows, A. Robert, M.D., and Joseph H. Krug, Jr., M.D. "Cyclodestructive Surgery." In *The Glaucomas,* ed. Robert Ritch, M.D., M. Bruce Shields, M.D., and Theodore Krupin, M.D. St. Louis, MO: C.V. Mosby Co., 1989.

Boyd, Benjamin E. "What Are the Contributions and Techniques of the Two New Highly Effective Laser Surgical Procedures for Glaucoma? What is the Update Evaluation of the 'Old' Laser Techniques for Glaucoma?" *Highlights of Ophthalmology* 16 (6) (1988) 5–14.

Fankhauser, Franz, M.D., Sylwia Kwashniewska, M.D., and Raphael M. Klapper, M.D. "Neodymium Q-Switched YAG Laser Lysis of Iris Lens Synechiae." *Ophthalmology* 92 (6) (1985): 790–792.

Gayton, Johnny L., M.D. "A 'Smart' Bomb for Glaucoma Treatment?" *Review of Ophthalmology, May 1995.*

Gimbel, Howard, M.D., Richard J. Mackool, M.D., Johnny Gayton, M.D., Andrew Iwach, M.D., and Martin Uram, M.D. "Endoscopic Cyclophotocoagulation in Glaucoma Treatment." A symposium. October 1995.

Goldstock, Bruce J., M.D., and Robert N. Weinreb, M.D. "Laser Treatment in Open-Angle Glaucoma." In *The Glaucomas,* ed. Robert Ritch, M.D., M. Bruce Shields, M.D., and Theodore Krupin, M.D. St. Louis, MO: C.V. Mosby Co., 1989.

Grayson, Douglas K., Sc.B., Carl B. Camras, M.D., Steven M. Podos, M.D., and Jacqueline S. Lustgarten, M.D. "Long-Term Reduction of Intraocular Pressure After Repeat Argon Laser Trabeculoplasty." *American Journal of Ophthalmology* 106 (1988): 312–321.

Greenidge, Kevin C., M.D. "Laser Therapy of Glaucoma." *Journal of the National Medical Association* 74 (4) (1983): 373–377.

Greenidge, Kevin C., M.D. "Nd: YAG Capsulotomy—Energy Requirements and Visual Outcomes." *Cataract* 1 (4) (1984).

Greenidge, Kevin C., M.D., Merlyn

M. Rodrigues, M.D., George L. Spaeth, M.D., Carlo Traverso, M.D., and Stanley Weinreb, Ph.D. "Acute Intraocular Pressure Elevation After Argon Laser Trabeculoplasty and Iridectomy: A Clinicopathologic Study." *Ophthalmic Surgery* 15 (2) (1984): 705110.

Hetherington, John, Jr., M.D. "Capsular Glaucoma: Management Philosophy." *Acta Ophthalmologica* 66 Supplement 184 (1988): 138–140.

Horowitz, Jed. "Laser Light on Glaucoma: The Therapeutic Burn." *Sight-Saving* Vol. 51 No. 2 (1982): 12–15, 22.

Hoskins, H. Dunbar, Jr., M.D., and Carl Migliazzo, M.D. "Management of Failing Filtering Blebs With the Argon Laser." *Ophthalmic Surgery* 15 (9) (1984): 731–733.

Hoskins, H. Dunbar, Jr., M.D., Andrew G. Iwach, M.D., Michael V. Drake, M.D., Bradley L. Schuster, M.D., Arthur Vassiliadis, Ph.D., J. Brooks Crawford, M.D., and David R. Hennings, M.S. "Subconjunctival THC:YAG Laser Limbal Sclerostomy ab externo in the Rabbit." *Ophthalmic Surgery* 21 (8) (1990): 589–592.

Klapper, R.M., M.D., and J.M. Dodick, M.D. "Transpupillar Argon Laser Cyclophotocoagulation (T.A.L.C.)." *Docum. Ophthal.*, Proceedings Series 36, 197–203. The Hague, Netherlands: Dr. W. Junk Publishers, 1984.

Klapper, Raphael M., M.D., Thaddeus Wandel, M.D., Eric Donnenfeld, M.D., and Henry D. Perry, M.D. "Transscleral Neodymium:YAG Thermal Cyclophotocoagulation in Refractory Glaucoma." *Ophthalmology* 95 (6) (1988): 719–722.

Kwasniewski, Sylwia, M.D., Franz Fankhauser, M.D., and Raphael M. Klapper, M.D. "Neodymium:YAG Microsurgery for Amelioration of Therapeutically Refractive Ocular Disease: Report of Two Cases." *Ophthalmic Laser Therapy* 2 (2) (1987): 88–93.

Latina, Mark A., M.D., Shlomo Melamed, M.D., Wayne F. March, M.D., Michael A. Kass, M.D., and Allan E. Kolker, M.D. "Gonioscopie ab interno Laser Sclerostomy." *Ophthalmology* 99 (11) (1992): 1736–1744.

Lieberman, Marc F., M.D., H. Dunbar Hoskins, Jr., M.D., and John Hetherington, Jr., M.D. "Laser Trabeculoplasty and the Glaucomas." *Ophthalmology* 90 (7) (1983): 790–795.

Mainster, Martin A., M.D. "Clinical Laser Physics." In *The Glaucomas*, ed. Robert Ritch, M.D., M. Bruce Shields, M.D., and Theodore Krupin, M.D. St. Louis, MO: C.V. Mosby Co., 1989.

Nataloni, Rochelle. "New Directions in Glaucoma Treatment." *Ocular Surgery News* 12 (12) (1994).

Quigley, Harry A., M.D. "Studies of Glaucoma Damage and Its Prevention by Laser and Surgical Therapy." *Eye-Gram*, newsletter of National Glaucoma Research, Beltsville, MD.

Ritch, Robert, M.D. "Doctor, I Have a Question." *Eye to Eye,* the newsletter of the Glaucoma Foundation, Vol. 6 No. 3, 1995.

Ritch, Robert, M.D., Jeffrey Liebman, M.D., and Ira S. Solomon, M.D. "Laser Iridectomy and Iridoplasty." In *The Glaucomas,* ed. Robert Ritch, M.D., M. Bruce Shields, M.D., and Theodore Krupin, M.D. St. Louis, MO: C.V. Mosby Co., 1989.

Schultz, Jeffrey, M.D. "Additional Uses of Laser Therapy in Glaucoma." In *The Glaucomas,* ed. Robert Ritch, M.D., M. Bruce Shields, M.D., and Theodore Krupin, M.D. St. Louis, MO: C.V. Mosby Co., 1989.

Schwartz, Louis W., M.D., George L. Spaeth, M.D., Carlo Traverso, M.D., and Kevin C. Greenidge, M.D. "Variation of Techniques on the Results of Argon Laser Trabeculoplasty." *Ophthalmology* 90 (7) (1983): 781–784.

Seedor, John A., M.D., Kevin C. Greenidge, M.D., and Michael W. Dunn, M.D. "Neodymium:YAG Laser Iridectomy and Acute Cataract Formation in the Rabbit." *Ophthalmic Surgery* 17 (8) (1986): 478–482.

Traverso, Carlo E., M.D., George L. Spaeth, M.D., Richard J. Starita, M.D., Ronald L. Fellman, M.D., Kevin C. Greenidge, M.D., and Effie Poryzees. "Factors Affecting the Results of Argon Laser Trabeculoplasty in Open-Angle Glaucoma." *Ophthalmic Surgery* 17 (9) (1986): 554–559.

Traverso, Carlo E., M.D., Kevin C. Greenidge, M.D., and George L. Spaeth, M.D. "Formation of Peripheral Anterior Synechiae Following argon Laser Trabeculoplasty." *Archives of Ophthalmology* 102 (1984): 861–863.

Uram, Martin, M.D. "Combined Phacoemulsification, Endoscopic Ciliary Process Photocoagulation, and Intraocular Lens Implantation in Glaucoma Management." *Ophthalmic Surgery* 6 (11) (1995): 19–29.

Uram, Martin, M.D. "Ophthalmic Laser Microendoscope Ciliary Process Ablation in the Management of Neovascular Glaucoma." *Ophthalmology* 99 (12) (1992): 1823–1828.

Uram, Martin, M.D. "Ophthalmic Laser Microendoscope Endophotocoagulation." *Ophthalmology* 99 (12) (1992): 1829–1832.

Ward, Amy. "Laser Surgery." Northwest Orient, July 1984.

Wetzel, W., M.D., U. Schmidt-Erfurth, M.D., G. Haring, M.D., J. Reider, M.D., and others. "Laser Sclerostomy ab externo Using Two Different Infrared Lasers: A Clinical Comparison." *German Journal of Ophthalmology* 4 (1) (1995): 1–6.

Chapter 7
The Final Battalion

Ashton, Paul, Ph.D. "Biodegradable Codrugs: A New Concept in Treating Ocular Ills." Presentation at Science Writers Seminar in Ophthalmology, sponsored by Research to Prevent Blindness, Orlando, FL, October 1995.

Buxton, Jorge N., M.D., Kevin T. Lavery, M.D., Jeffery M. Liebmann, M.D., Douglas F. Buxton, M.D., and Robert Ritch, M.D. "Reconstruction of Filtering Blebs With Free Conjunctival Autografts." *Ophthalmology* 101 (4) (1992): 635–639.

Campbell, David G., M.D., and Angela Vela, M.D. "Modern Goniosynechialysis for the Treatment of Synechial Angle-Closure Glaucoma." *Ophthalmology* 19 (9) (1984): 1052–1060.

Carenini, B. Boles, M.D., and T. Rolle, M.D. "Updating on the Surgical Therapy of Glaucoma." *Italian Journal of Ophthalmology* 6 (1) (1992): 31–35.

Duke-Elder, S., M.D. *Diseases of the Lens and Vitreous, Glaucoma and Hypotony*. Vol 2, *Systems of Ophthalmology*. St. Louis, MO: C.V. Mosby Co., 1969.

Gaasterland, Douglas E., M.D., Paul R. Lichter, M.D., Steven M. Podos, M.D. "Which Comes First? The Best Initial Therapy for Primary Open-Angle Glaucoma Is:" Articles based on related talks at the 1991 annual meeting of the American Academy of Ophthalmology. *Ocular Surgery News*, 1 March 1992.

Greenidge, Kevin C., M.D., and Karen Allison, M.D. "Filtration Blebs: Formation, Development, Maturation, and Complications." *Ophthalmic Practice* 8 (5) (1990): 188–192.

Greenidge, Kevin C., M.D., George L. Spaeth, M.D., and Carlo E. Traverso, M.D. "Change in Appearance of the Optic Disc Associated With Lowering of Intraocular Pressure." Presentation at the 88th annual meeting of the American Academy of Ophthalmology, Chicago, IL, October 30-November 3, 1983.

Henahan, John F. "Advanced Glaucoma Patients Fare Better With Surgery." *Ophthalmology Times*, 1 July 1991.

Herschler, Jonathan, M.D., Alice U. Claflin, Ph.D., and Gilbert Fiorentino, B.S. "The Effect of Aqueous Humor on the Growth of Subconjunctival Fibroblasts in Tissue Culture and Its Implications for Glaucoma Surgery." *American Journal of Ophthalmology* 89 (1980): 245-249.

Hoskins, H. Dunbar, M.D., Scott D. Magee, M.S. "An Information Collection, Management and Analysis System for Glaucoma." *Geriatric Ophthalmology*, May/June 1986, 15–19.

Jay, Jeffrey L,. M.D. "Rational Choice of Therapy in Primary Open-Angle Glaucoma." *Eye* 6 (1992): 243–247.

Katz, L. Jay, M.D., and George L. Spaeth, M.D. "Filtration Surgery." In *The Glaucomas*, ed. Robert Ritch, M.D., M. Bruce Shields, M.D., and Theodore Krupin, M.D. St. Louis, MO: C.V. Mosby Co., 1989.

Kidd, Martin, F.R.C.S., John Hetherington, M.D., and Scott Magee, M.S. "Surgical Results in Iridocorneal Endothelial Syndrome." *Archives of Ophthalmology* 106 (1988): 199–201.

Kronfeld, P., M.D. "The Rise of Filter Operations." *Survey of Ophthalmology* 17 (1972): 168.

Kronfeld, Peter Clemens, M.D. *Introduction to Ophthalmology*. C.C. Thomas, 1938.

Krupin, Theodore, M.D., and Scott M. Spector, M.D. "Setons in Glaucoma Surgery." In *The Glaucomas,* ed. Robert Ritch, M.D., M. Bruce Shields, M.D., and Theodore Krupin, M.D. St. Louis, MO: C.V. Mosby Co., 1989.

Migdal, Clive, M.D. "3 Reasons for Performing Early Filtration Surgery." *Review of Ophthalmology* February 1996: 8182.

Parrish, Richard Kenneth, II, M.D., and Robert Folbert, M.D. "Wound Healing in Glaucoma Surgery." In *The Glaucomas,* ed. Robert Ritch, M.D., M. Bruce Shields, M.D., and Theodore Krupin, M.D. St. Louis, MO: C.V. Mosby Co., 1989.

Rizzo, Joseph F., M.D. "Retina on a Chip." Presentation at Science Writers Seminar in Ophthalmology, sponsored by Research to Prevent Blindness, Orlando, FL, October 1995.

Savage, James A., M.D., and Kassim A. Khan, M.D. "Fine-Tuning the Filter: Adjusting Aqueous Humor Dynamics." *Clinical Signs* 11 (4) (1990): 3–15.

Sherwood, Mark B., M.D., Mordechai Sharir, M.D., Thom J. Zimmerman, M.D., and Jeffrey S. Schultz, M.D. "Initial Treatment of Glaucoma: Surgery or Medications." *Survey of Ophthalmology* 37 (4) (1993): 293–299.

Shields, M. Bruce, M.D. "Surgical Management of Coexisting Cataract and Glaucoma." In *The Glaucomas,* ed. Robert Ritch, M.D., M. Bruce Shields, M.D., and Theodore Krupin, M.D. St. Louis, MO: C.V. Mosby Co., 1989.

Solish, Alfred, M.D. "Indications for Molteno Implants." *Molteno Implant Newsletter* Vol. 1 No. 2, 1990.

Starita, Richard J., M.D., Ronald L. Fellman, M.D., George L. Spaeth, M.D., Effie M. Poryzees, B.A., Kevin C. Greenidge, M.D., and Carlo E. Traverso, M.D. "Short- and Long-Term Effects of Postoperative Corticosteroids on Trabeculectomy." *Ophthalmology* 92 (7) (1985): 938–946.

Tornqvist, Goran, M.D., and Liv Kari Droisum, M.D. "Trabeculectomies." *Acta Ophthalmologica* 69 (1990): 450–454.

Weiss, Daniel I., M.D., Robert N. Shaffer, M.D., and David O. Harrington, M.D. "Treatment of Malignant Glaucoma With Intravenous Mannitol Infusion." *Archives of Ophthalmology* 69 (1963): 154–158.

Chapter 8
The Cataract Connection

Gilmore, Michael S., Ph.D. "The Molecular Roots of Bacterial Eye Infections." Presentation at Science Writers Seminar in Ophthalmology, sponsored by Research to Prevent Blindness, Orlando, FL, October 1995.

Gwon, Arlene, M.D., Hiro Enomoto, Joseph Horowitz, and Margaret H. Garner. "Induction of de novo Synthesis of Crystalline Lenses in Aphakic Rabbits." *Exp. Eye Res.* 49 (1989): 913–926.

Gwon, Arlene, M.D., Lawrence Gruber, B.S., and Crystal Cunanan. "Lens Regeneration in New Zealand Albino Rabbits After Endocapsular Cataract Extraction." *Investigative Ophthalmology & Visual Science* 34 (6) (1993): 2125–2129.

Gwon, Arlene, M.D., Lawrence J. Gruber, B.S., and Christine Mantras, B.S. "Restoring Lens Capsule Integrity Enhances Lens Regeneration in New Zealand Albino Rabbits and Cats." *Journal of Cataract and Refractive Surgery* 19 (1993): 735–746.

Gwon, Arlene E., M.D., Robert L. Jones, Lawrence J. Gruber, B.S., and Christine Mantras, B.S. "Lens Regeneration in Juvenile and Adult Rabbits Measured by Image Analysis." *Investigative Ophthalmology & Visual Science* 33 (7) (1992): 2279–2283.

Gwon, Arlene, M.D., Lawrence J. Gruber, B.S., and Karen E. Mundwiler. "A Histologic Study of Lens Regeneration in Aphakic Rabbits." *Investigative Ophthalmology & Visual Science* 341 (3) (1990): 540–547.

Hoskins, H. Dunbar., Jr., M.D. "Management of Pseudophakic Glaucoma." *Glaucoma and Cataract Symposium*. Amsterdam, Netherlands: Kugler Publications, 1986.

King, Deen G., M.D., and William E. Layden, M.D. "Glaucoma and Intraocular Lens Implantation." In *The Glaucomas*, ed. Robert Ritch, M.D., M. Bruce Shields, M.D., and Theodore Krupin, M.D. St. Louis, MO: C.V. Mosby Co., 1989.

Mackool, Richard J., M.D. "Cataract Surgery Opens Window for New Glaucoma Treatment." Article based on an address by Dr. Mackool. *Glaucoma Support and Education Group Newsletter* Vol. 10 No. 1, 1996.

Mackool, Richard J., M.D. "Understanding Your Eyes." Patient information booklet. Astoria, New York: The Mackool Eye Institute.

Paton, David, M.D., and John A. Craig, M.D. "Management of Cataracts." *Clinical Symposia*, Vol 42 (4): 3–32, Cigba-Geigy Corporation, 1990.

Schneider, Pavel, M.D., Josef Flammer, M.D., and Phillip Hendrickson, Ph.D. "Does Glaucoma Surgery Accelerate Cataract Development?" *Cataract* 16 (1) (1994): 6–11.

Shaffer, Robert N., M.D., and Gerald Rosenthal, M.D. "Comparison of Cataract Incidence in Normal and Glaucomatous Populations." *American Journal of Ophthalmology* 69 (3) (1970): 368–370.

Chapter 9
Complementary Therapies

Angier, Natalie. "From the Body Itself, Hope for a New Breed of Antibiotics." *The New York Times*, 26 February 1991.

Arcanus, A.B. *Eye Diseases,* 6th Ed. Beaconsfield, England: Beaconsfield Publishers, Ltd., 1988.

Banker, Deborah E., M.D. *Self Help Vision Care.* Boulder, CO: World Care, 1994.

Barasch, Douglas. "The Mainstreaming of Alternative Medicine." *The New York Times Magazine,* Part 2, 4 October 1992.

Bergner, Paul. "Ginkgo Biloba: Tonic for the Ailments of Old Age." *Townsend Letter for Doctors,* April 1988.

Bettini, V., and others. "Effects of *Vaccinum myrtillus* Anthocyanosides on Vascular Smooth Muscle." *Fitoterapia* 55 (1984): 265–272.

Biddleman, J. "Bilberry, Huckleberry, Whortleberry, Etc." *Medical Herbalism* 6 (4) (Winter 1994–1995): 6.

Bravetti, G. "Preventive Medical Treatment of Senile Catarract With Vitamin E and Anthocyanosides: Clinical Evaluation." *Ann. Ottal. Clin. Ocul.* 115 (1989): 109.

Brody, Jane E. "Relaxation Method May Aid Health." *The New York Times,* 7 August 1996.

Buliero, G. "The Inhibitory Effects of Anthocyanosides on Human Platelet Aggregation." *Fitoterapia* 60 (1989): 69.

Campion, Edward M., M.D. "Why Unconventional Medicine?" *The New England Journal of Medicine* 328 (28 January 1993): 292–283.

Caselli, L. "Clinical and Electroretinographic Study on Activity of Anthocyanosides." *Arch. Med. Int.* 37 (1985): 29–35.

Chopra, Deepak, M.D. *Quantum Healing: Exploring the Frontiers of Mind/Body Medicine.* New York: Bantam Books, 1989.

Chopra, Deepak. *Perfect Health: The Complete Mind/Body Guide.* New York: Harmony Books, 1989.

Chopra, Deepak, M.D. *Unconditional Life: Discovering the Power to Fulfill Your Dreams.* New York: Bantam Books, 1991.

Cousins, Norman. *Anatomy of an Illness.* New York: W.W. Norton Co., 1979.

Cunio, Lauren. "Vaccinium myrtillus." *Australian Journal of Medical Herbalism* 5 (4) (1993): 81–85.

Dabov, S., G. Goutoranov, R. Ivanova, and N. Petkova. "Clinical Application of Acupuncture in Ophthalmology." *Acupuncture and Electro-Therapeutics Research* Vol. 10 No. 1/2, 1985, 79–93.

Egan, Timothy. "Seattle Officials Seeking to Established Subsidized Natural Medicine Clinic." *The New York Times,* 3 January 1996.

"Eyebright." In *Lawrence Review of Natural Products.* Austin, TX: American Botanical Council, April 1987.

Fironi, G., A. Biancacci, and F.M. Graziano. "Perimetric and Adaptometric Modifications of Anthocyanosides and Beta-Carotene." *Ann. Ottal. Clin. Ocul.* 91 (1965): 371–386.

Foderaro, Lisa W. "Hypnosis Gains Credence as Influence on the Body." *The New York Times*, 24 February 1996.

Gerson, Scott, M.D. "Ayurvedic Medicine of New York." 13 West 90th Street, New York, NY 10011.

"*Ginkgo biloba* Extract Efficacy in Early Stages of Alzheimer's Disease." *Herbalgram* 34 (Summer 1995): 13.

Goleman, Daniel. "A Slow, Methodical Calming of the Mind." *The New York Times Magazine*, 21 March 1993.

Gruson, Kerry. "The Long Road Back." *The New York Times Magazine*, 30 June 1985.

Harris, Alon, Ph.D., Victor E. Malinovsky, O.D., and Bruce Martin, M.D. "Correlates of Acute Exercise-Induced Ocular Hypotension." *Investivative Ophthalmology & Visual Science* Vol. 35 No. 11 91994): 3852–3856.

Harris, Alon, Ph.D., Victor E. Malinovsky, O.D., Louis B. Cantor, M.D., Patricia Henderson, M.D., and Bruce J. Martin, M.D. "Isocapnia Blocks Exercise-Induced Reductions in Ocular Tension." *Investigative Ophthalmology & Visual Science* 33 (7) (1992): 2229–2232.

Hay, Louise L. *You Can Heal Your Life*. Santa Monica, CA: Hay House, Inc., 1990.

Hollister, L.E. "Health Aspects of Cannabis." *Pharmacology Review* 38 (1) (1986): 1–20.

Huxley, Aldous. *The Art of Seeing*. Berkeley, CA: Creative Arts Book Co., 1982.

Jacobson, Stanley. "Mind Over Matters." *Modern Maturity*, December 1992-January 1993, 37–38.

Lagrue, G., and others. "Pathology of the Microcirculation in Diabetes and Alterations of the Biosynthesis of Intracellular Matric Molecules." *Front Matrix Biol.* Vol. 7 (1979): 324–325.

Lane, Benjamin Clarence, M.S. "Elevation of Intraocular Pressure With Daily Sustained Reading and Closework Stimuli to Accommodation." Thesis. Ann Arbor, MI: University Microfilms International, 1973.

Lietti, A., A. Cristoni, and M. Picci. "Studies on *Vaccinium myrtillus* Anthocyanosides. I. Vasoprotective and Antiinflammatory Activity." *Arzneim. Forsch.* 26 (5) (1976): 829–832.

Mairs, Nancy. "When Bad Things Happen to Good Writers." *The New York Times*, 21 February 1993.

McCaleb, Rob. "Ayurveda: Ancient Healing Art." *Better Nutrition for Today's Living*, December 1992.

McCaleb, Rob. "Bilberry . . . A Powerful Natural Antioxidant for Preventing Visual Disorders!" Herb Research Foundation.

McCaleb, Rob. "Bilberry: Microcirculation Enhancer." Herb Research Foundation, 29 April 1992.

Merritt, J.C., J.L. Olsen, J.R. Armstrong, and S.M. McKinnon. "Topical Tetrahydrocannabinol in Hypertensive Glaucoma." *Journal of Pharmacy and Pharmacology* 33 (1991): 40–41.

Merritt, J.C., W.J. Crawford, P.C. Alexander, A.L. Andoze, and S. Gelbart. "Effect of Marijuana on Intraocular and Blood Pressure in Glaucoma." *International Journal of Addiction* 21 (4-5) (1986): 579–587.

Morrazzoni, P., and M.J. Magistretti. "Effects of Anthocyanosides on Ptostacyclin Activity in Arterial Tissue." *Fitoterapia* 57 (1986): 11.

Moyers, Bill. "Healing and the Mind." National Public Broadcasting, March 1993.

Murray, T. Michael. *Healing Power of Herbs*. Rocklen, CA: Pima Publishers, 1995.

National Institutes of Health. "Complementary and Alternative Medicine at NIH." Information package, July 1996.

Packer, Mark, M.D., and James D. Brandt, M.D. "Ophthalmology's Botanical Heritage." *Herbalgram, Survey of Ophthalmology,* 36 (5) (March–April 1992): 357–365.

Passo, Michael, M.D., Linn Golberg, M.D., Diane L. Elliot, M.A., and E. Michael Van Baskirk, M.D. "Exercise Training Reduces Intraocular Pressure Among Subjects Suspected of Having Glaucoma." *Archives of Ophthalmology* 109 (1991): 1096–1098.

Pennarola, R., and others. "The Therapeutic Action of the Anthocyanosides in Microcirculatory Changes Due to Adhesive-Induced Polyneuritis." *Gazz. Med. Ital.* 139 (1980): 485–491.

Peres, Reyes M., S.A. Owens, and S. Di Guiseppi. "The Clinical Pharmacology and Dynamics of Marijuana Cigarette Smoking." *Journal of Clinical Pharmacology* 21 (8–9) (supplement) (1981): 201S–207S.

Ritchason, N.D. *The Little Herb Encyclopedia*. Pleasant Grove, UT: Woodland Health Books, 1995.

Rossman, Martin L., M.D. "The Healing Power of Imagery." *New Age Journal,* March/April 1988, 46–56.

Rotte, Joanne, Ph.S., and Keji Yamamoto. *Vision: A Holistic Guide to Healing the Eyesight*. New York: Japan Publications, Inc., 1986.

Scharrer, A., and M. Ober. "Anthocyanosides in the Treatment of Retinopathies." *Klin. Monatsbl. Augenheilkd.* 178 (1981): 386–389.

Schneider, Meir, Maureen Larkin, and Dror Schneider. *The Handbook of Self-Healing*. New York: Penguin Group, 1994.

Schneider, Meir. *Self-Healing: My Life and Vision*. London, England: The Penguin Group, 1987.

Selby, John. *The Visual Handbook*. Shaftesbury, England: Element Books Ltd., 1987.

Siegel, Bernie S., M.D. Peace, *Love & Healing*. New York: Harper Perennial, 1990.

Talbert, Lee, Ph.D., and Michelle M. Pauly. "Bilberry, an Extraordinary Vision Enhancer." American Institute of Health & Nutrition, 1991.

Trachtman, Joseph N., O.D., Ph.D. *The Etiology of Vision Disorders.* Santa Ana, CA: Optimetric Extension Program Foundation, Inc.

Ungerlieder, J.T., and T. Andrysiak. "Therapeutic Issues of Marijuana and THC." *International Journal of Addiction* 20 (5) (1985): 691–699.

Weiss, Rudolf Fritz, M.D. *Herbal Medicine.* Translated from A.R. Meuss, *Lehrbuch der Phytotherapie.* Portland, OR: Medicina Biologica 1988.

Wu, Zhen-zhong, You-qin Jiang, Su-mo Li, and Ming-ti Xia. "Radix Salviae Miltiorrhizae in Middle and Late Stage Glaucoma." *Chinese Medical Journal* 96 (6) (1983): 445–447.

Chapter 10
Eating for Healthy Eyes

Agamanolis, D.P., M.D., E.M. Chester, M.D., M. Victor, M.D., J.A. Kark, M.D., J.D. Hines, M.D., and J.W. Harris, M.D. "Neuropathology of Experimental Vitamin B_{12} Defieciency in Monkeys." *Neurology* 25 (1976): 905–914.

Altman, Lawrence K. "26,000 Cubans Partly Blinded: Cause is Unclear." *The New York Times,* 21 May 1993.

Altman, Lawrence K. "Vitamin Array is Found to Aid Elderly." *The New York Times,* 6 November 1992.

Angier, Natalie. "Chemists Learn Why Vegetables Are Good for You." *The New York Times,* 13 April 1993.

Angier, Natalie. "Free Radicals: The Price We Pay for Breathing." *The New York Times Magazine,* 28 April 1993.

"Aspartame Cause of Dry Eye." Conway, AR: The Health Resource, Inc., Summer 1995.

Aspelin, Arnold L., Arthur E. Grube, and Arthur R. Toria. "Pesticides Industry Sales and Usage: 1990 and 1991 Market Estimates." U.S. Environmental Protection Agency, Fall 1992.

Asregadoo, Edward R., M.D. "Blood Levels of Thiamine and Ascorbic Acid in Chronic Open-Angle Glaucoma." *Annals of Ophthalmology* 11 (7) (1979): 1095–1100.

Ausich, Rodney L., Ph.D. "Increasing Importance of Lutein in Diets." Des Moines, IA: Kemin Foods.

Balch, James F., M.D., and Phyllis A. Balch, C.N.C. *Prescription for Nutritional Healing,* 2nd Ed. Garden City Park, NY: Avery Publishing Group, 1997.

Banker, Deborah E., M.D. *Self Help Vision Care.* Boulder, CO: World Care, 1994.

Baxter, R.C. "Vitamin C and Glaucoma." *Journal of the American Optometric Association* 59 (6) (1988): 1438.

Busch, Eleanor B., and Bernd Busch.

The No-Drugs Guide to Better Health. Parker Publishing Co., 1983.

Bietti, G.B. "Further Contributions on the Value of Osmotic Substances as Means to Reduce Intraocular Pressure." *Transactions of the Ophthalmological Society of Austria* 26 (1967): 61–71.

"Bipartisan Agreement Reached Regarding Chemicals in Foods." *The New York Times,* 17 July 1996, A16.

Brody, Jane E. "Food-Nutrient Interactions: New Dietary Preferences Underline Their Importance." *The New York Times,* 7 November 1984.

Brody, Jane E. "Intriguing Studies Link Nutrition to Immunity." *The New York Times,* 21 March 1989.

Brody, Jane E. "New Respect for Vitmain E After Years of Faddish Aura." *The New York Times,* 26 May 1993.

Burros, Marian. "U.S. Will Focus on Reducing Pesticides in Food Production. *The New York Times,* 27 June 1993.

"Cataracts Linked to Diet." The *New York Times,* 8 December 1992, C8.

"Coffee May Increase Glaucoma Damage." Prevent Blindness America.

Davidson, P. Carl, M.D., Paul Sternberg, Jr., M.D., Dean P. Jones, M.D., and Robyn L. Reed, M.D. "Synthesis and Transport of Glutathione by Cultured Human Retinal Pigment Epithelial Cells." *Investigative Ophthalmolgoy & Visual Science* 35 (6) (1994) 2843–2849.

Davis, R.H. "Does Caffeine Ingestion Affect Intraocular Pressure?" *Ophthalmology* 96 (11) (1989): 1680–1681.

deCrousaz, S. "Vitamin B12 in Some Eye Diseases." *Ophthalmologia* 159 (1969): 297–316.

Dolby, Victoria. "Seeing Is Believing: Nutrients That Protect and Promote Eye Health." *Better Nutrition,* July 1996, 14.

Dolby, Victoria. "Zinc Deserves the Spotlight for Its Many Roles in Our Health." *Better Nutrition,* August 1996, page 12.

Duke-Elder, S., M.D. *Diseases of the Lens and Vitreous, Glaucoma and Hypotony.* Vol 2, *Systems of Ophthalmology.* St. Louis, MO: C.V. Mosby Co., 1969.

Etzel, Kenneth, Pei-Fei Lee, Tommy Yet-Min Lin, and Kwok-Wai Lam. "Factors Affecting Ascorbate Oxidation in Aqueous Humor." *Current Eye Research* 6 (2) (1987).

Evans, S.C. "Ophthalmic Nutrition and Prevention of Eye Disorders and Blindness." *Nutrition & Metabolism* 21 (1) (supplement) (1977): 268–272.

Fong, Donald, Kenneth Etzel, Pei-Fei Lee, Tommy Yet-Min Lin, and Kwok-Wai Lam. "Factors Affecting Ascorbate Oxidation in Aqueous Humor." *Current Eye Research* 6 (7) (1987): 357–361.

Goldberg, M.F. "Sickled Erythrocytes, Hyphema and Secondary Glaucoma: The Effect of Vitamin C on Erythrocyte Sickling in Aqueous Humor." *Ophthalmic Surgery* 10 (4) (1979): 70–77.

Higginbotham, E., and others. "The Effect of Caffeine on Intraocular Pressure in Glaucoma Patients." *Ophthalmology* 96 (5) (1989): 624–626.

Jampel, H.D. "Ascorbic Acid is Cytotoxic in Dividing Human Tenon's Capsule Fibroblasts." *Archives of Ophthalmology* 108 (9): 1323–1325.

Karstadt, Myra, and Stephen Schmidt. "Olestra, Procter's Big Gamble." *Nutrition Action Health Letter,* a publication of the Center for Science in the Public Interest, Vol. 23 No. 2, March 1996, 5.

Lane, Ben C., O.D. "Diet and the Glaucomas." *Journal of the American College of Nutrition* 10 (5) (1991): 536.

Lane, Ben C., O.D. "Myopia Prevention and Reversal: New Data Confirms the Interaction of Accommodative Stress and Deficit-Inducing Nutrition." *Journal of the International Academy of Preventive Medicine* U (3) (1982): 17–30.

Lane, Ben C., O.D. "Practical Dietary and Environmental Strategies in Support of Therapy for the Glaucomas: Intraocular Pressure (IOP) Risk Factors." Glaucoma Support Group Series, 17 April 1993.

Lane, Ben C., O.D. "Vanadium—Too Much Won't Build Better Vision." *Your Good Health Review & Digest* Vol. 2 No. 4, 1984, 55.

Lang, G., M.D., G. Richard, M.D., and R. Yee, M.D. "Effect of Radical Scavengers on Ocular Hemodynamics on the Visual Field in Primary Open-Angle Glaucoma." Presentation at ARVO Conference, 24 April 1996.

Langer, Stephen, M.D. "Antioxidants, Health Insurance for the Inside." *Better Nutrition,* July 1996, 54–58.

Lee, P., K.W. Lam, and M. Lai. "Aqueous Humor Ascorbate Concentration and Open-Angle Glaucoma." *Archives of Ophthalmology* 95 (2) (1977): 308–310.

Lefferts, Lisa Y. "Pass the Pesticides." *Nutrition Action Health Letter,* a publication of the Center for Science in the Public Interest, April 1989, 1, 5–7.

Linner, E. "Intraocular Pressure Regulation and Ascorbic Acid." *Acta Soc. Med. Upsal.* 69 (1964): 225–232.

Linner, E. "The Pressure Lowering Effect of Ascorbic Acid in Ocular Hypertension." *Acta Ophthalmologica* (Copenhagen) 47 (1969): 685–689.

Liu, K.M., D. Swann, P. Lee, and K.W. Lam. "Inhibition of Oxidative Degradation of Hyaluronic Acid by Uric Acid." *Current Eye Research* 3 (8) (1984): 1049–1053.

Mares-Perlman, Julie A., Ph.D. "Diet and Ocular Disease." Presentation at Science Writers Seminar in Ophthalmology, sponsored by Research to Prevent Blindness, Orlando, FL, October 1995.

Mehra, K.S., M.D., D.O. "Relationship of pH of Blood and Aqueous With Vitamin C." *Annals of Ophthalmology* January 1979, 83–85.

Norvell, Candyce. "Wanna Go Veggie?" *Better Nutrition,* August 1996, 60.

Null, Gary. "Oils and Fats." *Natural Living,* No. 5, January/February 1995.

Pauling, Linus, Ph.D. "On Good Nutrition for the Good Life." *Executive Health* Vol. 17 No. 4.

"Phytochemicals Can Be Hedges Against Disease." *Better Nutrition,* December 1995.

"Progress on Pesticides." *The Amicus Journal,* a publication of the Natural Resources Defense Council, 18, No. 3, 1996, 3.

"Public Citizen Wants Pesticides Off Our Food Shelves." Handout. Washington, DC: Public Citizen.

Rehac, S., V. Bartousek, and B. Dubznsky. "Vitamin B12 in Treatment of Diseases of the Optic Nerve." *Ophthalmologica* (Basel) 1958: 95–102.

Ringvold, Armund, Harold Johnsen, and Sigmund Blika. "Senile Cataracts and Ascorbic Acid Loading." *Acta Ophthalmologica* 63 (1985).

Rudolph, Michael. "A Growing Trend: Is Organic Food All That It Is Cracked Up to Be? That Is a Popular Question These Days." *The Energy Times,* July/August 1995, 48–57.

Sardi, Bill. "Nutrition and the Eyes." *Health Spectrum,* Vol. 3 (1994).

Schardt, David, and Stephen Schmidt. "Chromium." *Nutrition Action Healthletter,* May 1996, 10–12.

Scheer, James F. "Vitamin E." *Better Nutrition,* December 1992, 28–31.

Schneider, Keith. "Manufacturers Recycling Half of Chemical Wastes." *The New York Times,* 26 May 1993, A15.

Schuchman, Miriam, and Michael Wilkes. "The Vitamin Uprising." *The New York Times Magazine,* 2 October 1994, 79, 87–88.

Seddon, Johanna M., M.D., Umed A. Ajani, M.B.B.S., Robert D. Sperduto, M.D., Rita Hiller, M.D., Norman Blair, M.D., Thomas C. Burton, M.D., Marilyn D. Farber, Ph.D., Evangelos S. Gragoudas, M.D., Julia Haller, M.D., Dayton Miller, Ph.D., Lawrence A. Yannuzzi, M.D., and Walter Willett, M.D. "Dietary Carotenoids, Vitamins A, C, and E, and Advanced Age-Related Macular Degeneration." *Journal of the American Medical Association* 27 (1994): 1413–1420.

"Simplesse Applications." Manufacturer's product literature. San Diego, CA: Kelco Company.

Sternberg, Paul, Jr., Carl P. Davidson, Dean P. Jones, Tory Hagen, Robyn L. Reed, and Carolyn Drews-Botsch. "Protection of Retinal Pigmentary Epithelium From Oxidative Injury by Glutathione and Precursors," *Investigative Ophthalmology & Visual Science* 34 (13) (1993): 3661–3668.

"The Ten Worst Additives." *Nutrition Action Healthletter* Vol. 18 No. 5, 8, 9.

Todd, Gary. *Nutrition, Health & Disease.* West Chester, PA: Whitford Press, 1980.

Toufexis, Anastasia. "The New Scoop on Vitamins." *Time,* 6 April 1992.

"Vitamins for Vision." *Nutrition Action Healthletter* Vol. 21 No. 1, 4.

"Warning Labels." *The Trends Journal,* Vol. 5 No. 5 (Winter 1996).

Winter, Ruth. *A Consumer's Dictionary of Food Additives.* New York: Crown Publishers, Inc., 1989, 28, 29, 54, 55, 72–73, 146–147, 220–221, 228-229, 282–283.

Chapter 11
Grab the Reins of Responsibility

"A Way to Remind Doctors that 'Patients Are People.'" *Mayo Clinic Health Letter* Vol. 5 No. 9, September 1987, 3–6.

Allansmith, Matthea R., M.D., and Robert N. Ross, Ph.D. "Ocular Allergy and Mast Cell Stabilizers." *Survey of Ophthalmology* 30 (4) (1986): 229–244.

Belkin, Lisa. "In Lessons on Empathy, Doctors Become Patients." *The New York Times,* 4 June 1992, 1, B5.

Brody, Jane. "Reducing Household Hazards Can Help Older People Avoid Accidents in Their Own Homes." *The New York Times,* 29 November 1990, B17.

"Form a Partnership With Your Ophthalmologist." Article based on an address by Dr. Liviu Salmovici of the New York Eye and Ear Hospital. *Living With Glaucoma,* newsletter of the New York Glaucoma Support and Education Group, Vol. 7 No. 2, November/December 1993.

"Glaucoma and Blacks." Pamphlet. Prevent Blindness America.

"Glaucoma Testing." *U.S. News & World Report,* 23 December 1991, 71.

Green, Keith, Ph.D., D.Sc. "Detergent Penetration Into Young and Adult Eyes." Presentation at Science Writers Seminar in Ophthalmology, sponsored by Research to Prevent Blindness, September 1988.

Harris, Alon, Ph.D., Victor E. Malinovsky, O.D., and Bruce J. Martin, Ph.D. "Ocular Hypotension During Short- and Long-Term Hypocapnia." *Journal of Glaucoma* 3 (3) (1994): 226–231.

Kahan, A. "Developmental Implications of Ocular Pharmacology." *Pharmacology & Therapeutics* 28 (2) (1985): 163–226,

"Know Your Patient Rights." Brochure. Washington, DC: American Federation of Teachers.

Levin, Arthur A. "Adverse Reactions to Glaucoma Eye Drops." *Health Facts*, December 1987.

"Lightheadedness, Dizziness, Vertigo." *Secure Retirement*, November/December 1992.

"Loss of Near Vision With Age May Be Related to Glaucoma. National Glaucoma Research Report, Fall 1991.

"Managing Glaucoma Is a Two-Way Street." *Living With Glaucoma*, newsletter of the New York Glaucoma Support and Education Group Vol. 10 No. 3, June 1996.

Mandelkorn, Robert M., M.D., and Thom J. Zimmerman. "Effects of Nonsteroidal Drugs on Glaucoma. In *The Glaucomas*, ed. Robert Ritch, M.D., M. Bruce Shields, M.D., and Theodore Krupin, M.D. St. Louis, MO: C.V. Mosby Co., 1989.

McSteen, Martha A. "Reducing the Risks of Multiple Medications." *Secure Retirement*, November/December 1992.

"Medical Records: Getting Yours." *Public Citizen Health Research Group Health Letter* Vol 8 No. 9, 1992.

"Melanin Sun Lenses, Nature's Own Photoprotection." Manufacturer's product literature. Eritar Corporation, Inc.

"100+ Drugs Which Many People Should Not Use." *Public Citizen Health Research Group Health Letter.* Flyer.

"Patient Education Turns Fear Into Understanding." Article based on an address by Dr. Liviu Salmovici of the New York Eye and Ear Hospital. *Living With Glaucoma*, newsletter of the New York Glaucoma Support and Education Group, Vol. 9 No. 3, December 1995/January 1996.

"Patients' Rights and Responsibilities." Handout. New York: Manhattan Eye, Ear, and Throat Hospital.

"Questions on Eye Safety." Pamphlet. Prevent Blindness America.

Riffenburgh, Ralph S., M.D. "Doctor-Patient Relationship in Glaucoma Therapy." *Archives of Ophthalmology* 75 (1966): 204–206.

Ritch, Robert, M.D. "Proper Drop Instillation." Patient handout. New York: New York Eye and Ear Infirmary.

Rosenthal, Elisabeth. "When Hawks Turn Into Bats: New-Found Night Driving Woes." *The New York Times*, 28 July 1992, C6.

"Seven Principles of Taking Control of Your Medical Care; Part 1." *Public Citizen Health Research Group Health Letter* Vol 11 No. 6, 1995.

"Smoking of Cigarettes Is Linked for First Time to a Form of Cataracts. *The New York Times*, 14 September 1989.

"Time for Cinderella to Fight Back." *Living With Glaucoma*, newsletter of the New York Glaucoma Support and Education Group, Vol. 8 No. 5, May June 1995.

and Education Group, Vol. 8 No. 5, May June 1995.

"Understanding Your Prescription." Pamphlet. White Plains, NY: Will Rogers Institute.

"Use Medicine Safely," U.S. Food and Drug Administration, Department of Health and Human Services, DHHS Publication No. (FDA) 93-3201, December 1992.

"When Your Vision Begins to Change." *GLEAMS,* a publication of The Glaucoma Research Foundation, Fall 1995, Vol 13 (2).

"Work With Your Doctor to Manage Glaucoma." *Glaucoma Watch,* a publication of Otsuka America Pharmaceutical, Inc., Vol. 1 No. 1, Winter 1993.

"You and Your Doctor, How to Get the Best Care." *Consumer Reports,* February 1995, 81–88.

Zagelbaum, Bruce M. "Preventing Sports-Related Eye Enjuries." Presentation at Science Writers Seminar in Ophthalmology, sponsored by Research to Prevent Blindness, Orlando, FL, October 1995.

Chapter 12
Support Services—There's Help Out There

"Accessing the Internet." Patient handout. New York, NY : American Foundation for the Blind.

Bereck, Judith. " Tools for Blind Students." *The New York Times,* Education Supplement, 6 August 1995, 16.

Caputo, Brian J., M.D., and Jay L. Katz, M.D. "The Quality of Life of the Glaucoma Patient in the Light of Treatment Modalities." *Current Opinion in Ophthalmology* 5 (11) (1994): 10–14.

"Computers and Their Effect on Your Eyes." Pamphlet. Chicago, IL: Prevent Blindness America.

deCourcy-Hinds, Michael. "Finding Better Health of Horseback." *The New York Times,* 12 September 1993, 34.

Fischer, Michael L., O.D. "Legal Gray Areas in Low Vision: The Need for Clarification of Regulations." *Journal of the American Optometric Association* 64 (1) (1993): 12–14.

Garrett, James F. "Historical Background." In *Vocational Rehabilitation of the Disabled: An Overview,* ed. David Malikin and Herbert Rusalem. New York: New York University Press, 1969.

Hollander, C., O.D. "Patient's Guide to Vision Rehabilitation for the Partially Sighted. Patient handout. New York, NY: Sight Improvement Center, Inc.

Hoppe, Elizabeth, O.D., M.P.H. "Evaluating the Laws Defining Blindness." *Journal of the American Optometric Association* 63 (6) (1992): 390–394.

"Is Your Computer Screen Harming Your Eyesight?" *Prevent Blindness News,* Spring 1995.

"Jobs held by people in AFB's Carrers and Technology Information

Bank." Patient handout. New York, NY: American Foundation for the Blind.

LaGrow, Steven J., Bruce B. Blasch, and DelAune. "The Efficacy of the Touch Technique for Footfall and Surface Plane Preview." Unpublished paper on mobility training.

LeClerc, Paul. "Electronic Data for All the People." *The New York Times,* 17 August 1996, 19.

Leventhal, Jay D. "Blind, Not Incompetent." *The New York Times,* 12 August 1992, A19.

Levine, Mindy, consultant, National Association for the Visually Handicapped. Summary of an address given to the New York Glaucoma Support and Education Group. *Living With Glaucoma,* newsletter of the New York Glaucoma Support and Education Group, Vol. 10 No. 3, May 1996.

Lewis, Peter H. "Putting Disabled in Touch." *The New York Times,* 20 February 1990, C9.

"Living With Glaucoma." *GLEAMS,* a publication of The Glaucoma Research Foundation.

"Living With Low Vision." Life Sight Flyer. Chicago, IL: Prevent Blindness America.

"Magnification Programs for the Computer Screen." Patient handout. New York, NY : American Foundation for the Blind.

Newman, Marilyn. Unpublished paper comparing touch technique with RoboCane in mobility training.

Peters, Jennifer. "After the Examination: Care of Low Vision Patients Beyond Ocular Services." *Journal of Ophthalmic Nursing and Technology* 11 (1) (1992): 13–16.

"Richard Karn Speaks Out on Eye Safety at Home." *Prevent Blindness News,* Winter 1996.

Rigsbee, Lois. "The Glasses Come Off: Grooming Strategies for Women With Low Vision." *GLEAMS,* a publication of The Glaucoma Research Foundation, Fall 1990, Vol. 8 (3): 3.

"The Sightless Learn Dancing, and More." *The New York Times,* 31 May 1989.

"Synthetic Speech Systems." Patient handout. New York, NY: American Foundation for the Blind.

"Visual Aids and Information Material." Catalog. New York, NY, and San Francisco, CA: National Association for the Visually Handicapped.

Zagelbaum, Bruce M., M.D. "Preventing Sports-Related Eye Injuries." Presentation at Science Writers Seminar in Ophthalmology, sponsored by Research to Prevent Blindness, Orlando, FL, October 1995.

Glossary

accommodation. Adjustment of the eye to focus on objects at varying distances.

acetylcholine. A substance that transmits nerve impuses across nerve junctions. Acetylcholine medications constrict the pupil.

acetylcholinesterase. An enzyme that breaks down acetylcholine to form acetic acid and choline.

acuity. Clearness. Visual acuity is determined by the smallest object that you are able to see at a specific distance. The Snellen chart is used to measure visual acuity.

acupuncture. A traditional Chinese therapeutic technique using fine needles that are inserted under the skin at specific sites that correspond to different organs and systems.

adenosine triphosphate. An organic compound that is an energy source in many metabolic reactions, especially those related to muscular activity.

adrenergic drug. One of a class of drugs used to control glaucoma by increasing aqueous outflow and decreasing aqueous production.

agonist. In ophthalmology, a term used to describe the action of certain medications.

aldehyde. Any of a class of highly reactive organic chemical compounds obtained by oxidation of primary alcohols.

amblyopia. "Lazy eye." There are a variety of reasons for this condition.

angiogram. A photographic image of blood vessels.

angle. In the eye, the area in the anterior (front) part of the eye where the iris and cornea meet.

anterior chamber. The front portion of the eye that contains the aqueous humor.

antioxidant. A chemical compound or substance that inhibits oxidation reactions.

aphakia. Absence of the eye's natural lens.

applanation. Flattening of the cornea to assess the level of pressure in the eye.

aqueous humor. A watery fluid produced by the ciliary body that fills the anterior chamber of the eye. Also called the aqueous fluid.

argon laser. A type of laser used to treat glaucoma by placing minute burns on the trabecular meshwork, iris, retina, and/or abnormal blood vessels in the eye.

beta-adrenergic blocker. Any of a class of drugs that block the stimulating effect of epinephrine. Used to treat glaucoma, these drugs inhibit the secretion of aqueous humor by the ciliary body. Also called beta-blockers.

bioflavonoid. Any of a group of aromatic biological pigments or compounds, widely distributed in higher plants, that account for yellow, red, and/or blue pigmentation. Many have antioxidant properties.

bipolar cells. Retinal cells that connect the rods and cones with the ganglion cells.

bleb. A reservoir created in a glaucoma filtering operation to aid in the drainage of fluid from the eye.

blind spot. The area where retina joins with the optic nerve, forming a funnel, and from which the nerve extends to the brain. This area of the retina is not sensitive to light.

calcium-channel blocker. A type of drug used to treat high blood pressure by decreasing total peripheral resistance.

campimetry. A method of detecting defects in the central portion of the visual field.

capsule. The transparent sac attached to the ciliary body that contains the lens.

capsulotomy. (1) A surgical procedure performed as the first step in extracapsular cataract extraction. (2) An Nd:YAG laser procedure performed to correct capsular clouding after implantation of an intraocular lens.

carbonic anhydrase inhibitor. A chemical compound that suppresses the formation of the enzyme carbonic anhydrase in the eyes, decreasing the formation of aqueous humor.

carotid artery. Either of two major arteries in the neck that carry blood to the head.

catabolize. To break down a complex substance into simpler substances.

cataract. Opacity of the crystalline lens.

catecholamine. Any of a group of natural substances in the body that stimulate the sympathetic nervous system. Among them are epinephrine, norepinephrine, dopamine, and nomethylepinephrine.

cholinergic. Activated by or capable of liberating acetylcholine.

choroid. The highly vascular tissue layer beneath the retina; provides the blood needed to nourish the retina.

ciliary body glaucoma. Malignant glaucoma following surgery caused by aqueous humor becoming trapped behind the vitreous.

ciliary body. A ring-shaped structure that joins the iris and choroid.

ciliary muscles. Finger-shaped extensions of the ciliary body to which the zonules are attached.

ciliary processes. Layers of cells arranged in folds to make up the ciliary body. They are responsible for the production of aqueous fluid.

Circadian rhythm. The biological clock.

collagen. A fibrous protein found in the connective tissue, including skin, bone, cartilage, and ligaments. There are four types of collagen in the eye.

cone cells. Light-sensitive cells concentrated in the macula.

conjunctiva. The mucous membrane lining the insides of the eyelids and covering the exterior part of the eye.

convergence. The eyes' effort to maintain binocular vision; seeing objects with both eyes simultaneously.

cornea. Clear tissue that makes up the forward central part of the eye, responsible for the majority of the eye's focusing power.

corneal edema. A condition in which the cornea swells with water and becomes cloudy.

corneal endothelium. The innermost layer of the cornea. Only one cell thick, it regenerates rapidly if damaged.

corticosteroid. A steroid produced by the adrenal cortex; cortisone derivative.

"count fingers" test. A test of low visual acuity, determined by a person's ability to count fingers presented over two feet away.

cow's eye. A bulbous eye that can occur if trapped fluid expands the flexible tissue of an infant's eye.

cup. In ophthalmology, a concave area in the optic disk that represents nonfunctioning retinal cells.

cupping. A term used to describe the appearance of a damaged optic nerve. It is one of the measures used to evaluate progression of glaucoma.

cyclodestruction. A general term for the use of either extreme cold or laser energy to destroy part of the ciliary body.

deoxyribonucleic acid (DNA). A complex nucleic acid that contains the genetic "code" within each living cell.

diabetic retinopathy. A condition associated with diabetes mellitus in which blood vessels proliferate over the retina.

digital tonometry. Judment of intraocular pressure by pressing a finger against the eyeball to test its resistance.

DNA. Deoxyribonucleic acid.

dry eye. A condition brought about either by a defect in the composition of the tears or incomplete closure of the eyelids, resulting in corneal dryness and discomfort.

electroretinogram. A record of an ERG test.

electroretinography (ERG). A technique for measuring the retina's response to light.

endocapsular. Occurring or appearing within the lens capsule.

endothelium. The innermost tissue lining of many structures, including blood vessels and the cornea.

epithelium cells. Membranous tissue, usually a single layer of closely placed cells, that covers most internal surfaces and organs and outer surfaces of the body.

ERG. Electroretinography.

exfoliation. A general term for processes whereby flakes of tissue are shed in the eye.

extracapsular. Occurring or appearing outside the lens capsule.

extracapsular cataract extraction. Surgical cataract extraction procedure in which the anterior lens capsule is partially or completely removed.

extraocular muscles. The muscles attached to the outsides of the eyeballs and the insides of the eye sockets that are responsible for moving the eyeball.

fibroblast. A connective tissue cell. Fibroblasts form the fibrous tissues of the body, and also proliferate at sites of chronic inflammation.

filtering operation. A surgical procedure to open a channel through which the aqueous fluid may pass.

floaters. Dark specks or lines that appear to float before your eyes. They are caused by cells or other nontransparent material floating in the vitreous fluid and casting shadows on the retina.

fluorescein angiography. An imaging technique in which the dye fluorescein is injected into a vein and its circulation tracked by x-ray. It can be used to assess circulation in the retina and choroid.

fovea. The area in the center of the macula that provides the clearest and longest-distance vision.

free radical. An atom or group of atoms having at least one unpaired electron, making it highly chemically reactive. Free radical activity is necessary for many biological processes, but if not properly contained, it can lead to tissue damage.

fundus. The interior of a hollow organ such as the eye.

ganglia cells. A group of nerve cells that give rise to the optic nerve.

glutathione peroxidase. A compound synthesized from the amino acids glutamate, cysteine, and glycine, that is widely distributed in animal and plant tissue. It destroys peroxides and free radicals; is a cofactor of enzymes; and detoxifies harmful compounds.

glycogen. A carbohydrate that is the form in which glucose is stored in the liver.

Goldmann visual field. A machine that uses a kinetic approach to measure the field of vision.

goniolens. An optical device used for examining the anterior (front) section of the eye.

gonioscopy. Examination of the anterior chamber using a goniolens.

haptic. A hook on an intraocular lens implant to hold the implant in place.

Humphrey or Octopus visual field. A computerized visual field testing machine that uses a static approach to measure the field of vision.

hyaloid face. The thin membrane that surrounds the vitreous and interfaces between the anterior and posterior sections of the eye. Also called the hyaloid membrane.

hyaluronic acid. A component of the vitreous and aqueous fluids.

hyperopia. Farsightedness.

hyperplasia. A nontumorous increase in the number of cells in an organ or tissue.

hyphema. Bleeding into the anterior chamber of the eye.

hypotony. Low intraocular pressure.

intracapsular cataract extraction (ICCE). Surgical cataract extraction procedure in which the lens and lens capsule are removed.

intraocular lens (IOL). An artificial lens that is implanted in the eye after surgical removal of a cataractous natural lens to correct refractive error.

intraocular pressure (IOP). The pressure within the eye. High pressure, above 25 mm Hg, is considered suspect for glaucoma.

IOP. *See* Intraocular pressure.

iridectomy. Surgical removal of part of the iris, performed to control intraocular pressure.

iridotomy. Creation of a small puncture in the iris. A laser is often used for this procedure.

iris. The pigmented vascular ring-shaped structure in the front of the eye that controls the amount of light passing from the pupil to the retina. It attached at the outer edge to the ciliary body.

iris root. The portion of the iris that is attached to the ciliary body.

ischemic optic neuropathy. Obstruction of blood flow to the optic nerve.

lacrimal apparatus. The system that produces tears and allows them to drain from the eye. It includes the lacrimal glands, the puncta (the opening inside each upper and lower lid), the lacrimal sac, and the tubes and ducts that drain tears into the nasal passages.

laser. A device that uses a concentrated beam of light to cut or burn objects, including tissue. Lasers are used for a number of procedures done to treat glaucomatous conditions. The word is an acronym for light amplification by stimulated emission of radiation.

lenticular. Like a lens; usually refers to the crystalline lens of the eye.

lysozyme. An enzyme that occurs naturally in tears and is capable of destroying some bacteria, thereby acting as a mild antiseptic.

macrophage. A type of white blood cell that removes debris, dead tissue, and foreign substances from tissue.

macula. A small yellowish area of the retina where rods and cones are most densely packed. The macula is responsible for fixation.

magnetic resonance imaging (MRI). Computerized scanning using a strong magnetic field; often used in diagnosis of nerve fiber disorders.

malignant glaucoma. A condition in which the ciliary body rotates and blocks off the flow of aqueous fluid. It is most likely to occur as a complication of filtration or cataract-removal surgery.

miosis. Constriction of one or both pupils.

MRI. *See* Magnetic resonance imaging.

mydriasis. Dilation of one or both pupils.

myopia. Nearsightedness.

nanophthalmos. Abnormally small eyeballs.

narrow-angle glaucoma. Glaucoma characterized by a buildup of aqueous fluid in the anterior chamber resulting from closure of the angle. It can be a result of the structure of the eye (shallow angle) and/or other ocular bodies inserting into the angle.

neovascular glaucoma. Glaucoma associated with the abnormal formation of new blood vessels.

nerve fiber layer. The layer of tissue in which retinal nerve cells converge to form the optic nerve.

neurotransmitter. A substance used to transmit signals from one nerve cell to another.

occipital lobe. The rear part of the brain; responsible for visual perception.

Octopus visual field. *See* Humphrey or Octopus visual field.

open-angle glaucoma. Glaucoma in which the angle is open, but the outflow of fluid is otherwise impaired, resulting in a buildup of aqueous fluid in the anterior chamber.

ophthalmologist. A medical doctor who specializes in the treatment of eye diseases, including surgery.

ophthalmoscope. An instrument for examining the back of the eye.

optic nerve. A bundle of nerve fibers that connect the retina to the visual cortex of the brain.

optic neuropathy. Degeneration of the optic nerve.

oxidation. A chemical reaction in which an oxygen molecule encounters another substance and snaps up or sheds one of its electrons to combine with that substance.

pallor. Unnatural paleness. In ophthalmology, it is a term used to refer to paleness of the optic nerve head, which may indicate lack of blood flow.

PAM. See potential acuity meter.

parasympathetic nervous system. Part of the autonomic (involuntary) nervous system; it is controlled by the neurotransmitter acetylcholine.

periocular injection. Injection into the eye.

phacoemulsification. Part of a cataract removal procedure in which ultrasound vibrations are used to liquefy the cataractactous lens, which is then extracted through a tiny incision.

phagocyte. A scavenger cell that engulfs and absorbs waste matter and invading microorganisms in the body.

photocoagulation. Condensation of protein material by laser beam. In ophthalmology, it is used primarily to treat retinal detachment, destroy abnormal retinal blood vessels, and destroy part of the ciliary body.

photon. The smallest unit of light energy; sometimes described as a particle or quantum.

phthisis bulbi. Shrinkage of a damaged or diseased eyeball.

pigmentary-dispersion glaucoma. Glaucoma associated with the flaking off of pigment from the iris; the pigment disperses into the anterior chamber and causes blockage of aqueous flow.

plateau iris. A configuration of the iris that may result in blockage of the trabecular meshwork.

pneumotonometer. A tonometer that uses a puff of air to measure intraocular pressure.

POAG. *See* Primary open-angle glaucoma.

posterior chamber. The portion of the eye behind the iris containing the crystalline lens and vitreous humor.

potential acuity meter (PAM). A device used to measure potential visual acuity in eyes with cataracts.

prelaminar layer. The spot where the nerve fibers converge to take a 90-degree turn to form the optic nerve.

primary open-angle glaucoma. Open-angle glaucoma not associated with any other underlying disease process.

prostaglandin. Any of a group of body chemicals synthesized from fatty acids and serving as mediators of many physiologic processes.

pseudoexfoliation syndrome. A condition in which white flakes appear on the tissues and structures of the eye and clog the outflow passages.

ptosis. Drooping of the upper eyelid.

pupillary block. Blockage of normal aqueous flow through the pupil from the back to the front of the eye because of tight contact between the iris and the lens or vitreous face.

retina. The innermost layer of the eye, comprised of light-sensitive tissue.

retinal detachment. Complete or partial separation of the retina from the choroid.

retinol. The form in which the body utilizes vitamin A and stores it in the liver. Retinol is needed by the rod and cone cells.

rheumatoid arthritis. A connective tissue disease producing pain and inflammation of the joints; it is also associated with thinning of the sclera, red and dry eyes, and juvenile glaucoma.

rods. Light-sensitive cells that primarily serve for night vision.

Schlemm's canal. A ring-shaped network of passages through which aqueous humor drains into the bloodstream.

sclera. The tough, fibrous, white tissue that forms the outer layer of the eye.

scleral spur. The band of scleral fibers located between Schlemm's canal and the ciliary muscle, which serve in part as anchor for the ciliary muscle.

sclerostomy. Surgical creation of a hole in the sclera for the purpose of producing another channel for fluid drainage.

scotoma. An area in the visual field where vision is impaired or absent.

shiatsu. A form of massage based on the principles of acupuncture;

instead of needles, pressure of the thumbs and forefingers is used to stimulate specific points on the body.

slit lamp. An instrument that projects an elongated beam of light on the structures of the anterior segment of the eye, allowing a doctor to view the eye's interior.

Snellen chart. The standard chart used to measure visual acuity.

sphincter. A general anatomic term for a circular (ring-shaped) muscle, such as the pupillary sphincter.

superior oblique muscle. The muscle that moves the eyeball outward.

superior rectus muscle. The muscle that moves the eyeball upward.

superoxide dismutase. An antioxidant enzyme.

suture. Stitching; the thread used to close an incision following surgery.

tendon. A strong fibrous band of tissue that attaches muscle to bone.

tonometer. An instrument that measures intraocular pressure by assessing the eyeball's resistance to flattening (applanation).

trabecular meshwork. The meshlike structure through which aqueous humor drains, located in the anterior chamber angle where the cornea and iris meet.

trabeculectomy. A surgical procedure in which tissue is removed from the trabecular meshwork to create a new channel for the outflow of aqueous fluid. Also known as filtration surgery.

trabeculoplasty. A procedure, usually performed by laser, that modifies the trabecular meshwork to increase fluid outflow.

ultrasound. The use of high-frequency sound waves for diagnosis and/or treatment.

uvea. Pigmented tissue of the eye that contains the majority of blood vessels. Composed of the choiroid, ciliary body, and iris, it is considered a whole system.

vasoconstrictive. Tending to constrict blood vessels.

visual cortex. The area of the brain responsible for interpreting visual information; the cerebral end of the visual pathway that begins at the retina. It is located on the occipital lobe, in the back of the brain.

visual field. The area in which objects can be seen when the eyes are fixed on a central point. It is generally circular in shape.

vitreous humor. The transparent gelatinous mass that fills back of the eye.

zonular fibers. Tiny ligaments that attach the edge of the lens capsule to the ciliary body.

zonule. A zonular fiber.

Resources

EDUCATION

Center for Medical Consumers
237 Thompson Street
New York, NY 10012
212–674–7105

Maintains a medical reference library to assist consumers with decisions regarding treatment.

Hadley School for the Blind
700 Elm Street
Winnetka, IL 60093
800–323–4238
http://www.hadley-school.org

Offers in braille or cassette free course materials leading to high school diploma, continuing education, or Carnegie units.

National Eye Health Education Program
Box 20/20 Vision Place
Bethesda, MD 20892-3655
301–496–5248 or
800–869–2020 (to order publications)
http://www.nei.nih.gov

Promotes community health education and awareness. Publishes *Outlook.*

For additional information on schools for the blind and special education programs for the blind and visually impaired in your area, consult with your local board of education and your local school district.

INFORMATION

Diet and Nutrition

Alliance for Food and Fiber
800–266–0200

Recorded messages on various topics, including pesticide use, healthy eating, and safe food handling. They will return calls to answer questions not covered in the recorded messages.

American Dietetic Association Nutrition Hot Line
800–366–1655

Nutrition help line staffed by registered dietitians. Recorded messages cover a variety of topics from the amount of fat in your diet to the milligrams of caffeine found in a chocolate bar. If you need more information, you will be referred to a consulting dietitian.

HCF Foundation
800–727–4HCF
Publishes brochures and a free newsletter relating to diet and diabetes, cholesterol, heart disease, high blood pressure, and cancer.

U.S.D.A. Meat and Poultry Hot Line
800–535–4555
Registered dietitians will answer questions about safety, labeling, and nutritional value of meat and poultry.

University of Alabama at Birmingham
800–231–DIET
Gives dietary advice and sends out fact sheets.

General Health Issues

The Health Resource
564 Locust Avenue
Conway, AR 72032
800–949–0090 or 501–329–5272
http: //www.thehealthresource.com

For a nominal fee, assembles summaries and references on any medical subject.

National Health Information Center
Office of Disease Prevention and Health Promotion
P.O. Box 1133
Washington, DC 20013-1133
800–336–4797 or 301–565–4167
fax 301–984–4256
http://www.nhicnt.heal.org

Provides referrals to private and public organizations for more information on particular health problems.

Natural Healthcare Hot Line
Natural Healthcare Institute
Herb Research Foundation
Box 201660
Austin, TX 78720
303–449–2265

Information about herbs and health; ask for an information specialist.

Patients' Rights Hot Line
215 West 125th Street
New York, NY 10027
212–316–9393

Provides information on patients' rights. Similar hot lines exist in many other states; consult your local telephone directory. If there is no such service in your area, contact your state health department and ask for the specific department that oversees your area of concern.

Public Citizen
1600 20th Street, NW
Washington, DC 20009
202–588–1000

Publishes a booklet entitled *Medical Records: Getting Yours.*

Glaucoma and Other Vision Problems

American Academy of Ophthalmology
P.O. Box 7424
San Francisco, CA 94120
415–561–8540
http://www.eyenet.org

Provides information materials on glaucoma and cosponsors the National Eye Care Project for persons over sixty-five who are medically underserved (800–222–EYES).

American Council for the Blind
1155 15th Street, NW, Suite 720
Washington, DC 20005
800–424–8666 or 202–457–5081
(3:00–5:00 p.m. Eastern Time)

Provides resource lists on services for the visually impaired, and is a strong advocacy group. Also has special interest groups for the visually impaired.

American Foundation for the Blind
11 Penn Plaza
New York, NY 10001
800–232–5463 or 212–502–7600
e-mail majordomo@afb.org (to receive network updates, legislative alerts, discussion of policy and program developments, etc.)
http://www.afb.org/afb

Publishes numerous pamphlets, books, brochures, legislative updates and alerts, and the *Directory for the Blind and Visually Impaired in the United States and Canada,* which lists state commissions, low-vision services, public libraries, and other organizations throughout the country serving the blind and visually impaired. It is headquartered in New York City and also has regional offices in Atlanta, Chicago, Dallas, San Francisco, and Washington, DC.

American Optometric Association
2420 North Lindbergh Boulevard
St. Louis, MO 63141
800–365–2219 or 314–991–4100
fax 314–991–4101

Provides literature and doctor referral information.

The Associated Blind
135 West 23rd Street
New York, NY 10011
212–255–1122

Provides information free of charge to visually impaired persons.

Association for Macular Diseases, Inc.
210 East 64th Street
New York, NY 10021
212–605–3719

Publishes a newsletter and other information on macular diseases. Membership fee.

College of Optometrists in Vision Development
P.O. Box 285
Chula Vista, CA 91912-0285
619–435–6191
fax 619–435–0733

Recommends practitioners; provides informational literature.

The Glaucoma Foundation
33 Maiden Lane
New York, NY 10038
800–GLAUCOMA (toll-free worldwide) or 212–504–1900
fax 212–504–1933
http://www.glaucoma-foundation.org/nyo

Publishes a quarterly newsletter, *Eye to Eye*; a booklet, *Doctor, I Have a Question*; and a patient's guide. Also provides listings of eye doctors in specific geographical areas and funds glaucoma research. Will respond to written or telephone queries.

Glaucoma Research Foundation
490 Post Street, Suite 1042
San Francisco, CA 94102
800–826–6693 or 415–986–2162
http://www.glaucoma.org

Publishes the informational newsletter *GLEAMS* and a booklet on glaucoma; sponsors a glaucoma network; funds glaucoma research.

The Lighthouse
111 East 59th Street
New York, NY 10022
212–821–9200
http://www.lighthouse.org

Publishes *Self Help Mutual Aid and Support Groups for Visually Impaired Older People: A Guide and Directory*, a manual that lists groups throughout the nation.

National Association for the Visually Handicapped
22 West 21 Street
New York, NY 10010
212–889–3141
fax 212–737–2931
e-mail staff@navh.org
http://www.navh.org
also at 3201 Balboa Street
San Francisco, CA 94121
415–221–3201
fax 415–221–8753

Provides information for visually impaired persons.

National Federation of the Blind
1800 Johnson Street
Baltimore, MD 21230
410–659–9314 or
800–356–7713 (in New York)

Strong advocacy group that also provides informational services.

Optometric Extension Program Foundation
1921 East Carnegie Avenue
Suite 30
Santa Ana, CA 92705
714–250–8070
fax 714–250–8157

Provides informational literature and referrals to optometric practitioners.

Prevent Blindness America
500 East Remington Road
Schaumburg, IL 60173
847–843–2020 or 800–331–2020
(Monday–Friday, 8:00 a.m.–
5:00 p.m. Central Time)
http://www.preventblindness.org

Maintains a free center for information on a broad range of eye health and safety topics. This organization is headquartered in Illinois but has affiliates throughout the country.

Vision Foundation
818 Mt. Auburn Street
Watertown, MA 02172
617–926–4232 or
800–852–3029 (in Massachusetts)

Engages in advocacy work and provides information on self-help groups. Provides a vision resource list in large print or cassette form.

Products and Technology

American Foundation for the Blind National Technology Center
11 Penn Plaza
New York, NY 10001
800–232–5463 or 212–502–7600

Evaluates and provides information on reading systems for the blind and visually impaired.

American Telephone & Telegraph
800–233–1222

Provides information on telephone equipment adapted to special needs.

Closing the Gap
P.O. Box 68
Henderson, MN 56044
507–248–3294
http://www.closingthegap.com

Publishes reviews of hardware and software appropriate for persons with disabilities six times a year; also holds an annual international conference. Membership and subscription fees.

Consumer Product Safety Commission National Injury Information Clearinghouse
5401 Westward Avenue, Room 625
Washington, DC 20207
800–638–2772
Provides information on product safety.

Contact Lens Association of Ophthalmologists
523 Decatur Street, Suite 1
New Orleans, LA 70130-1027
504–581–4000
http://www.clao.org

Provides information on contact lenses.

Resources for Rehabilitation
33 Bedford Street, Suite 19A
Lexington, MA 02173
617–862–6455
http://www.rfr.org

Publishes resource guides including *Living With Low Vision* large-print resource.

Other

American Association of Retired Persons (AARP)
601 E Street, NW
Washington, DC 20049
202–434–2477
TTY 202–434–6554
fax 202–434–6499
http://www.aarp.org

Will send disability literature on written request; also offers a resource guide, Americans With Disabilities Act (ADA) guidelines, and travel guide. Membership fee.

Department of Aging
2 Lafayette Street
New York, NY 10007
212–442–1111

Provides a free brochure on helpful public programs for people over sixty living on fixed or limited incomes. Similar departments exist in most other states; consult your local telephone directory.

National Institute on Aging Information Center
P.O. Box 8057
Gaithersburg, MD 20898-8057
TTY 980–222–4225
fax 301–589–3014

Publishes a pamphlet on aging.

LOW-VISION AIDS

American Foundation for the Blind National Technology Center
11 Penn Plaza
New York, NY 10001
800–232–5463 or 212–502–7600
http://www.afb.org/afb

Adapts, evaluates, manufactures, and sells special aid devices and products.

Arkenstone, Inc.
555 Oakmead Parkway
Sunnyvale, CA 94089
800–444–4443 or 408–245–5900

Sells reading machines/systems.

Can-Do Products
Independent Living Aids, Inc.
27 East Mall
Plainview, NY 11863
800–537–2118
fax 516–752–3135

Sells various products; free catalog available.

C-Tech
P.O. Box 30
2 North Williams Street
Pearl River, NY 10965-9998
800–228–7798

Sells reading machines/systems.

Henter-Joyce
2100 62nd Avenue North
St. Petersburg, FL 33702
800–336–5658

Sells reading machines/systems.

IBM Special Needs System
P.O. Box 1328
Boca Raton, FL 33429
800–277–9449

Sells reading machines/systems.

Inwave Optics, Inc.
29 West Milwaukee Avenue
P.O. Box 5113
Janeville, WI 53542-5113

Manufactures prescription glasses that expand peripheral vision.

Kurzweil Educational System
411 Waverly Oaks Road
Waltham, MA 02154
800–894–5374

Sells reading machines/systems.

The Lighthouse Low Vision Products
36-20 Northern Boulevard
Long Island City, NY 11101
800–829–0500

Sells various products; free catalog available.

Maddak, Inc.
6 Industrial Road
Pequannock, NJ 07440
800–443–4926
http://www.maddak.com

Sells various products; free catalog available.

Maxi Aids
42 Executive Boulevard
P.O. Box 3209
Farmingdale, NY 11735
800–522–6294 or 516–752–0521

Sells various products; free catalog available.

National Association for the Visually Handicapped
22 West 21 Street
New York, NY 10010
212–889–3141 fax 212–737–2931
http://www.navh.org
also at 3201 Balboa Street
San Francisco, CA 94121
415–221–3201 fax 415–221–8753

Provides and advises on visual aids; conducts lectures and holds an annual showcase and counseling center. Free large-print catalog available.

National Federation of the Blind
1800 Johnson Street
Baltimore, MD 21230
410–659–9314 or
800–356–7713 (in New York)

Sells various visual aids and appliances.

Optelec-Joyce
6 Lyberty Way
Westford, MA 01886
800–336–5658

Sells reading machines/systems.

TeleSensory
455 North Bernardo Avenue
P.O. Box 7455
Mountain View, CA 94039-9951
800–804–8004 (for products for the visually impaired)
800–286–8484 (for products for the blind)
http://www.telesensory.com

Sells both black-and-white and color closed-circuit television systems.

Visuaide
841 Jean-Paul-Vincent Boulevard
Longueuil, Quebec J46 1R3
Canada
514–463–1717

Sells reading machines/systems.

RECREATION

The Arts

Art Education for the Blind
160 Mercer Street
New York, NY 10012
212–334–3700
fax 212–334–8714

Through use of tactile information teaches the visually handicapped to "see" paintings. Conducts workshops and consults with museums, working on a twenty-volume art history textbook for the visually impaired, "Art History Through Touch and Sound."

Hospital Audiences, Inc.
220 West 42nd Street
New York, NY 10036
888–424–4685 (toll-free worldwide)

Publishes "Access for All: A Guide for People With Disabilities to New York City Cultural Institutions." Also has a program for the legally blind in which a sighted individual accompanies the person to theatrical performances and describes the action to him or her.

Reading Materials

Choice Magazine Listening
85 Channels Drive
Port Washington, NY 11050
516–883–8280

Offers free service for persons unable to read regular print. Every other month, subscribers receive 4-track cassettes containing eight hours of articles, fiction, and poetry. Cassettes are playable on Library of Congress talking book cassette player, which is also free of charge. Readings cover well-known print magazines.

Doubleday Large Print Home Library
501 Franklin Avenue
Garden City, NY 11434
800–688–4442

Large-print books.

Matilda Ziegler Magazine
80 Eighth Avenue, Room 1304
New York, NY 10011
212–242–0263

Provides tapes and braille; free.

National Association for the Visually Handicapped
22 West 21 Street
New York, NY 10010
212–889–3141
fax 212–737–2931
e-mail staff@navh.org
http://www.navh.org
also at 3201 Balboa Street
San Francisco, CA 94121
415–221–3201
fax 415–221–8754

Maintains a large-print lending library.

National Braille Press
88 St. Stephen's Street
Boston, MA 92115
800–548–7323 or 617–266–6160

Sells braille publications; free catalog available. Also provides transcription services.

National Library Services for the Blind and Physically Handicapped
Library of Congress
Washington, DC 20542
800–424–8567
http://www.loc.gov/nls

Provides braille and recorded books and magazines for the blind and physically handicapped; talking books, plays, catalogs and bibliography, music scores, and music instructional materials. Materials may be accessed directly from the library.

The New York Times
Large Type Weekly
Mail Subscription
P.O. Box 9564
Uniondale, NY 11553

Offers a weekly large-print newspaper.

Soundelux Audio Publishing
37 Commercial Boulevard
Novato, CA 94949
800–227–2020

Sells books on tape; free catalog.

Random House
201 East 50th Street
New York, NY 10022
800–793–2665 or 212–751–2600

Sells large-print books and audiotapes.

Reader's Digest
Large-Type Publication
P.O. Box 6389
Louisville, NY 40206
800–877–5293

Sells a large-type version of the monthly magazine.

UlversCroft Large Print Books
Helen B. Boyle
279 Boston Street
Guilford, CT 06437
800–955–9659

Sells soft-cover large-print books, including mysteries, romances, Westerns, and classics.

For additional sources of reading material, check with your local public library or consult the *Directory of Services for the Blind and Visually Impaired in the United States and Canada,* published by the American Foundation for the Blind (see page 285).

Other

The Laboratory of Ornithology
159 Sapsucker Woods Road
Ithaca, NY 13440
607–254–2400

Produces a bird song tutor on tape

that may be purchased from the Laboratory or borrowed from National Library Services.

Visions Services for the Blind and Visually Impaired
120 Wall Street
New York, NY 10022
212–425–2255

Camping programs for the blind and visually impaired. Services limited to metropolitan New York residents.

North American Riding for the Handicapped Association
P.O. Box 3 3K50
Denver, CO 80233
303–452–1212

Teaches horseback riding to the blind and visually handicapped. Has 460 centers throughout the U.S. and Canada; will send a list of centers in your state upon request.

SERVICES

Low-Vision Services

Unless otherwise specified, these agencies provide one or more of the following services: rehabilitation services, training in independent living skills, vocational training, and counseling and support services.

American Foundation for the Blind
11 Penn Plaza
New York, NY 10001
800–232–5463 or 212–502–7600
e-mail majordomo@afb.org (to receive network updates, legislative alerts, discussion of policy and program developments, etc.)
http://www.afb.org/afb

Provides professional services relating to issues of employment, aging, rehabilitation, orientation and mobility, education, low vision, early childhood and multiple disabilities, advocacy; also provides talking books; maintains a circulating library; conducts research.

The Associated Blind
135 West 23rd Street
New York, NY 10011
212–255–1122

Provides services free of charge to visually impaired persons.

Catholic Guild for the Blind
1011 First Avenue
New York, NY 10022
212–371–1000 extension 2017, 2020

Serves the New York metropolitan area only. Check with your local Catholic Charities for more information.

The Deicke Center for Visual Rehabilitation
219 East Cole Avenue
Wheaton, IL 60187
630–690–7115

Provides visually impaired people with tools and training to function independently. Some optical services may be provided free of charge.

Glaucoma Research Foundation
490 Post Street, Suite 1042
San Francisco, CA 94102
800–826–6693 or 415–986–2162
http://www.glaucoma.org

A national support network for glaucoma patients.

Guide Dogs for the Blind, Inc.
P.O. Box 151200
San Rafael, CA 94915-1200
415–499–4000

Nonprofit organization that provides traning in the use, handling, and care of guide dogs, plus follow-up services, at no charge to the blind or legally blind.

Helen Keller Services for the Blind
57 Willoughby Street
Brooklyn, NY 11201
719–522–2122

Serves the New York metropolitan area only. Literature available on request.

Jewish Guild for the Blind
15 West 65th Street
New York, NY 10024
212–764–6200
also at 75 Stratton Street South
Yonkers, NY 10701
914–963–2024

Serves only those areas listed.

The Lighthouse
111 East 59th Street
New York, NY 10022
212–821–9200
http://www.lighthouse.org

Provides a variety of services to the blind and visually impaired. Also has facilities in Staten Island, Queens, and Westchester, NY.

National Association for the Visually Handicapped
22 West 21 Street
New York, NY 10010
212–889–3141
fax 212–737–2931
e-mail staff@navh.org
http://www.navh.org
also at 3201 Balboa Street
San Francisco, CA 94121
415–221–3201 or 415–221–8753

Provides services for visually impaired persons.

Visions Services for the Blind and Visually Impaired
120 Wall Street
New York, NY 10022
212–425–2255

Provides rehabilitation services; self-study kits on tape (ask for GIL publications).

Medical and Optometric Services

State College of Optometry
State University of New York
100 East 24th Street
New York, NY 10010
212–780–4900

Will provide a complete eye examination by a licensed optometrist in your home if you are a senior citizen unable to leave home because of a disability or illness.

The Hill Burton Program
Health Resources and Services Administration
5600 Fishers Lane, Room 1119
Rockville, MD 20857
800–638–0742 or 301–443–5656 or 800–492–0359 (in Maryland)

Depending upon income, provides health services at no or reduced charge.

National Eye Care Project Eye Care Hot Line
P.O. Box 6988
San Francisco, CA 34131-6985
800–222–EYES

Provides services to U.S. citizens or

legal residents sixty-five or older who do not have access to an ophthalmologist. Medicare assigment accepted as full payment.

Other

Access Resources
351 West 24th Street, Suite 9F
New York, NY 10011-1517
212–741–3758
e-mail accessrs@ix.netcom.com

Mediates disputes related to the provisions of the Americans With Disabilities Act (ADA), which mandates reasonable accommodations be made for people with disabilities in such areas as employment, public accommodations, and public transit. Also provides ADA and disability training to companies.

Life Line Systems
640 Memorial Drive
Cambridge, MA 02139
800–543–3546

For a monthly fee, provides a service in which personal emergency assistance can be summoned by pressing a small button worn on your person, using a system specifically designed for the visually impaired.

Medic Alert
2323 Colorado Avenue
Turlock, OK 95381-9015
800–863–3420

For an initial registration fee and an annual renewal fee, provides an emblem engraved with an ID number and a twenty-four-hour hot line number to supply vital medical information about the registered individual in emergencies.

For further information on agencies in your area that offer services to the blind and visually impaired, check the publications of the American Foundation for the Blind (see page 285). In addition, your state Department of Rehabilitation may provide such services as instruction in braille, daily living skills, independent travel, job preparation and placement, and medication consultation. If you are a veteran, you may qualify for rehabilitation services provided by the U.S. Veterans' Administration. The Veterans' Administration also produces audiotapes on subjects from medical care, housing, and living arrangements to consumer issues, financial matters, health and nutrition, and long-term care. You can also check with your local telephone and electric companies to see if they will provide large-print statements, and consult state and local commissions and other public agencies that offer job counseling, rehabilitation, and placement services.

SUPPORT GROUPS

The following groups are sponsored by Prevent Blindness America:

California:
Linda Creel
President and CEO
3702 Ruffin Road, Suite 201
San Diego, CA 92123-1812
619–576–2122
fax 619–576–2123
e-mail 104706.1104@compuserv.com

Georgia:

Jenny Pomeroy
Executive Director
455 East Paces Ferry Road
Suite 222
Atlanta, GA 30305
404–266–0071
fax 404–266–0860
e-mail 104706.1102@compuserv.com

Massachusetts:

Laura M. Riedinger
Executive Director
375 Concord Avenue
Belmont, MA 02178
607–489–0007
fax 617–489–3575
e-mail 104706.1077@compuserv.com

New York:

Joseph Basile
President and CEO
160 East 56th Street, 8th Floor
New York, NY 10022-3609
212–980–2020
fax 212–688–9641
e-mail 104706.1076acompuserv.com

Meets ten times a year, publishes "Living With Glaucoma."

Oklahoma:

Martha Pat Upp
Executive Director
6 Northeast 63rd Street
Suite 150
Oklahoma City, OK 73105
405–848–7123
fax 405–848–6935
e-mail 104706.1115@compuserv.com

Texas:

Elaine Barber
President and CEO
3211 West Dallas
Houston, TX 77019
713–526–2559 or
888–98SIGHT (in Texas)
fax 713–529–8310
e-mail 104706.2523@compuserv.com

Virginia:

Timothy Gresham
President and CEO
9840 Midlothian Turnpike
Suite R
Richmond, VA 23235
804–330–3195
fax 804–330–3198
e-mail 104706.1107@compuserv.com

In addition, The Lighthouse (see page 292) sponsors support groups for persons afflicted with low vision throughout the country.

TRAVEL AND TRANSPORT

Greyhound offers a free travel ticket for a sighted person accompanying a low-vision or blind person (pay for one ticket, get one free.)

Handicapped parking permits/placards are available from your state's Department of Motor Vehicles at no charge.

Para-Transit Service: It's the law. If the public transportation system serving your area cannot accommodate you, your community must provide para-transit by van, taxi, or some other vehicle.

Index